Windmill

A Novel

By Rob Bignell

WINDMILL

Copyright Rob Bignell, 2012

Atiswinic Press
Ojai, Calif. 93023
http://inventingreality.4t.com/windmill.html

ISBN 978-0-9858739-2-9
Library of Congress Control Number: 2012919207

Cover Design by Rob Bignell

Manufactured in the United States of America
First printing October 2012

For Mom and Dad

"The wind bloweth where it listeth, and thou hearest the
sound therof, but canst not tell whence it cometh, and
whither it goeth; so is every one that is born of the spirit."
- John 3:8

"Howl, howl, howl! O' you are men of stones
Had I your tongues and eyes, I'd use them so
That heaven's vault should crack. She's gone forever."
- Shakespeare, *King Lear*, v, iii, 259

Prologue

What Carl Steinar remembered most was the thick and spoked blood, splattered across the car's windshield as if a child's painting of a red sun. At first, the young farmer simply did not register the finality inherent when a car and truck are crushed to half their lengths upon a crossroads breaching the prairie's great open spaces. He still believed there was a chance she might be alive despite the tightening of his stomach as he pushed past the state trooper.

Kneeling before the car, however, all he could see was blood. His wife appeared to be asleep, but he knew that crumpled body, jammed between the driver's seat and projecting steering wheel, had simply lost too much vital fluid for it to be true. Then a mist of lavender netting covered her, as if she was a bride about to wake, and Carl Steinar realized he was viewing Gwen through his tears. In a single moment, every memory of their few short years with one another surfaced: the first night together; of how she loved Nebraska's yellow sky and the wind's glorious cry, of her soothing hands as she caressed his neck; of their two little boys. He stumbled back, lay fetal position in the middle of the road, and shaking his head desperately tried to hold back the weeping.

Suddenly, he saw only a vast splay of white, and the air

rushed from his lungs in a great howl.

Chapter 1

Though dust spiraled in thick furrows off the gravel road then across the vast, barren fields, Peter Steinar hesitated climbing down the windmill. He instead left his father and brother standing below to watch the approaching burgundy-colored car as sunlight and wind burned the land raw in a river of heat.

"Here must be that news reporter now," said father, beckoning for him.

Peter rolled his eyes but began his descent. Upon reaching the ground, his father handed him a handkerchief. It did little good. Red granules of prairie loam whirled upon the wind like thick swarms of gnats, and the old man blinked slowly. Peter searched for a hint of anticipation in that vacant face, saw only a thick line drooping beneath zombie eyes and skin damp from the swelter.

As the car rolled into the yard, the three men stood in place. Their sweat, acrid like sour milk, hung thick in the air while they stared at the woman driver. The dark shade of a cottonwood hid her features, then the door creaked, and she rose from the car like dawn between mountain crags. She was small with narrow shoulders, yet her blackberry-colored hair fluttered about, filling the horizon. The eyes, a smoky topaz, blended with her creamy complexion. She possessed a thin, sovereign nose. Peter admired her dimples, round and modest in their sweetness. The woman extended a hand to his father. "I'm Abbie Blaire, from the Guthrie County Register," she said, her voice peaceful, like a strummed harp. "You must be Mr. Steinar."

Her hand felt warm to Carl. Embarrassed, he did not allow his own large, cracked palms to linger. "Carl Steinar," he said, a hint of richness in his almost whispering voice. "These are my sons, Peter and Lyle."

She smiled as each sibling nodded in turn then reached for a notepad tucked in the pocket of her blazer. Wind swept back the jacket's lightened side, and Peter glimpsed the curve of her lithe hips. His throat ached. He had seen her before, had heard her voice.

"So this is the windmill?" said Abbie, gesturing toward the metal pyramid at the yard's center. Her slender hand broke their stares.

"That's the windmill," Carl Steinar said. He rubbed his eyes, the pupils expressionless as a cow's.

"And it still works?"

"Oh yes, she's still going," Carl said, "like a train whistle on a lonely night."

Abbie's eyebrows rose and after a silent moment she turned to Peter, hoping for a less enigmatic response. He glanced away, felt shame over his dust-laden face, at the soaked spots stretching beneath his armpits, at his dull, tousled hair. Yet, his father had insisted that the windmill needed oiling, and with Carl Steinar, the old, spindly tower always came first, even if inconveniencing everyone else.

"Maybe we should go inside, where it's cooler," Peter said.

At that, Carl and Lyle Steinar sauntered toward the farmhouse, and Abbie found herself standing alone in the hot sun with Peter. "Sure," she said as grinning.

The arid wind beat steadily against Peter and Abbie as they crossed the lawn. A swing set, its red and white barber pole stripes faded and flaking, sat next to the tree nearest the gravel driveway. Its lone metal swing creaked with each gust. When the boys had reached their teens, the yard and its three cottonwoods, once an adventureland of great games and climbs, became just another chore of constant mowing. Lyle often thought he could get out of that mundane task if the yard somehow became a woods, so sometime during his eleventh year he carefully cut around a seedling centered between the cottonwoods, allowing it to grow. Many times Peter forgot it was there as he had not played in the yard for some time and would walk right over the sapling, its thin but sharp points scratching his wrists. Then he'd pause for a moment, stare at the puny tree, and as breathing the whiffs of fresh wheat aloft the wind, contemplate yanking it out. Peter did not want to cause trouble with his younger brother, though, so he simply held his burning wrist against his mouth, letting body warmth soak the pain and salt of his broken skin.

The wind died as they entered the stuffy house, dark from the drawn curtain and yellowed Cape Cods over the kitchen sink. Boxes and stacks of newspapers lined the walls. Abbie noticed one pile topped by an edition dating back some 15 years. The furniture appeared at least that old as well, and for a moment Peter reproached himself for suggesting they go inside. Sitting at the dining table, he pushed away dirty dishes and an open cereal box, whole Lyle, his eyes caked with gray dust and belly sticking out even farther than usual, slumped in a chair across from him. Their father lolled into the living room, however, his mouth hanging open as if a senile old man trying to gain his bearings.

Peter only glanced at Abbie, avoided looking directly at her in fear that she'd see the black dirt worn into the hems of his jeans and beneath his fingernails. He thought her to be at most a year or so younger than himself. Then his eyes gazed upon the gray floor; here I am, he thought, a man in my mid-twenties, and she's probably already done more things, gone more places, than me.

In the living room, Peter's father picked up a standing frame picture of his deceased wife, examined it longingly, and gazed at Abbie then again at the picture. He swabbed his eyes once more, and for the first time the nubile reporter noticed his forehead was heavily creased, like an overfolded map. At length, he sat on the sofa, stared toward the gun cabinet.

"Well, let's begin," Abbie said, her notepad covering a ketchup stain in the small space cleared by Peter. "How old is the windmill?"

"Oh gosh, almost a century now," Peter said. "It's not the first one built on the farm, you know. You see, long ago, each farmer was on his own when it came to supplying water, so great granddaddy dug a deep well and set up a windmill to pump water. That was back in the 1880s maybe. How long ago was it, Father?"

"More than 110 years ago," Carl Steinar said softly from the living room. "He was a Norwegian immigrant, promised by the railroads that this was a great utopia." Then he suddenly quieted, as if losing interest, and turned on the television.

Abbie's mouth parted slightly, but Peter broke in. "Most others in the area were Germans and Swedes, so great-granddaddy often got cajoled about being different," he said then continued nonchalantly about how the first well wasn't deep enough so a new windmill replaced it, this time made out of steel, a mighty impressive addition at the time, and the one that sill stood to the day. She noticed a slight twang in his voice, considered it more interesting than the answer. With each passing moment, much about this young farmer intrigued her: He was rawboned, even loose-limbed, she thought, but surrounded with an aura of hardness, much like the old movie star, what was his name – Gary Cooper? Yes, that was it. She thought the little scar above his mouth, barely noticeable when he spoke, endearing. Professionalism, she told herself, professionalism. Reporters do not take a liking to their sources; they simply provide information, that is all. Yet, as scribbling his words down with a fine point pen, she never once stopped looking at him.

"Say, that's some trick," he said.

She bit her lower lip lightly. "What is?"

"Being able to write without looking at the page. Aren't you worried your lines won't be straight?"

Abbie nervously itched the back of her neck. "I've never thought about it, actually...Perhaps you could explain how the windmill works."

Captivated by her thin fingers, Peter did not speak; he sensed that somehow they had touched him. Abbie's eyes crinkled at the corners as she glanced at him.

Lyle sat up, loose hair strands falling over his brow. "The wind turns the blades, which in turn cranks a turbine," he said.

Abbie shifted her attention toward him. "What happens when the wind changes direction?"

Peter cut off his brother. "There's a fantail that moves the blades so they always catch the wind."

Lyle drooped as Abbie turned back to Peter. Just like my brother, the youngest Steinar thought, always slamming a door in my face. His lips pursed.

Peter explained the windmill's workings then answered Abbie's questions about how it still was used on the farm, maintenance they performed on it, and why they bothered to keep it when there were more modern conveniences, and a host of others. Though sometimes Peter stumbled for words, a great patience ran through her gaze, and he had to keep resurrecting the likelihood that her behavior was simply a matter of occupational courtesy and nothing more.

Abbie wanted quotes from the other two Steinars but found neither willing. "Mr. Steinar...Carl–," she said, looking toward him as a black-and-white western blared from the television. "What does the windmill mean to you, personally?"

He turned around slowly, surprised someone would ask him that. Often he'd thought about it himself, but nothing came from his lips. Abbie watched him struggle, wondered if the deep, crescent rings under his eyes held the answer. In the gray interior of the farmhouse, his normally pale face appeared rough, like rope. He possessed a no-nonsense demeanor, she sensed, maybe one that was a little too hard, like he would sink if tossed into water. Then he spoke slowly, cautiously. "You can see the windmill" – except in the particular strum of his voice he said "wind-meal" – "standing above the farm buildings from a mile away. Isn't that something?"

Abbie's eyes narrowed slightly as pondering the answer. She decided not to ask a follow-up. "Well, I think I've got everything I need," she said as standing. "Maybe we could go outside for some photos?"

Peter nodded and stood, but Lyle and Carl remained seated.

She peered at Lyle, who breathed passively. "I'd like the whole family in the picture," she said.

Lyle rose sullenly. "Come on, Father."

Outside, a torrid wind swept in wide tracts as the sun hovered above. Peter's brother and father lagged behind him and Abbie.

"If you don't mind me asking," she said to Peter as pulling a camera from her car, where's Mrs. Steinar?"

"Mrs. Steinar?"

"Your mother?" she said hesitantly. "She should really be in the photo, too."

Peter leaned against the windmill. "Died in a car accident. She's been gone for some time now."

Her face went flush. "I'm sorry. I didn't mean to–"

Peter waved her off. "You didn't know."

Before either could speak, Lyle and Carl arrived, and almost blushing Abbie quickly lined them up. Behind the three men, the windmill's paddles chirred in the hot August wind, the orange rust specks shifting against the pure blue sky like the images of a kaleidoscope. The fantail twitched slightly as the wind curved, but the whirring never ceased. Abbie backed up, held a hand over her eyes to shield them from the bright sun. The cloy scent of butter-and-eggs wildflowers wreathed through the air, gliding along the wind, and her hair swept back and leeward, unveiling a soft, peach-colored neck. Peter imagined his cheek curling against it.

*****

With the chores done and the day hot, Carl Steinar decided once Abbie left that they would rest. He settled into the recliner, Lyle went to the porch, and Peter headed to his bedroom.

As Peter's head lay upon a pillow, Abbie's presence lingered in his mind like dew atop grass on a pleasant morning. For several long moments, it hid from his eyes the peeling paint that hung from the ceiling. Sometimes they would flutter down as he slept, but he never told his father about the need for a new coat. Nor did he mention the need for a new mattress as the one on his childhood bunk had flattened over the years from his growing weight, or for new bedding as his twenty-year-old sheets were discolored and the spread ragged. He never would tell his father of such things, for they were remnants from another time, from when all the world was a great garden.

Peter's memories of his mother were vague, amorphous as melted candlewax. He closed his eyes, recalled her swiping at the cutting board with a knife, alternately rhapsodic and swinging chop bouncing through the house, of her combing her hair straight, of her smiling broadly, but there was little more. So instead his unconsciousness supplemented the truth with a dream cast and reshaped across his long youth. In that vision, she was gray like a gypsy moth, floating amid clouds and lily pads. They were at the creek, where the rising sun whitened only her face and shoulder blades as it washed the brown from the cottonwoods. The sweep of her arms through the water remained quiet, however, and he barely could make out her voice, a sonorous, echoing call. Then she smiled, eyes aglow, and looked right at him, mouthing his name. He swam toward her, the scent of wild water filling his nostrils, then swallowed a spoonful of it, sandy and impure. Despite his strokes, he could move no closer – she was like a warm hand that could not be reached as you hung over an abyss, and his arms strained harder, faster, until he had to fly straight up and catch his breath. Still, she hovered there, mutely calling his name. Then the wind blew, lifted her blackened hair, and as the gust brushed against his cheeks, it propelled him back. "Mom!" he shouted, "Mom!" but another blast struck, and she dissolved in the chill.

His eyes blinked open, stared at the thickening streak of mildew across the far wall. No, he would not need to tell his father about that either. After all, one day soon he would leave the farm, maybe even Nebraska. Though uncertain where to go, at that moment he thought it might somehow involve Abbie.

*****

Sitting on a porch step, Lyle glared at the empty plain surrounding the cluster of bins and sheds as an acrimonious dust blew across the horizon. Though away from his brother and father, the two still angered him, like they were taunting bullies standing on the sidewalk as he tried walking to school. They always found a way to exclude him, to cut him out of their precious lives. He thought again of moving into town, of taking a job at the stockyard. Nothing prevented him from doing so, yet he felt oddly tethered to the farm. But when one felt loyalty to others, he wondered if it also did not imply at least a sliver of lover for them. As the years passed, Lyle slowly realized that what really moored him to the homestead was something to which only his father and brother could provide a link.

A band of dark always covered the memory of his mother. His strongest recollection was not even of her but of the blueberries she'd purchased the morning of her death. They sat upon the kitchen counter, ripe and plump, dew glistening upon an indigo pile in a pea green carton made of the same hard paper that eggs came in. She'd probably plan-ned to use the blueberries at lunch, he imagined years later, pouring them over vanilla ice cream for dessert. As the sun rose toward noon, so also did their scent, until any breath taken in the room wafted with their richness. It was the smell of June, forever imprinted on his mind.

Lunch never came, though.

As the hours lilted through the sordid afternoon heat, the blueberries soured. They sat quiescent on the counter for two days until Aunt Amita came over and quenched her nostrils at the odor. Cradling him, she held the gray and squishy blueberries at arm's length then dumped them in the garbage. The berries thumped against the trash can's walls, rolling to the bottom, and he thought of what a waste not eating them had been.

A great waste, he mused, like my own life; it's as if I'm dying of dry rot. He decided to go see Jackie Kine the next day about taking a job at the stockyards.

*****

Years of toiling had bent Carl Steinar.

As a Woolite commercial played for the fourth time that afternoon on the television, he stared into the empty space of his living room and thought of the determination, of the incredible privation, to which his father and granddaddies held tight so they could survive year after year, just to build the farm. After more than a century of their hard work, it stretched for 1,842 acres about his clapboard farmhouse. His granddaddy had constructed the home during the First World War's high prices and good times, deliberately designing it so the front door faced the churning windmill that constantly shifted in the ever changing but always present breeze. Just beyond the farmhouse and windmill sat the red barn and crumbling granary, each added following the next great war. Two decades after that, when Carl was just a boy, the pole shed and modern silos were erected, their silver caps glowing in both day and moonlight, as if stars. Surrounding the home farm, broad fields crossed the prairie swells for a mile in every direction. All spring, golden sunshine warmed and irrigation wells moistened the red humus, and by early summer the wind blew in the heady scent of blossoming wheat. Through autumn, those same winds carried the bawling of white-headed cattle let loose to graze upon the dormant crop. Wire fences marked three boundaries of the farm, and to the southwest a shallow creek outlined the fourth side. Along that stream, where the grass never shriveled from the hot winds, lay the remnants of the first Steinar homestead – decayed wood and an ill osage orange tree, it tough-wooded and bushy in branches only.

Carl Steinar had once loved and been proud of his farm. It never meant more to him as during those few years with Gwen in the late Eighties, despite the sliding wheat prices and ever-rising costs conspired to destroy the spread just as blizzards, dust bowls, and locusts had dealt devastating blows to his forefathers. Yet, a cow could be replaced, the soil replenished, and the wheat replanted. It was not so with a wife.

Gwen had grown up on a nearby farm, was a country girl through and through from her first pair of bib overalls as an infant until that fateful hour she ran an errand to town for combine parts. She loved the wind's sound and hung chimes everywhere to capture it. Through the day and into the night, those hollow bars sang magically, as if fairy dust flung from a wand. Of all the composers she loved, her favorite was the windmill; she'd once said its purling reminded her of a beating heart.

He clicked off the television and sat quietly in the dim room, listening for the windmill's whir. It was still there, a mother calling softly to her child, even after all of those years.

Rising, he lumbered to the bathroom, his joints aching, the old wood floor creaking. He swiveled the sink faucet onto hot. As the basin filled, he rummaged through the medicine bottles and after-shaves finding a lone razor blade.

Even in the ashen light, it glimmered. He held out a wrist, and without blinking, scraped the blade against his flesh.

A drop of blood fell into roiling water below.

Chapter 2

To Abbie Blaire, there was no worse fate that caring for a broken man. She had watched her mother spend ten years proving so. Not that Abbie's father appeared other than physically injured to anyone after his accident, of course; he did not drink any more than usual, did not become addicted to painkillers, did not outwardly abuse his family. He'd not surrendered on life, just merely clutched to an unreasonable passion. To the casual acquaintance, all he suffered from was a slight limp in the right leg.

Peter Steinar in contrast did not falter at all, Abbie mused, but stood tall as a Titan rocket. She replayed her first wild breath upon seeing his broad hands, his high cheekbones. He was perhaps a bit too formal, she admitted, yet also admirable for being a man who did not mince words. A great enthusiasm entwined his voice. She recalled the artfully mussed look of his sun-dried hair, entertained the notion of running her fingers through it all afternoon. Then there was his large chin and those eyes, peaceful and content though something ghostly about them, and his shyness when he gazed at her, so unlike his younger brother who kept leering. Despite the dust that had settled upon Peter from working outside, a strangely familiar scent, like a field of wildflowers in July, emanated from his frame. She

thought of the redness of his lips, of his long eyelashes, wondered why a local girl hadn't yet snared him. He'd forgiven
her so easily for the faux pas about his mother, though Abbie saw how at that moment his eyes grayed, like the under-
sides of clouds. She sensed he would need her.

Indeed, she found herself certain that a deep longing,
like a disease that dissolves and rots from the inside, was
ravishing him, at least psychically. Abbie had seen it in her
own father: his long, empty stares, his suddenly dulled palate as he slouched over the dinner table, in the sonorous
tone of his voice. Then there was how he kissed her mother,
their lips barely meeting, the meaning of their touch pur-
poseless. For blackening their three lives, for hanging on,
she hated him.

On her first day in Felton just two months before, Abbie's break with the past has begun. She spent the first
hours setting her few belongings in specific, permanent
places. Growing up, she'd lived on five different air bases,
each of them distant and desolate posts alternatively in re-
gions of great sand and of imposing ice. The few communities in her life were the orderliness of school libraries,
the quick roar of jet fighters overhead, and ceaseless change
itself. All through her teen years she yearned for the seemingly dull lives of those in the small towns neighboring the
bases. Finally, after four college years of never-ending
moves between dorms and summer rentals, she vowed once
and for all to experience the quiet, uneventful life.

As Abbie entered the county courthouse, she thought
its Corinthian capitals and soaring granite columns beneath
the Monticello dome were more at home in the 1950s than
the beginning of a new millennium. The whole town felt that
way to her, and during most of the last half century, Felton
had appeared almost exactly as she saw it at that very mo-

ment. She loved the old, turn-of-the-century buildings rising two-and-a-half stories above the street, appearing like a Christmas diorama minus the snow; she enjoyed hearing the two retired bachelor farmers yakking away on a bench out front of the pharmacy as the old pond mill clacked away in the distance. She relished watching clerks and merchants busying themselves behind store windows, delighted in smelling fresh bread and rolls as passing the bakery. On Saturdays, she'd stroll the farmers' market picking up snap beans, ripe strawberries, and long ears of corn.

Abbie sifted through her scribblings of sheriff's reports from the police blotter as waiting for the county clerk's office to open. Two speeding tickets, firecracker complaints, neighbor dog loose in garden. Tame, peaceful stuff, the way life should be. Lost in satisfaction, she did not see Peter when he walked in.

He noticed her, however. Though a claw barrette held back Abbie's hair, a couple of errant strands fell across the eyes anyway, and her lips shined red like raspberries. Just then she glanced up, and her eyes brightened as if sunlight upon a pool. He wore tight, faded blue jeans and a white T-shirt. She quietly giggled to herself over the bits of chestnut hair peeking boyishly beneath the bill of his cap.

"Hello Peter," she said loudly, and he cantered over to her.

"Got a big scoop?" he said, noticing her reporter's pad full of notes.

Abbie smiled, pushed the strands out of her face. "Morning rounds. If you call police briefs big, then yep, I've got the scoop.

"And you?"

"Heading down to the Soil and Conservation Office. Forms."

They said nothing for a few seconds, then as the county clerk's door creaked open, Abbie hesitantly rose. So this is it with him, she thought, just another friendly face. "I enjoyed visiting with your family yesterday," she quick said.

Peter beamed. "Say, being that you're new in town and all, would you like to go for a ride sometime?"

Abbie paused, her brow crinkling. Perhaps it was not over. "A ride? A ride where?"

Peter's face reddened, as he glanced at the floor. "I mean show you around the county. I've lived here my whole life."

She grinned playfully. "Is that what you do for fun in Felton, go for rides?"

His face turning mockingly stoic. "We don't allow 'fun' in Felton."

She tittered.

"Meet you at two then, this afternoon?" he said. A shaft of sunlight split through the courthouse window, and rosy from the red carpet cut between them.

She nodded, tried to appear restrained. "Would the Register office be okay? You know where that is?"

"Hey, I'm the one giving you the tour."

She laughed then waved to him and was off.

Stepping into the clerk's office, Abbie let go a silent "Yes!" She'd had many successes, many accomplishments through her life – winning spelling bees in elementary school, her first freelance article placed at the top of page one, graduation with honors from college – yet somehow this felt sweeter.

Abbie had experienced such pleasure all through childhood, right up to that one autumn day in junior high. She and her father were walking through an air base hangar. Despite a new training bra and menstruation's onslaught, vestiges of childhood still clung to her like snow in crevasses on a spring day. First Lieutenant A.J. Blaire, dressed in flyer's suit, rubbed her head with his hand, messed up the hair. She tried shaking loose but couldn't. Not that she really wanted to, anyway; it was all part of the game.

"Now, Scruffcake, watch me fly off into wild blue yonder," he said, grinning and smelling of lavender.

He ambled out of the hangar toward his fighter jet, climbed a ladder into the cockpit. A ground guide gave him the thumbs up as the glass canopy closed. Then the jet fired on, a powerful roar. Abbie squinted though she didn't really feel the heat shooting out of its engines. She beamed, wanted to tell all of those towering adults in the hangar that was her father the magnificent Lt. A.J. Blaire, who flew many times faster than sound, who protected them and all of their families. They gazed upon her, their smiles wide as the prairie's horizon. Suddenly the jet bolted across the runway and into the air.

The jet's nose pointed level with the distant horizon and not toward the heavens as during previous flights, though. The airmen around Abbie tensed. At 500 feet, mere fractions of a second later, the plane arced downward then suddenly spiraled toward the ground. An explosion rocked the wings. The airmen about Abbie ducked, but she remained standing, could only gasp, the shock too horrendous for screaming. A small and fragile figure shot out of the smoke, a white and red striped flinging from the back. He floated toward the ground, though not stiff and commanding as in the movies, and hit with a thud as the jet crashed several yards down the runway, the metal wreckage afire. The man did not rise from the tarmac. Her face paled as the rescue crews scrambled. The windsock at the runway's end fell limp.

An investigation followed. Trying to be a hero by saving the plane, her father had ejected too late, and the explosion flung shrapnel through his right leg. Lt. A.J. Blaire would be cleared of any charges. He'd even walk again, though with a limp. But he'd never fly again, and for him that was worse than death.

Now Abbie Blaire wished for an adulthood without the fast-paced lifestyles of jet jockeys, their constant travel, their unending calls of duty to far off places like Somalia, Bosnia, Kuwait, Iraq, Afghanistan, places so far away and difficult to find on maps. She sought a serene landscape, one in which nothing and no one changed. For her, Felton, Nebraska, was just such a place, though any of a thousand other towns might had done as well. Felton simply had the job opening. And just maybe, she thought, I've found a friend here. She crossed her arms, gazed at the president's picture on the clerk's wall. All she had to do now was convince the editor to give her the afternoon off.

*****

"Father feeling better?" Peter said as swinging open the front door. He wasn't really concerned about his old man, thought it was probably just a little heat exhaustion or a touch of flu, but he was too excited not to speak.

Only stagnant air and grayness like steel wool met him, though. "He's better," Lyle said after a moment. His back remained rigid, lips tight. "Let him rest awhile."

Peter's eyes lingered upon Lyle for a moment, gauged this new attitude. The elder of the Steinar brothers found strange the previous night's events, odd like how a halo forms about the moon before a snowfall – it was something that caught your eye. Actions had transpired while he'd been asleep dreaming again of his mother. Apparently Lyle found their father nauseous in the bathroom, had helped him to bed, later had brought dinner to him. His brother even had cleaned up their father's mess. That probably was a first, Peter supposed. "You seem awfully considerate as of late," he said.

Lyle harrumphed. "And you seem awfully chipper."

Peter shrugged then bounded up the stairs, his body waving like a flag. Lyle sneered and followed him to the bathroom. He figured that all would be fine if Peter just didn't stop at the master bedroom; he'd have to keep his brother occupied and so watched him change shirts, spray on cologne, and prance as if covered in pixie dust.

"So what's this all about?" Lyle said, motioning at the cologne.

"I'm showing Abbie around the county."

"You mean that reporter who came out here yesterday?" He raised his brow. "Like a date?"

Peter paused from scrubbing his face, fought back the urge to grit his teeth. "I'm just showing her around."

"You're acting like it's a date."

Peter thought back to the last time he'd went out with a woman who interested him. It was the summer after graduation. He was down at the drive-in with Laura Jean, a week before she was to leave for college. He proposed not going. She got mad, called him stupid for staying in Felton. All those years later, he supposed she'd been right about leaving. After all, he couldn't imagine her living on the farm nor could he see himself wiping drool off a baby of theirs. He dried his face and brushing past Lyle headed downstairs.

His brother traipsed after, like a shadow with a will of its own, and stood at the bottom of the steps. "Gonna eat lunch with us?"

"Nah," said Peter.

Then from upstairs came a creak. Peter and Lyle knew

it only could be made by stepping on the warped board between the bathroom and the master bedroom; thanks to that tripwire, they'd been caught coming home late many times when teenagers. Lyle stared open-mouthed as his father plodded down the steps into the living room.

"What are you doing up?" Lyle said.

"I'm taking a break."

Peter glanced at him. "From what?"

"A break from my nap."

Carl Steinar's face lacked color, as if cut grass withering in a ditch, and Peter wondered for a moment what had happened to the hard-bitten man who'd once told him "Don't curse the chaff when it strikes your face – it shows which way the wind is blowing." The stupidity of those words and all of his other maxims annoyed Peter. With his father it was always the future. On occasion, though, Peter let one eye slip backward. Grabbing a soda from the fridge, he did not say goodbye as marching briskly into the yard. Peter believed he had much to be angry about, yet somehow he always found himself forgiving. Outside, the wind remained still.

In the living room, Lyle examined the black husk of his father, knew he couldn't leave the farm now, not unless he wanted to see his old man dead. Nor could he just leave this to Peter, who never gave a damn about anyone. Lyle suddenly knew what being the fly buzzing against a window pane was like; the wide world was before him but there was no way he could enter it now, especially with the invisible force of emotions holding him back. He promised himself to find a way of handling this.

Slumped in the recliner, Carl Steinar sensed that his standing had diminished in his youngest son's eyes, but he'd come before the bar of meaninglessness and unable to scale it, felt no obligation to explain himself. Lyle never would understand anyway, he decided, so he simply stumbled into the living room chair and rested.

His son stared at the red slash across the wrist. "Why'd you do it, Father?" he said finally, hands trembling. "Why'd you try killing yourself?"

Carl Steinar simply gazed into the pallid recesses of their house and remained silent.

*****

The highway rose as it approached the horizon, and though no mountains were present, the easy, gradual climb toward the distant Rockies was unmistakable. All that stood for Peter and Abbie to see was the colossal sky, forever looming ahead and above. Wind roared against the pickup truck, gushing over their faces and rolling hair locks back until they stood like erect flags as yellowed papers and crimped sale receipts rippled upon the floorboards. When Abbie first got in, she had to push away a mud-caked fencing pliers, and now her feet competed with a hot wire testers for space. Ahead of them, sun-baked cracks and the occasional rubber of some teenager's squealed tires lined the faded blue road.

Abbie already had seen most of the places he showed her, yet she found his gentlemanly manner and bright eyes too boyishly sweet for any protest. She glanced occasionally at the pale, pink scar above his mouth and wondered why he hadn't grown a mustache to conceal it. Her imagination drew blanks as she tried thinking of ways he might have gotten it.

"Have you ever seen a twister out here?" Abbie said over the wind and a Dwight Yoakam song. Perhaps in a bad storm he'd been hurt, she thought. Sunglasses sat perched atop her forehead.

"A couple of times. Except they don't sound like freight

trains."

She looked at him quizzically. "Oh? What are they like?"

"A river, out of control."

Peter resisted staring at Abbie's breasts, beveled in the heat. He admitted an intense sexual desire for her, yet an equally powerful longing that had nothing to do with carnality also surged inside. He'd once felt something similar when out of boredom at the North Platte mall he paged through an art book and saw a full spread painting of a nude goddess, her red hair wavering about in the breeze, hands covering vagina and a breast, angels heralding her birth. Mesmerized, he stared at it for a long minute, then when his brother approached with Hot Rod magazine in hand snapped the book shut in embarrassment. He never found the picture again. In a way, Peter thought, Abbie with her creamy neck bared and her scent earthy as if a patch of blooming sunflowers was much like that goddess.

"I have a weird question for you," Abbie said suddenly.

His head perked. "Oh?"

"The wind – if it ever stopped, would you miss it?"

Peter chuckled. "Why do ask that?"

She smiled devilishly at him. "Just wondering."

"All right then." He considered her question for a moment and nodded. "Yes. Yes, I would. Like water itself."

Abbie leaned an arm against the window, gazed silently at the passing prairie. She wondered if he meant anything more than the obvious need of liquid in life. Water, food, shelter, clothing – it went without saying, didn't it? Yet one could not read too much into what he said, she thought; besides, his exactness, his directness, was what she found attractive about him in the first place. Perhaps he simply hadn't understood the full implication of the question.

Then Peter pointed toward the lower part of the windshield. "Look over there." A white clapboard church, its tall spire jutting into the sky, sat a field away near a winding gravel road. Next to it was a collection of clunky, weathered headstones. "That's the church my family used to attend," Peter said. "It's the oldest one in the county. Not in terms of being the first established but being the oldest building still housing a church."

Abbie gazed at the solid structure. Upon moving to western Nebraska, she had expected to see herds of a thousand buffalo grazing beneath the sun's heat and wheat fields lit a brilliant gold the year round. It was not so. Still, meadowlarks sang among the grasses, and sprays of wildflowers perfumed the air. Abbie had predicted the land's flatness, yet never did she imagine its utter vastness or how it rolled so pathetically into the horizon. Neither had she dreamed of the constantly blowing, arid wind; she thought there would be a gentle breeze, the scent of fresh baked apple pie from some kitchen windowsill always loft it.

"You go to a different church now?" she said.

Peter was quiet for a moment. "We don't go at all."

Their drive floated through the afternoon like that, making small talk, of seeing all the things that gave meaning to the loves of small town people upon the Great Plains. He showed her the shuttered, rotting one-room schoolhouse now serving as a town hall, an abandoned hand pump at a farm destroyed by a tornado in the 1940s, the ancient grange hall, the myriad windmills with their fans like rosettes in the sun, the long white sand roads that led nowhere. She thought of how the few trees upon the undulating prairie all stood wide and healthy – there were no spindly trees, no saplings – and how their truck always seemed to close in on a site but never quite reach it.

"So you actually like Felton?" Peter said.

"Sure. It's the first place I've lived where bottled water didn't taste better than the real thing."

He grinned. "But why come out here? We're so far from anything."

"I want a quiet life. I want openness."

Peter nodded. There was nothing quite so beautiful as the green farmland spread beneath he amber glow of an early evening sun, he thought. Well, almost nothing quite so beautiful. He glanced at Abbie, noticed how with the hair pulled back her neck appeared longer.

"Don't you like Felton?" she said.

He nodded. "You're not supposed to admit it, you know."

Abbie laughed. "I won't tell anyone so long as you don't say that I like it, too."

She peered out the window. There were no natural landmarks to guide them, and something about the prairie loomed severe and mysterious. Yet, she thought, here I am with this lithe man, his babyish eyes clear, in the vast, dreary flatness, discovering freedom. She found the prairie's immensity delightful simply because it frightened her. Then his hand crept toward her knee and patted it. She did not push it away as he left it to rest there.

*****

Despite that his mother's touch once soothed him like warm water upon a streambed's pebble, Lyle possessed virtually no memories of it. When his father attempted suicide, though, he feared it might be God's way of ensuring the pain from those recollections would not pass him. As he pondered such punishment, the dim house was quiet just as the night before, and the evening before that, and the one yet before that. His thoughts shifted to Abbie – he loved how her pupils flashed like coins in a stream, how her voice lilted a fluid, expansive lyric – and on all that his brother had said during the interview about the windmill, the farm, the family. Yes, Peter liked that reporter, too, Lyle told himself, but he also knew his brother could no more hold on to something good than an old woman could keep her footing on ice. Then Lyle heard in his mind the running faucet and saw the trickle of water streaming down the steps' center. He stood, followed the imaginary line upward, but when the bathroom door came into sight, his father was not slouched over the sink.

Lyle let out a sigh of relief as his heart's rapid pound slowed, then ran a finger over the edge of the white sink where blood, red like a cardinal in January snow, had settled from his pale father. He had pulled him onto the toilet, and when the old man's chest rose then fell, Lyle realized he wasn't too late. He held up his father's calcimine face at the chin. The pupils were slack, and he shivered at the stench of his breath. Lyle wrapped a towel around the slashed wrist to stop any further bleeding. His father couldn't have lost much blood, so he surmised the cut wasn't very deep. He searched the medicine chest for a bandage and finding one reeled it about the slender cut. Absorbing blood, the gauze hung about his wrist like a clump of wet red clay. Wind buffeted against the thin window as his father's shadow fell long across the sunlit bathroom. In the summer heat, mildew swelled at the cramped room's corners. Then Lyle lifted his father, heavy as a sick calf, and slung an arm about his shoulders. He passed Peter's room, heard him snoring through the slightly ajar door. At the master bedroom, Lyle laid his father on the high bed, checked the wrist again for blood. It continued to coagulate, and the half-soaked bandage stiffened weave by weave as it dried. He returned to the bathroom and meticulously wiped away any sign of the incident.

An hour later, exhausted and unable to eat, Lyle sauntered into his own mutely lit room. He tugged at his shirt.
Heavy with sweat, it stuck to his back. Then he stared out
upon the indigo sky, watching stars prick through the
sheath as the rising moonlight speckled the lawn with silver.
All through that long night, he listened for his father's
breathing. Lyle decided by dawn that he'd have to spend the
rest of his life on the farm looking after the old man. Finally,
he cried himself to sleep.

Chapter 3

Carl Steinar took over the farm when his father suffered a heart in 198-, the year before Peter was born. It was about noon. Sitting behind the wheel of his tractor, Carl thought blithely of dinner as listening to the farm report on the cab radio. The air smelled old and dry, like the ring of dirt about a pulled vegetable; summer had fallen from reach. Then his pickup truck thundered out of the red dust roiling upon the field before him. He slowed, watched the truck bounce across the furrows, made out Gwen's face in the driver's seat as it reared then jolted to a stop. She jumped out, ran toward him, the ends of her white cardigan fluttering in the wind. He bounded from the parked yet running tractor.

"Oh God, Carl, it's your father!" she shouted over the machine's clattering. "Something's happened. We've called an ambulance."

Carl's eyes widened, and grabbing her lithe hand he bolted for the pickup. They left the tractor in the field, motionless and still burning fuel.

Inside the farmhouse, his mother, her face heavily veined, lay over the still body. Carl rushed to it, tried not to push her aside though he needed space to gauge his father's condition. Despite a slightly ajar mouth, the old man emanated no breath, and with each passing moment his face grew more wan. Carl's hands trembled as he kneeled over the body. "Father?" he said, trying to conceal the shakiness in his voice. "Father, can you hear me?" His tongue grew dry and coppery. He knew from the lack of sweat along his father's brow and the glassy eyes beneath it that there was nothing to be done. "What happened?" he asked, as if possessing such knowledge would give him the power to raise the dead.

"He was just heading out to the grain bins..." his mother stuttered between sobs. "He was just..."

Gwen placed a hand upon Carl's broad shoulders. "He just stumbled then reached for the wall and fell."

Carl shook his head, found his own skin growing clammy and cold. All those years his father had spent struggling against the elements, against the greedy bankers and politicians sitting in their expensive suits and leather chairs so far away, and his own body had betrayed him. He fought back a tear.

"Do you think he'll be all..." Gwen started, but her words trailed off as he turned to her. For a second, his eyes caught the light like a dull stone.

Though the death jarred Carl Steinar, in the following weeks he threw his all into readying the crop for the next harvest, in continuing and finishing what his father had begun for him. A month after the heart attack, his mother declared she no longer could stand living in the house that conjured so many memories of her dead husband, and the following morning, as frost lay like arsenic sprinkled upon the lawn, they saw her off on a bus to live with his brother Gil in Omaha. At sunset, as the evening star lay low in the crisp sky, Carl contemplated his future and shuddered.

Without either parent, he grew increasingly more dependent on Gwen. The young farmer never spoke his feelings to her, though, never described how the loss of his father and his mother's abandonment of their home tore at him like wolf upon its prey over and over until only bone was left. Somehow she already understood his pain. And somehow her mere presence healed him of it. After returning from a hard day in the field or pole shed, he often caught her scatting as going about chores, sometimes to one of her jazz records, once in a while to a tune imagined in her head, occasionally to the wind. He would stand in the doorway and simply listen, letting her reaffirmation of life warm his face like the rising sun after a cold night. Then, in the evening when the daily tasks were completed, he'd find her sitting at the kitchen table organizing scrapbooks and family albums. He would lean over her shoulder, the nape of her neck sweet like blossoming sunflowers, and pressing cheek to cheek, their lips would meet and linger as if each pair were honeysoaked. With the passing days, his existence swam farther and deeper into the placid, sweet-tempered stream that was his wife, and there, as if a baptized man, he was reborn.

Hand-in-hand, they gradually decorated the farmhouse, that autumn painting the walls a mint green then piece-by-piece replacing the previous generation's icons and erecting their own symbols, from the dining room table atop a braided oval rug Gwen purchased in North Platte to a new bedroom set, its headboard an arch of brass bars. When at last she suggested that the living room needed a picture to replace the faded one that had always hung there, Carl readily agreed, and so they began a long search for just the right portrait to emblematize their joint destiny and heritage. Unable to find it, they begrudgingly settled on a wedding gift picture of two pheasants grazing about a bush. For her birthday in April, he bought a puppy, a collie that she named Jesse. All his life he would remember how her eyes glistened as she raised Jesse from the box, still round with puppy fat, his caramel eyes sheepish and heavy-lidded, the coat silky white and muted orange.

What followed became the most joyous year of Carl Steinar's life. There were reminders of his parents – mother's melancholy phone calls home, some artifact from childhood stumbled upon in the pole shed – but none troubled nor elated him more than the softball league games played in the field next to the country church and the cemetery where his very own father rested. As staring down the pitcher when at bat, he'd find the array of cracked and worn tombstones distracting, but when the willowy voice of Gwen, her belly now round with child, rose through all of the cheers, and his eyes narrowed on the task at hand. The crack of stick against the ball threw his spirit into an epiphany, for she'd allowed him to overcome the horror of loss, allowed him to laugh in the face of emptiness. She really had been the one to smack that ball deep into centerfield; he'd merely been the tool, the extension of her sublime being. Afterward, as the teammates slapped him on the back for the homerun while their families enjoyed chicken and hamburgers charcoal grilled in the open air, he refused to drink beer since Gwen couldn't due to pregnancy. The guys cajoled him to lighten up, but each woman there swooned and wished for the same quality in her own man. Sometimes, as the sun shined like a glowing tangerine, he'd gaze at the thin break in the grass marking the baseline heading into first and feel guilty again about playing and laughing so near his father's grave. Then he'd smile and know this was the way his old man would have wanted it.

*****

Felton, Nebraska, was established as a water tank stop

for the Burlington-Missouri steam locomotives when the Texas cattle drives ended during the 1870s. More than a century later, its downtown and main street still ran parallel to the railroad tracks. Pawnee Indians lived in the region until briefly forced out by Sioux, but with the advent of trains and the white man's buffalo hunts, they soon left as well, opening the region to immigrants from all across northern Europe. Most of the starving peasants found the wind that forever blasted over the boundless horizon the single aspect of the prairie that they could not impose order upon, and so it became unbearable. Many left. The townsfolk who stayed owed their destiny to it, though. Felton became the county seat when during President Grover Cleveland's first term when a tornado destroyed another village up the tracks. Since Felton possessed a stream large enough to power the flourmill's two burrs, people eager to erase bad memories resettled there, and businesses quickly flourished. For the next hundred years, it remained predominantly Lutheran, with a small Roman Catholic congregation. By the early 1980s, it suffered from the great crisis befalling all archaic farm communities in the dawning Information Age. When Abbie Blaire moved to town, the nearest hospital was 30 miles away, the school superintendent taught driver's ed, and the Lutheran pastor did a circuit of parishes.

Felton was still a small town where no one locked their doors, though, and Abbie, having lived all her life on security-minded air bases, liked that. As she ambled on her morning rounds through the snug air, the barber stepped lackadaisically from his shop and called her name. She glanced over her shoulder and waved in return. After a few steps, she scolded herself for not stopping to talk; the habits of her fast-paced college days till ran deep.

Then she saw Peter, walking down the street straight at

her, and she deliberately looked at the sidewalk. They collided.

"Are you all right?" he said blushing. "I'm sorry – I thought your saw me. Looks like you're in a rush."

Abbie gazed upon his nicked and dirty yet virile frame. My grimy little farmer, she thought as suppressing a giggle. The wind blew rich and sonorous. "My, you make it to town an awful lot," she said, leaning closer.

Peter gazed at the young woman. Warmth filled her glowing eyes, and her breathing eased outward like the undulations of calm water. She wore a soft white blouse with an indigo-colored blazer. "Parts today," he said.

"So you're the Steinar errand boy then?"

"Yeah," he said grinning.

"I enjoyed your nickel tour of the county."

His face reddened again. "You really do like it out here, don't you?"

"It isn't rushed; it's as if there are no problems."

"Life just rolls on lazily?"

"Compared to the city." Abbie stepped aside. She had felt this way toward boys during school day crushes. There was so little to say, yet she couldn't bear for the moment to end. "Guess I better get back before the editor thinks I've been kidnapped." She lingered for a few seconds, though.

"I'll walk you back," he said.

"Okay," she said, her smile washing away his uncertainty. The sky hung huge and bright over them. They remained silent, passed the gift shop then the beauty parlor where the hairdresser blow-dried the coiffure of a woman who looked like her mother, Mary Dawn. Abbie imagined that whenever they spoke by phone, her mother was gazing at a college picture of her, the one in which she stared back with the cynical eyes of angry youth, a second-hand beret tilted over the brow. In another room sat her father, an empty, black hull that each morning subsisted on a cup of coffee and a nearly stale muffin to keep his weight down, then spent his days constructing plane models, reading the Air Force Times, and sifting through Internet garbage, a man reduced to a tuft tossed about the wind.

At the newspaper office, Peter stepped in front of Abbie before she ascended the concrete stairs leading to the main doors. "Say, no tour of the county would be complete without seeing my family's farm," he quick said. "Would you like to stop by again? Last time you saw just the house and the windmill."

Before Abbie could answer, she sneezed. "Must be ragweed."

Peter pulled a handkerchief from his back pocket, handed it to her. "The goldenrod is blooming."

"My, you're prepared for everything," she said playfully as taking the handkerchief.

"No, not everything. Sometimes I just guess as going along."

She gazed up at his eyes, they dark yet soulful. So far his divining had been pretty good, she thought. "Well, I guess I'll just have to take you up on you offer then. I have to return this handkerchief, after all."

*****

Like a hobbled horse, Carl Steinar shifted slowly through his chores that following afternoon. Peter thought all the while that his younger brother was prowling behind their father, and sometimes he even found Lyle blocking his view of the dotty old man. Peter supposed poor lighting could have been playing tricks on his eyes, for even at the height of summer, an ashen glow permeated the pole shed thanks to the discolored roof and an unreachable, burned out bulb high in the swallow-infested rafters. Cobwebs and straw lurked like shadows across the corners of the shed, filled with farm machinery and a suffocating heat.

As Lyle leaned against the grimy top of a double drill, he examined the musty fertilizer bags, their odor sharp and pungent like cow urine just sprayed a grimy red toolbox at his father's feet, who stretched out on the dirt floor beneath the implement, pounding away at a colter. As the battering echoed through the shed, swallows fled their nests and swooped out of the wide, open doorway. A dryness filled the three men's throats.

"I suppose we'll have to listen all afternoon to you telling us about your date," Lyle said.

Peter had said nothing to them about his time with Abbie. "Sounds to me like you're asking."

From beneath the drill, their father held out an arm. The cuff of his sleeve slid down a couple of inches. Lyle's eyes bolted to it; the wrist was unblemished, like a polished white stone, and he sighed in relief. "Hand me the locking pliers," his father said despondently.

Lyle dug through the box, gave him a tool, then glanced at Peter. "Not really," Lyle said. "Just wanted to know if you showed her the levee down by the creek."

The levee, Peter thought. Old Sutter Road led down there. It was no more than a small berm tucked far away from the main highway. Back in high school, he and Laura Jean Strom often would go there and make out. How long ago was that, he pondered, six years ago? Had it really been that long?

"Nope, we didn't," Peter said.

"Sounds like you're slipping," Lyle said, and then eyeing a bug creeping along the ground, he stomped on it. Lifting his boot, he considered the squashed insect for a second then wondered why his brother was always the lucky one, able to get a date just a few hours after meeting a woman. Probably saw how attractive I found that reporter and raced right over just to prevent me from asking her out, he figured. It was always that way with Peter. Lyle remembered when he was six and got the notion of riding the combine with his father. When he started walking through the cut golden fields, husks and chaff swirling about on the wind and landing on his sweaty neck, Peter ran over to him and asked what he was doing. Lyle foolishly told him. As the combine rattled upon the horizon, Peter headed for it, his longer legs pushing ahead. Realizing his mistake, Lyle broke into a run, and upon hearing the footsteps Peter also ran, far outdistancing him. Lyle screamed at his brother to stop, but he was answered only with a wheat kernel fluttering into his mouth. He spit it out, tried running again, but tripping, landed chin first in the dirt. A sharp straw poked his cheek. He rose, brushed himself off, watched his father stop the combine so peter could climb aboard for a ride to the end of the row. He refused to weep.

Be patient, Lyle told himself, don't let your anger show. He supposed the same would be necessary when dealing with his old man.

"Feeling better, Father?" Peter said, though he little cared. Carl Steinar never would back off him, always kept pressing until cornering him. Yet, Peter knew until he asked questions there'd be no way of ascertaining what his brother had been up to the past week.

Lyle quick glanced at his brother. "Father's feeling fine."

Carl Steinar stopped hammering, and a silence, eerie as a greening sky before a tornado, filled the shed. He thought of how in front of the café in Felton he'd often pass the pair of bachelor farmers that were a town landmark, each sitting half a foot apart, one wearing a beaten cowboy hat, the other a new seed cap, both of them dressed in denim, work boots, and gray hair. Their eyes were sullen, as if wondering what kind of cruel joke life had played on them, and they breathed with heavily punctuated wheezes. They smelled clean in their button shirts, pen and notepad sticking from each front breast pocket, but once the sun angled past 10 a.m., reducing the shade to a sliver, an acrid stench much like dog breath quickly emanated from them. They talked of people leaving town, of wheat prices, of girls they knew long ago, of the general doom befalling Felton and all the Great Plains. On occasion, one would rise and buy the other a soda; typically they took turns doing so, but neither spoke of any formal arrangements toward this end. Should one fall behind a day, though, it was sure to cause the slighted party to privately complain about the other being cheap. Eventually, their rears grew sore from sitting on the hardwood bench, and they rose, took care of their errands, then headed to the café for lunch. Carl Steinar always thought of them as cut meat spoiling in the hot sun. He wasn't going to be like them, ever.

"Actually," Carl said from beneath the drill, "I haven't felt better in quite a long time. No, I haven't been quite so certain about things in a while."

He continued hammering.

*****

When Peter had told his father about breaking up with Laura Jean, the old man only harrumphed and after a brief pause said, "When a creek runs dry, there's nothing left but rock." Then he returned to pouring seed into the planter. Peter's eyes glared, and realizing a great desert separated them, merely shook his head. Six years later, he no longer cared what his father might think of his personal life, and so the next day he strolled with Abbie upon the farm in the broad daylight, out beyond the pastured cattle contently chewing the wheat stubble, down toward the water and its medicinal-scented cottonwoods, across the windfall path lined with clover, linen and elderberry. Still, as they closed upon this intimate place of his childhood, he found breathing difficult, like a chestnut had been lodged in his throat.

Gazing at Abbie, a warmth flushed across his body, and the day's glory engulfed him as it had years ago. In the thinness of her mouth, the primness of her frame, she possessed a fluidity that he admired, like a field of stars twirling through the seasons. A lark chattered away as they walked. The prairie suddenly sloped downward, into a series of draws, all green and lush, and he heard the constant trickle of water at the bottoms' center. His pace rose into a near scramble as they descended, and the sun glinted off the vert blades pricking their ankles. Nearing the cottonwoods, ash trees and box elders hugging the water, a strange waft of moistness filled his nostrils, as if they'd left a wasteland for the tropics. A miniscule husk flitted against Abbie's lip, and swiping at it she worried that the tall weeds along the creek's bank might be poisonous. Then she saw how a well-worn path worked its way to a clearing beneath a tall cottonwood. She sensed he'd been here many times and wondered why.

Below the clearing, the aquamarine creek flowed like a stretch of gauze cloth before them. She gasped. "It's beautiful," she said.

Peter listened closely for the high-pitched croak of a frog, the long groan of buzzing insects. In childhood, they'd often lulled him to sleep. Even when dozing, there was the certainty of the creek, of how it ran like a blood vessel, surging and flowing, the very liquid of life itself. That late in summer, though, all was quiet as the wind barely ruffled the water's low, sluggish surface. He'd often wished his mother had been buried there. In a way, he supposed, she had.

"It's called Skriftlig Creek," Peter said. "The Omaha used to call it 'The Tadi.' It means 'wind.'"

She nodded, smiled widely, flashingly. Her dark hair shined like a plum held to the sunlight.

"It flows into Medicine Creek," he continued. "She's small, but ours is one of the few in these parts that never goes dry."

The grass swayed to Abbie's footsteps as she stepped into a flat red rock hanging over the warbling creek at the bank's bottom. Peter stood his ground, flicked a stone into the stream. "The water soothed me...my fears," he said. "I guess that sounds strange."

Abbie glanced back at him, shook her head. With Peter standing on higher ground, it was as if she were stopping to look at a statue. His face glittered like a stone, and he stood tall and erect, a towering officer. "Do you ever feel alone?" she said.

Peter chuckled. "When you live out here on the flats, it's hard not to be alone."

A smile stretched across her face as if it were dawn rising. She raised her face to the sun, and her fluid hair fell back like pure wine. Peter watched her for a moment then turned his eyes to the creek, its current bouncing and swinging like a little child in the distance.

"I enjoy the silence out here," he said.

Abbie's brow scrunched into furrows. "But it's not quiet out here," she said. "Don't you hear the water and the wind?"

He examined her for a long moment.

"There's a rhythm to it."

Peter listened intently to the breeze as it whistled across the creek like a lark in the field. His pupils widened, and he suddenly understood what his mother loved about it and that old windmill.

Chapter 4

At dawn, Lyle leaned against the windmill's cold metal rungs and trembled. He wondered if Peter knew. Despite their father's preference for long-sleeved shirts even on the hottest of days, the crag upon his wrist was not difficult to see. Lyle thought that certainly by mid-morning, as the sky's two-toned vista dissolved into a depthless blue, his brother would know; perhaps Peter was looking at it that very moment inside the farmhouse while the two men readied themselves for the day. Or maybe a spot had been missed in the bathroom, and curious where the blood came from Peter might ask. What would their old man say?

Strands of Lyle's bangs poked from beneath his cap and flopped in the breeze. He raked a finger along a crossbeam, examined the thick coat of dust covering the swirl upon his skin, wiped it with a rub against the thigh. The windmill's beams ran in lines true and straight before him. When a boy, he'd always viewed the steel structure as a model, a paragon of adulthood: towering, firm against the elements, at times even musical in its playful clatter. The weak scent of coffee spilled from the farmhouse as its front door opened, and Lyle heard first his brother's sprite feet upon the porch followed by their father's own dolorous steps. He did not face them.

Above, the windmill beat steadily like the continual striking of the chisel, and his father passed, bound for the machine shed. The two men gazed at one another, and a flicker of mutual comprehension appeared in their eyes. It vanished instantly, though, as if smoke twirling in a quick wind. Lyle fell into step behind his old man, tried to determine what had gripped his consciousness.

He glanced over his shoulder to see if Peter was coming. Between them, the windmill hovered black against the shimmering gold sky, the blades clacking slowly to the dry, perpetual breeze. Silhouetted, the bars appeared to bend, as if the whole contraption was ready to collapse under its own weight. A spray of wheat husks and dirt fluttered like ashes as he stared into the rising August sun, it a flaming bonfire red. Just as the iron beams of that windmill were bolted to one another and the foundation they stood upon, so Lyle knew he also was pegged to the farm. He canted his head downward, let the wind tumble out of the west to rip away then resettle layers of dust and earth as it did every moment for all of eternity. His brother's steps grew louder, closing upon him.

*****

Carl Steinar's arms ached and his shoulders burned from tearing apart the combine's header that morning, but it was a good pain, one that he could suppress. The repair really wasn't necessary – even with a slightly bent divider the machine would run fine – but his work extended the harvester's life for yet another season. One more chore completed, he thought, one more day half done. Years ago, getting out of the thickening heat if only for an hour would have felt good, but now he saw little difference between the clammy skin of the Stygian indoors and being soaked in his own sweat under the brilliant August sun. The scent of old straw, heady upon his senses, flittered upon the open air.

He hoped Lyle would not force him to live through that night. Tormented by the possibility, he drifted behind as if a phantom. Lyle opened his mouth to speak, but Peter beat him to it. "You okay, Father?" he said. "You look kind of tired."

For a moment, pride surged through Carl Steinar. He'd raised his sons to be wholesome, to be dutiful. Gwen would have approved. "You know it's been a good morning's work when the body is tired," he said.

"Just muscle strain," Lyle said, looking at Peter.

The two sons stood next to one another for a long, quiet moment. That's just the way I like to see them, side-by-side, united, Carl thought. Yet he knew it also was a dangerous union, especially then. "Of course it's just muscles," he said, his words a half-growl. "And it hurts like the mischief."

In the house, he leaned back in the living room recliner and stared at the opposite graying wall where a painting hung of two pheasants grazing about a bush. The couple had planned to replace it one day with an aerial photograph of the farm; men came around at least twice a year to sell them one, but they always put if off: too expensive, didn't like that exact shot, wheat prices might be low this autumn so they needed to save. He could imagine one of those pictures hanging there right then, a wide pan of his combine breaking across a half-harvested field, a cloud of yellow husks rolling over the golden grain and stretching almost as far as the main farm, the red barn and windmill rising through the small cluster of cottonwoods, the narrow creek with its line of brush and stout trees marking an edge of their property.

Their farm.

"The county fair starts Wednesday," Peter said, sitting

on the couch adjacent from his father.

Carl nodded. Will Lyle make me live through that, too, he wondered. He knew there was one to blame for his youngest son's tenacity but himself. He'd always ensured consistency in their lives, provided support and sustenance, had helped them to understand what it meant to be a man: to be strong, stoic and fearless, to never show pain, to not grieve openly. So this was the cruel irony of fatherhood, he thought, to have raised one's children so well that they served you too perfectly in old age. Perhaps I should have hated my sons. Still, where would that have gotten me – an infirm man hanging on to every excruciating breath until death overtook me?

"Just act" was the Steinars' unspoken motto; there was no need for useless talk. He thought of their ritual breakfast of long ago when the three sat together at the kitchen table before parting, a coffee mug warm in his big hands, small spoons full of cereal and dripping milk upon the tongues of each boy, until they grew and their appetites moved to forkfuls of eggs and sausages then coffee of their own, first with sugar and cream, and finally without. Such mornings were quiet as each of the Steinar males focused upon the meal at hand so he'd be prepared for the numerous chores ahead. That shared time remained pregnant with unspoken intimacy, Carl knew. Yes, I've raised them into men, he thought, and spent nearly two decades of spring, summer, autumn, and winter doing it. Then he recalled how the coldness of those winter mornings rang against him. Still, he persevered, and that also filled him with pride.

"I'm thinking of taking Abbie," Peter said. "I'll probably ask her tonight; I'm going over there for dinner."

Lyle shot him a look from the living room entry.

"Well son," Carl Steinar said, his voice long and pondering. Abbie? That reporter? Why in the latest Register there hadn't been anything at all about the Steinars or their windmill, and he wondered what really had brought her to his farm. Then, with a derisive undertone, he finished his thought aloud, "Always sell your grain first."

Peter's eyes rolled. The boy understood his advice. It alluded to granary weevils that hollowed out kernels. If one kept his wheat too long, the weevils would make the grain worthless.

"Whose turn is it to make lunch?" Lyle said quickly.

The other two Steinars glanced at him, then the father waved him off. "I'm not all that hungry."

"I don't want to fill up," Peter said as rushing past the kitchen table to the staircase.

Lyle shrugged.

Carl stared at the empty sofa his eldest son had occupied. He and Gwen had joked of how they'd have two sons and a daughter, one for each cushion. The boys would care for the land when the couple reached old age while the girl would marry into a proud farming family, one like the Steinars with a long, noble history upon the Nebraska plains. That hasn't come about, either, he thought. Now his two sons had grown apart from him and from one another. He gazed at the living room's picture window, watched how the wind buffeted against it. The breeze reminded him of music, of life. Both always were a matter of the moment, like breath drawn in and exhaled, a here-and-now constantly improvised. Yet, paradoxically to him, the quality of life in itself was timeless, unchanging. He turned his gaze into the vacant shallows of the room, his eyes tender as blackberries.

*****

When Abbie Blaire met her beau Peter Steinar at the door, he held out a succulent bloom of lavender and pink asters. Stammering that it was for her, she accepted with a beam and resisted prancing about. He followed her inside, the smell of baked chicken wavering about them as he glanced around. She'd painted the walls a light peach and had decorated her apartment in a sand castle motif, from kitchen towels and posters to the throw upon the sofa. He fixed upon a framed poster in the living room of a bright ocean scene.

"I love that picture," Abbie said, "especially how it freezes the moment."

Peter nodded. "You have a nice place."

She swiped away a strand of hair straying in her eyes. "If you look close enough, everything is slightly run down," she said, then with a smirk, "so don't look too close at anything."

He grinned. "Nothing's ever beyond repair."

For a moment, they stood, smiling at one another, and then she glanced away and thought of what disrepair her own life was in. She wondered in the hour before Peter arrived if the perfect dress, if the most alluring perfume, had been selected. Half of that prep time was spent sifting through the vanity drawer for the right hue of eyeliner, rogue and lipstick; she needed to get organized soon, for throwing contents of unpacked boxes into chests and closets was barely better than leaving it in cardboard. With the back of her hand, she brushed again at the offending hair strand, pondered if braiding it wouldn't have been better. Amid all of the evening's careful planning, she desired to feel free, as if wind upon the prairie.

"I should look in on dinner," she said.

Peter followed her to the kitchen.

"We're having chicken," she said as leaning over a wok where boneless strips fried in garlic and barbecue sauce. As sprinkling water and sunflower seeds onto it, then working a wooden spoon through a small pot of snap beans, she could feel the burn of his eyes admiring the delicate curve of her hands, the fall off her hair. The wok came to a boil, and she dished the strips and vegetables into two plates, carried them to a round café table tucked against a wall. French bread and a wine bottle sat between the place settings.

They took their seats, avoided looking directly at one another, said nothing. Her sheath dress, it blue like the sea, pinched tight at the waist. She watched Peter split a bite of chicken off one end with a fork, and he glanced at her as he chewed. Her eyes caught the light as might jasper, and their silverware scratched against the plates. She took a snap bean into her mouth; their pods had toughened not had the seeds inside grown into hard stones. Outside, thunder boomed a great distance away.

"Is the meal all right?" she said as tearing off a hunk of bread and buttering it.

He nodded, gave her a foothold to latch onto.

"Jill Lierley down at the office recommended the recipe. It apparently goes way back in her family."

"I went to school with her son."

"I understand he's going to college over in Lincoln now."

Peter said nothing for a second. "Yeah, Lincoln. Say, you never answered my question the other say. Not really any-way."

"What question was that?"

"About why you became a reporter. I mean it must be exciting and all, but why in Felton? The stories here would be so–" He paused for lack of a word.

"Banal?"

Peter wasn't certain what she meant. "Dull."

"A girl has to start somewhere." A smirk again covered her face, but Peter's brow crinkled. For a moment, his uncertainty did not register with her as she gazed upon him, his hair a shade heavier than nut brown, the mouth tender and smile grateful, and wondered at how he was never embarrassed yet boyishly shy, at how his breath fell upon like honey spread atop bread pulled hot from the oven. He ate heartily. Outside, rain suddenly rushed downward, then after a few moments fell at a more patient pace.

Abbie's dimples widened, and she leaned slightly forward as looking directly into his eyes. "Felton is peaceful," she said. "My whole life was spent moving all over. I would give everything to have the quiet life. I really mean that."

Peter grinned, watched her eat. She chewed slowly, her mouth moving in small circles. For the first time that evening, he noticed that her slender arms were bare. "The meal is very good," he said. "You'll have to ask Mrs. Lierley for some more recipes. Maybe I could throw together one of them for us some night."

"You cook?"

"I had to if I wanted more than canned food growing up. Father never had much time, and my brother was too lazy."

Abbie reached for her wine glass, realized it was empty. "Oh, I'm sorry, I never served the wine, you must be thirsty," she said, pouring it from the bottle. "'Wine will wear down stones as well as water, but wine makes life richer.' That's what my dad used to say."

Peter looked confusedly at her.

"It's a metaphor. You know, when two unlike things are compared."

"Very unlike in this case."

"Not really. You see–" A cat cried from outside before

she could explain. "The neighbor's little beastie must have been left outside. Well, anyway, what about you? Have you ever thought of living somewhere else?"

Peter took a sip. "I'm grounded here. Where would I go anyway? What would I do?"

Abbie leaned back in a chair, bared a knee as the wind rose, splashing rain against the window. ""You've never thought of leaving Nebraska?"

"Well, I'd be a liar if I said no to that. Sometimes I really want to leave this place, you know, never look at it again."

"You mean take a vacation?

He chuckled. "No one from Nebraska vacations."

"People in Lincoln and Omaha do."

"The big city's not for me."

"Me either."

"The cat whined again, and Abbie glanced at the window. "The Jantzens must not be home. Certainly they'd have heard it by now and let it in."

Peter stood. "I'll go get it."

"Wait, I'll go with you," she said, grazing his arm with hand as she rose.

She grabbed an umbrella from the entryway closet. As they opened the front door, a tabby sat on the stoop, its begging face looking up at them. He reached down, but it darted toward the curb.

"Hey, come back here," he said stepping into the sleek wind.

Abbie giggled, and joining him outside, bent a leg behind her to remove a high heel. With an umbrella in the other hand, she almost lost her balance as Peter glanced back at her. He laughed, long and fulsome.

"What?" she said, slipping out of one heel then repeating the awkward act with the other foot.

"You look so funny doing that."

Her mouth curved long and wide. "I can't very well go out onto a slick surface in high heels," she said. Seeing him laugh was good, she decided; Peter too often possessed a serious demeanor in his voice, his expressions.

They traipsed along the sidewalk together, calling for the cat. The street in front of them stretched like a ribbon of shimmering black, and the locks of his hair shined iridescent in the street lamp's glow.

"I think it's gone," Peter said. "Sorry."

"I'm the one who should be sorry. You've gotten all wet."

He shrugged. In her bare feet beneath the umbrella, she appeared fragrant and warm.

"So tell me, Peter Steinar, have you ever tasted prairie rain?"

"What do you mean?"

She sidled closer to him. "You know, when you were a little kid, did you ever stick your tongue out and try to catch raindrops? Like this?" She tipped the umbrella back upon her shoulder and leaning forward slightly stuck her tongue out. Raindrops splattered against it.

He roared in laughter again, the corner of his eyes crinkling in pleasure as he watched her. "Well, no, I'd say I haven't, but once–" At that moment, a wind gust batted them, pulling Abbie's umbrella before her. Pushed inside out, it spun in her hands like windmill blades. She shrieked, shook the rain from her arms as bringing the umbrella back over her head. "Guess I don't need an umbrella now," she said, tossing it over a shoulder."

"Might as well give up on the cat, too," he said. Rain dripped from his chin. He turned back to the apartment, but she did not move.

"You were saying there was something else you did during a shower?" she called to him, her mouth curling slightly.

He placed his mouth against hers, and they kissed deeply, tasting the moisture that had collected upon one another. Abbie guided an arm around his shoulder as he slid a hand upon the small of her back. She squeezed tight against him, his lips like a steaming petal, and although they did not move, she felt as if they were swirling.

*****

For a moment, they heard only their heartbeats. As Abbie combed the rain from her hair, it hung loose down the back of her dress; she stared at Peter then placed a palm upon his cheek and leaning forward brought her moist lips to his once again. He swooned, as if swallowing a mouthful of wine, and his arms glided about her back to steady himself, to draw her nearer. Even in his wet hands, warmth rose amid them, as if they'd lassoed all the sun's energy.

She pulled back, ran a fingertip beneath his eye. "Perhaps you'd rather do that than talk?"

His dimples flared. He took her whispery hand, it so light that a mere touch he half fancied would send him floating, and stole her away toward the bedroom. A gentle rain pattered outside, and then the comforter's pattern of leaf and life, the peach bed sheets cuffed over them, spread before the pair.

He guided Abbie to the edge of the narrow bed, and her eyes gazed at him wondrously. As he breathed her natural, earthy scent, it like sunflowers in bloom, the tension upon his face eased. Her dress, air blue and luscious as a silk sheet, wrapped tight about her frame. Then their teeming lips glided across one another, and he tugged at the concealed zipper centered upon the blades of her back. She raised her arms, and he pulled the garment to her hips, unveiling her firm breasts, perched in white silk bra, then with his thumbs he stretched each side of the dress and removed it from her body. Her raven hair swayed as she stepped out of the covering pooled upon the floor.

Canting toward her, he unclasped the damp bra and cupping a breast kneaded it between his firm yet gentle fingers. She closed her eyes, moaned. Then he stopped and held his arms above his head. She started with his top shirt button, measuredly undoing it, as if fearing too quick of a move would tear the thread. As unclasping each one, she pulled the shirt's opening away to unveil more and more of his chest. He studied her face as she concentrated on each button with the utmost care. At the belt, she untucked his shirt, undid the last button, the glided her hands up his torso and beneath the fabric. His warm body trembled. She pulled the sleeves back, and he held his arms behind his back so the shirt came off inside out. As it fell to the floor, she leaned toward him, and his lips streamed along her neck, it supple beneath his mouth, then his tongue drew a slow circle around a nipple, curled upon it, and took it inside him. Her eyes glazed, and tipping her head back, she gasped. The palms of her hands flattened against the bedspread. She stretched her fingers like a kneading cat as he pinched the breast with his lips. He moved up and down, tenderly nipping, savoring the milkiness of her skin. She smoothed the back of his neck with a hand, and entangling her fingers in his feathery hair, pressed him against her chest. Twirling his short locks, she patted his head with her palm. His hands shifted to her waist, and he gazed for a moment at her blue panties, tight against her creamy thighs, a damp gray spot at her slit. She let go of his head and canted back as he quickly wriggled her hose off, suddenly impatient with the preliminaries and intent on seeing her nude.

Then she sat up, and they gazed at one another; as their eyes locked, she undid his jean's snap, drew the zipper down, then rolled the denim away, working his boxers with them. Her eyes shifted to his bulge, and he stood, one leg at a time to step out of his boots, pants and socks. He returned to his knees and as embracing, their tongues tasted each other's mouths. Suddenly he felt as if the brakes of his truck had gone out. Pulling at the sides of her panties and un-peeling them, he eyed her honeyed patch, a triangle of matted and curled hair. Placing a hand upon each thigh, he spread her legs apart. The size of her patch widened, revealed two oblong bumps cutting vertically between the legs. He shifted her rear closer to the bed's edge and lowered his head, drew in a strong musky whiff of her. His fingers spread her labia, and he inserted his tongue. Her heat pressed upon his mouth; she groaned loudly as reclining, eyes half-shut, her hands grasping uncontrollably at his head.

And then he was atop her. She thought his body light, found herself flying. Their arms wrapped around one another, and as their ankles interlocked they found a rhythm. To Peter, it felt as if they were riding upon a winged horse.

Chapter 5

The sun broke through the horizon's gray sheath, illuminating Peter's pickup truck in bonfire red. His eyes gleamed. The farmstead – a mere patch of green trees, silver storage bins, and a lone farmhouse – rose from the expansive plain before him, then suddenly the windmill glistened, its metal shining with ever more brightness, for the sky over his home darkened a hue from a new arm of the previous night's storm. To the north where the clouds had given way, the sun blazed like a flame against blue velvet, and light webbed across the sky as dew shimmered upon the fields. A wholesomeness vibrated through the countryside and consequently him, inspiring a sense of lucidity that he'd found missing so many years. He yearned for the moment to last forever.

As he opened the farmhouse's screen door, though, the luster gave way to a stained brown like that of withered mustard seed. Closed curtains and blinds shuttered the windows. Peter felt his way along the wall, brushed a hand over a chink, knew the kitchen was a mere step away. Tiptoeing, he checked for his father and brother. That late in the morning, they'd already be aware of his absence, and he thought their watching him as he returned somehow cheapened Abbie. But only the faucet's intermittent drip met Peter. Probably left on again by Lyle during one of his late night drinks, he scowled to himself. Turning it off, he pulled the kitchen's Cape Cods slightly aside but did not spot the two. A band of clouds approached the sun, and he caught his ghostlike reflection, the face thin and at moments insubstantial, then rubbed the back of a hand against the bristling whiskers upon his chin.

His feet stepped lightly upon the stairs, his body weightless as a moth, and the top landing entered a murky hallway. Passing his father's room, the old man lay curled upon the bed, a green woolen blanket pulled tight about his body; Peter found odd the sight of his father resting, as if a five-legged calf – not improbable, for he himself had seen one born many years ago, but highly unlikely. He gazed against the door, the trim pressing into his shoulder, and gazed upon his father. The room smelled of rain drizzling from a black sky. He glanced back into the dim hall, saw his brother's room empty, wondered where he was. Peter's mouth grew dry, and he headed to the bathroom sink.

In the mirror he again caught his reflection, but what before had appeared airy and colorless now loomed solidly. Stubble grew thick and swarthy upon his cheek; he pondered how Abbie could stand its scratch. Sliding open a cabinet drawer, his hands fumbled for shaving cream and razor. The scent of aloe rose about him as he sprayed a mound of liquid gel into his palm then spread it across his face. His stomach hungered for her cool, kindly touch. The dark beard made him look dirty, he thought, and a sense that he was soiled in more than appearance pinged him deeply. He pulled the razor blade again across his cheek, and in the clear swath his skin glowed, as if a polished white stone. Though he'd enjoyed the night, now in the farmhouse's confines it felt vaguely cannibalistic, like he'd consumed a loved one to incorporate that person into his very own being. His lips frowned at the notion – certainly that wasn't what their passion had been about, he thought – and as grimacing, the razor nicked his chin. A drop of blood splayed against the sink's eggshell basin.

Dabbing the cut with a tissue, he winced, then held the blade under the running tap to clean it so he would continue shaving. How could I be so damned careless, he thought to himself as keeping his face muscles taut while drawing the razor through its last motions, this time slowly. He wiped his head clean with a towel. The new dryness numbed his nerve cells, and he rinsed the sink of his whiskers and bloodstains. In the bathroom's cheerless light, the water's roiling reminded him of his and Abbie's laughter when she told of how her car didn't work if wet and the troubles she'd gotten herself into because of it. As he shut off the faucet, water gurgled down the drainpipe. He recalled how she listened, her eyes bright, to his stories of Aunt Amita taking care of him and Lyle growing up. Then, with a forefinger he skimmed the cragged rip upon his chin; the skin around it felt smooth, as when he traced her sleeping shoulders. Peter closed his eyes, saw her body wrapped in a warm glow, pupils glazed in delight. As his eyelids rose, in the pitted and gouged plaster about the mirror he spied a speck of dried blood.

He leaned close to it, knew his own simple nick couldn't have splashed that far. The pinpoint appeared congealed, as if it had been there for days. His throat tightened.

Suddenly he dashed downstairs, told himself he had to get out of the house, that he needed fresh air. Peter took a seat at the top of the porch steps, they worn down the center. To the west, the sky continued darkening, like denim soaking water. On the warm spring nights through the summer evenings when he was a small child, his father and mother would sit upon the porch, holding hands and staring moony-eyed at the lush plain and humming windmill. His body went lax, as if collapsing from a deep, drawn-out kiss.

Behind him, the screen door creaked open, and his brother swaggered out, hair ruffled from slumber and sat on the steps next to him. His tattered white T-shirt, a hem of it stained long ago with grease, remained untucked. Peter looked off into the distance, wondered where his brother had been all of that time.

"Father's sure been sleeping a lot lately," Peter said.

"It sure looks like you're not," Lyle said, smirking. "At least not last night, anyway."

Peter turned away, folded his arms. Something had taken over his brother, he sensed, some newfound confidence.

"Was she as good as Laura Jean?" Lyle said. "It'd be hard to be as good as her, I suppose."

Peter's heartbeat rose as his eyes hardened, and he whirled toward Lyle. "'Suppose' is about all you could do when it comes to women." His brother's face fell half-white, as if ice cracking, and slowly rising he went back indoors. Peter found his anger flowing, like blood from an open wound, and the cut upon his jaw tormented him like a biting fly. He scratched at it.

Soon the steel gray of impending rain drenched the sky, and after several deep inhalations, Peter also turned for inside. Sauntering up the steep stairs, too exhausted for work, he decided to sleep the day away. His brother lay snoring in his room, still dressed in dust-laden clothes, the boots on as well, looking like a large boulder in a quarry. Peter fell into his own bed and closed his eyes to shut out the gray, to let his mind blanket the real world's blackness with the colors of his dreams. He imagined himself secure in the bosom of Abbie's love, her breath a soft trill, his face tucked between his head and shoulder. With each passing image, a warm sensation grew inside him, overtaking the pain. Asleep, he dreamed of his mother rising from water, her hair luminous beneath a yellow moon.

*****

Lyle doubted if he could stand another night remaining half-awake, listening for his father. A week had passed since Carl Steinar tried killing himself, and though Lyle had taken to mixing crushed pills of diphenhydramine in the old man's food, doing so did not provide enough comfort to let him also slip into deep slumber. Lyle knew he needed to get away, to empty his head. So when Carl announced that they would build a new rout weeder that morning, Lyle proffered that he'd like to check on some cattle in town and could pick up some welding rods along the way. His father was all too happy for him to go.

As Lyle clomped along the stockyard's catwalk, sweat forked down his face like wax on a melting candle. Nebraska's hot, dry weeks had arrived, would last through early fall. He leaned against the warm railing, a gold line streaking a dozen pens long, the raw scent of cattle below mixing with the sawdust under their hooves. They lowed and shook huge heads, stared dumbly at passersby, chewed cud. Still, it was a fine bunch, Lyle knew, and he imagined all the steaks that would carved out of their languorous flanks. If I leave the farm, I'll have to come up with new ways of keeping tabs on father, Lyle thought. He knew that would be difficult. Perhaps he could continue living on the homestead until certain all was right again.

"Well if it ain't ol' Sleepy," said a husky voice as a hand the size of a grizzly paw slapped Lyle's back.

Lyle and Jackie Kine grinned at one another. From under Jackie's cowboy hat, tufts of red hair billowed like the flame of a small campfire, but his eyes appeared non-threatening, though more alert than somnolent. He'd been a senior on the football team when Lyle, just a freshman, had made varsity; the younger Steinar recalled the many bruising hits Jackie had laid on him in practice. No malice was intended, though. Jackie's little brother was in the same class as Lyle, and the three boys often hung out together drinking beer, playing baseball with roadside mailboxes, sticking angry wasps down each other's shirts. Back then, everyone talked of how in a year or two Lyle would lead the conference in rushing and bring glory days back to Felton athletics. So nobody understood why he didn't go out for the team his sophomore year. Jackie Kine knew, though.

"They still talk about you during games," Jackie said.

"We're still losing that bad?"

"Most think you could have been all-state."

Yeah, maybe I would have been all-state, maybe even more, Lyle thought. So I made a stupid choice, but then I'm not smart or good-looking like my brother. Peter always got the A's and the girls: North Platte dolls visiting at bonfires, girls from all over Guthrie County during the annual fair, and for the longest time Laura Jean. Not one of them was ugly either; Peter got the kind of women that guys lapped at. Then there was me, the bulky little brother, flying out on the road every weekend, trying to prove that nothing in the world bothered me, not even death itself.

For a moment, Lyle and Jackie leaned against the railing, stared at the yard below. The sun beat bright against the labyrinth of fences, raised even more of the beastly stench to the men as chaff and dust from an open hay bale puffed outward and onto their drenched faces. Their nostrils pinched shut, and both lips pursed tight to keep it out.

"Let's go to the sale barn," Jackie said.

Lyle followed him down the catwalk as a hot wind fluttered over them. He craved those nights when his truck windows were rolled down, when he flowed with the cool wind across the smooth prairie in those mad teenage road races. For him, life was motion, and only then did he ever feel power surge through his body. The auctioneer's fast-paced rattling echoed through the arena as Lyle and Jackie Kine found seats near the top. A number of farmers watched the half-dozen cattle herded by cane into the sales pen below, but most talked amongst themselves while a couple even pulled straw cowboy hats over their brows to snooze. A man stepped past them, his heavy cologne momentarily masking the smell of dried cow dung emanating across the yards. He and Jackie nodded at one another as Lyle glanced at the electronic price board above the exit.

"Now what do you wanna leave that nice spread of yours for, Lyle?" Jackie said.

"I'm thinking of striking out on my own. I need a little seed money."

"The old man won't help?"

"Don't want to ask."

Jackie Kine examined Lyle for a moment, wished for a good beer to help cool off. "There ain't any seed money to be found here."

"No openings?"

"No pay," Jackie said, shaking his head. "This ain't the kind of place a farmer's son comes to work at. It's for farmhands tired of their bosses or drifter cowboys who get local girls knocked up."

Lyle leaned back in his seat, the thin cushion giving quickly under his weight. He sighed.

"It's not that I wouldn't give you a job, Lyle, if I had one to give. You're a good man. Never been in trouble, at least legally, and you're a hard worker. You'd have to be if you grew up on Carl Steinar's farm; that man never stops working."

Lyle turned away, scowled. "Well, there's always Joe at the elevator, I suppose."

Kine examined his old friend closely. "You haven't heard? Joe Audun packed up his family and left town just this week."

Lyle slowly turned his head toward his old friend. "He quit?"

Kine nodded. "Said he needed better paying work. But it's more than that. There's no future in Felton. He went for his kid's sake."

"Kids aren't something I have to worry about."

"Not now anyways. Should the time ever come, though, don't you think they'd be better off on that farm? At least you've got land to sell if worse came to worst."

"I'll have to share it with my brother."

Kine shrugged. "Still better than being at the mercy of some boss man. At least you're in charge of your own paycheck."

Lyle sighed. He knew all about being at the mercy of someone else's whims.

*****

Never had Carl's heart beat so fast. Hovering at Gwen's beside, he stared at her painfully contorted face. *Breathe in, exhale, breathe in, hold it, exhale, push, exhale* – he couldn't remember the order. Though the space about his wife's sweat-laden brow remained dark, the rest of the room glared as nurses darted and the doctor buzzed about her, and Carl found himself caught up in the fury, all nervous and excited at a single instant. It was like the thrill he felt the moment before breaking out the combine to harvest. He leaned against her bed rail, the sterile gloves itchy upon his hands, and knew that despite his starting all of this with a quick thrust and release deep inside her tiny frame, it was now entirely out of his control, like a river that had been released from the floodgates and could not be stopped. And yet, he was responsible for the life and all that would follow in only a few more moments. Such omnipotence simultaneously inspired and repulsed him as he watched his wife take large, deep breaths like those of an athlete during an underwater swimming race. "Breathe in, exhale, breathe in, hold it, that's good honey, exhale," Carl repeated, though he hadn't said it for several long seconds. Gwen didn't seem to be following his instructions anyway. His forehead flushed, and gripping the metal railing tighter, he swooned. The heater at the North Platte Hospital had been turned up much too high, Carl told himself, then shook his head at the realization that he was rationalizing his sudden wooziness. Over the years, he'd seen many animals give birth on the farm never once had the sight of blood or the grunts and bellows of the female in labor sickened him. No, it is not revulsion I feel, he told himself, it is something else, as if the very wind has taken over my muscles, taken over my heartbeat.

"Breathe in, exhale, breathe in, hold it, exhale," he found himself saying over and over, more to control the rhythm of his own lungs than to guide his wife's. A tentative peace came to his body. *Breathe in, exhale.* The doctor and nurses focused on the gap between Gwen's uplifted knees, and then, involuntarily, she held her breath, turned purple across the face, and suddenly relaxed. A tear welled in her eye as their newborn wailed. Carl glanced again at the bed's end, and into the firmament their doctor held a slick, squirming form, no larger than a little girl's doll. The eyes upon the scarlet body pinched tight as its miniscule fists squeezed air then let go. Before Carl could comprehend what had occurred, a nurse wrapped the infant in a soft blue blanket and handed it to him.

"He's a boy," the doctor said as Carl released his held breath.

Quavering and grinning broadly, he brought Peter to his Gwen. As she cradled the baby, Carl smoothed the damp hair out of her eyes, and for several long moments they gazed rapturously at their first son. They named him Peter, after his grandfather, just as Carl had been named after his. And so, in a single brief heartbeat, the Steinar name was continued for another generation. Carl knew his father, gazing down from Heaven's rafters, smiled proudly upon him.

*****

A bright computer screen stared back at Abbie as she tried writing the Steinar windmill piece. No words came, though, and she flipped through her scribbled notes, looked for a way to start. She wanted to write a story that Peter would be proud of; not knowing how it could be done only made beginning all that more difficult.

The editor cast her a glance as fumbling with the file cabinet in the newsroom's back. She wondered if after not hearing any tapping of the keyboard for a while he'd come to check on her. It was unlikely, she knew, but her nervousness undermined any sense of security. With the weekly newspaper's deadlines, though, there was plenty of time to work on the article, she told herself. And Abbie planned to take it, for she knew that if patient enough, the words would come.

The editor stepped toward a desk behind her, and pausing there, read from a manila folder. She typed the Steinars' names on the screen. It was an old trick she'd learned in college: When struck with writer's block, start with the basic facts – name, age, where they live, what they're doing – then fill in the gaps from there, for each accompanying new fact resulted in another divide that required yet another statement to bridge it, and so on the story went, like wind across the earth, only ending after running out of its own oomph. This time, the words failed her. It was as if the names stood like unmovable boulders snug against one another. She thought back to grammar school days, when sitting alone in her cold room, waiting for her father to return, and she lost herself in words. Paragraphs and book reviews and essays – they all spun so easily from her pen into the willowy loops and lines of cursive letters upon the page. Teachers always returned her papers with gold stars and A's affixed atop them, and such praise became a surrogate for her father during the intervals between his visits home. Now she abandoned any belief in him ever returning. Her thoughts fell to the first long strip she'd made to Felton, paralleling the Platte River most of the way. A softness kissed the land, and it opened all arms to her: warm light, wheat sprung up from the soil, the clean scent of Rocky Mountain snow melted into rain. The town was so tiny – it'd be a mere neighborhood in Omaha – and she could drive across it in a few minutes! And all of the buildings, so quaint! Felton rose like a little play village, a fantasy town surrounded by boundless sky. She coveted it. At the interview, Cary Sutherland, Guthrie County Register's editor, thanked her for coming all that way. He wore a polyester tie, had hair the color of freckles, was almost laughable in his small town politeness, but when he told her "Your work is very impressive," he said so with speckles of admiration in his eyes, and Abbie knew he meant it. She blushed. Then he listed everything that a college girl from a big city wouldn't like about living in a godforsaken place such as Felton, as if he himself hated the town, and upon finishing he straightened her resume and clippings on his desk, tamped them against the hardwood top, and stuck them back into the envelope she'd used to mail them. He asked if she really could live "here." She nodded, gave some half-sensical answer about how the town couldn't be that bad, that there must be plenty of things to write about "here," and besides, she wasn't much of a big city girl anyway, had always preferred the quiet, peaceful life, and while making this up as going along, in the back of her head his words "Your work is very impressive" kept ringing. When she finished the answer, he offered her the job.

She bit her nails as staring at the computer screen, a pencil precariously balanced between her fingers. With this story, she vowed, her editor would again be impressed. So would Peter. He deserved it, too, and she decided this story would be her gift to him. For just when Felton was becoming all of those things Cary Sutherland had warned about, Peter entered her life. he listened to what she had to say, he could cook, and he knew how to make love sweetly to her, so sweet she felt as if she were flying. She closed her eyes. Places such as Felton unfortunately were disappearing, she thought.

That was how to start the article, Abbie realized. Though towns like Felton and the lifestyles they offered vanished each year across the great stretch of prairie, strong men – compassionate men like Peter Steinar – worked to preserve them. With her story, she would help him in that effort. Her fingers tapped the keyboard lightly, tentative like the first rain drops on a tin roof, and then as the ideas multiplied, so also did her speed until a downpour sounded.

Chapter 6

Though most of Carl Steinar's memories had grayed, he recalled the death of his wife with the utmost clarity. That day, the strong scent of fresh wheat flowed beneath the gleaming sun as a warm west wind shook buds from the tress. A quilt of garnet, amethyst and sapphire wildflowers covered fallow pastures from where a brown thrush sang. Gwen had just returned with the boys from the weekly run to town when, hands and shirt dappled with grease, he approached from the shed. "I need you to run back into Felton and get a part," he said. "The damn combine's acting up again." Her mouth narrowed. She had a trunk load of groceries and lunch already wouldn't be ready on time.

Carl noticed her quiet displeasure. "Leave the boys with me if that'll help. I really need the part now rather than later." He grabbed two brown bags from the trunk, bread loaves and celery stalks sticking out, carried them to the house.

"All right," she said, unstrapping Lyle's car seat. As the middle of five farm children, accommodation was a skill Gwen had naturally acquired. With it befell the ability to soothe, a perfect balance against Carl's high-strung tendencies. He'd come to depend upon this power of hers and often was amazed at the many ways she manifested it. Though she spoke softly, Carl always listened as her voice rose luminously, like a choir, and her hair, dark as a river at night, rippled in silky wisps past her jaw's fine contour. When she smiled, the corners of her eyes crinkled sweetly; he found it more nourishing than wine. Anger simply wasn't in her personality, and the few times she did boil, her dimples, slightly curved like flower petals, undercut the rage.

Still slender after two pregnancies, Gwen's face shined that spring day just as it had since he'd first wanted her in high school. Though a claw barrette pinned back her hair, a loose strand still fell over the eyes. She smelled of country sage. Hurriedly, Gwen stuck away the frozen foods and those needing refrigeration, left the canned and boxed goods for later. She knew interruptions such as running quick errands simply were a part of farm life. The inability to accept that fate was why her eldest sister Amita couldn't entirely enjoy the country life and ran an antique store in town.

"I've already called the part in," Carl said as hauling two more brown bags into the kitchen. "They said it'd be ready."

She nodded, placed a carton of blueberries on the counter as peter stood upon a chair, digging through the unpacked bags for his candy bar.

"Yum," Carl said as staring at the berries. "Can't wait to have those."

They gave one another a peck upon a cheek then she was off. Outside, the windmill's blades wobbled in the slight breeze as Carl carried Lyle's baby seat to the swing set, placed him on the ground beneath a cottonwood's shade. "Peter" he said, "play on the swings and watch your brother until your mother gets back. It's too hot in the pole shed for a baby."

Peter took a seat on a lone plastic swing. His feet

dangled as he chewed on the chocolate bar melting between his fingers.

Perceptibly, the day's temperature rose. Carl worked on this and that, every few minutes peeking out of the scathing shed to check on his two sons. Peter busied himself at the swings pretending to be in a great car race as Lyle slept. Eventually Peter tired of his imagined game, and the gaps between his father's glances widened. When the shade shifted far enough so Lyle lay in the full sunlight, Peter dragged the baby seat back into the edge of darkness. The boy's stomach growled as the swing creaked behind him, and he found himself slipping into uncertainty. His movements grew cautious. Then the house phone range, clacking like the windmill when quick gusts burst through its blades, and Carl rushed from the shed.

The sun passed a degree overhead.

Suddenly Carl spurt from the house, ran toward Peter. The little boy's eyes shot up as he stumbled back. Before he knew it, his father had grabbed an arm, scooped up Lyle in the baby seat, and was pulling them toward the pickup truck.

Carl Steinar drove faster than Peter had ever seen before, and as gravel spat from under his the tires, he thought even a bit recklessly. Sweat dripped along his father's neck until he no longer smelled of lavender. Then Carl cranked the steering wheel hard, almost fishtailing as cutting onto an intersecting road without stopping. Peter's small hands gripped a protrusion near the door handle to keep from being thrown around, and the plastic stuck to his perspiring palm. Dust rose around the pickup truck, spilling into the cab and his lungs. They passed the Bris farm, its yard full of scampering kids and life, then ignored another stop sign onto a blacktop highway. Lyle let out an urgent cry, and Peter suddenly was afraid to ask what happened.

Then they came upon it, a tangle of vehicles and people and cones all over the road, chaotic like images upon a spinning top. Carl quick pulled off to the side, jumped out. A cop car's red and blue lights darted like flares into the sky, and Peter's mouth grew dry. Very quietly, he slid from the truck and followed his dad past the crackle of police radios into the sweaty throng of adults. The sun had arced past its highest point, and their shadows grew long as the wind throbbed swiftly, like his heart.

A state trooper blocked Carl as Peter, like a raindrop slipping its way down through ceiling rafters, worked through the crowd toward them. "I'm Carl Steinar," his father said. "The sheriff's department called and–"

The trooper, uniform stiff and neat, placed a hand on Carl's shoulder. "Another motorist fortunately had a cell phone and called immediately after the collision, but by the time anyone could get here, it was…it was already too late."

"I want to see my wife," Carl said.

"Please sir, just wait," the trooper said.

Carl Steinar pushed past him, sprang toward the truck and car, the bumpers knotted, each crushed to half of their lengths. Peter ran after his father, but the trooper nabbed the boy's wrist. "Hey son, you need to stay back," he said.

Peter stared at his father kneeling before the wreck. To the boy, the crunched automobile with its moss green frame and sun-worn 4-H bumper sticker looked very similar to the one his mom drove. Is that why my dad's staring at it, Peter wondered, because he's trying to see who it belongs to? Yet there was more to his father's gaze, as if his eyes were enormous white caves being hollowed out of canyon walls as the river of life crashed at and flowed around them. Then his father stumbled back, sat fetal position in the middle of the road, shaking his head desperately. He howled, as if pain.

Peter's body shook. He glanced up at the trooper who still held his arm. "Is my mommy in there?" he said.

The trooper's face paled as he stared at the boy. Letting go, the officer edged away, said nothing. Several firemen carrying percussion bars rushed past Peter toward the car. Two of them went to Carl Steinar, lifted him, helped him to an ambulance. The trooper returned and brought Peter to his father, whose blank eyes stared at nothing as his mouth quivered. Peter felt the whole world slip from beneath them.

In the days following Gwen Steinar's death, Carl spoke meekly as he pondered where the Lord had been for his wife. He could not erase from his mind the sight of Gwen weltered in her blood. Aunt Amita, Uncle Joe, the whole Vann family, many friends, even Gil, attended her wake at Birger Funeral Home.

"How bad was the wreck?" Gil whispered to Uncle Joe.

"It looked as if someone had run over half of it with a tank."

Aunt Amita gave brief eulogy. "She always complained the land was 'level as an ironing board,' but she really loved the fields and the way the wind whistled across them, strewing the bluebells' pollen all about; my sister often said it reminded her of a soul in flight." Amita paused, glanced at the stained glass. "She loved to see those windmill blades spin, hear them whirl, knew it meant the wind was being harnessed into something purposeful, something beautiful."

The next morning, as a weak light split across the countryside's thin soil, the Steinar family sauntered into the Lutheran church. It walled the prairie's great open spaces, buffeted the party against the flaming wind. Throughout the funeral, Peter shifted upon his hard seat as if a branch in a storm, but his father paid it no attention, just stared mindlessly at the wooden floor, his face wan. Next to them, Aunt Amita cradled Lyle, rocking him in her arms, lulling him at times with a long, soft "Shhh." Finally the pastor said, "From Ecclesiastes: 'He that observeth the wind shall not sow, and he that regardeth the clouds shall not reap.'" They sang the Commital, and, as the organ played, filed out beneath a swollen sun. At the burial, Carl could barely stand; Uncle Joe discreetly slung an arm about his wait and help him up. The roads home were long as they crossed the great yawn of land. An eastern wind blew. Once on the farm, after all the formalities had finished, Carl Steinar stared out upon his sprawling land, hundreds of acres flat in every direction, most of it barren of wheat, the rest of it scrubland feeding his cattle, and thought, "This is all mine, mine alone. Whatever am I going to do with all of this by myself?"

He gazed at the sky, and his heart hardened into a small stone.

*****

For a good part of childhood after Gwen died, Peter and Lyle were deeded to their Aunt Amita. Though already possessing a brood of four, she readily took them in, as if it were a duty to her sister. She was a godsend for Carl Steinar, for with all the farm work, he had no way of caring for two moppets. In any case, he didn't really know how. The first time he attempted breakfast, more broken eggshells than blueberries ended up in the pancakes. Then there was the laundry with all of the whites dyed pink after he mixed in a red shirt. Aunt Amita's participation was good for Lyle, too; almost as if he hadn't lost his mother; indeed, never once did he cry for her. He merely accepted his aunt's warm caresses as if his mother's own.

Hair ragged and graying prematurely, Aunt Amita barely resembled her youngest sister. With Gwen gone, she was the only one of the Vann siblings left in Nebraska. As soon as the others were old enough, they scattered across the country like leaves in the wind. Peter thought the aunt's soft, rounded cheeks similar to his mother's, but Amita's brows were thick, almost furry, and the bridge between her eyes flattened into a broad expanse spilling onto a large, bulbous nose atop long, thick lips. In her husky, fast-paced voice, she was quick to curse when someone upset her, and Peter had to grow use to it and his uncle's swearing, often done in jest, sometimes in tirades. Worse for Peter, his aunt smelled like the cattle she and his uncle raised, musky and all barn, and that prevented him from wanting to fall into her bosom. Neither were her meals particularly pleasant, for she often cooked heavy dishes void of flavor, like meatloaf or plain pork chops. She fed the children bread and butter sandwiches for snacks. The cooking did not seem to bother Uncle Joe. Every morning he'd wipe his breakfast plate clean by sopping toast across the bacon grease, and with increasing frequency as the years went on, he turned sideways when passing through doorways. Languorous and sullen like a log, he largely ignored his nephews, not to mention his own children, and spent his days outside with the wheat and cattle. For him, food and farm alone defined life, gave him vigor. Indeed, Joe and Amita rarely went out, but when they did, it always was to the Chuck Wagon Café where talked only of farming and no matter the time of day ordered by name the Broncobuster, the triple-patty hamburger a quarter foot tall. When not eating or working, his eyes held at best a dull gleam, as if his universe were blunted.

Peter remained unobtrusive whenever at Aunt Amita's. That time mostly was during summer harvest, autumn planting, and each night after school for an hour or so. Despite not liking her house, it at least was warm, as is even a run-down motel, its vacancy sign swinging in the cold wind, to a weary traveler. Perhaps the worst part of being with Aunt Amita was his cousins, especially when they hollered "Mom!" and received a terse answer. Dagan was the same age as Peter but swore all of the time in imitation of Joe and Amita, both of who got angry with him for it. After punishing him, he'd always chastise Peter for not cursing. Two years older was Brady, whose hair lay brown like the tips of grass during a drought. He'd taken to always saying "You oughta know by now" just as his own mother often said, except he wasn't mocking her but attempting to claim his dominance in ways besides age and size. Between Dagan and Brady stood Gretel, the lone girl in the bunch. Somehow she always lost her sandals, and being a girl, she naturally took the brunt of her brothers' abuse. Finally there was Galen, just a year older than Lyle. All of his toddler clothing, broken toys, and unread books were on to Peter's younger brother.

Throughout that first long summer with Aunt Amita, Peter's vision grew increasingly grainy though he did not need glasses. He spent each night with her until after dinner, when his father would pick him up. Following the silent ride home, he'd go to bed, only to be awaken at dawn's first stretch for cereal, the trip back to Aunt Amita's, and a day of utter boredom at her antique shop. Peter dealt with it all by remaining quiet, by gradually making do with as little as possible. He did not nag for candy bars nor ask for special gifts. He did not argue with his aunt's clothing selections or complain about the meals served. All considered him a golden child.

The dreams started during that first harvest, when his busy father only saw him briefly for breakfast. He could not tell where he was, could barely make out his mother's gray form, camouflaged like a moth against weathered wood. She smiled at him, that much he could see, and his eyes glowed, that much he knew. He tried swimming toward her, but an invisible fence pushed him back. Repeatedly ramming into the phantom barrier, he screamed in frustration then suddenly awoke, shivering and drenched with sweat.

With each passing day that winter, he spent more and more time pressing his face against the chilled window of the bedroom, the pane so cold his nose sometimes turned blue, and with sunken eyes he'd stare at the blinding expanse of glittering white snow, watching and waiting. His memories one by one crystallized, however, like the very ice threading down the glass, the vision through them distorted at the edges but sharp at the center. After a while, Peter fancied he could smell the ice; it reminded him of the creek in late spring, its water still fresh from the melt but indolently declining in volume. If his mother reappeared, even for a moment, the little boy swore to himself that he'd tell her he loved her.

*****

Lyle lurched straight up in bed. The shock of consciousness rang through him, and his head reverberated as Carl Steinar, standing in the doorway, called for him again, voice pounding like a giant's steps across a field. Lyle rubbed his eyes; the old man had awakened before him. Slowly the room came into focus, and each object steadied. "After breakfast, you need to run into town, pick up some insulators," said Carl, hands on hips. His eyes glared like a strong beam, and for a moment, the youngest of the Steinars almost quivered.

Doubting if he could slip any pills into the old man's coffee with him up, Lyle pondered how he might get out of going. Rising, he slipped on his jeans then tucked in his shirt and grabbing the wallet from the dresser glanced again at his father in the hallway. Despite the sour taste in Lyle's mouth, the moment possessed a certain sweetness, much like alcohol when imbibed, a quick flush of honey followed by a deep, long burn. His father stood stiff, like a steer, and Lyle found himself admiring him. Maybe, he surmised, now that the old man was back in command, all was right again. Perhaps there would be no need for the sleeping pills.

Then his father shook Peter awake. "Up and at it," the old man said as Peter stirred, "we're going to work on the fence line." Lyle waddled into the slate-colored hallway, rubbing his temples as yawning. His father stepped out of Peter's room at the same moment, and with eyes euphoric as Moses gazing at Mt. Sinai, the old man exhorted, "Better to be the hammer than the nail." Lyle's heart surged. He sensed a newfound spirit, an enthusiasm, in his father; perhaps it meant he now could find his own freedom. Lyle closed his eyes. He could not believe himself for here he was, venerating the strong Carl Steinar over the weakened, emasculated version of the old man. But Lyle knew he always had.

He thought back to the summer before kindergarten. A wind moved delicately yet with force, fluttering sunlight smacked against him, and he rolled through the air. Landing on his back, he saw Peter atop him, tearing the blossoms from his hands. "Get off me!" Lyle screeched, but the pain in his ribs seared, like a foot kicking a cold bucket in winter, and rather than tossing his older brother off him, he tried holding on to his flowers and suppressing the hurt. Peter's fist struck his face over and over until he cried, wails rising from his mouth full of dirt, his eyes squinting shut from the blinding sun.

Then the pressure of his brother was lifted from him, and he saw his father's face, hard and angular, the eyes swirling like an agate's marks. Peter lay upon the ground weeping as their old man leaned forward and with a firm grip of the arm raised Lyle until he had no choice but to stand or fall again. Though grass stains, shame, and remnants of musty leaves covered his body, he chose to stand. He wanted to spit the first from his mouth but unsure how his father would react thought better of it. Suddenly he desired to collapse into his father's huge frame, to be held and caressed. As if his father were reading his mind, he found himself picked up and carried back toward the house. He tucked his chin against his father's shoulder, swallowed the loam upon his tongue, and closed his eyes.

Lyle blinked as trying to breathe in the farmhouse's stench; with it closed up, their collective breaths had turned it pungent like a wet cow, musky and sharp. He wished the ache in his burly neck would go away. Waking up was indeed a prime example of his father's phrase "an act of will," he thought; the utter stillness of sleep, as if an animal safely hidden from a ferocious beast, always was preferable. His father often spoke against such a view, as if life's joy came in the challenge of reshaping the world. Why not simply let things be, Lyle wanted to ask him. Besides, one could not will the wind. It merely blew and blew over the earth until fading into oblivion.

Peter moved languidly into the hallway, his strength low as a stream during drought. He kneaded his temples, winced at the glaring white light from the window. Passing him, Lyle descended the narrow and practically vertical staircase into grayness. He decided Peter could watch their old man for once.

*****

Dirt and sweat smudged Carl's white T-shirt, its cotton stretched to the limit about his waist and underarms, as Peter trudged with him along the fence marking the farm's westernmost section. Their footfalls crunched against the dry soil as a trail of red dust spun behind him. The grit struck to Peter's grimy arms, and brushing at it with his wet hands only left smears. They meticulously examined each metal pole, judging if it were leaning, shaking it to determine looseness, and if it failed on either account, with a wrench of the hand and the pound of a mall hammer, it was straightened; then they tightened the three strands of barbed wire about the post, first in the middle, next at the bottom, and finally across the top. As a child, Peter often had walked the fence line, Carl knew. Though wind constantly swept across the plain, the farm hadn't changed much since those days, he thought. Each time they parked their truck near the fence line, the bull wandered close enough that they could hear him graze as he guarded his herd, just as their bull did 30 years ago when he helped his own father repair the barbed wire that swept across the gray horizon.

Carl paid neither the bull nor the sky any heed, though. With rough and calloused gloves wrapped around the mall hammer, he whacked each pole into the ground with a certain deliberateness. His face remained hard and brown, like petrified wood, and he wore the seed cap's brim close to the eyes through there was no sun to block. Odors of sweat and seed grain rose strong from his flesh, but never once did he pull the collar away from his neck or wipe the beading perspiration with a handkerchief. He always wore a long sleeve shirt, no matter the weather, and never complained of it, even on a hot day such as that one.

Only in the fields did Carl sense any completeness in his life. He loved the feel of fertile land beneath his boots, of how he could drag his heels across it and claim victory. Like his father and granddaddy before him, he had shaped this land into something usable, something profitable, just as a potter's thumb wields wet clay, and yet it hung perilously close to neo-desert. Each day one could see the fragility of their existence as red dust curled in a broad ribbon across the naked plain. There were plenty of reminders that people had failed before them, like the abandoned, rusted pickup truck out on the Dickens homestead or the crumbling firehouse rising from the prairie grass just a mile out of Felton. The soil spawned life and death. Its intentions were cloaked, and should a man believe he was destined to rule it, the wind would sweep up the carmine dirt and quietly smother him. A man had to fight and subdue the land as if he were to taste its fruits. Even though a plow's furrows last a millennium, cutting them alone was not enough.

Yes, this is as good of a place as any to die, he decided.

They got into the pickup, moved further down the fence line, their bodies bouncing across the uneven ground. Carl parked near the top of a slope so the truck could have more space to gather speed. One had to be careful, make it look like an accident or the life insurance would be no good. Peter jumped out, eager to be finished, but Carl lingered, being sure to leave off the truck brake.

"Why don't you take that leaning pole over there," he said to Peter, pointing at a distant one to their left. Peter nodded, and Carl headed for a main wooden post in front of the truck.

While Carl worked, he eyed the pickup truck as it balanced precariously upon the knoll like a large boat slopping upon the sea. One might as well had blamed the wind for an illusion of movement. Then it eked forward over the wheat stubble, and suddenly gaining speed, headed directly for him.

Hearing the creaking of gears, Peter glanced up. He

broke into a full run, the mix of thin green and brown grass crackling beneath his boot heels, and dove for the truck door. His foot slipped as he tumbled into the cab, and though the door slammed against his leg, cutting skin, he managed to grip the steering wheel and turn it hard left. The truck fishtailed as he grabbed the emergency brake handle and cranked it up. His chest lurched against the steering wheel, and the pickup truck stopped, only a few inches away from his father.

As Peter caught his breath, he looked up. Carl just stood there, no twisted look of fear upon his face, no balling of body in horror, not even a wince. The pickup did not move, and Peter got out, asked him if he was all right.

Carl faked a nervous roll of his eyes, patted the truck's hood. "Must not have put the brake on," he said as keeping his arm with the scarred wrist behind his back. "She's never done that before, even when I've forgot."

Peter stared long and hard at his father. Color remained absent from the young Steinar's face.

"Guess we could wait on the north section until tomorrow," Carl said.

Peter nodded. "Yeah, we're going to wait."

Chapter 7

Peter barely spoke a word the whole way to the fairgrounds. It bothered Abbie, but she remained quiet as his pickup truck bumped along the prairie road. Above, the sky had cleared, and from miles away the midway glittered while behind them patchy daubs of purple filled the horizon. Abbie crossed then uncrossed her hands. Her thoughts flittered like a bird hopping from branch to branch, uncertain of where to rest, and she drew in a long breath. Odd, she thought, how this was so much more difficult than talking to someone for the newspaper that you didn't even know. Finally she turned to him, asked if everything was all right.

"The fair's not much," Peter said quickly. "Felton doesn't have the sass and brass of bigger towns."

Abbie smiled; she'd already been to it several times for the Register, photographing the 4-H blue ribbon winners, manning the newspaper's grandstand booth. No, it wasn't like the big expositions in Omaha, nor had he answered her question either. Still, the fair held a certain charm, like the twinkling of stars of the zodiac, and she liked the way Peter explained everything to her as if it were all brand new. They parked on a freshly mowed field and from the wooden gate passed through living history displays of artillery and rows upon rows of farm equipment as heading toward the carnival rides. A woman on stilts ambled by, and gaping they looked up.

Abbie admired how the peach glow of the setting sun broke through Peter's light shirt so the muscular outline of his body shined. His presence sang to her. They paused as coming to a packed crossroads, and she shifted her large black purse, vowed the next time she'd take less. When one is more stable, more permanent, she thought, one didn't need to carry so much – or was it the other way around, that those on the move traveled lightly, carrying little baggage?

"Do you like petting zoos?" Peter said.

Abbie nodded.

"Let's go."

There, a dozen kids and their mothers clung around pens of rabbits, lambs and ponies. A goat poked its muzzle through the boards, and giggling Abbie leaned toward the fence. Her hands cautiously reached for then caressed its hairy jowls. The beast stunk faintly of straw and musk. She canted yet closer, eyeballed it. The goat's slick tongue jut out, its rough tip slathering her cheek. She squealed then broke into laughter with Peter as slobber dripped from her face.

"Last time I listen to you about going to a petting zoo," she said, grinning and wiping the damp cheek with a tissue from her purse.

"There's a bathroom near the arena," he said, his eyes suddenly distant again.

They walked toward a sweeping wooden building, watched kids struggling to get livestock to follow in a circle. Crowds began to fill the rickety bleachers as she entered the lady's room.

Twisting on the dual faucets, Abbie swished her fingertips under the water to test its temperature. Satisfied after a couple of adjustments, she dabbed a paper towel into the stream then brought it to her face, careful not to spoil the makeup. Sometimes trying to understand Peter was like entering a deep cave with only a small candle to light the way, she thought as the cheap brown paper rubbed across her cheek. With each moment, she found her confidence growing increasingly porous – he hadn't yet even said if he loved her or not – and wished she could wipe away his veneer just as the paper was doing at that very moment to her blush. After a second, she daubed the spot dry, and pulling a compact from her purse, quickly blotted the exposed region of her face. Powder rose up in tiny poofs. His eyes hung so sullenly; perhaps I'm not being amatory enough, she decided. With the blush reapplied, she threw out her chest and tugged at the blouse's hem so it fit more tightly around her torso. The barn's fecund smells, mixed with oats and wet straw, settled in the evening's cool as she exited.

Together, she hooked her arm into his, and hugging a shoulder against his larger frame, they passed stand after stand. At one, they could get a picture taken of themselves atop a Harley for $5, another sold snake oil, and a third hawked Hoover vacuum cleaners.

Peter glanced at her. "What do you think so far?"

"It's fun," she said, wondering if he'd finally broken from his moody spell. Perhaps her closeness had worked. "It's like a little adventure."

He chuckled. "Adventure? In Nebraska?"

Abbie tossed her head back in laughter. The bright orange and red spokes of the Ferris wheel filled her vision as they stepped past the cotton candy booth. All about them music wafted from the calliope and organ grinder, and she grabbed his warm hand, pulled it about her waist. "Want to go on the Ferris wheel?" he said. Her eyes lit up, and she felt

like a little girl again. As their Ferris wheel car swung upward, Abbie fancied herself a bird in free flight. The carney
stopped the ride every few feet for others to board, and at
the top, high above the fairgrounds, the wind swayed their
car. She gripped Peter's wrist as her stomach and eyes rolled. He smiled, took her hand, but she pulled it away and
wrapped her arm around his then leaned against his frame
as holding his sleeve tight. He nuzzled her forehead, quick
kissed it. Then with a jolt, the ride took off, turning faster
and faster until spinning lissomely. She knew it was all right,
scolded herself for doubting.

Disembarking, she swooned, as if caught in a mini-tor-
nado, and focusing upon him tried to regain her balance. He
did not stare back, only gazed far ahead, as if his eyes were
concentrated upon an object across the horizon. What was
up with him, she wondered. Had he just used her for sex and
now was bored, sticking with her out of some warped sense
of duty and obligation? Maybe he was try to fool her into
having his way again tonight? She straightened herself, refused to let her shoulders slump. A barker shouted at them
from a game booth, urged Peter to win a big pink elephant
for his gal. Above them, the greenish glow from the fair's array of lights covered the clouds. Finally, she tugged at his
shirt, and he glanced at her.

"Look, there's a fortune teller," Abbie said as pointing.
"Let's get our fortunes read."

She grabbed Peter's hand, tugged him toward the
striped canvas tent before he could speak. The medium
stood near the entrance, the edge of an orange flap fluttering at her ankles, and tried smiling beatifically. "Yes, yes, my
two lovebirds, come learn your future," the woman said,
faking a vaguely Eastern European accent. Abbie stifled a
giggle as Peter bought their tickets.

The glow of a crystal ball lit the purple and red canvas behind the fortune teller as they took seats about a round table. Peter noted an extension cord running along the crushed grass to beneath the tent wall, but then the woman's flashing hands drew him to the crystal ball as she introduced herself.

"I am Tatanya," she said, her breath stinking faintly of Polish sausage. She wore a white peasant blouse. Jewelry hung from her ears and slim wrists, jangling as she shifted. A scarf, tied like a gypsy's, held back her thin, walnut-colored hair, and heavy swaths of black makeup covered dim eyelids. Incense wafted over them as she grinned crookedly. Then she leaned over the crystal ball, moving her hands within an inch of the glass as if caressing an electrical field. She crooked her head, and Peter caught the haggard face chewing gum at the edge of her mouth.

Before he could laugh, though, she spoke. "Oh, I see good things for you two," she said, her voice rising like a meltwater creek in April. "You have just met one another, have you not?"

Abbie whispered a yes.

Tatanya was good at pretending that something could be seen in the ball. Peter glanced at Abbie while she peered intently at the fortune teller's sliding hands.

"You are at the beginning of something very great, something very momentous," the fortune teller continued. "I see many changes, many good changes, ahead for you."

"Do you know what those changes will be?" Abbie said softly.

The fortune teller peered closer into the ball. "The ball often is not so specific. But it appears that these changes will take you back home, just as the bird which flies south for the winter returns to its very nest the next spring."

The bridge of Abbie's nose wrinkled as both she and Peter straightened in the folding chairs.

"Say, how do I know you're really telling us the truth?" Peter suddenly said. Abbie's startled eyes rose then her face reddened as she glanced at him.

The fortune teller leaned back. "The crystal ball tells all, for those who know how to see."

"And how–"

She stood. "I am sorry, but I see no more!" With that, she moved to the tent's entrance and lifted the flap.

Outside, Abbie ribbed Peter. "I can't believe you asked her that," she said.

Peter examined her face. "The crystal ball tells all," he said as exaggerating the fortune teller's fake accent and rubbing his hands about an imaginary ball, "for those who know how to see!"

Abbie stopped walking. A new bank of clouds hid the moon's glow. "Are you angry about something? Did I do something to upset you?"

He shook his head, spoke between gritted teeth. "No, everything's fine."

She touched his elbow, caressed it. "No it isn't. What's bothering you?"

He swiped her hand arm away, spun out of reach.

*****

It was Aunt Amita who boxed and hauled away all of Gwen's belongings, just five short months after the funeral. Always practical, Aunt Amita knew from the moment she was told of her sister's death that Gwen wasn't coming back; her wait until mid-winter to clear the house was merely an acknowledgement that Carl might need to grieve. So the one day each week that Aunt Amita visited to clean, she arrived extra early and brought a carload of boxes with her.

Moving swiftly for she could not afford a wasted moment, Aunt Amita marched to her younger sister's closet while Carl sat in the living room. She did not ponder over each garment, merely tossed them into the boxes, as if wheat shoveled into a bin. Despite her speed, they all fell neatly in – barrettes, purses and shoes, hair brushes, perfumes and skirts, earrings, makeup, sweaters – boxes and boxes of which, as they filled, deprived Peter's memories of substance. Soon the closet was empty as a January field with nothing left behind but a lone hanger. Through it all, Peter merely sat there, bitter-eyed, hatred beating in his heart. Years later, he would wonder if that afternoon were a beginning or an end. Like the wind, such moments held no definitive points.

*****

The day after the fair, Peter could not stop thinking about either Abbie or his father; it was as if two forces tugged violently at him from opposite directions. He gripped the steering wheel harder, tried to steady himself as he drove to see old Cornelius Skerry, the one neighbor who his father still spoke routinely with. It would have to be a quick stop, Peter knew, as he'd told his father of needing to pick up some papers at the conservation office, and his planned fib about long lines would go just so far. If only to avoid his father's third degree, he'd not had been in a rush to get back, but earlier that day the latest Register had arrived. Plastered in five columns across its front page was Abbie's story of the family and their windmill, accompanied by a picture of the three men standing in front of the spindly tower. When Peter brought it in from the mailbox, Lyle crowded near his father, who sat at the kitchen table. Carl Steinar waved off his eldest son, though. "I'll look at it later," he said. Peter handed it to him nevertheless; it was only proper for him to read the article first. Then Peter joined his brother, and careful not to graze one another, they skimmed the story over their old man's shoulders.

"STEINARS' WINDMILL HEARKENS BACK TO PIONEER DAYS" the headline read, then after Abbie's byline, it began: "Out on the vast, windswept plains of Guthrie County, little has a chance of lasting forever. Indeed, the countryside is populated with articles of a failed past: an abandoned farmhouse, hand pumps for wells on homestead ravished long ago by tornadoes, broken wagon wheels left by pioneers. On the Carl Steinar farm, however, one memento has survived for a century and with the family's loving devotion, likely will last for at least another hundred years: a 1910 model Dempsters windmill."

Peter blushed as his feet seesawed on the kitchen tile. The article not only was slightly overwritten, but as reading down the columns, he found himself the most frequently quoted of the Steinars and in one paragraph even described: "...a young man in his mid 20s, his hair a shade heavier than nut brown, never embarrassed yet boyishly shy." Still, the article was quite accurate, and between the lines it hinted at a great power that Peter innately was drawn to; his spirits rose, swirling and spiraling as if smooth jazz pouring from a saxophone.

Then Carl Steinar harrumphed indignantly. With a slap, he set the paper on the table, the side featuring the headline and picture face down. His mouth crunched bitterly.

Peter's brow furrowed. "Don't like the story, Father?"

"No, I don't. The 1910s weren't pioneer days, first off. And every farm around here has a windmill going back that far – what's so special about ours? Then there's the matter of who is quoted the most; you can tell who she's fond of."

Lyle nodded. "She even described you." He crossed his

arms.

Peter turned to his father. "Well, sure, everyone's got a windmill, but ours actually runs, as good as the day it was put up. And she isn't saying it was built during the 1800s, just that it recalls those days."

"Well, maybe so," said Carl Steinar, sardonically stretching his syllable. "But it wasn't fair how she quoted you more than Lyle. I've always believed in the equality of my sons and expect that others will treat them as I have."

Peter frowned. It was just like his father to douse a good moment's flame.

The truck bounced over the heat-cracked road that cut in a straight line across the land, flat as a table in all directions. "...never embarrassed yet boyishly shy," Abbie had written. Is that what she really thinks of me, he wondered. After blowing up over the fortune teller, he'd apologized profusely, said he was just exhausted from working all day in the field, and suppressing all thoughts of his father had been able to salvage the evening. By night's end, Peter almost had forgotten about him, but she only allowed a goodnight kiss at her front door, and guilty over his poor behaveior, he did not press.

Though he missed the tender rhythm of Abbie's breathing, Peter knew he couldn't be concerned with her now. His old man was in need, demanded attention. Carl Steinar was overbearing and refused to be close, but he'd made sure the boys' basic needs were met – "You always take care of your own first," he once said, and that never was lost upon Peter. Cornelius Skerry would know what, if anything, was going on. The two old men were friends long before Peter had been born and was the only one he trusted to aerial spray his crops though others charged less.

Cornelius Skerry's gray shed loomed at the end of a

gravel driveway, the wide doors splayed open. Peter's truck engine sputtered to a stop, and the day's heat quickly pressed against him. A stench of grease and burning garbage hung in the air. Peter couldn't tell why his old man liked this Cornelius; their relationship had started had begun as utilitarian – he'd taught Carl Steinar to weld – and from there it grew into the spraying contract then into friendship. Cornelius just had a way about him where the old man was concerned. As Peter stepped from his truck into the bone-dry yard, dust filled his nostrils.

Rotund and neckless, Cornelius Skerry tottered out of his shed like a punching bag with feet. His thick, flat lips grunted a question that implied "What do you want?" and a greeting all in one.

"Cornelius, we've got to talk," Peter said.

The old man paused, not so much from the urgency in Peter's voice as from the sweat that the hot sun wrung from him. After taking off his glasses and wiping them with a handkerchief stained long ago by oil, he finally spoke. "What's going on?"

Peter stepped toward him, hoping the proximity would demonstrate his seriousness, but after catching a whiff of Cornelius' acrid underarms, he stopped. "It's about my father."

Cornelius cleared his throat, long and loud, then after rolling a glob of phlegm in his mouth, spat. "What about him?"

Peter leaned back, felt like when he was a little child in school with his hand half-raised in the air, going up then down. "The other day, while we were in the field together, he was nearly run over by a pickup truck. The emergency brake was left off and the truck was parked on a slight knoll near the creek. It rolled straight at him, and he didn't even flinch. It was like he wanted to be run over by that truck. Has he said anything to you? Anything odd or strange?"

Cornelius frowned. "Now just sit and hold still for a while. Your father is a fighter, would never try to off himself. Why he's a human pit bull – once he takes a chomp of something, he never lets go."

Peter nodded. His father was persistent, that much was definite. One time several years ago, he'd wrestled a stubbornly uncooperative calf nearly twice his weight into the dehorning chute. Though the animal bellowed and kicked as if the devil itself had grabbed it, Carl Steinar, his teeth gritting, never once let out a sound, not even a grunt. With an arm wrapped around the calf's belly and the other about its neck, he marched it straight across the pen, his back never bowing. The calf landed in the chute with a thud then Carl patted its rough hide as if to acknowledge it as a worthy opponent. "You can't trace the wind, boys," he said as shoving the calf's head into the stock. "You've got to grab on a hold of the earth, make something of her. That's how a man's worth is measured." The smell of his sweat, musky yet sweet like raw honey, rose through the shed, and Peter's frame surged with pride at the certainty such masculinity exuded. His father paused for a quick second, and with a handkerchief wiped his brow, but the other hand, its wrist quivering as if a racehorse waiting to break from the gate, maintained hold of the dehorning shears. "And one more thing," the old man said just before raising the tool to the terrified calf, "the only thing as important as a hard day's labor is working together as a team to finish the task at hand. Teamwork and cooperation – they can never teach you enough of that in school. Mark my word, though, it's far more important than most of what you'll learn there." Peter's throat clenched as the shears clipped off a horn stub in one quick slice.

He examined Cornelius for a second. If anything really was wrong, Peter decided, Lyle would tell him; it was a brother's obligation. "Yeah, you're right," he said.

Cornelius slapped him on the back, good and hard. "Of course I am," he said. He chuckled, and his breath, like wet mud clinging to a boot, hung between them. "Now you get on back to the farm and get your chores done before that old bastard makes you stay up half the night finishing them."

Peter grinned. He now had one less problem to worry about.

*****

Sweat glistened at the V below Lyle's neck as the three Steinars hovered along the fence line, finishing the job started the day before. Sunlight glinted off the barbed wire. Like his brother and father, Lyle wore a collared shirt, jeans, and cowboy boots, but beyond that, he felt no connection to them. He eyed his father's wrist; the cut upon it had evolved into a jagged pink scar beneath the cuff. Lyle knew he could take a job only when certain his father wouldn't try suicide again.

"Jimmy Hayes makes nine dollars an hour at the stock-yards," Lyle said, "but the best part of it is when the hours are up, the day is done."

Peter harrumphed. "That's a hell of a way to live, quitting even when there's work to do."

His father pulled a wire strand tight around a pole, cinched it off. "You can't make that much."

Wind swept Lyle's forelock upward. "Don't worry, Father, I'm not leaving."

Carl only continued to work the next wire. Lyle examined his face, it worn like a barn fatigued by time, and tried to determine if the old man was really scared of him going.

He knew his father never worried about farm loans being denied despite a poor year, never concerned himself with low grain price or rising costs, at least not so long as those pressures lasted only short term. So what troubled him now, Lyle wondered. His leaving? Losing control of a son? The old man probably tried to kill himself just to keep him there.

Groggy, Peter turned over the five-gallon pail they'd used to carry tools that now stuck out of their back pockets. "Is the truck brake on, Father?" he said after a moment.

Lyle's eyes perked. He'd thought his brother had been hanging a bit close to their father, as if an overprotective parent concerned about a child's reckless meandering.

Carl Steinar looked up. "The truck is all right."

"I just don't want another accident to occur," Peter said.

Lyle stepped toward his brother. "What happened?"

"The pickup truck nearly ran him over. Rolled down the knoll at him."

Lyle stared nervously at their father.

"I forgot the emergency brake," Carl said. "That's all."

"Where was this?" Lyle said, eying him.

"Out on the southwest side, near the creek," Peter said. "He didn't tell you last night?"

"Say, who told you that you could make nine dollars an hour at the stockyards?" Carl said, looking directly at Lyle. The best way to avoid a confession, he knew, was to throw one's own deceit back at them.

"I didn't say I'd make nine dollars," Lyle said.

"Then who said this Hayes boys made nine dollars?"

For a moment. Lyle stumbled over his words. "Jackie Kine."

"Jackie Kine?" Carl said. Jackie, he recalled, had been the star quarterback on the Felton football team when Lyle got the starting job. The old man never understood why his son quit despite making varsity, but it didn't really matter. It kept him on the farm. "He wouldn't tell you a cock-and-bull story like that, would he?"

Peter glanced at his father. "Aren't you changing the subject?"

Carl eyed his eldest son. "I'd say the foal has lost her spots," he said.

Peter sneered.

With that, Lyle took off his gloves and tossed them into the toolbox. He was a prisoner on the farm, he knew, no better than the cattle kept inside the fence he repaired. Maybe, he thought, I should just let the old man off himself.

Chapter 8

As Lyle drove the blue stream of road breaking across the prairie's red clay, a hot wind burned at Carl Steinar's arm. The old man did not complain, only knew that he must remain patient, that he could not dart for a flame like some insect. Then their bodies jerked as the truck bumped over the railroad tracks marking Felton's village limits, and they crossed the short bridge over the creek that gave the town its reason for existing, at least a century or so before when it had been founded. Ahead of them, a steeple loomed; the church had been built on a knoll, the highest point in the city. Safety from floodwater there, the old farmer supposed, though he couldn't imagine the creek – neither deeper than his knees nor wider than his stretched-out body – much overflowing its banks. His son turned right and entering the old downtown parked near the barbershop for the monthly haircut. Carl knew he had to keep up a front lest Peter discover his true intentions.

A dense smell of oil and hair filled his nostrils as he stepped past the striped poles and opened the screen door. The barber motioned for him to take the center chair despite that two bachelor farmers already were seated against the wall. Lyle joined them, looked like one of their sons. Carl turned away from the trio. "Just a little off the top and sides," he said. As the barber pinned a sheet at the back of his neck, the bachelor farmers in their down-home plain speak talked of crooked state politicians with bought-off votes and the heroic school board member who declined his salary to save the district money; all the while, hair fell from Carl Steinar like chips struck from a marble block, and a country song played on the radio. Between the buzzing clippers and snip of the scissors, he tried listening to the tune, but each time the barber paused, providing the white-walled room with a brief silence, the two old men with their mildewed complexions butted in. They smelled of farts and dirt, wore no deodorant so far as Carl Steinar could tell.

"Say Carl, was it your son I saw the other night at the fair with that pretty news reporter from the Register?" the barber said, an ah shucks glint in his eye.

Carl didn't respond for a moment. "That was him, all right." Imagining those two there was too cruel an image for the old man; it roused in him a vision of he and Gwen as a young couple, hiding low in the wheat field, he playfully ambushing her as she called his name, the constant pecks and endless hugs, the red juice of a shared strawberry upon their chins. His memory knotted with thoughts of her.

Light broke through the shop's blinds like a shallow breath. "She's a real Brenda Starr, uh?" one of the bachelor farmers said then took out his false teeth and wiped them with a handkerchief.

Carl remembered the first time he brought Gwen home. She wore a floral print dress with sandals, and a strand of her hair kept waving in the breeze as his pickup truck sped across the prairie. Pretty as a full-blown rose, her tender skin mingled with the air about them. On the homestead, his father sat at the kitchen table, determining his cash flow, estimating the price of crop per bushel and what a reasonable yield would be. It was all a guess, of course, just like it was a guess to Carl how his old man would react to Gwen when he introduced her to the family, but it was calculated, and for that the father admired him. Indeed, he'd always revered his second son, Carl, even before the bookish elder Gil left to college in Kearney, dreaming of business management, of work done from behind a desk and not upon the land.

When Gwen entered the farmhouse, Carl's father gasped, as if seeing for the first time a woman he wouldn't soon forget. He accepted her from the start, not so much as a daughter for that would be intimate to a man of his generation, but more like a niece. When speaking, he'd look at her, his eyes beneath the short-cropped gray hair gentle, his voice rational, as if he didn't want to reveal that being in her presence was like discovering gold in the mountains. Should he smell from chores, he'd spend a minute longer freshening up in the bathroom, from which he'd emerge with horn-rimmed glasses in hand, wiping the lenses with a cloth. Even at the dinner table his manners improved a notch as he made an effort not to slurp the soup or to chew on a toothpick afterward. Most interestingly to Carl, his father would pat him on the back whenever the young couple left for their date, as if he were on close, personal terms with his son. Carl supposed that in a sense they were, for he understood his father's hard philosophy. The world was full of ruthless enemies – weather, grasshoppers, bankers – and only a steady, unyielding willpower could fend them off and allow one to survive. Somehow, though, Gwen gave Carl a certain confidence that disproved the need for such regimentation.

When they stepped outside that first night, hand in hand, Gwen paused. "Let's just stay for a moment and look at the windmill," she said.

For a moment, Carl wanted to laugh. The rattling old contraption, he thought, Still, he looked up at it simply because she did, and within the briefest of moments a new way of viewing the world, a new meaning of life, fell upon him. Its simple, American Gothic framework, the eight foot diameter of the fan, the curved steel blades rotating counterclockwise, it all stood for something more in Gwen's wonder-filled eyes. That windmill, he realized, represented him and all the Steinars who had come before, was a monument to their determination, their courage, their achievements. As he gazed in awe of it, Gwen leaned closer, and whispered against his cheek, "Isn't it beautiful?"

The barber twirled Carl toward the picture mirror. "Well, what'd ya think of that?"

Carl nodded, and as the barber pulled away the sheet, a chill ran up the old farmer's back. He stood, paid cash, and with Lyle left silently.

Outside, the wind squeezed Carl's body as they passed the barbershop pole, it spiraling ever upward. Glints of sunlight shimmered upon the sidewalk as he headed toward the pharmacy, Lyle lugging along behind him. No, he thought, Abbie and Gwen might look alike, but the former was not the latter's equal and never would be. Why, nobody could be like his Gwen; yes, the two women were different as a whisper to a shout. Reaching the pharmacy, he slipped quarters into the soda machine, listened to their clink and double bass burp of a can released and sliding down the door. No, he told himself, Peter needed a true country girl, one like Johanna Bris or her sister, Astrid. Carl knew his first priority, though, was Lyle. He handed him a soda.

They leaned against the wall, and as the red brick scratched at Carl's back, he stuffed a hand in his pocket and glanced at the bench below him. Trees rustled in the wind, but protected by the buildings his stony face no longer felt the brunt of the breeze. A car passed, and for a few moments he inhaled its sooty exhaust. This isn't so bad, he thought as sliding onto the hard wood bench. He sipped his cola. Actually, it's not much different than my life right now.

*****

Though Peter had turned to the window, Abbie thought he still was listening. For a moment, she watched him examine her reflection, it superimposed over a full moon low on the horizon, and knew that despite the thinness of her image, he could make out the dimples' upward flare as she smiled. She sensed her quiet power over him. Then with a whispery hand she petted Peter's leg, and he returned his gaze to her, to the real woman on the floor.

"Though we lived on each air base, it wasn't always possible to be with him," she said.

Sprawled across the sofa, Peter nodded. Abbie sat upon two pillows before him, one knee pulled to her chest, the leg cradled by arms crossed at the wrists. Her eyes glanced at him, they full of adoration like a child's pupils before breaking into a gleeful titter. Moonlight caressed her supple throat. He leaned closer, and chin to kneecap she gently rocked against her leg. Thirst unfolded in her throat, and she breathed in the cinnamon candle's scent, hoping it would break the dryness. She did not want the moment to disappear.

"For some time, we didn't know if he was going to even live; they didn't tell us anything when they went into surgery, just did what they thought was best to keep him alive," Abbie continued. Her eyes drew back. "They made the right decision, of course; they're not to blame for anything. It's just...well, after that, he changed – it was as if I'd lost him."

Peter crawled onto the floor next to Abbie and wrapping his arm about her slim waist, pulled her into him. He caressed her hands. "At least he didn't die."

"No, worse happened. He survived. It was a living death."

"You still have him."

Abbie shook her head. "I don't have him at all. The man he was died in the crash. He's just a husk, now."

"Have you ever gone back? To where the accident happened?"

"I couldn't go if I wanted," she said. "It's a restricted area – I'm lucky my father was able to get me in the day he crashed. What about you? Have you been to where–"

Peter tensed. "I've been there. A couple of times."

She wondered, hesitantly, if it would help her to go there as well, if she could bury her own memories with his. Then she touched his knee. Perhaps you could show me–"

Peter shook his head like a little child; he seemed to shrink away, she thought.

"We don't have to if you don't want," she said, running her fingers upon her fingers upon his temple then down his cheek. She understood in part why he didn't want to.

He pushed her hand away. "Why are you always pressuring me?"

"Pressuring you? What do you mean?"

"You're always talking about your father, always asking about my mother. What's you obsession with it?"

"It's important to me. To us."

Peter's eyes slanted away from her. "My mother's death…none of that is important to me."

Abbie examined him, tried to see the light inside his eye. "That's not so," she said. Her cheek fell to his knee, and she pressed against it.

Peter jerked his leg away. Outside, the moon had risen

above the tree line, and its full silver light filled the window. "No, it really isn't," he said.

She searched his face for an explanation. Peter had said he loved me, she thought to herself, would he not then trust me as well? "Look, you're angry right now," she said. "You have to talk about it. If not with me, then with your father or your brother."

"Around my father it's best to be silent." His mouth pinched tight, projected outward.

"You're not around your father now." She caressed his shoulders.

He shrugged her away. "It sure seems like it, though."

Her eyes widened, but then they thinned as her hands resisted rolling into tiny fists. "Look, we don't need to turn this into a pity party. You're unjustly taking out your anger at the death on your father."

Peter gazed upon her, his face white, then as it regained color, his lips narrowed. He rose, the vessels upon his temples bulging, headed toward the front door.

The littlest skip of the heart boomed through her. She scampered after him. "Peter Steinar, you come back here, now."

He swung around, stood firm. "You don't tell me what to do." He stared at her like an angry bull protecting its herd.

Abbie's face boiled red, and clenching her fists she scowled. "Your swagger is such a brave act."

Peter raised an eyebrow and paused, unsteadily. His lips parted for a split second then sealed. Hand quivering, he turned the doorknob and stepped into the moon's silent light.

*****

Driving through the listless night, Peter bent his cheek to the window. His body shimmered with the truck just as it had years ago when the sash shook in the winter wind and the cold walls of the Steinar house rattled. With the arrival of each winter, there was the listing of things desired and the circling of that magical date on the calendar, but there were no stories behind neither the yellowing ornaments nor caroling but for one holiday before she had left them. Every year after that, Carl Steinar put up the tree only the week-end before Christmas and through his frugality by and large dismissed the holiday. Then came Peter's eighth winter, and his father, a slight glint in his eye, announced on Christmas Eve that Mina would spend the day with them. Who was Mina, Peter wondered. The next morning, there were the usual four gifts beneath the tree, two of them for each of the boys. They opened them, a stocking cap and jackknife for Peter, a toy tractor and a sweatshirt for Lyle. About 9 a.m., a car pulled into the driveway, as a spray of snow spiraled off the crackling ice, their father rushed out the door, not even bothering with a coat. Peter pressed his face against the living room's frigid window to see. She wore a cowl tunic top in green velour. Then she embraced his father. From her trunk, they pulled armfuls of presents and approached the house across the wind-rippled snow. Looking over Peter's shoulder, Lyle's eyes brightened like a star in the evening, and he thrust his head forward to get a closer look.

Inside, the two adults set the barrage of gifts upon the kitchen table, and before the woman could do more than pull down her hood, Carl wrapped his arm around her.

"Boys," he said, "you know those nights you've been spending with Hannah, the babysitter? Well, I've been spending those evenings with someone, too. This is her, Mina. She's going to be with us for Christmas, like I said last night."

The boys stared up at her. She smiled, her cheek burning red from the cold.

"Are those presents for us?" Lyle said, pointing at them.

"Now Lyle–" Carl began, his voice severe, but Mina cut him off.

"Why yes they are," she said, kneeling before Lyle. "You must be Lyle, the youngest one."

He nodded.

From the table, Mina took a box wrapped in green paper with pine trees stamped upon it. "Then this one is for you." She held it out to him, as if a glass slipper upon a silver platter.

Lyle gasped, and clutching it, tore at the paper. Inside was a toy dump truck. He slid it to the floor, and wide-eyed shifted it back and forth across the tile, making truck noises.

Mina turned to Peter. "And you must be Peter. Your father has told me so much about you, about what a hard worker you are. Would you like one of your presents, too?"

Peter shook his head.

She pursed her lips. "Are you sure?"

He looked away from her, stared at the kitchen sink full of dirty dishes.

Carl stepped toward him. "Peter, Mina is talking to you. It isn't proper to not answer someone when they're speaking to you."

"Oh Carl, it's all right," Mina said. "He's probably just a little shy."

They left the presents to wait until after dinner.

With the drifting snow, their drive to the Holiday Inn at North Platte was long, but it was the closest open restaurant that Carl could find, for in Guthrie County people ate Christmas meals with their families. The buffet stretched the entire length of the dining hall, its turkey, crisp salad, glazed ham, mashed potatoes, and a hundred other food enticing

the boys. The hotel wafted with the delectable scent of cinnamon, pine and orange cream. As the four sat at a table,
their plates brimming before them, they said little. Then
Lyle, loosely holding a fork between bites of turkey, turned
to Mina. "I like molasses cookies," he said.

She smiled and nodded. But before Lyle could speak
again, Peter shoved an elbow into his ribs, stared at him
with squinting eyes.

Lyle remained quiet. All he knew of his mother was her
humming, vague like a mist covering the moon, and how a
wisp of her hair would flutter across her eyes in the warm
current, though he was uncertain if the latter memory actually had anything to do with her. Lyle suddenly realized he
didn't know what to say to a mother.

Mina was demure yet big-boned, a typical Felton farm
girl. Peter could tell that she'd tried to keep her dark-com-
plected figure slim, but the large hands and breasts were a
dead giveaway. His father grinned the whole time, and when
glancing at her, she'd smile back, but the boy's quietness
and refusal to answer any of her questions with more than
averted eyes and a murmur quashed any festiveness among
the four. Peter particularly disliked the talcy scent of perfume. He scratched at the wool of his sweater as they ate,
and when Carl told him to knock it off, the boy only picked
at his food, letting the ham and creamed corn grow cold.

Carl never went out with Mina again.

*****

With each step, Peter crunched and flattened the grass
beneath him as he tried for the hundredth time to clear the
image of Abbie from his head, but she possessed a certain
liquidity, a clarity and gracefulness that permeated his
thoughts. He recalled her breath, it full of tang and balance
like the wind, felt the silkiness of her hand. Perhaps they

could get back together, he told himself, but if they did he definitely would maintain a distance; she had become too close, he thought, that was the problem. What gnawed him most at him was how when he'd left her eyes appeared dusky as the melancholy of an approaching storm. It hollowed away at the layers of his certainty, each level through the years so painstakingly set then mortared. Indeed, during Peter's youth, he longed to know about his mother's childhood, about the day she married his father and the months she carried him in her belly, so he often spent hours inventing legends of her. Fantasy, however, did not have the same pull as truth, and he searched for a way to discover the latter.

One day while his father worked in the fields and Lyle napped, Peter sneaked into the attic where photo albums were kept in boxes. Opening to the middle of a dusty blue volume, he found between the laminated pages a gray-toned newspaper clipping of a beautiful, dressed-up teenage girl. Her dark-colored hair was pinned up and back, revealing slender golden rings upon petite ears, a narrow face with round chin, and a creamy, bare neck below which fell a long dress that glittered despite the photograph's lack of color. She stood beneath a tall cottonwood and on thick, luxurious grass, like those at parks, and in her white-gloved hands and forearms cradled a bouquet of roses with baby's breath and ribbons. He read the caption: "Gwendolyn Vann, 16, wears the silk brocade dress that she sewed and won first place for at this year's Guthrie County 4-H and FFA Fair. Guthrie County Register photo." It was his mother! He gazed at the picture then slowly lifted the plastic covering. It made a tearing sound as he pulled it gingerly away from the sticky background. The glue holding together the two pieces stank vaguely like Aunt Amita's soups. He hid the clipping under his shirt so it could be spirited back to his room and looked at whenever desired.

Often he did steal looks at the picture, but never when the father or bed-wetting brother were around, for he wanted to keep this special knowledge of her secret. Soon every feature of his mother as a teenager was committed to memory; he added the detail of her eyes being bright as a lantern to each of his invented stories about her. Peter told no one in his family about these stories. There was little opportunity for nothing ever was said among the Steinars about their loss, not even when the family made its infrequent sojourns for the cemetery. At night while Peter lay in bed, he'd suppress the need to talk to his father about her, to tell how he didn't believe he'd told her he loved her enough, to explain that he hadn't meant to forget showing her the picture he drew, to ask if he himself was going to die. Peter knew that his father needed the sleep.

So the boy resigned himself to fantasy, and the creek became the pages upon which he escaped. He could induce a memory of her there. She'd glide in, almost transparent, on a current. The strength of those visions lured him back in time after time. First, though, he had to skirt the sandy field, its brown clumps bright in the hazy sunlight, feel the rays' warmth rising upon his neck. If he pointed his head toward the fallow section, green with weed and grass, sometimes he'd catch a sweet whiff of prairie bluebonnets, but then he tended to drift onto the plowed furrows, and his shoes sunk in the dirt, coating them red. So he kept his eyes forward, maintained a straight course. In the distance, a neighbor's tractors hummed, and a pickup truck occasionally slashed down the road. With each step, however, those sounds of the real world diminished.

He'd wait all winter to go there, then finally in April when the wind had shed its chill and he heard the first singing robin, he was on his way. Like a hermitage where one could hide, he'd sit under the cottonwood, its down parachuting in windrows across the sky, and watch the creek, which swelled like a river flowing over its stones, smoothing their rough edges. The meadowlark's lilting song announced summer's arrival, and he'd leave the farmhouse in the morning when dew covered the green grass and wheat, never looking back until reaching the fragrant and supple creek. Sometimes he'd bring a book, other times he'd toss sticks into the creek and watch them overturn, spill and rock. Occasionally he'd simply listen to the insects drone in the chest-high grass. One summer week, he crawled along every inch of the shoreline, looking for a black widow spider, none of which lived in Nebraska, though he didn't know any better. It was then that he first noticed how the caddis fly skimmed along the water's surface, how in daytime the poplar leaves flashed and dazzled, how every year the cottonwood grew a couple of feet higher. A few times he'd get hungry, but always he stayed until the creek mirrored the sunset and the chirp of crickets filled the night air.

One day, as the cottonwood branches caught the sun's light, his mother appeared. She remained vague, as if he were seeing her through a kaleidoscope or splay of broken glass, and a mist, like the folds of a white gown, surrounded them. He called to her. She drifted closer, and he stretched his hand to her, but she was many times farther away than he thought. She shook her head no, as if to warn him against reaching, then cold bawled over him, and she dissolved like ash swept away in the wind. He thrashed madly at the water, shouting for her as the fog lifted. She did not reappear, though, and the water where she once stood merely rippled outward as the wind carried Peter's wailing voice far beyond the creek.

When autumn arrived, he'd bid farewell to his imaginary friends – the trout, the frogs, the wild walnut trees, the turtles – and gaze sadly as the water ribboned onward, fallen leaves flitting downstream upon its surface, to a wide, shallow bottomed river he'd never seen. Then the October of his tenth year, he realized there'd be no more lullabies among the wheat fields. As his feet crunched through the dry grass, the branches bare and silhouetted in the distant, setting sun, he looked hard at his refuge. Next spring, his father said, he'd have to start helping around on the farm. A cold wind slapped his body, and he sensed it might be the last day of Indian summer, that there would be no more going to the creek. He paused for a moment, took in a deep breath of the butter-and-eggs wildflower, of the prairie grasses, then watched the clouds purple above the orange sun. He plucked an errant wheat stem from the ground, scraped off its head between his fingers, and stuck it between his teeth. Just as my father does, he thought. The boy spit out the stem and walked languidly back to the house.

Chapter 9

Lyle tapped his fingers against the sofa's armrest, but his father did not seem to notice. If only I could sleep, the youngest of the Steinars thought, I wouldn't mind doing nothing. But the old man remained awake, the gleam in his eyes like a candlelight about to be flicked out, and it became a simple matter of outlasting him. Lyle stared off into the kitchen where the Register still sat on the table, the side containing the article about them face down, just as his father had left it two mornings ago. Jealousy soaked his cold body at the thought of how that reporter described his brother. To think, Peter and some woman who'd moved to town only a few weeks before, mad in love with one another – no wonder he hadn't recognized what really happened out along the south fence with the truck. He pondered if his brother could be that stupid. Or perhaps their father simply was faking it, had not made it so obvious. But why? He must be trying to manipulate us, Lyle reasoned, just as he always has. But what was he positioning them for? To stay on the farm? That seemed like folly. He gazed at his father, could almost make out the sound of stillness that permeated the ashen house. It was a low-toned hum, the kind he imagined a prisoner might hear waiting day after day in his cell.

"Wanna go do something, Father?" Lyle said.

Carl Steinar merely sat there, as if bundled up against a mistral wind. "We've done enough for the day, don't you think?"

Lyle raised his brow. Most times he'd had agreed with his old man, but now he found himself lost. He shifted uncomfortably. "Like you always say, Father, 'The dog who turns his nose up at the bone loses it to some other mutt.'" It was a bit of reverse psychology, he knew.

For a moment, Carl Steinar rubbed his chin, as if reflecting upon the notion. His response ended there, though.

Lyle leaned forward. "Father," he said quickly, "you know I want to leave the farm." His tempo slowed. "That doesn't have to be."

The old man stayed still for a long moment then slowly turned to face him. "What are you proposing?"

Lyle sat erect at the newfound power to evoke a reaction from his father. This was no time for meditation or introspection – it was the moment that counted – and exhilaration suddenly burned in him. "I'll stay," he said, "if you can assure me that you'll never try anything again like you did in the bathroom last week. Or like you did a couple of days ago to Peter with the truck."

His father looked directly into his eyes, as if trying to penetrate them. Then a faint blush ran across the old man's face, though only briefly. He nodded. "That sounds reasonable."

Lyle gazed upon his father's expression – it was the same determined glint that the old man got in his pupils each July, just before the harvest, when he'd straighten his back, and crossing his arms stare out at the field, knowing that with only a few more days of hard work he'd be set for the next year. Lyle's body flushed. He'd experienced such anticipation, too, during his freshman year after making varsity, when he would run out of the locker room at game time, the verdant green field feathery soft beneath his feet, a rosy glow from the setting sun across all of those faces on the bleachers. He smiled at his old man. Loyalty, Lyle knew, was important, but a price had to be paid for it. There was give-and-take. Certainly his old man understood that – hadn't he been the one who long ago told Peter and him to "Make sure your 'straight-up' deal doesn't have any 'sharp curves' in it"? All little children and their parents exchanged something for loyalty, for mutual nurturing, Lyle told himself, but he no longer was a kid. Grown-up, he did not have to bear the oppressiveness of his old man's lifestyle, of the farm's demands, didn't even have to call the old man "father" if he didn't want to; and as an adult, he could expect something more in return for his allegiance. Now that I've asked for acknowledgement, he thought, look where it has gotten me. He suddenly believed his father's tyranny was no stronger than gossamer.

*****

Carl Steinar knew how to resolve problems. When machinery broke down, he could tear it apart then put the pieces back together so they worked even better; should a cow grow sick, he would diagnose the illness after a few simple observations and heal the beast as if he were a crack country vet. With the boys, however, his solutions did not always show Solomon's wisdom. Still, in the short they were practical and effective. A case in point: Peter and his mother.

Throughout elementary school, Peter lied about her. The first tale – that he had a living mother – was innocuous enough. Then the stories evolved to how well she baked brownies and cookies, which he told whenever classmates brought birthday treats. Sometimes he described how she worked in North Platte and that was why no one ever saw here. Then one day she was an actress in L.A., busy making movies and unable to come home. The lying did not bother Peter; he knew the stories were not true and discerned no difference if his schoolmates were the wiser, so long as they accepted him. Soon the school requested his father come in for a conference.

The day Carl Steinar arrived, an autumn wind scattered dried and broken husks all about the playground. Until the teacher's phone call, he'd never had any trouble with Peter; his eldest son earned above average grades and rarely talked of school, except for the time in second grade when he came home all excited as his teeth were red from a fluorine tablet taken during health class to test their cleanliness. When Carl reached Peter's classroom, he knocked on the door then leaned in, catching sight of his pencil sharpener, neatly arranged rows of little desks, and the teacher, a young woman maybe the age of Gwen when she died.

"You must be Mr. Steinar, Peter's dad," the teacher said as rising. Her dress looked like a finger painting as she glided toward him.

They sat across from one another at a low table, and she described Peter's lying. Her face was narrow, pleasant, each feature small yet defined. He liked the way she combed her bangs over the forehead while the rest of the blonde hair was pulled back into a brief ponytail. Her voice rang as if a soft bell, certain but mildly sweet, and he found her easy to listen to. Then there was her perfume, light yet lingering as the scent of prairie rose in spring. She sat still as he tried explaining his son's behavior, yet he could not, for why Peter did not respond positively to this woman who reminded him so much of Gwen, not necessarily in appearance but demeanor, in effect, alluded him. He stumbled over his words, paused to regain his mental footing, and she leaned forward, touched his wrist. "It's all right, Mr. Steinar," she said, "you needn't explain – that's not the point of our conference." He found himself staring at her delicate fingers, and though they rested against him for only a slight moment, it felt to him like several. The interior of his body surged, as if an electric current had snapped on, and his mouth grew dry with guilt.

Carl looked away from her as recalling the way he stroked Gwen's angelic hair at night. He tried focusing on the floor puzzle of a school bus, on the bulletin boards filled with bright, primary shapes and colors. Then his blood roiled in anger at seeing beauty in another, as if it were an offense to the memory of Gwen, to her simply yet lyrical beauty. "Peter was at the accident," he said.

The teacher's brow furrowed. "Oh, I'm so sorry," she said and canted her head sympathetically. "Has Peter had any counseling or therapy?"

Carl glanced at the floor, shook his head.

"If the lying continues or worsens, you may want to consider it."

His hands contracted into fists. "I don't allow lying," he said. "It's wrong, and I've always taught him not to. I don't know what's gotten into him."

"It may not be as simple as that," the teacher said as he rose.

His eyes glared at her. He wanted to kick the table, to topple it and all the tiny desks, to strew their contents across the classroom. His desire for violence surprised him; usually he was gentle as the ticks of an old grandfather clock, or so he had disciplined himself to be. One found peace through suppression.

"He won't lie anymore," Carl said, his voice trembling as he stepped through the doorway. Behind him, the teacher's eyes widened dubiously.

Picking up the boys from Aunt Amita's store that evening, Carl Steinar didn't know if he was more mad at himself than at Peter. Where had I gone wrong, Carl wondered. He's provided continuity for Peter, had modeled the virtue of never showing grief, had never let up in his demand of Peter that he also not reveal it. The death simply was something to put behind them, like a bad crop.

"I talked to your teacher today," Carl said.

Peter just sat there, indifferent like a boulder that occasionally sticks out in the middle of a field, brought there tens of thousands of years ago by gigantic glaciers.

Carl wiped his own forehead with a handkerchief. "You're not going to lie anymore, do you hear?"

Peter nodded, and Carl glanced at him, tried to gauge his sincerity, Doing so often remained elusive for Carl. Control of certain feelings, various thoughts, like anxiety, pain, melancholy – the only way to elevate oneself above the pure rage and passion of animals – also meant never admitting to having such emotions. He realized the boy possessed hidden feelings that could not be fathomed. This truth forever wrapped any understanding of his son's life in a cloak of uncertainty.

At home, Peter did not go inside with his father but played near the windmill. After a while, Carl glanced through the window for him, saw his slender body standing still, the head cocked upward. A young black hawk had perched itself atop the shed, and Peter gazed at the magnificent creature as if it were a serpent. Violently powerful, the claws looked to be as large as the boy's own hands. Its smooth, paddle-shaped wings fit beneath the neck like a cape pulled tight. Unlike any other bird the boy had seen, though, it had huge, dime-sized eyes, and for a moment Carl thought maybe his own awe had enlarged the creature to monstrous proportions. Occasionally its wings fluttered, but always the hawk returned to stillness so that the long feathers stretched behind it like coattails, and the down-turned beak jut ominously outward.

Then Carl noticed his son's outstretched arm, how the boy was trying to coax the great hawk down to him. The father knew that trying to get a bird to sit on your arm, even a gentle one like a sparrow or a mourning dove, was im-possible. Wind alone possessed a hawk's existence, for all the creature ever did was glide upon it, using the currents to its advantage rather than fighting it, and mastering that feat alone ensured survival. At that moment, he realized that only the very young and the very old truly appreciated a bird's flight.

*****

Peter hadn't said he loved her, though there'd been plenty of opportunities: after a jukebox dance at the High Life Bar, during the throes of steamy sex, as ascending the Ferris wheel in their open air cart. Perhaps he couldn't, Abbie thought, for whenever she gazed longingly at him, his lips came together firmly, like he wanted to speak but too much pain prevented him from saying nay words. Some-times as they embraced, she held her ear close to his mouth, hoping he might whisper it to her, yet all he caught was his breathing, an expansive shallowness whose warmth with each exhalation flooded her cheek but then rapidly cooled.

Her head shot up; a sharp wind whirled about the mer-ry-go-round and swished the empty swings as if ghosts played upon them. She trembled, and a copperiness filled her mouth. Too much of her own life had been spent linger-ing with phantoms.

Resting upon the wooden carousel, its seat nicked and

red paint faded, Abbie let go a long sigh, and though for a moment the fresh air lifted her, as her feet lackadaisically kicked at the ground, the vision blackened. Glancing up, her father's fine-hewn body stood silhouetted in the sun, then, propelled by his muscular arms, the merry-go-round spun, and she laughed as tipping her head back to draw in the breeze. He chuckled, twirled it faster, and a strand of nut-brown hair fluttered. She imagined herself a cloud upon the sky. Then it slowed, and as Abbie wobbled off, he lovingly rubbed her scalp with his large hands.

"Want some ice cream, kiddo?" he said.

She nodded then nearly stumbled over her still tottering legs. He howled with laughter, grabbed hold of her shoulder, and hugged her body close.

Despite regaining balance, Abbie's head reeled dizzily with excitement. Then she gazed up at him. "Daddy, what's it like to fly?"

He paused for a moment, as if deep in thought, then spoke. "It's like gliding atop a restless rhythm, almost as if the air were alive, and you roar through the sky so fast you can hear yourself moving, and all awhile the silver clouds above shine like mirrors." Abbie stared at him enraptured, not fully understanding but still adoring the opulent timbre of his voice. She supposed flying might be like spinning on the merry-go-round.

As the carousel of her adulthood teetered to a stop, she sensed how all the world around her refused to be stilled. One could not control time, could not control others, any more than her own hands could grab hold of the wind and keep it from flowing. Despite Peter's solidarity when he held her in his arms, he too was like the wind. She roused from memory the feeling of his broad hands caressing her bare torso as she leaned back into him, the night surrounding them like a veil of black satin, his body sweetly ringing with the scent of cherry almond. Being with him was as if their souls ran together, feeding off one another's energy. Blood rushed to her head, and she rubbed her temples, couldn't tell where or even when she was anymore. Awash in heat, her thoughts would drowsily.

A few sunny blocks later at the Tastee Freeze with her father, he handed her an ice cream, its cone already slick and gooey in the hot sun. She licked chocolate chips off the mound's sides then whorled her tongue around the edges, tried to reduce them before more melted upon her fingers. Then they ambled through downtown, peering into store windows, the occasional sound of a jet overhead catching his attention. Finishing the cones, they drifted into an alcove of shops with public restrooms. When she emerged from the ladies room, hands clean, he stood inside a millinery and through the window waved for her to join him. "I think I've found the perfect hat for me," he said when she met him. He slung a Russian shapka atop his head and eyebrows raised, struck a sophisticated pose. She giggled as he danced a jig, instantly stopping whenever a shopper passed, then once out of sight, beginning again. Laughing uncontrollably, Abbie had to hold her gut from guffawing so hard, and she nearly choked on her bubble gum, which only caused her to laugh with even more force. She never wanted to be weaned from him.

Then Abbie had no choice but to leave the nest. After the accident, he wouldn't take her anywhere again. Too ashamed of his limp, he never left the house, just spent all of his time building model airplanes, though never of the one he crashed in.

She pondered what Peter was ashamed of. Certainly he suffered from a sense of ignominy – it always was a heartbeat of anger – for she heard the quiet fury roiling in him, like a boxer desperate to be let loose so he could punch. The wind twisted through the green blades before her, and Abbie listened to it roar like a turbulent river across the lush sweep of prairie. The wake reminded her again of the past, and she watched a swath of grass reverberate until a new thread of wind sliced through it then died. She herself had possessed such inklings of shame and hatred. Yet, Abbie knew that no strand of wind was so great that it would last across all of time, and soon she would forget.

She closed her eyes, imagined herself flying above the treetops across the prairie. Upon the land's gentle rise to the west swayed a green sea, each blade the ray of a blaring wave. A wholesomeness vibrated through her and across the countryside, a purity that she'd found missing for so many years in her life. Then upon the horizon it appeared, a gleaming break in the flat landscape, the grain bins golden, a windmill clutching the clay soil beneath it just as time clung to space. It was the Steinar farm, and as she neared, anise-scented goldenrod rose from the bright orange fields that spread for miles around their homestead, and freshness itself broke through, shimmering, singing and humming, like her father before the accident, for the coronal farm rang airy and clear. Well, she joked to herself, all except for the kitchen.

Then Abbie daydreamed of living on the farm. Life there would be rooted, would ring with tradition. She saw herself sitting at a table, the fresh scent of grain upon the breeze drifting through the open windows, soft light playing across the hardwood floors. Peter sat next to her, he grinning as telling a mildly funny anecdote from the day, and then their laughter rose as he expounded more and more upon the tale. If she wanted such a life, Abbie knew she'd have to remain strong, like a petal that despite a brutal wind refuses to tremble. She wound a lock of hair about her finger, and opening her eyes, decided the time had come.

*****

Carl Steinar shook as Abbie Blaire stepped from her car that evening. He and his sons had finished working on the planter, and following a long afternoon in the boiling shed, he'd planned for them an evening of quiet solitude amid the farmhouse's coolness. Peter excitedly shouted Abbie's name, though, and picked up his pace.

The collar of her blue blazer flapped in the wind, and she blushed, her face like a red sun upon water. When Peter reached her, she said nothing for a moment, just replayed his voice in her mind, listened to each slow and deliberate word, each punctuated with a twang. "I hope you don't mind me just showing up like this," she said, pausing after her first breath. "Another story brought me to the neighborhood."

"No, not at all," Peter said. His eyes lingered upon her as she delicately swished away a wisp of hair with her hand. She spoke so formally, he thought; he wanted to apologize to her again, to forget about the previous night's disaster.

When Carl Steinar finally caught up, he glared at Abbie. "Why didn't you call first?" he said.

Peter stared open-mouthed at him. The Steinar boy did not like surprises, yet his father seemed full of them lately. Peter's belly twittered once more, just as it had the night of the truck incident. Yet, every time his mind reeled with the notion of some conspiracy, he circled back to reality and scoffed at the idea of his father killing himself; nothing ever bothered his unemotional old man. It was an accident, plain and simple. He glanced at Abbie, her body taut and glowing, a honey-scented perfume lilting toward him, and he watched her high and perky breasts rise as she breathed. Lyle stepped between them.

Peter spoke. "Father, she said she was already in the area."

The old man merely grunted.

"Christ, Father, don't be so friendly," said Peter, his voice like hot ash.

Lyle scowled at his brother.

Carl's hand quivered, though not from his son's rebuke, as his eyes remained latched on Abbie. Three weeks before, she'd arrived like a phoenix, reminding him of everything he had worked so hard all those years to forget. When unable to stand his memories any longer, he'd taken the only course he knew. Then, just as all those years ago, he had collapsed at the sight of blood. Carl found himself staring at the ground, and looking up, examined Abbie as well as his eldest son. The old man's frizzled hair waved in the wind, and his sweat smelled vaguely of sauerkraut, like he hadn't bothered to bathe. He remained mute as stone and eyed the girl, almost longingly.

Peter turned from his father. Maybe something was wrong with his old man, he pondered.

Abbie glanced at the old farmhouse. Sunlight glimmered off the white clapboards, showing water stains and the swashes of dust slapped across it by wind. She stared at a second story window, its shade drawn, wondered if that was where Peter slept. The quiet and stale air of such a sealed room worried her. Above the window, a triangular roof pointed into a blue sky, it hot like a stove flame. She sucked in her dry breath, turned to Peter. "Actually, I was hoping we could speak in private."

His brow furrowed as Lyle's upper lip crinkled. "Okay," Peter said. "Just let me go inside for a minute and wash up.

You can wait on the porch if you like."

She gazed upon him for a moment, measured the tone of his voice. "All right."

As they headed for the front door, Carl stared at the windmill that so often reminded him of his troubles, watched how its firm, thin lines blackened beneath the sky's splotches of violet and rose. The paddles teetered slightly in the air's stillness, and occasionally it squeaked, the sound like a quick tear of metal. He ran an arm across his forehead, wiped the sweat away, and wished the mill would turn, would react to a wind. For a moment, he half-fancied climbing it and twirling the paddles himself, but of course that was idiotic. He smacked his lips to relieve them of their dryness and continued staring as the stale air suffocating him. The night would not bring wind, nor would it bring coolness. He gazed at Peter and the young reporter as they passed his wife's trowel, still on the porch all these years, the handle weathered, the blade speckled orange. For a moment, he considered that they looked just like he and Gwen must have on the day it was left there.

Abbie leaned against the porch railing, waiting for Peter. The other Steinars hung back, cautiously watched her from a distance, like she were a phantom appearing at the window of a long abandoned house. What had he told them about her, she wondered. Waves of heat rippled over the fields, and she began wringing her perspiring hands. Then the screen door swished open, and Peter stepped outside, drying his cheeks with a towel. His jaw was set beautifully, she thought, like an early morning's calm.

"You wanted to talk in private?" he said.

She nodded. "About last night."

"I'm sorry. There just were some things on mind and–"

"You can tell me about them if you like."

He looked away. "There's not much to tell. It's just that ...look, I'm sorry."

Abbie examined him for a moment. "If you feel uncomfortable about it now, you don't have to say anything. Just answer me this one question, though." She paused.

He gazed at her, his brown rankled. "What question is that?"

"Do you love me, Peter Steinar?"

Chapter 10

After school, Peter, and when old enough, Lyle, would amble downtown to Aunt Amita's store where they'd stay until it closed, after which she drove them home to their father, who by then had finished with the chores and made supper. Peter's cousins also would plod along to the musty old shop, its wooden floors worn and the plaster walls cracked. Once there, Lyle and the cousins retreated to the dark void of the basement where they played Chinese football or Simon Says and stayed out of Amita's way. Peter, however, lingered upstairs.

Aunt Amita sold country-styled decorations and occasionally Amish pieces shipped in from Iowa. She'd started the business with inheritance from her parents' deaths, figured it was a good idea to diversify since Joe only grew wheat, but like all businesses in rural towns its fortune rose and fell with the farming economy. That meant it mostly fell. She was persistent, however, and Peter observed this. Soon, he started imitating her, did the sweeping and straightening, then anything, just to keep busy while the others played below. He disliked the basement's damp scent, the old cobwebs, the way dust curled in the dark corners like little mice hiding from the light. When people came into the shop, they'd compliment him for being such a good helper and his hard work. One day, Aunt Amita started introducing every customer to the boy just to show him off; it helped her sales, but she also knew it gave him the attention he no longer received at home. She was right, for following each smile and acclaim he only worked more diligently, unconsciously thriving upon it as if he were a tree bending toward sunlight.

And so Aunt Amita helped Peter learn his manners in the absence of a mother. Since the grandparents had all moved to Florida or Omaha, or had died, this godmother who smelled of camphor and oatmeal cookies was all the boy could depend upon. As if sensing this, whenever around her he kept his ears perked, like a cat expecting something to happen. She did not mind her nephew's constant company for often he was the ideal child that her own children never could be. Though she loved all of her offspring dearly, their faces always seemed to be full of smudges, and with slumberous eyelids and glazed pupils she constantly scolded and reminded them to tuck in their shirts, to pick up their toys, to keep their heads up. She often cited Peter as the virtuous model they should follow. He wished she would not, for that only further isolated him. Despite all of his aunt's attention, Peter knew she never was truly a mother to him. Though she did not realize so, the hugs of her own children always were tighter and longer than those given to Peter and Lyle. He suspected she was but borrowed.

One spring as Peter swept the floor, his eye caught what appeared to be a snowflake in the window overlooking the street; he set down his broom, and mouth agape, stepped toward the fluttering. It was a gray moth, trying to break through the glass. The boy stretched a finger outward but did not touch. Then he kneeled, leaned closer. It really was no more than two sets of overlapping wings, the antennae like feathers, its head and legs clothed in thick bundles of hair. Amid the utter quiet, the flittering of its wings resounded loudly. Sometimes when it rested on the sill, Peter's finger could sneak up from behind and caress its spiny back. Then it would suddenly swoosh up and torpidly loop about as if to catch a glimpse of what had harassed it and, after hovering momentarily, glide toward the nearest glow upon the window. Peter watched the moth circle, his eyes rolling as it tracing the patterns of a great wind. The moth smelled like country sage, he thought.

*****

In the kitchen's pale light, Lyle heard a thump from behind. It sounded vaguely of distant thunder, and as he turned, his father stood but a step away, still and hard.

"What are you doing?" Carl Steinar said.

A blue caplet slipped out of Lyle's cupped palm, bounced on the counter. For a moment, both of them stared at it as cola bubbled in a nearby glass. The old man's calloused hands rose, and he pointed accusingly at his son. "I trust you to make dinner, and this is what I find?"

"It's not gonna kill you."

"What is it?"

Lyle said nothing, turned back to the counter, scooped up the pill. His hands trembled.

"I asked you a question," Carl Steinar said. His eyes narrowed into small black stones.

Lyle gazed at the cola – it seemed to fizz more with the diphenhydramine in it – and he found himself counting his breaths. With Peter in town, he had thought it would be safe to slip the pills into his father's drink. Tomato soup burned on the stove.

Then Carl grabbed Lyle's still curled hand, pried at his fingers. The old man's nails were sharp, like flint.

Lyle shoved him against the refrigerator, stared directly into his eyes. "They make you sleep, all right?" Lyle shouted. Then his head tilted slightly as he examined his father's
pupils. They did not show surprise but hung like withered
grass. Lyle understood something of him right then, of how
when feelings were at issue, words were oddly unnecessary,
just as he'd suspected all along. So it was, Lyle realized, between he and his own mother, a woman of who virtually no
memory existed whatsoever inside him. Still, thoughts of
her remained buoyant in his mind though no solid surface
stood beneath them. He knew, of course, that his father possessed emotions; the exchange of them merely escaped their
relationship, as did a butterfly fluttering away from the dog
that leaped after it. Had my mother bathed me, he wondered, I must have been, for several months at least. Peter told
him about her death, of the blueberries she had left out for
dessert. Was that all she had willed to them, a cardboard
crate of rotting fruit? This mother had acted as if she'd always live, like she'd always be there for them. Lyle found
moving his legs difficult, as if he were slogging through a
dark swamp. He let go of his father.

Released, the old man's knees wobbled, and he slid onto the cold floor, stared at the empty white ceiling and the
nothingness between. Tears seeped along the creases of his
face.

Lyle gasped at the sight of his stricken father. It reminded him of many years ago when as a child he heard a
faint crying in the quiet. Creeping down the stairs, he peeked about the living room entry into the kitchen, spied him
flat across the tile, lowing like a calf upon a distant field. He
did not know what to do, was too small to save him. With a
long, drawn sigh, the young boy stepped back and ever so
softly returned to his room.

Fourteen years later, Lyle kneeled at his father's side. "What do you want me to do, Dad?" There was a long pause, filled with no sound but Carl Steinar's occasional sobs. Then Lyle continued. "Well, Dad? Do you want me to let you kill yourself?" The old man did not respond, remained distant as an uneasy dog. Outside, wind randomly struck at the chimes hanging upon the porch.

*****

Lyle left quietly, as if no more than a rustle on a winter's night, offering Carl Steinar the opportunity he'd wished so long for, especially after his youngest son's betrayal. He did not rush to the bathroom, though, merely sat upon a kitchen chair and leaned over the table, a propped elbow holding him up. Closing his eyes, he massaged his forehead with a broad, open palm. The hand burned cold, as if it were a stone exposed to the January air. The sourness of soup, seared in a pot, wafted about him, and when the throbbing along his temples did not cease, he gave up fighting and opened his eyes.

Through the sink window, he watched the dust blowing from his son's truck as it sped down the driveway onto the main road. He nervously rubbed the red, swelled marks of hard work upon his hands. What would Solomon do now, he wondered. What would his old man do? He thought back to when a child, during a drought year, to his father's lowest point. Or had it been his highest? Young Carl Steinar sat upon the porch, knees bent inward and knocking on occasion against one another, as his father, head down, walked steadily up the long gravel drive, feet crunching against the blinding rocks, the sun's heat pressing. He defied the malignant universe with clothing that covered his entire body – oil-stained cap, plaid shirt, denim jeans, heavy work boots – he opposed it with his proud bearing, a quiet profile, so upright and firm. For such efforts, he was but rewarded with acrid sweat and a thin layer of grease that flowed across his flesh as dust from the baked fields filled his nostrils. But he continued on, as if oblivious to it all.

Out beyond the yard, he kneeled, scooped his hand into the parched dirt. More of it drifted upon the wind than stayed in his cupped palm. He sighed. The sun dried his skin to leather, and as his waxy eyes stared into the plains, it bright as a nuclear blast, he surveyed the field about him, every inch reduced to brown stubble. For a moment he must have wondered if God had forsaken him, Carl thought all those years later. But though grit stuck to the old man's dampened cheeks and the earth smelled of dried and curled parchment, his voice never once choked. Even with the order disrupted, he refused to see himself as a victim. And so his father rose, back erect, and accepted the truth, it as taut and thorny as the barbed wire that lined their farm. Each day, he carried on, never drawing his arms tight about himself, determined to outlast it, but the rainless days only swarmed like locusts.

Carl remembered it as the last year that his father raised chickens, for the fowl withered in the heat, and after that he didn't bother. Then in late September, the hay reserved for winter was fed to the cattle. Amid the grasshoppers' interminable song, Carl even heard his father pray for rain. Eventually it came, as did the government relief check, and life returned to normal for the Steinars. But it did hurt the old man, that much Carl knew, for much as he tried hiding it, one still could see the pain trickling from the corner of his eyes, so voluminous that no amount of restraint could keep it from overflowing its container.

Now he himself had reached that point.

His ancestors left no diaries or journals to tell of those

years. And what if they had, he thought; the certainly misogynist writings probably would crack and crumble in his soul until he could no longer stand to read them. Carl knew there was one thing that he still shared with his father and grandpa: He always wanted to pass on this culture to his children. Destiny was no longer in his hands, though.

At least, Carl Steinar thought, the old man had mother to fall back upon, to prop him up. Carl scratched at a boil on the side of his neck, and in the quiet he listened to the wind's murmurings. They sounded like his own faint heartbeat. For a moment, he thought of life and its crosscurrents, always swirling back upon itself, upon the past. Thinking of his childhood, of his son's futures, he was like time itself, bringing an end to all things, devouring its own offspring. Can I devour myself, he pondered. Lyle had called him "dad." He'd always demanded that be called "father," did not know why, only knew it was what his own father had expected. A few simple presumptions led to so few wants, so few needs, Carl told himself, and since Gwen's death, he had desired less and less. Now he wanted almost nothing at all.

*****

He stood around the corner from her. It was coincidental, Abbie knew, for she hadn't been followed to Kjopman's Grocery. Felton was a small town, and certainly something like this could happen, she told herself. The question now was what to do about Peter Steinar being in the same tiny store. She considered her options: Hide, either by fleeing to the bathroom and waiting an indeterminate amount of time until she thought it was clear, or by simple avoidance stay in the back corner where she could duck down a couple of different aisles while discreetly watching for him; of course, there was the possibility of meeting him, either by carefreely going about her business until he noticed her and said something, or by walking straight up to him and risking a confrontation. She cast her head down, pretended to read the back of a tomato soup can as mulling the alternatives. He'd already told her he didn't know how he felt. Then a shadow cast itself upon the label, and she looked up.

"Peter!" she said, and her mouth remained slightly ajar even after she spoke.

For a moment, he grinned like a little boy, then his mouth quickly flattened. "Abbie," he said with a slight nod. His tone sounded restrained.

"How are you?"

"Getting along fine."

Her brow crinkled as she gazed up at him, half-smiling. What did he mean "fine," she thought, wasn't he going through what I am?

"I just wanted to thank you for the article on the windmill and my family," he continued. "It was nicely written. And very flattering."

The corners of her mouth flared. "Oh – thank you, I –"

"And I also wanted to apologize for that night I stormed out of your place." His feet shuffled, and he tucked both thumbs into his jean pockets. "Guess I took it all a little too personally."

Her face flushed. "I...I understand," Abbie said, though she didn't, at least not completely. "I said some nasty things, too, I guess. Perhaps we could–"

He stared at her for a long second, then finished the sentence. "Could put it behind us?"

"Yes. That's what I'm trying to say."

He nodded again. "I can."

"Good – I can, too, of course. In fact, I have." She paused for a moment, composed herself. "Perhaps you would like to get together again. Watch a movie, get a bite to eat or something–"

Silence hung between them, and though Peter did not speak, he broke it by slowly shaking his head. "No, I don't think that would be so good."

Her body suddenly chilled. "Oh – but…"

"Maybe we could just be friends."

"Friends? Well, I suppose – I mean, I just thought that–"

"I've got a lot that I need to work out right now," he said. "You probably could tell that. I…I enjoyed my time with you, Abbie, I really did, but–"

She gazed into his eyes, tried to conceal her welling. "But?"

He looked away. A circular reflecting mirror behind him caught the slumping of his back as both hands slid deeper into his pockets. "Well, like I said, there are some things I need to first work out."

Her chin trembled, and sucking in air from her mouth, she did not breathe for a second after her muscles tensed then steadied. She saw herself as an eighteen-year-old, gazing upon her father in one, desperate last attempt to draw him back. As usual, he did not look up when she stood at the door. Then she called for him, and he glanced at her. His mouth remained a flat line, the lips hard as she stepped inside. Though Mary Dawn always kept the house well dusted, a dimness covered the study. He wouldn't let his wife stay too long there.

For a moment, Abbie remained uncertain what she'd say to her father and merely stared at him. His complexion had dissolved to a dull white, as if he'd been locked inside a cabin for a particularly long winter, and wrinkles stretched from beneath his eyes all the way to the temples. He breathed shallowly, like an asthmatic. Regaining her composure, she darted to the window and opened it, hoping his stale, salve-induced scent would disappear beneath the blossom-filled breeze, but he turned his back to the outside air, as if having tasted the bile of soured love and wanting no more. She reached for his hand, desired to stroke it with her supple fingers, to let him know someone understood. His limbs only hung flabbily upon the armrests, though, and she wondered if they were even his anymore or just artificial like the rod that kept his leg bones connected so that they appeared normal.

After a long, drawn minute, Abbie sat measuredly in the chair across from him, a desk separating them. How many times have I already tried this, she pondered. Then the teenage girl sat upright and decided this would be the last. "I'm going to college next year," she said.

He nodded. His arms and hands remained still, did not fidget. Why, he was no more alive than my childhood dolls, she thought.

"We don't have much time left together," Abbie said.

He gazed at her, his eyes murky – if only she could make them gleam again – and he exhaled a stale breath. She remembered the one time almost a year after the accident when they had gone out in public, when she'd chased the dandelion, and he angrily wrenched her from it, negating all they had once been. His fingers had dug so deep into her arm that they left bruises.

She set her hands upon the desk, and dust stuck to the fingers. "You wouldn't want to do something, would you? Go somewhere?"

In the fading light, his body gathered shadows, and she wished he could cut loose from the stake of his damaged leg. He shook his head.

Abbie remained quiet for a long while, merely canted her head downward. What was there to say anymore, she wondered. Every day he just sat behind his desk, keeping the leg out of sight, acting nonchalant, carrying on his silent fight. What happened to his former brashness, could it have dissolved that fast? Her head tilted back for a moment to take him all in. Sweat flattened the sprigs of his short-cropped hair, and his distant expression emanated a great boredom.

Suddenly he pushed away from his desk. "Abbie, I can't go anywhere," he said. "Not the way I am."

Her hands coiled into fists as she squeezed her eyes taut, like two contracting lines of light. She rose.

Before she could tell him that he could leave, that there was nothing to be embarrassed at, that she deserved to be seen in public with her father, the fast-paced shuffle of Mary Dawn's feet interrupted her. In a blur, her mother hustled to behind the desk and clapped the window shut. "Abbie, go on now, let your father rest," she said. "He doesn't want to be disturbed."

Mary Dawn fluffed up the pillow behind her husband's back then sprayed mountain mist air freshener in two brief sweeps across the room. Setting down the can, her lithe fingers began kneading his shoulders. A yellow haze hung in her mother's eyes, as if a weak sun on a gray day. She was like a hive insect, merely living out its role to her husband's plight, Abbie thought.

Then Mary Dawn clucked her tongue. "Really now, Abbie, you know better than to bother your father. Go on now, let him rest."

Abbie glowered at them, her face venomous, then stomped out.

Peter's hand reached for her wrist but stopped shy of it. "So being friends would be all right, then?" he said.

She nodded. This was a public place, she was an adult,

there would be no storming out this time. "Friends then," Abbie said, but she did not smile saying it.

Chapter 11

As if a gargantuan red phlox, dust bloomed all around Lyle's truck when it barreled into the yard. Peter could not see him through the cloud, but he heard the pickup door slam shut, then a few short seconds later the porch screen swung open and with two beats clattered to a close.

Lyle sauntered into the kitchen, looked about. He did not see their old man. "Where's Father?" he said, attempting to mute the anxiety in his voice, careful not to say "Dad." He couldn't let Peter know of his concerns, he told himself; the bastard only would twist it to his advantage. Still, he knew keeping such a secret would be difficult at best. Peter had an eye for vulnerability and might recognize it in him. He would have to remain in the shadows, as he had when his brother returned after spending the night at Abbie's. From the sink he drew a glass of tap water.

Peter looked up from his newspaper, examined Lyle suspiciously. His brother's tone once again chipped at the confidence cemented by Cornelius Skerry's words. "Should we be worried where he's at?" Peter said.

Lyle's lips pinched tight. It's another one of my brother's tricks, he told himself, an effort to bait me. "You care for our old man?" he said after a few seconds. "Why start now?"

Peter's fists curled. It was bad enough that his brother

moved just as their father did when hail destroyed a crop – never thinking about it, only continuing onward, plain and simple – but now he had to tolerate his insolence as well.

Lyle took a seat at the kitchen table, directly across from him, fingered his glass of water, the sides beading with condensation. Their glances veered away from one another, Peter's toward the newspaper, Lyle's to the kitchen window. Outside, the yard dust settled upon the earth, like wind bending down a stem. Lyle pondered what Peter found enticing in reading the paper each day; he did not like rituals himself as they always reminded him of his own isolation. He unconsciously tapped his fingers against the table, his pace growing louder and faster with each thought. For years, he'd seen mothers carrying candlelit birthday cakes at neighborhood parties, had watched TV shows broadcast from Denver or Omaha thanks only to a backyard satellite dish. Peter set down the newspaper, crossed his arms. Lyle slowly turned his head to him, stopped tapping. Peter's brow furrowed; their father had been away for quite some time.

Lyle paid Peter's words no countenance, for he'd given up on him long ago. It happened in the wheat field that stretched beyond the window before him. Lyle was maybe three, old enough to reach the front door's knob. A bright yellow sun filled the sky, lifting the gold out of the blossoming wheat, its ripeness heady upon the wind. Peter had sneaked out again, and this time Lyle was intent upon staying with him. He would no longer taste the dry-mouthed emptiness of being alone, at least not for that afternoon.

Circling the house, he spotted Peter in the wheat field, heading toward what he thought was the creek, and raced after him. The tall stems scraped against his legs, a mere sensation at first neither bad not good, then due to his soft young skin a slight annoyance, and finally a painful chafing of flesh as Peter, aware of being followed, sped up.

The wheat rustled in massive waves beneath the gusts, and Peter disappeared from sight. Tears welled in Lyle's eyes, but he refused to bawl. As he pushed the terror deep inside him, he found it easy not to weep at all. He sighed, and though his innards ached from the compacted bulk of his emotions, the urgency of his loneliness had disappeared. As the years passed, other feelings gradually vanished from his existence, all except anger.

Lyle brought a hand to his cheek as gazing upon his brother. He held back the waves of hatred swirling inside, but like rock dikes not constructed high enough, moment by moment he found himself desperately adding more and more stones. Lyle felt such scorn as well toward his old man, the one he always had to call "Father," even as an adult – but he'd made a deal with him and would keep his end of the bargain – in any case, it was Peter who was to blame, Peter who never cared a whit for anyone other than himself.

Lyle's fist rose beneath the table like an underwater wave, and as his wrist trembled, the other hand brought it back to his leg's side to unfurl. Outside, the windmill's blades fluttered.

Then the telephone rang, shattering the silence like a rock through a pane glass window. Peter answered it and for a brief moment listened.

Perhaps, Lyle thought, it was their father. Then Peter called to him as holding the phone out and quick added, "It's Jackie Kine."

Lyle snatched the received from him, stepped away. Between them, the phone cord's right coils stretched to a barely straight line, as if water cutting a path through earth.

*****

Peter discovered the creek one spring day during grade school. He'd always known it was there, had heard his parents talk of it. While aboard the combine with his father, he'd often glimpsed the distant blue sash that ribboned ever onward through the amber wheat. By the time he was six, his father would let him amble alone into the fields and explore. One warm April weekend, he followed an amazing stream of cottony down that parachuted in windrows across the sky, leading him to the waterway. The down sailed from a cottonwood that clutched its high bank, and he sat beneath the tree, pretending snow was falling. As the days grew longer and increasingly warmer, he returned, listening to the lark's repeated song of lyrical five notes as watching the stream gently drawl southward.

By summer, he found the creek an extraordinary place to escape the open prairie's constant wind. Sometimes he'd bring a book to read under the cottonwood. Other times he'd toss sticks into the creek, examining them as they moistened, rocked, then overturned while the poplar leaves upon the opposite bank flashed and dazzled and above him the cottonwood leaves danced. He spent a whole week along the shoreline one August looking for a black widow spider while the crickets chirped steadily in the chest-high grass. As the sun slowly arced overhead, he watched the trout swimming in the stream, listened to the frogs croak from their muddy crevices, poked at the turtles curling into their shells, tasted bitter seeds from the wild walnut, squished the stream's sandy bottom beneath his toes. He grew to understand the cottonwood, the fresh water, and the caddis fly skimming its surface like a child knew the warm embrace of his parents. Thanks to winter's forced absence, he noticed from year-to-year all of the strange and wondrous changes along the creek, like how its course veered a little more to the east and how the cottonwood rose a couple of feet.

Sometimes when loafing under that old, favorite tree, Peter could induce a memory of his mother. She'd glide in on a current, almost transparent, the edges of her body wavering like hundreds of little white pennants. Even as a ghost, her lips were red like raspberries. He leaped into the creek that she hovered over, dog paddling toward the visage. She smiled broadly, an opus of approval at his efforts to swim toward her, though each time he failed. His head would bob under the water, as if caught in a flashflood's waves, but once he rose above it, gasping for air, her form grew increasingly vague and amorphous, like a bird's shadow. If only he could fix her sinuous motion, if only he could move forward! Then she dissolved, burned off by the prairie sun.

In autumn, as the fallen leaves flitted downstream upon the creek's surface, he'd occasionally remember the day his mother died, and with each image gently rewrite the text of that event. He did not resurrect her, at least not at first, but instead reconstructed the gaping holes torn wide by an array of miniscule emotions, like the moment when his eyes were dry and he wanted to speak but could not think of anything to say. Peter knew that times such as her death demanded something be said, yet as a child all he could imagine was: "You always hear about this on TV, but you never think it's going to happen to you." It felt good, at least in his imagination, to say something, but then his own mind betrayed him as his father glared. "Oh shut up, boy, would you?" he shouted, then turned to the trooper and pushed past him. It was all Peter could think of his father saying at a moment like that. One could not blame his father, though, for he was angry, and rightfully so.

*****

They always spoke of it as their farm, but it really was

only the old man's, from the farmhouse's dust-speckled clapboards to the cattle in their weary wanderings, from the rooster weathervane creaking atop the barn to the open plan that through their sweat yielded silos full of golden wheat. Still, amid the thorny heat Lyle marched, searching the eastern field for his old man. The wind, jaunty and propulsive, bounced in his ear. One day, father had promised, this would be all his and Peter's, too. Lyle did not know if he wanted to be part of that.

Wild sunflowers bloomed along the barbed wire. In just a couple of months, as autumn settled across the prairie, they would droop over the fence. Perhaps his old man wished to see them on more time, to drink them in with his eyes while they still stood in their glory. It was as good of a theory as any; he really didn't know where his father might have gone. Slipping outside after Jackie Kine's phone call, Lyle had surveyed the yard. His old man's truck remained on the brilliantly lit gravel, but no sounds emanated from any of the farm buildings. Wind already had blown away any sign of their footsteps. He checked the machinery shed, found only the swallows flitting languorously, then moved to the cattle barn, where the few young heifers who preferred the shade to their herd's company crowded the gate at his arrival, anxious for an offering of hay. Lastly, he stalked the silo bins, his boots crunching the dry grass, scaring mice back into their dirt hovels. His father was nowhere to be found. And so, with a listless sigh, he headed in the direction opposite of the afternoon sun, toward the horizon where darkness would fall first.

There were any number of directions his father might have gone. Perhaps he'd even walked onto the road and hitched a ride somewhere. That was unlikely, Lyle decided; his father never would just up and leave the farm. Still, the old man had surprised him more times in the past two weeks than in all of their 20 years together. Lyle paused, held a hand over his eyes to block the profuse sun and scanned the level earth before him. Clouds hovered high above the prairie swells, and upon the plain lay nothing but emptiness. He understood in part the source of his father's stress; a simple bad run of weather, entirely out of his control, could make all of the efforts meaningless. Working the land required discipline, levelheadedness. One had to be sensible, practical. It was a mighty defense against distress and panic but demanded a stoicism gray as stone. The back of his throat ached for water.

His feet remained constant, though. After an hour, once Lyle had reached the eastern fence line and turned south, he paused. In one direction loomed his duty to father, in the other the lure of soft sleep. His arms burned red from the sun. Either way, he'd have to amble over the dry clay field. Wind rang like bell tones across the plain, and his tired mind turned sluggishly. He disliked how the dirt ground into his teeth, despised how his skin perspired in the hot sun, hated how his nostrils clogged until all he breathed was dead, desert soil. I should have taken the tractor, he thought, or his own pickup truck. Why didn't I, he wondered; if I had, perhaps the old man already would have been found. They could be drinking beer now on the porch, half burying their bottles in the dirt to keep them cool.

They? There was no "they" on the farm. His father talked, his sons listened politely. Lyle shivered in spite of the prairie's swelter. With each passing year, his father spoke less and less, even to his good friend Cornelius Skerry. The sun pinpointed Lyle like an eagle upon its prey. No, I must continue looking, he told himself, and shepherding his worries and tears to a recess deep in his mind, he walked, the dust from the sweltering plain clouding his heels with each footfall.

Reaching the uneven ground near the creek, his step bouncing like a rickety roller coaster ride, uneven and resile, except it was all slow motion. He stopped again. Below the verdant knoll, he could make out the bauble of the sluggish water as above him the wind roiled unabated. A thin cow path wound its way to the creek, and he pondered if his father had gone there. Following it, the fauna's lush scent rose around him. He turned sideways, gingerly descended the steep bank that the cattle could take in a single step. Before him stood cottonwoods, willows, and all manner of trees pleasant to the sight. He did not sit upon the water's banks, though. For all he knew, his father already had returned to the house and was waiting so they could perform some new chore. On a farm, there never was a short supply of work. Lyle's head fell into his hands, but he refused to cry. Oh! The futility of such a search, he moaned to himself. The field dust upon his palms slipped into his wet mouth. He was trapped, like a shutter clattering against its latch.

After a moment, he turned; the time had come for returning to the plains. His heavy feet slogged up the knoll, the grass rustling against his boots then crinkling as the forest of creek-fed green gave way to clay furrows, the wheat stubble brown at the base. So also did the air grow more arid, and he found breathing increasingly difficult as the sun's full brilliance shined upon him. He headed north, only slightly hopeful, as if wandering a desert at dawn. Then, in the distance, a silhouetted figure appeared, and as Lyle's pace quickened and his lungs beat rapidly from the exertion, there was his father, standing mid-field, trembling like fence wire in the wind.

*****

As Carl Steinar walked the fence line, he gazed at the crimson furrows undulating in a giant sweep toward Skriftlig Creek, echoing the water's curved flow. "You've got to grab on hold of the earth, make something of her – that's how a man's worth is measured," he told himself yet again. A slight breeze warbled over the soil, occasionally swirling dirt and pollen from one row to another. He forced himself to accept that Lyle had been drugging him all of the time. Face trembling, he lingered, then breathed the black loam deeply to regain control. He almost could taste the sweet bread that would spring from the fallow field in only another season. Still, his son's actions were tantamount to poisoning. Kneeling, he rubbed a palm full of dirt upon his hand, let the moist grains clump between his fingers.

Perhaps I should forget about the boys, he thought, just let it all blow away, like dust upon the prairie wind. He tossed the dirt in his palm, watched a good portion of it swirl upward and across the plan while the bulk fell directly to the ground. Yet, he wondered, how did Lyle know what was good for him; the boy always was making stupid decisions like quitting the football team back in high school, even though by not going out the next season, Lyle served his dreams well. If Lyle had gone all conference or obtained a scholarship, he'd probably be away right now, unlikely to ever come back. After some time, Carl Steinar glanced up, gazed at the crooked and disintegrating path to the creek. There's simply too much to battle, he thought, too many enemies for one man to fight alone. How could he ever control his son, who after slamming him into the fridge flew out of the house in a rage, taking off to who knew where? No, he whispered as slowly shaking his head, no, giving up on the boys would be a disservice to Gwen, to her memory. He had to continue marching across the fields, had to assure himself that he was wrong about his son.

As he walked, the throb of his heart rose just as it did every week before harvest. During those few days in July's 40 mile per hour winds and 95 degree temperatures, from the moment that meadowlarks and turtle doves called at dawn until the crickets chirped at night, he'd prepare the combine for the great event: adjusting the header, greasing, fueling. Carl supposed he became grouchy before the harvest, but deciding to wait or not was tricky, a choice that the whole next year's comfort rested upon. For others, it seemed a joyous time. Young adults who'd left Felton often would take their vacations in July, right during the wheat harvest, and come back for a week-and-a-half just to help. No one was returning to his farm, though.

In those days immediately before the harvest, he would march to the field, the wheat rippling in the wind, and run the heads of grain between his fingers, seeing how the shell separated, all to determine its dryness. Then, with the tongue he'd lift the kernels from his palm to gauge their hardness and maturity. Dissatisfied, he spat them to the ground and returned to his shed, went over the combine with grease gun for what seemed like the hundredth time. On the fourth straight day of this, he and Peter – years ago it was he and his father – stepped gingerly along the field's edge, eyed the spot that would determine the harvest's success. There was no real science behind the selection, merely a sense that a certain plot appeared more average than the rest of the auric straws. Then, as if instinctive, they'd simply stop and lean over a section, and tilt a group of stems into the sunlight. They'd run their fingers over the velvety stem and along the head, across the scaly kernels and then along the lengthy silk beard. Sometimes a husk would slip off under their touch, quietly flitting to the black dirt below. The wheat had a certain scent to it when ready for harvest, a sort of sweetness yet musk, like warm honey, that urged them to the combine. Knowing the precise moment of when to harvest was everything, for a miscalculation of even a day would mean a poor grade and low prices.

Then Carl broke a straw in half, and stripping the head off, stuck it between his teeth like the long cigarette of a wealthy, top-hatted aristocrat. It was indeed time.

They tromped back to the homestead and entering the dim pole shed started the combine, rolled it forward into the bright sun. It snorted and thumped then roared and purred. Carl Steinar turned the throttle low and peeked out the door. "Sounds just like last year, wheezes in all the same spots," he shouted down to Peter. Then the old farmer was off to make a swath for a sample cut. Afterward, he unloaded the grain into a long truck, and ambling up the semi-trailer's ladder with a coffee can in hand, dipped it into the mound for his wheat sample. He and Peter, and later Lyle as well, hardly able to avoid speeding, drove into town for the first testing. Other farmers with the same anxieties milled about the co-op, sipping coffee and waiting their turn, too, watching the meter as a machine weighed each sample, the minute or two of its work seemingly like an hour, but on virtually every test, lights flashed 13.8 percent, a magical number.

It also meant time was running out.

Returning to the farm, Carl found that the custom harvesters had arrived, as if on cue. Their five campers, six semi-trailer trucks, four grain carts, three pickups, and eight combines lined the edge of a fallow field near the roadside. They were a motley bunch: retired farmers, college students on break, a husband and wife with their three daughters. Each told tales of sitting out rain for a week, of pulling into a farm after a devastating hailstorm, of trying to combine frost-damaged crops, each jostling to maintain control of the narration as others embellished the story. They were like old friends. Most of them returned every year, traveling a northward migration from Texas into the Dakotas, as if cowboys on a cattle drive. Each morning for almost a whole week they'd wait for the dew to evaporate before combining, followed by the bump and whoosh of their machines, most of them quarter-century 6600 John Deeres but one a mighty new 9500 John Deere, leased every summer by Carl Steinar for just one week. Then came the work, the harvest's hot, itchy dust swirling everywhere and worry about every cloud on the horizon. Carl listened to the radio for weather and grain market reports as moving across the fields, an acre every 37 minutes, on occasion rustling rabbits and pheasant out of the wheat as chicken hawks lurked overhead, waiting to swoop upon a flushed creature. The bin filled in 111 minutes. Peter and Lyle would climb onto the combine as he filled a grain truck, and he'd always have to caution "You be careful going up and down that ladder!" These words had been said a dozen times every harvest, yet still they climbed with abandon. Or the two boys would romp barefoot with the three Cairn daughters in the backs of the trucks, letting the warm wheat sift through their toes like sand on a beach. Though not wanting to, the harvesting crew would have to quit its labors at two or three in the morning for the moisture content rose so high the elevator wouldn't accept it, and so under a black sky, the skunk's scent upon the wind and bats wheeling about in the yard light, they'd call it a day for a few restless hours of sleep.

Finally the week passed, and the fields were reduced to long sways of stubble. The Steinars and the harvest crew said their good-byes, and soon the coolers and boomboxes at the edge of windrows were picked up, and the mobile village disappeared, leaving only the imprints of their tires upon the grassy roadside. Then Carl would glance at the weathervane and shout, "Let the storms blow! Let them blow!" He'd pay the bills and let each boy pick out a toy in Felton. That was the extent of the celebration, though. Other families would leave on vacation, take off in their cars and pickups while the Steinars stayed home. The boys, content with their new play tractors and dump trucks did not mind, however.

Carl Steinar rose and lumbered along the fence line, wheat weed scratching against his jeans, his feet cracking the stems with each step. The open air smelled good, he thought, clear and fresh like the great sky above, and for a moment his heart surged. Then he paused, leaned his hand against a fence post. He was not supposed to feel that way, was not supposed to feel anything at all. Kneeling again, he picked a wheat straw, stripped away the head and placed the stem between his teeth. The power in his knees surprised him. I should have bent over, he told himself, let the pressure destroy my back. Damn!, he thought, the farm still makes me feel...His mind drifted into oblivion and an aching filled the gray murkiness that he'd become comfortable with during the last eighteen years.

Yes, Lyle's betrayal pained him, and gazing out upon the great sweep of land before his eyes. he found it almost unforgivable. He sniffed back a tear in the headiness of the sun's warmth. There was so much one couldn't know about others; he recalled the weeks after Gwen died when he boxed all of her jazz records and brought them to the attic – he knew she loved those exuberant swings of rhythm but never really understood how she became a lover of such music. Tears slunk down his face; you might as well toss chaff into the wind, he decided. Then a form appeared upon the horizon, a faint smudge at first, it nearing as cresting the knoll and gaining solidity like some creature rising from a thick smoke.

Chapter 12

At the age of twelve, Abbie tottered between being daddy's little girl and the stature of womanhood. The awkwardness it brought her often burned hot as a red flame. Though small-framed, whenever looking at her classmates she thought herself a tall, ugly weed. Her skin paled from being indoors too much, her eyes squinted whenever in the sun, and her breasts – no larger than half-lemons – sprang out just enough so that she was recognizable as female. Sometimes, as her father recuperated in their small Omaha residence, she'd fall back upon the comfortable ways of the past and play with dolls, especially when Mary Dawn, who had taken a job as a discount store clerk to support the family, returned home and hoping to clean the house unhindered shooed her onto the porch. It was there that Abbie garnered the interest of three neighborhood boys, who though unsure of their place as they too edged toward adulthood, knew it could be at least temporarily fixed if they defined someone else's position. Their red pupils lingered upon her as they hovered along the sidewalk like gnats about a street lamp. An ill-fed mutt scampered at their ankles. Though Abbie kept them in the corner of her eye, she did not worry that they would come onto her own porch. They always remained a discreet distance away, and so far none of them had bothered her at school.

One summer evening, Mary Dawn called Abbie inside – her father wanted a glass of water, and she was too busy with vacuuming and dusting, would she get him one? Abbie had no second thoughts about it, gladly obeyed.

Coming out onto the porch, Abbie heard the quicksilver steps of someone ducking from their walkway. She did not catch a glimpse of him – she assumed it was a he for the steps were heavy, forceful – but she did hear the stifled sniggering and giggles from around the hedges that fenced in the yard. Then her feet kicked something hard, and she looked down. Her face whitened like the moon: it was her doll, the legs torn off and gone. She glanced up, mouth agape, as the boys' laughter rose and they clambered out into the open, waving the two legs high over their heads in taunt. Her face burst into tears, and she scampered back inside, wailing. Even over the vacuum's high drone, Mary Dawn heard her daughter. She shut off the machine, asked what was wrong. Cheeks red and swollen, between gasps Abbie explained in a falsetto whine what happened. Her mother kneeled, gave her a hug. "Oh, come now, sweetheart," she said, "you really are getting too old for dolls anyhow." Abbie spun away, wished for her father to appear, to balance the scales. He did not – would not, she knew, not any more. She ran to her room, slammed the door behind her, did not come out for dinner, even when Mary Dawn cautiously sauntered in and asked if she was hungry. As night fell, Abbie rubbed the damp, salty corners of her eyes and gazed out at the wind-tousled trees. A storm was approaching, and she was a cold, angry sea.

The next day, Abbie set about on her plan to exact justice. She did not view it as revenge, saw only that she had been wronged, and in the absence of any adult assistance, would have to make right on her own. Perhaps that was what being an adult meant, she thought – taking care of things – and feeling that she was on the cusp of womanhood, she came to believe that this act would be an initiation into it. Forehead creased, the girl spent the morning spying on the boys from afar, seeking a way to show them her new might. Their day was spent ambling about, seeking amusement, snatching away any interesting object that one of them might possess: an alligator clip, an odd stone, a half-eaten candy bar. She even watched them urinating on a wooden fence in an old, litter-filled sandlot. Still, after two days of intermittent shadowing, no plan emerged. She decided to drop the whole notion; there were better things to do with her time. Besides, she risked being found out, and it only meant they'd do something else mean to her.

That night, though, the drive for revenge smoldered in her eyes, like one of the pinpoints of starlight that shined through her bedroom window. Abbie did not want to harm the boys, just let them know that she was capable of it, let them know that they could not define her. In the yard, trees trembled as the wind roiled. To be reduced to a mere plaything, an object used for another's entertainment, that hurt far more than the destruction of any doll. Her mouth grew dry. Revenge, she suddenly understood, required not directly hurting the other but something that he cherished. The air turned moist outside, a sure sign of another approaching rain. Then a neighborhood dog barked at a rattling gate, and in a flash she knew exactly what to do.

The next day, she again discreetly traced the boy's steps, out past the five-and-dime where they filched gum, then down by the creek which they tossed pebbles into, each stone hitting the water with a *kerplunk!* and finally through the sandlot, where the sun upon the tan dirt lifted

the temperature to a near swelter. Gradually, the boys separated, and as they did, she discovered which one owned
the mutt. She followed him to his house, and as crouching
behind a fence watched them play fetch with a stick.

At last, the boy went inside when a woman's voice told
him dinner was ready. Abbie leaned around the pickets'
edge as the dog sat outside. Quietly, she called to it.

The mutt perked its head, then as Abbie patted her
thigh twice and softly called once more, it trotted to her. She
cupped its jowls in her hands, caressed the cheeks. The mutt
stunk vaguely of wet leather boots. Then it sniffed her face
and wagged its tail while she told it in a voice barely above a
whisper what a good boy he was. She backed away, and with
confused eyes the mutt raised its muzzle. Abbie smiled.
"Come on," she said, double patting her thigh again. She took
another step, and so in return did it. Kneeling, she clasped
and petted its face, then standing, returned to her walk. The
dog followed.

Abbie's feet fell lightly upon the cement sidewalk as she
headed home, a little girl smelling sweet like summer berries, and at one side "her" dog, its coat the color of those
shapka hats her father used to dance a jig in. No one would
suspect a thing. The taste of orange bubble gum that she'd
chewed earlier in the day still lingered upon her breath.
What she was about to do, though, was a very womanly
thing, she told herself.

Entering the yard only a few blocks later, Abbie tied a
rope around the mutt's neck and fastened the other end to a
natural gas pipe oft a side of the house. She would have to
work quickly for her mother would be home soon. As to her
father, she did not worry; he never left his room anymore.
The dog let out an urgent yelp as she scampered for the
house. Within a few moments, she returned to the mutt,

holding in her palm a battery-operated hair clippers. Its metal blades glinted in the light as she turned it on. The dog cowered at the noise, it droning like a distant jet fighter. Abbie placed a hand about the nape of his neck to keep it steady, then with the other began running the clipper over its spine. Hair fell in clumps and floated upward into her face as if stuffing shaken from a pillow. The dog's eyes rounded into confused circles. Moments later, Abbie was done: A hairless stripe ran straight down the mutt's back, as if it were an inverse mohawk. She untied the dog, and it bolted out of the yard, ran for home.

Scooping up hair from the grass, she disposed of it in the kitchen garbage then meticulously cleaned the shears, dabbing hair oil on it so its scent returned to that of her father's. Finally, she sauntered onto the porch, and picking up her legless doll that had lain on the wooden deck for three days, having weathered two nighttime thunderstorms in the interim, she brought it to the trash pail and watched it thump down the side until coming to rest upon old banana peels and coffee grounds. She closed the lid, leaving her girlhood companion in the deep black well.

*****

Darkness filled the Steinar boys' primary school days. Their father, busy with chores and fieldwork, found little time to play or talk, and without a mother, they had only Aunt Amita's thick, clumsy arms and the musky scent of her sweaty bosom for comfort. Still, they venerated him for his persistence, and they respected her, understood after hearing stories of how some classmates' separated parents did not visit one another – let alone their own children – that she was doing more for them than most ever would. So the boys did whatever their aunt asked, half out of fear that she, too, might abandon them.

But when Aunt Amita nonchalantly told Peter to get the broom she'd left in the basement, his eyes shrank, and he stood absolutely still. Peter did not like going there, but she gently nudged him toward its door, knew he needed to socialize with children his age, not just the adults that visited her store. After a moment, he trudged toward the basement stairs, but, Amita rejoiced, he was going never-theless. Her sister's son was indeed brave, she told herself.

Peter's feet tentatively fell upon each step, and a sensation as if he were tumbling overcame him.

Then, holding onto the loose railing, he caught a glint of something shiny in Lyle's small hands. Propelled by curiosity, he descended the stairs with a sudden urgency as his cousins ran about and shouted in play. Lyle tried to hide the object, but youthful urges to examine his newfound prize prevented him from being discreet.

"What's in your hand?" Peter said to him.

Lyle looked up, his eyes trembling. "Nothing." He tried to shift both arms behind his back. Peter stood directly in front of him now. "You've got something, and I want to see it."

"It's nothing important."

"So what is then?"

Lyle hesitantly held out an arm. He uncupped his soft palm, unveiled a shard of glass the size of his cheek.

Peter almost gasped. "Give that to me."

Lyle carefully withdrew his hand. "No. I found it, and it's mine."

"You'll hurt yourself"

"I won't."

"You will. You're too little. Now give it to me."

"I am not too little."

Peter placed a hand upon his hip, extended his arm.

He'd grown impatient with this game. "Give it to me now. "

"No." Lyle turned away and examined his piece as if there was little Peter could do if only he refused.

Then Lyle felt his arm twist, like it were being pulled out of its socket, and as his widened eyes caught sight of the might that attacked him, he saw Peter squeezing his wrist hard, trying to force his hand to drop the glass. Lyle screeched, held the shard tight. His cousins circled them, cautiously stood back in respect of the sharpness that would not be surrendered.

The pain in Lyle's forearm neared a level of unbearability. He tried to break away, but Peter's grip was tight. Suddenly, as if in panic, Lyle flailed his arms madly, and Peter, knowing his plan would not work, let go.

He did not step back, though.

As Lyle's arm came up, a point upon the triangular piece of glass slipped outside his palm and caught Peter above the lip, diagonally slicing a half-inch. It sharper than any thorn, Peter stumbled back, heard a wind rushing like some mighty sound from heaven, and then the howl of pain swallowed his body. He swung a hand to his mouth; the cut felt like a freshly plowed furrow – and finding his fingers wet, he pulled the tips away, saw blood. It was as if his flesh were melting.

The door at the top of the basement steps sprang open, and Aunt Amita descended, her body decreasingly silhouetteted as she neared. "What is going on down here?" she hollered. "What is all of that screaming?"

Amita's children shrunk back, leaving a great part that led directly to her two nephews. Peter covered his mouth, tried to conceal the blood that seeped onto his backhand as Lyle shook, eyes agape at the power of his glass shard. She gasped, pulled his fingers away, saw lips soaked with blood.

"How did this happen?" she shouted, and when no one answered, she shouted it again.

Brady stepped forward. "Lyle did it," he said meekly.

She glared at the youngest of the Steinars, watched him shift both hands toward his back. Then, in a motion swift as a snake's strike, she grabbed hold of his wrist and squeezed loose the shard. It fell to the floor, a smoky cloud of red upon one tip.

"Where did you find this?" she said, forcing him to look at it. "Don't you know better than to pick up sharp glass?"

She swatted his behind, and he screeched. Then she turned to Peter and examining the cut for a moment, rounded him toward the stairs. "Let's get this washed up and disinfected," she said. "Everything will be all right."

Lyle twirled in anger, his face red and scrunched up. "It was an accident!" he screamed, his fists rolled.

Brady stepped forward. "It really was an accident, Mom," he said. "Lyle didn't mean to cut his lip."

She scowled at him. "And where were you during all of this? You're the oldest. It's your responsibility to make sure nobody gets hurt."

Then she led Peter up the stairs, slamming the door shut behind her. In the tiny bathroom upstairs, she sat him on the toilet and with a paper towel dipped in hot water, swabbed away the blood. Though the pain stung, he refused to curl up and cry.

*****

A rough wind blew over Peter as he hammered another nail into the pasture gate, connecting two grayed boards that had seen their share of weather. He'd purchased new latches and screws earlier that day at the hardware store as soon as coming across them in their worn cardboard boxes lining the grimy shelf; most farmers went with the sturdy metal gates, but he liked the old-style ones such as those his grandfather had erected decades ago. The task would give him the opportunity to take his mind off Abbie, he told himself, and for some time it worked as he planned the operation, identifying the supplies needed, analyzing precisely what must be replaced, and estimating time to completion. Once the mundane steps of actual repair were underway, though, he found there was too much time to think during the pounding of nails and the marches back and forth to his truck bed. Sweat trickled down his brow, and the eyebrows caught his perspiration like a berm along the creek as he continued banging until the head of the nail fell evenly with the board's plane. In the distance, the Steinar's bull eyed his labors suspiciously.

Peter grabbed a piece of lumber from the pile sticking out the end of his pickup truck. The wood's rough surface still pressed into his hands despite wearing work gloves for he'd taken the boards out of the pole shed. Some of them were not so good, much like the high school girls who'd remained behind in Felton after graduation, he joked to himself. He wondered if his father's inane frugality had infected him as well. I just as well could have purchased new lumber, he thought, yet here I am, squeezing the buffalo on the nickel until it bellows, just like my old man. He remained hesitant over hating him or not. So it was with Abbie, too. She made quips as frequently as his old man rattled off pithy sayings; yet her gibes were just the opposite in tone, full of irony, their meaning wind-like and insubstantial, not stone cold certainty. They made her alive, more real.

Across the horizon, the cattle marched slowly yet surely, sometimes lagging but always moving in one direction, the flanking bull examining Peter. Their lowing barely reached his ears. He was little interested in their procession beneath the tepid, yellow sky, the sunlight diffused by haze, and surrounded by all of that clover, sweet as it blossomed, he was unsurprised by their mutual nonchalance. How could any animal not taste the impressive freedom of the bountiful range? And yet, he knew it also was filled with much emptiness.

It did not have to be, he thought.

He paused for a moment, let the wind press against his sweat-stained shirt. A columbine wavered alongside the post closest to the gate, its dainty petals extending backward in a long spur from which delicate blue-green leaves sprouted. It only made him think again of Abbie, of how like that wildflower she was fragile in appearance but beneath it quite tough. This girl, he thought, had him all caught up, like he were a husk aloft a breeze. Such a ride in the past would cause him to overflow with joy, but he just wanted to settle upon the firm earth and regain his bearings. He placed upon the board a hinge, the sun-heated metal warm in his hands like a pot pulled from an oven, and screwed it into place.

He glanced up. The bull had inched much closer, stood upon the slightest of knolls a few yards away. The beast lowered its head to show off, as if a weight lifter flexing his muscle. Its intention did not fall for what before merely had been a soft snout transformed into a solid triangular mass of black from which curved two crescent horns, their points narrow and sharp. He snorted loudly then kicked a hoof against the prairie floor. Miniscule clouds of red dust drifted up from the bull's pawing leg.

Still, the Steinar boy stuck to his task. How many times before had he been in this pasture and never been rushed? He thought again of Abbie, of her glittering hair, and how in the sunlight it reminded him of ripe wheat, a fine, burnished gold. Peter set a nail to the board and struck it, but as the hammer arched up, he caught out of his eye's corner the beast bearing straight toward him.

As his torso twirled about to see the bull's furious rush, his mouth went dry. He leaped for the pickup's bed, banged his knee against the unevenly stacked lumber, and the bull pulled up, a mere foot from the tailgate. The beast's musky scent boiled in the hot air as its red eyes flashed. Peter grabbed a board and swung at it. The wood caught the bull's nostrils, and it swirled back, the pupils wide in amazement. Peter hurled the board again, and the bull, though out of reach, jumped back once more as the wood swooshed past. Breathing hard, Peter stood ready to bat, but his new enemy hung back, unwilling to step up to the plate, yet also unwilling to give ground. They stared steely-eyed at one another.

"So, it's a stalemate then, is it?" Peter said, his grip upon the board relaxing.

The bull pawed at the ground once more, frustrated at its inability to strike. Peter chuckled but knew he was a prisoner as much as the beast before him. He decided his best defense remained in patience. It was just a matter of waiting the bull out, for soon it would rejoin the herd, already flowing like a soft wind deep into the pasture without him. Then the opportunity to escape would arise. He wondered how long that would be, and already found himself bored just standing there, watching the bull amid the great plain, it immense like the floor of an evaporated ocean. The wind struck him repeatedly in its unexpected starts and stops. After a while, the bull's eyes no longer gleamed, and Peter sat, still holding the board just in case it charged.

"Well, how long shall we wait?" Peter said to it.

The beast did not answer, merely kept its dull but angry eyes upon him. For a while, Peter remained content to wait, just to prove his superiority. But as the sun gradually passed overhead, his stomach began to flitter and his body shift. He wrung his hands together. Still, he knew it was no time for desperation.

Then the bull stared at him in a sidelong glance, as if trying to discern what he was up to, just as Abbie had done at Kjopman's Grocery when they agreed to be friends. He had hoped she would say that wasn't how she wanted it. The wind blew wide and sullenly, a long wail across the bald plain. He watched the beast's marble-like head swing away from him. Abbie lingered in his head like a ghost that refused to be exorcised from a house. His skin grew clammy, despite the heat. Like with this bull, he and Abbie had reached a standoff; he could see that now. The beast's musky scent waned as it gradually stepped back. Perhaps it had given up, Peter speculated, maybe my perseverance has paid off. He smacked his lips, wished for a beer, and ever so slowly crept to the edge of his truck bed then eased himself to the ground. The bull flashed him another look but did not charge. In case it should rush, Peter remained at the tailgate, straightening the boards, picking up whatever tools he could. Then the bull moved off, headed back to its harem. Peter sighed. If only life could be so neatly arranged, he thought as shaking his head.

*****

Coach pushed them hard during that frowzy September week. But Lyle was determined to start Friday's game against the Indians. In his two seasons of playing junior high football, he'd always started and ran over every opponent as if a wronged man intent on exacting his revenge. Though Coach Lampert moved him directly to varsity during his freshman year, he remained a backup, needed to learn the system. Lyle detested himself for not being among the elite;

he wanted to be a winner, too.

His chance came two games in when the starting running back broke his arm. Though his replacement, Lyle soon found that he'd have to work for the job. Coach simply didn't think he was ready, even told him that. So, for a whole week of practice, he competed against another backup, a junior who though slightly smaller knew the playbook. "Competition's good for a person," growled Coach Lampert, his gray forelocks waving in the wind. "Builds strong minds 'n bodies." Lyle believed him. And he wanted to start.

Suddenly Lyle became the most motivated player on the team. He was the first on the field for practice and the last off. During calisthenics, he ran faster and stretched farther. In blocking drills, he hit tackling dummies, pushing them longer than ever before. In scrimmages, he performed like the playbook described for he passed on sleep to memorize it. On running plays, he penetrated the line with force, mashing the linemen like a speeding semi-trailer. Each practice was a two-hour exhibition of brutal strength and determination.

At Thursday afternoon's workout, he committed the final act resolving his status for Friday's game. Near the beginning of scrimmage, he broke through the defensive line and charged for the end zone. Only a linebacker stood in his way. Hitting him squarely in the ribs with his left shoulder pad, his nemesis crashed to the ground with a loud thud as Lyle scored. The wind knocked out of him, the backer writhed painfully. Trainers rushed onto the field to see if he had broken anything.

"That's the way to pound em!" shouted Kent Cairn, the center. "You gotta make the sonufabitch hurt, make em know you're not just another freshman off the bench."

Lyle stared in amazement at his power, nodded mind-lessly. "Think he's hurt?"

"That would be a fuck if Tom got hurt so he couldn't make tomorrow's game," Cairn said. "We might not win. Hey, don't let it bother you. To hell with it. You had a good hit, scored. That's all that counts. "

"Guess you're right," Lyle said, turning away from him and glancing at the sidelines. Old man Lampert and his assistant, Coach Holter, looked at him with approval. They knew he had been working hard all week.

In the shower after practice, as sweat and pain dripped down Lyle's body, Coach Lampert told him he would start. Filled with jubilation, Lyle burst out singing every verse he knew of "Louie, Louie." His aching body fell into the bliss of victory.

Friday's game didn't start well for him, though. He'd played little in the first two games, and his inexperience showed itself vividly. When the center snapped the ball he hesitated. Should Jackie Kine turn right to hand off the ball, Lyle shifted left. Early in the second quarter, Felton drove deep into enemy territory, largely off a couple of passing calls. The Indians firmed though, giving Felton a third down on their 20-yard line. Lyle's teammates knew that if stopped again, they'd have to settle for a field goal attempt, and one from that far out was nearly impossible for small school teams.

Lyle readied himself for the play, following the count and Jackie Kine's hand, which twitched slightly the second before Cairn snapped him the ball. Lampert was gambling, called for a draw with Lyle as the runner. As Kine took the ball, an Indian rusher broke through the Felton line. Kine dropped back, handed the ball to Lyle. Like a train at full throttle, he burst forward, but with an even blow to the chest, the rusher leveled him.

On the ground, Lyle shook his head. Though standing two inches taller than the rusher, he had been knocked down with ease, as if just another backup off the bench. Shame crept over him.

He glanced at Coach Lampert for support, but the old man just shook his head in disgust. Lyle's head bubbled in anger; he swore that no Indian would get the best of him again.

Knowing a field goal could not be made, Coach Lampert opted to try another a pass on fourth down. He kept Lyle in to block. Kine scrambled for a couple of seconds, rifled the ball to a receiver. The Indian defender stepped in front of him, picked off the ball. He scurried down the sidelines as Lyle and several of his teammates angled for him.

Fast with youth and flushed with anger, Lyle corralled him off. The Steinar boy's conditioned reflexes did not stop him, even when certain the Indian player, cheered on by raucous fans, would step out of bounds. He'll pay for it, Lyle thought through gritted teeth. Lyle's heart pelted through his jersey, and like a crazed animal on a hunt, he lurched forward, focusing the complete weight of his drive into the butt of his helmet. Struck, the Indian's small body bent backwards, collapsed to the muddy ground. Lyle senselessly completed the tackle with a crushing blow from the shoulder pads.

He picked himself off the still body and stared at it. That Indian would think twice before he returned another interception against Felton, Lyle told himself. His teammates rambled over and slapped him on the back. "Way to go!" they said. "Good job!" "Way to let him have it!" He had prevented the receiver from scoring a certain touchdown, they told him.

Lyle only peered at the downed Indian, though. The player lay motionless on the ground, and Lyle waited for him to stand, but his lame, curled body remained in the muck. What was the matter with him, Lyle wondered, why didn't he get up? The Steinar boy shivered, and the strength of his muscles sagged. Was the Indian player all right? A numbness spread through Lyle's body. Just what had he done?

The Indian trainers ran onto the field, quickly kneeling around him. Lyle stood over them as they checked their player's condition, taking off padding, feeling his bones for fractures. He had only been knocked unconscious, they said, and the downed player began to stir.

Lyle sighed in relief.

Chapter 13

Lyle rose upon the plains like a storm approaching from the west, a silhouetted figure marching atop the furrows, growing increasingly taller with each step. Carl Steinar shivered as if a bough in the wind; he'd not expected anyone to come looking for him, yet there was no other explanation for his son's behavior. So the old man stood his ground, the dry scent of sand-colored husks and stems wafting all about him, grit binding itself to the edges of his teeth and eyes. When the two met, neither spoke, and they sauntered in step toward the farmhouse.

Carl wished he could get along better with his son, knew Lyle was more like him than Peter, did not possess that restlessness and desire to explore that his eldest child so frequently exhibited. He still loved Peter, but in much the same way he respected old Cornelius Skerry, out of a mutual admiration for what the other was not. Carl longed for Cornelius' carefree lifestyle, and his friend wished to be the self-disciplined Steinar; their regard for one another blunted any natural friction that would flare between two such disparate personalities. And so what if Peter liked to wander, Carl thought, while he himself preferred the nest's comfort? His son always returned.

Carl spoke without shifting his gaze. "Where did you

drive off to?"

Lyle hesitated for a moment. "To see Jackie Kine, at the stockyards. He wasn't available."

Carl nodded. "Guess he's a busy man these days."

Lyle remained silent.

They marched on. The sun's brightness pressed against Carl's back and the nape of his neck as he tried to recall the last time he'd walked with his son from this direction, between the creek and the farmhouse. It was years ago when he had gone looking for his boys. Trampling across the plain, the red dust loosely striped across the buff-colored loam, he found them only after a long search, and just in time, too. As Lyle squirmed on the ground, trying to hold on to a bunch of wildflowers, Peter struck his brother's wailing mouth over and over. Carl's face glared as a heat rose inside him, bubbling like a wicked rapids. To think, his own sons fighting, two brothers who one day would jointly run this farm he so desperately held together with his dear sweat and fiber. But he said nothing of this, only let his anger speak, and tossed Peter off like an empty gunnysack. Lying in the grass, the boy suddenly bawled, and Carl's eyes flashed at him like razor blades. Why, it was hardly a long distance that he'd been thrown, Carl thought as his mouth crooked and pupils rolled back in disgust at the boy's fragility. Then he bent over and with a firm grip of the arm raised Lyle until his youngest son had no choice but to stand or fall again. The boy chose to stand, and for a moment, pride over his younger son's spirit surged through Carl.

He slung Lyle into his arms, carried him back toward the house. The boy tucked his chin against Carl's shoulder as Peter staggered behind, whimpering. But Carl only cantered steadily toward, listening to young Lyle's breathing, it soft and delicate like his lost Gwen, exhaling and inhaling, he imagined, like a young boy should. Lyle already possessed the signature looks of a grown Steinar man – the thin, still lips, a hardened brow – traits passed down through the father from the boy's grandpa, who got them from who knew where, maybe even a woman, Carl speculated, but that did not matter. For the next generation, the Steinars would appear like they had during the past several decades, the way that people in Felton thought a Steinar should look. Carl quietly ran his rough hand through the boy's hair, it slight yet velvety like gramma grass, the bangs falling half way across the forehead, then he leaned forward to kiss his son's temple. But his nose crinkled, and he stopped an inch short. The boy did not smell like him or his father; what he emanated was neither bad nor odd but merely a lack of that Steinar scent in the way a desert is deficient of water, there but not sufficiently present. What does he smell like, Carl pondered, and then it came to him: like blossoming sunflowers. He gasped slightly and withdrew, his mouth instantly drying in terror.

Carl Steinar would never kiss his son again.

Far ahead of the two men, their clapboard house and its cluster of farm buildings shimmered in the heat. So, all these years later, Carl thought, his son still had tried to prevent him from committing suicide, even had gone searching for him. The field turned almost slumberous in its utter quiet, and sweat beaded along Carl's forehead as his eyelids hung heavily. The boy had tried so desperately to conceal the blue caplet, then when exposed defended himself so vehemently; what was he up to? There was no escape from his son's watchful eye, Carl told himself. The earth stank of bread too dry to eat, and the back of his throat ached with thirst. He wished there had been a kitchen door to open so his son would have had more warning to hide the pill.

*****

Abbie's hair flung wild and spiraling as a slight gasp escaped her lips. She no longer cared what

Peter thought or felt, only that his warm mouth continued to press upon the nape of her neck as his hand caressed her midriff; the attention alone balanced against his lack of words. She had not intended for the evening to end with them naked in one another's arms, coiled like serpents let loose upon her bed sheets, but that was the course it had taken. Some yearning from deep inside allowed her to feel great satisfaction that it had, though...

During the previous two days, Abbie had scratched around the idea of phoning Peter herself. Knowing his father didn't much care for her, though, she doubted if any message would get through. Eventually the notion of a face-to-face meeting wheedled to the top of her thoughts.

Then, coming home late from the Register Friday night, she spotted his pickup parked at the High Life Bar, and wringing her hands, decided to spy on him.

She twirled the ends of her raven-colored hair the whole way across the gravel lot; he hadn't called in seven days, and that was not a good indication of his interest. Reasons abounded why he might not had spoken to her, she knew, and so her reporter instincts of first hearing both sides before passing judgment wormed through the internal naysaying until she had no choice but to take action.

The collective voices of those filling the High Life drowned out the screen door banging shut behind her. A smoky haze filled the dim bar, with the only lights an orange glow hovering above the pool table and over the liquor bottles stacked behind the bartender. As she headed for the bar rail, blouse and jeans tight about Abbie's frame, the faces of nearly every cowboy and farmer there narrowed upon her body. This was a man's domain, and amid the jukebox music, it loud like a train chugging down the tracks, they far outnumbered the women. Her spine prickled. The fume of a farmhand's cigarette crossed her path, but other than pinching her nostrils she paid it no heed, could not afford to. At the bar, she turned her back to most of the crowd but in the mirror could see a couple of them still staring. Sweat trickled upon her temples. She fanned herself with the wave of a hand, cast her eyes about for Peter. Two other women, both suntanned blondes, held glasses of liquor a mere stool away next to the dartboard. Her heart slowed for a moment; she was not entirely alone.

And then he appeared, his solid frame between two standing farmers whose balance shifted from one foot to another just as she glanced toward the end of the bar. Her face brightened. Still, she kept her place, tried not to gawk; it was certain to attract attention, and for the moment that was not her objective. He sat hunched over the bar rail and a beer bottle, and she knew he was unaccompanied. Abbie turned to the door. Knowing he was by himself was good enough, wasn't it, she asked herself, but before taking a single step, she leaned against the counter, told herself that rationalizing a way out of there was merely masking fear. Abbie stood straight up.

No, she wouldn't lose a man who could make her feel as if she were flying.

...Abbie could not sense the sweat pooling beneath her back for her body seemed to hover above the mattress as his mouth caressed her inner thigh. She grasped his hair to keep him there. Her heart pounded swiftly, and she found herself rising, as if given wings. Then his fingers spread her fold. He was a mist that she flew through…

"A beer, something light," Abbie said as the bartender asked her what she'd have. "And send one down to that cowboy at the end of the bar, the one whose hair is a shade heavier than nut-brown. "

The bartender glanced at him. "Sure thing, miss."

She put on her best smile, kept her eyes wide and fixed upon Peter as the bartender brought first her then him a beer. She leaned one leg forward, bent it at the knee as the other remained straight. Though the jukebox played raucously and the farmers struck pool balls as clinking their beer bottles against table tops, once her attention focused upon him she heard none of it. He grinned back, and for a moment she flushed, then regaining control of her expression, batted her eyes. She flipped her head back slightly, let the loose bangs over her brow flutter so the face cooled. Then he waved for her to come down.

Abbie's dimples flared. With a swing in her step, she headed directly toward him. All else in the bar appeared but a blur.

"Well, howdy pilgrim," she said in a mock western twang upon reaching him.

Peter's gaze lingered upon her as he pushed his beer away in favor of the new one the bartender had brought. He patted a barstool for her to sit on.

"That's quite brave of you," she said, "calling a strange girl over here. Could be dangerous."

"Not too dangerous for local consumption, I hope." A constricted gleam came to his eyes, if only briefly, as it he was trying to suppress his joy.

Still, her body tensed as she sat next to him. Though he'd been receptive enough, they were only friends. His lavender scent overpowered the odor of sticky beer on the tavern's floors and walls. "I'm sorry," she said, "about–"

He waved his hand. "There's nothing to apologize about. Really."

Fret showed in her eyes. She wondered if he was so angry with her that he didn't even want to hear it. Maybe I've underestimated him, she thought. "Is it because 'friends' don't have to say they're sorry?" she said.

"Things happen. Often no one means anything by them." Her posture relaxed, and she leaned toward him.

"'It's a little something my father often told me," he said. "I was never sure I really believed it, but now I guess so."

She smiled. For a moment, he seemed unreal, as if fog, or mere ether.

...Then Abbie's head arched as he entered her. From her lips rose a moan, and a headiness filled her face, which as he thrust lightened to less than the density of air, as did all of her body but for the pulse point between her legs where they joined. Her hands – she could hardly feel them at all though she knew they existed – grabbed for the bed sheet, kneaded it as if to anchor herself upon the earth as she levitated, losing all contact with her senses: the beer-laden breath that now only vaguely flushed warm upon the mouth as she exhaled, the guttural sounds emanating from deep in his chest that seemed far as a distant memory, the perspiration that glistened across her brow and breasts but like dew upon a leaf could not touch her soul...

Peter set his bottle down. "Perhaps tomorrow night you'd like to meet me at the High Life Bar."

"I don't know," she said with a smirk. "It's macaroni and

cheese night. I can't miss that."

Peter chuckled. "I'll take that as a 'yes,' then."

Abbie took a gulp from her own beer. It rolled at the bottle's neck like seafoam.

"Something happened to me, earlier today," he said. "I was in the field, rebuilding an old plank gate. Our bull rushed me."

Abbie's brow knitted in worry. "Are you all right?"

"Oh, no physical harm done," he said. "I made it to the back of my pickup in time, but he kept watch over me for a good half hour or more. Neither one of us would back down. I suppose we were both kind of stubborn. It got me thinking about us, though."

"How so?"

"Well, this 'friends,' thing. Despite what I said, I don't want to just be friends. You don't either, I suspect."

Abbie cautiously shook her head.

"Being friends because we got into an argument, that's like a standoff. As I waited for that bull to go on about its own business, I decided that if given another chance with you, I'd take it."

She tucked strands of her hair behind an ear, then tilted her head slightly as gazing upon him.

Keeping a smile upon her face was not difficult; just hearing the sweet tang of his voice was enough to raise one. The problem was smiling too widely, as if a lover's clown. She held her warm hands together, crossed at the wrists, found that even it showed her giddiness. Tittering, she leaned toward him, close enough to catch another whiff of his lavender cologne. She almost could taste his body, the nape of his neck a lush peach, so succulent between her lips.

...In bed, she rolled onto her tummy and arching the

back, propped her torso up on both elbows and gazed at him. Her hair was sweat-laden and mussed up. He said nothing, though, as her lips parted mischievously. The dampened sheets pressed against her smooth belly, and she wondered if he could see enough cleavage. The musk of their sex hung heavy in the room. She swung her bare legs upward at the knees, crossed them over the ankles, inched toward him. Their mouths met, and as her head swirled, she could not tell if it was wine or his being that caressed her tongue…

Sitting at the bar railing, arm touching Peter's, she felt comfortable, like the bird returned to its warm nest high aloft the branches where no creature could harm her. His eyes grinned at her. "Want to dance?" he said.

Abbie held out a hand, and Peter led her by it to the dance floor. Placing his palm about her waist and the other in mid-air for her own fingers to entwine, they began to stomp a two-step, then spun. Her hair swirled. A breeziness overcame her, and as she glanced down, her feet seemed to skim the floor. The bar's worn barstools and time-bruised walls suddenly turned all jazz and glitter as they twisted about each other like strings in a knot. Abbie found herself returned to a better time. She threw her arms around his head. "I'd like to take a walk again with you on your farm. "

He nodded. "I think I'd like that, too."

At that, her heart whirled, and Abbie felt as if she were holding the edge of the world. Suddenly she did not trust herself, sensed that they'd probably end up spending the night together. Abbie rested her chin against his hard chest. She giggled.

He glanced at her. "What?" he said as grinning.

…Her eyes hung half-shut in contentment, and she

smiled back. His lavender scent, amplified by the sweat of their passion, drowned her senses. She no longer could tell if the swirl in her head emanated from their simultaneous orgasm or from the beer. Then with her finger she gently traced the slight scar above his lip, as if to say let me into your heart. "Oh, Peter Steinar," she said finally, "I love you so much. You can tell me as much or as little about yourself as you need to. Just promise that one day you will tell."

*****

After Gwen died, Carl Steinar almost never went to the tavern, so the discovery of his boys' mid-adolescent drinking binges shocked him. He found the need for liquor based either in celebration or sorrow, yet there was no time for either extreme in his life. So that first night when the boys arrived home after the late show had finished, beer breath betraying their secret, he stared at them, his jaw firm. He'd always kept tough curfews, and from a distance they apologized, tried telling the story of some girl whose car had broken down and how they gave her a ride home. He let it go. Hung over or not, they'd still have to do chores in the morning, and that alone would teach them a lesson, he thought.

It did not.

After the third late night in two weekends, he discreetly followed them to see exactly what they were up to. He vaguely understood; after all, he'd once been a teenage boy himself. From overhearing snatches of his sons' conversation, he knew their friends gathered every Friday night at the abandoned German-American State Bank out near the edge of town. So an hour after the boys left, he drove within a half mile of the red brick building and set off across a scrubby field along the creek's woodline. He felt his way through the deep night, darkness like a shawl across the land. Branches scratched his hands, and on occasion he tripped over rocks and discarded boards. Sometimes, invisible litter crinkled beneath his feet, and for most of the way he could smell the grass stains and sand upon his hands from when he had fallen. He would have preferred to been tucked beneath sheets rather than out in the cold, even though his unshared bed hardly offered much more warmth. Then his foot stepped into a puddle and mud splattered against the ankles. He paused for a moment, the water soaking through the leather boot, and tried not to draw attention by tiptoeing out of it, cringing at the squish of his wet sock, which he'd convinced himself echoed louder than it really did.

Then he spotted them. His brow rose.

The brick bank sat on a plot bordering the creek, and its walls hid the teens well from the roadside. Should the Guthrie County Sheriff's deputies decide to get out of their cars and make a bust, two trails led to an easy escape through the water. Confident he had not been seen, Carl knelt behind a bush and watched them. The teens played their boombox of heavy metal music loud, even when cars passed, and they rambled on between beers about teachers, the latest movie, their parents' stupidity. By midnight, they'd paired off, and heavily drunk couples swooned and cuddled and necked, though Carl doubted they loved one another. It simply was something to do.

Carl Steinar threw up his hands. Yes, when growing up he'd enjoyed a beer or two out back, yet these teenagers drank neither to celebrate nor to drown their grief but to merely drink. He suddenly found his sons ambiguous, like art or mystery. Not so long ago they savored simple apple juice, but now like a fishtailing truck each had turned away from him, was out of control. For so many years he'd believe in his personal infallibility, yet here it was, proof that he'd somehow failed as a father. What had Lyle once said, not so distantly in the past to him? "How long will it take for me to look like you?"

Then the wind rose like a trumpet, loud and angry. Eyes sunken, Carl turned away, his face a satin red. He found the sand slipping away from beneath him, as if surf were washing the ground away. What would his boys do with no Virgil to guide them? He did not realize that for his sons there always was the warmth and safety of the lit house awaiting them, as if they could return to the womb. He retreated into the bramble.

Six hours later, the boys entered the living room, the bang of the door behind them a spike in the silence. Their father sat awake in his chair as snow scrawled across the television screen. Dried mud rounded the hem of his jeans. They suddenly stopped speaking in mid-sentence and stared at him. He said nothing.

The next morning, Carl Steinar stirred his sons awake bright and early for chores. Lines hung deep below the boys' eyes as they moped about the kitchen then the farmyard. While Carl and Peter fed the cattle, a quietness like that of a rare prairie day filled the old man's ears. His lip quivered for a moment as he and Peter glanced at one another. Carl set down his shovel, traipsed toward the grain bins, Peter following. They looked in the pole barn and the calf pens. Then, in the hay shed, they found Lyle sprawled asleep upon straw bales, the dog licking his face. With a finger like a bull's horn pressing into the side of an upstart stripling, Carl Steinar poked his youngest son's ribs. Light blinded Lyle as his eyes flashed open. "I hear that it was quite a hullabaloo at the old bank last night," the father said, his voice a heated syncopation. "If you want to hang with that crowd, that's fine, but you're still going to do chores the next morning." He fixed his eyes upon his son. "You best check on the calves."

Brushing chaff off his coat, Lyle grabbed a pitchfork and drifted toward the calf pens. Peter grinned demonically at his brother, eyes full of victory, muttered a snide comment toward him. Less than a breath later, Carl grabbed his elder son's arm, wrenching the boy sideways so he faced him. Anger roiled through Carl Steinar like ocean swells; has all my hard work and long hours led only to this, he wondered. "You just knock it off, too," he said, his voice hissing. "You were out all night as well."

Peter began to argue back, but Carl cut him off. "My sons are free to say what they please, but remember, this farm isn't a democracy." He stomped off.

Lyle and Peter continued forking hay to the cattle as the lowing beasts bunted one another's heads for position and snorted their fetid breaths in thanks to the Steinar boys. Unwilling to face one another, the two boys held in their grumbles. Then, inexplicably, a bang, loud as an exploding artillery shell, echoed through the barn. Peter burst through the slim door into the blazing sunlight as Lyle lumbered behind. Their father swung a sledgehammer at the windmill, and a large echo resounded in the prairie's vastness. A corner post depressed beneath his blow. Peter ran at him, each step in the dry August heat parching his throat. Grabbing a shoulder, he spun his father toward him. The old man's face swelled with red as they stared at one another. Then he resisted, and Peter strained to hold the hulking arm as the father's spit dripped onto his bare arm and burned. The sledgehammer bounced onto the dirt, barely missing the boy's foot, then the two men fell under one another's weight and rolled upon the ground.

*****

Carl Steinar placed one foot on the disk. Resting his elbow upon the uplifted knee, he stared into the barren horizon as the morning wind rustled against his shirt. Around the lone leg still planted on terra firma, dirt billowed as if coyote pups chasing one another about a tree. The raw breeze burned his cheekbones, but he resisted the onslaught. Then, as the gusts rested for a brief moment, the old farmer spit though he did not chew tobacco. He hoped Peter did not smell the nervous sweat beading beneath his arms.

The door to the shed rattled as Carl gazed solemnly upon his son. They locked eyes. "We ought to check the heifers, see if they've taken to calf," Carl said.

Peter crossed his arms. "It can wait 'til tomorrow."

Carl Steinar looked up, cocked an eyebrow. After a moment, he snorted. "Why, what else have we got to do today?"

"I have plans with Abbie this afternoon."

"This afternoon? Doesn't she ever work?"

"She's a reporter. When there's a night meeting, she gets the afternoon off."

"I know she's a reporter." He returned to pounding rivets out of the disk, his face concentrating upon the point his chisel struck. "There's not much to her," the father said after a couple of taps. "She's a little skinny."

Peter recalled the big-boned woman his father had once brought home for Christmas. What was her name? Mina, he thought, yes that's it. She looked nothing like his mother. He wondered if his father really preferred women that way, wearing plus sizes. Had he not liked his own wife's slenderness, not appreciated the femininity inherent in it? He scanned his father's face, tried to determine what the old man really was saying. Rutted like a rock wall, it did not twitch even when sparks flew from the clashing metal. Perhaps such a feature was admirable, Peter thought, a sign of his stubbornness that holds out against defeat, but the boy himself was determined.

"She's meeting me here, about one," Peter said.

His father did not break a beat in his work. "No matter which way or how hard the wind blows, we still must plant and reap, then plant and reap again, and again," he said.

"What's that supposed to mean?"

"It means this afternoon we're checking heifers. "

"I don't think you heard me. Abbie is meeting me here, about one."

The old man looked up, his pupils narrowing, and set down his chisel and hammer. "That girl isn't allowed on my farm. "

Peter's mouth dropped. "What?"

"You heard what I said."

Peter placed his hands upon his hips. "We're going steady. If she isn't allowed on the farm, then neither am I."

For a long moment, Carl Steinar examined his son, measured the red in his face to see if the expression backed up his words. He gambled. "You've heard. Now do as I say." The old farmer turned away.

"No sir," said Peter, a bull pawing the ground as it snorts. "I won't."

Carl turned steadily, and though silent his pupils roared as he stared evenly at Peter.

"I will leave the farm, go work at the stockyards," Peter said. Anger seethed through him like an unrestrained wind.

"There you go again, looking for the payoff but not the pitfall. Nah, you'll be on this farm all of your life."

Peter grabbed his old man's shirt at the chest, pushed him back against the shed's tin wall. The metal reverberated as the boy's nostrils flared. His father's face suddenly turned vacant, though, like a fallow plot, and Peter's brow wrinkled then his eyes drew back in bewilderment. The old man would not fight back. Peter let him go, stared at his own hands. Beyond them, the windmill clattered mercilessly in the breeze, as if phantoms were madly turning the blades. Carl Steinar lowered his head to regain a sense of equilibrium.

Chapter 14

Lyle Steinar scowled as if a baby with colic. Standing behind a row of currant bushes outside the machine shed, he watched Peter and Abbie cross the field hand-in-hand. Even from his distant vantage, he could see their bodies glowing with passion, like they'd harnessed and compacted all of the sun's energy into their very beings. With each step, the space between the two lovers shortened until they paused and gazed into one other's eyes, then their walk continued as they repeated the behavior without realizing so. Lyle suddenly found himself lost, as if walking circles in a blizzard. Before this Abbie had arrived, there was an order to things on the farm, from the very moment dawn flushed the stars out of the sky through the falling of evening's black hush.

He recalled the harmony of the Steinar breakfast. Despite the weighty tone of each morning's gathering, once the luminous sun broke through the kitchen curtains and covered the table, serenity reigned. There always was the constant of coffee and toast, then the chores stretching beyond into the distant day, yet even back then he knew something was missing. Did nostalgia now fill that hollow sensation, he wondered, creating a fondness for the past? He spat on the dusty ground, turned back to the shed.

Rolls of rusted barbed wire lined one wall, and to reach the shade in which his father sat, Lyle had to step around the lawn mower, the scent of gas and grease strong, then navigate a maze of hastily tossed tools, buckets, and used paint brushes. Near the edge of where light slanted into the building, he spotted at eye level before him a spider hanging by a single thread from the rafter. He swiped at it as if a cat upon prey, and the spider's hard back cracked between his fingertips. After a moment, he examined it, a pool of red about a flattened black husk on his thumb and forefinger. It reminded him of when as young boys he and Peter ate ripe berries plucked from the bush outside, and the juice would trickle across their fingers and palms like a victim's blood upon the murderer's hands. As life itself, the tiny fruits tasted tart upon his tongue.

Lyle turned to the compressor he'd been using to blow dust and debris from the combine. Not so long ago, only we Steinar men crossed these fields, he muttered. His father shifted upon a turned-over pail in the sweltering shed. The old man stunk of cold salt, as if he'd experienced a hot sweat during sleep and the slickness had evaporated beneath a long, chilled wind. Lyle's face crinkled in disgust. Was he planning his death again? How could one ever guess when he'd strike next? Lyle's shoulders drooped, as if an over-loaded bag were slung upon it. Would his father run himself into a combine, crash the pickup? He tossed down the compressor hose, ran his hairy wrist across a wet brow. He knew all too well why his old man was upset; after Abbie had arrived, he'd quit any notion of checking the heifers. Maybe giving his father a chore to do would provide him with purpose again, a task that like slumber would break his thoughts. Lyle understood how not seeing the world about him with all of its myriad connections was best; life remained much easier, much less complicated, if one stuck to the task at hand, if one kept himself numb during the times in-between. It was a lesson he had learned from his father. Perhaps he needed to reteach it to him.

"Dad, we need to replace the auger on the combine," Lyle said to him.

He stared at his old man, whose body remained still as stone. Despite deep etchings upon his father's dusty face, no sign of urgency registered.

"Do you want to drive?" Lyle said.

No response came. Lyle stretched his hands about his father's ribs, raised the old man to his feet. Carl Steinar breathed deeply, like a runner before the race's start. They sauntered toward the truck, then Lyle let him go and took the lead. The sun shined upon them like rock rubbing against grindstone. He wished his father would walk faster, then climbed into the truck. What business was it of his if Peter wanted to surrender his birthright, if his father could not cope with it? The corner of Lyle's upper lip rose slightly; blood rushed around his eyes and into the temples. No, it had always been, always would be: one had a duty to those who tended to you – take care of the land, and it'll take care of you, his old man always said. Still, Lyle's thoughts remained stuck, as if in a feedback loop. Couldn't his father see that he loved him?

Carl Steinar turned the ignition, whirring the truck to a start. Dust roiled through the open window, clotted Lyle's nostrils. He did not need to ask if they would go to the salvage yard for parts; new ones simply were too expensive. As they reached the hardpan and gained speed, lines upon the faded blue road passed swiftly beneath them. In spite of the hot-as-a-torch air, his father shivered. Dusty, Lyle's high school girl friend, never had shown fear when they ran their races; he'd give her that much. The thin reflectors marking a neighbor's driveway whirled past.

Back then, life and death were like a lottery to him. He ignored the road's deep potholes and their dangerous curves around telephone poles, merely flew across the horizon toward a definitive line. After the ride, all of the teens crammed themselves into the wooden lot, as if frightened of the prairie's open spaces. Lyle would shift about, his hands having nothing to do, as they enveloped him in their adoration for winning yet again. Amid it all, his shoulders slumped; the boy thought of them like he did his brother and old man, always hurrying him along like he were a steer sent to market. Inevitably, the diphenhydramine caplets would make their way into his palm, and upon swallowing them he'd lumber off behind the wild plum bushes, drop his drunken carcass onto the earth, then wrap himself so deeply in sleep that pain ceased coursing through his body.

Slowly, the red dust layered across the withered grass came into focus as his old man's truck entered the junkyard. As they slogged into the office, its owner, Kerry Halvard, stood behind a counter, and a small fan too noisy for its size blew directly on him. The three exchanged acknowledging glances. "We called earlier about an auger for a combine header," Lyle said. "Damn thing barely got us through the last harvest." A tape measure clinging to Halvard's belt bounced as he nodded that the part was available. He waved them toward a back door, and the two Steinars followed him behind the counter, winnowing with every word he spoke about which combine they might cut it from. As he grabbed a safety goggles and gloves from a wall peg, a large dark oval of perspiration showed at his armpit.

Heading into the combine graveyard, they marched past tour rows of varying models, all of them missing parts, some half-buried in weeds, each discolored by the sun and stinking of rotting wheat kernels. Halvard pointed toward a great mound of olive metal. "That one?" he said. Lyle nodded, and as Halvard went for his pickup truck, a dirty blue handkerchief tucked about his belt flopped. The truck's clatter drowned out the rush and whistle of hot wind slamming into the two Steinars. Lyle stared at the grasses shriveled from dryness, or perhaps, he speculated, from the rust that dribbled off the hulking machines during when there had been some precipitation. A gust blew exhaust from Halvard's pickup into his face. His nostrils pinched tight until the smoke passed. Parking the truck, Halvard lolled to its bed, where a grimy generator sat bolted to planks. The scent of gasoline hovered in the dry air.

Halvard wiped his forehead with the handkerchief "Grain prices have got to go up soon; I've got 12 people on my payroll and will have to lay off two of them soon if they don't."

"Twelve? That many?" Lyle said.

"Makes me one of the largest employers around," Halvard winked. "Just the other day, old man Dawson stopped by and offered to sell me all of his equipment. He's 65 and has no one to take over the farm."

They leaned under the rusted combine, searching in the grayness for the frame's bolts. Halvard grunted as his beer belly weighed heavily on the knees. "I think there's one here," he said, pointing. Carl bent toward the finger for a closer look, nodded, then backed away as Halvard fired up the generator and acetylene torch. Sparks flew from the combine's underside as the smell of melting iron filled the air. Lyle's mouth tasted coppery from inhaling the odor. A bolt fell out of the header, smoldered in the grass. Halvard gingerly tamped it with his worn boots, then with a heel kicked it into the dirt and hastily buried it.

"Bernie Alien's foreclosure auction is Thursday," Carl said. "We're going – not to buy but to show our solidarity."

Lyle's brow rose at the thought that his father had come out of his stupor so quickly, and he examined the old man's face. Perhaps there was nothing to his antics, maybe he really just needed to stay busy. His face swelled with anger. It was like the quiet rage Carl felt at him for not pursuing football; though never saying anything about it, Lyle still could sense the skin beneath his father's shirt burning whenever autumn and talk of the Huskers or Felton's chances in conference play reared. The thought must had settled upon him as well that playing football meant being good at it, and being good at something other than farming meant leaving Felton. That was not something Lyle was ready to do or Carl ready to permit, however. Still, the tension did not leave Lyle's mind as they loped back to the shop. It raised memories of when he played football five years before. Unlike dreams, those images held an intractable vividness, like how the crowd's anticipatory cheers rose as the Felton Pioneers approached the ball. The linemen bent into the stances as Jackie Kine brought his hands under the center then barked the count. Lyle's knuckles dug into the ground and he slipped the mouthguard against his tongue, readying himself His knees twitched. Then as he was about to sniffle in the cold autumn air, the line sprung forward and Jackie wheeled toward him. He jut ahead, and as Jackie thrust the ball into his hands, he cradled it, as if it were an infant, and spurt ahead with all the power his legs could muster. Then his shoulder slammed against the back of his own man, and as white mesh filled his vision, he could not push him, no matter how hard he tried. Suddenly he felt his chest fall forward as someone gripped his ankles and pulled his feet off the ground. The side of his helmet slid against the lineman's thigh, and as his face bounced on the grass, dirt spit into his eyes then his mouth as he swore.

They'd lost the game.

Now Lyle wondered if he'd lost his father.

*****

Smoothed by years of use, the steering wheel slipped through Carl Steinar's fingers as he turned off a whole section before the Williwaw and Visne roads crossing. Lyle sat in the passenger seat, the faint smell of junkyard and grease tube upon him. Going that way extended his trip from Felton by a few miles; when heading there on his weekly sojourn, it meant entering town out near the school rather than by the mill where he usually wanted to end up. Still, his sons never once mentioned the odd route he took. Perhaps they too recognized how it marginalized the crossing they avoided, in the same way that a man must turn both eyes away from his house as it burns.

An azure ray of late afternoon sun hit him as he angled across the plains. Like a thousand or more times before, just to keep his mind off things, he recited each of the crops and soil types seen along Visne Road: the wheat, the rich scent of the mollisol giving way to the light colored aridsols, the occasional patches of oats and rye. Sometimes he avoided Murnan Road as well, for butter-and-eggs wildflowers grew along the shoulder, and that reminded him of Gwen gardening. Memory, when he thought about it, lay severe and mysterious, like the prairie itself, each a great sweep of unbroken and unbounded land that one never could leave so long as alive. Memories always returned, like the seasons, sometimes late, sometimes early, sometimes out of sync with the calendar, but they always returned.

He wiped his brow with the back of a wrist as catching

first sight of the grain bin announcing his farm's existence. Though summer's heat had reached its climax, he shivered. The sultry afternoon reminded him of when his older brother, Gil, had left the farm. Ah yes, his older brother, moving about goods and dollars electronically and abstractly rather than putting all the tangibles down on paper with a simple pencil like a man in touch with reality would. Gil had picked out his best to wear that August day Carl and their father took him to the bus station; why he'd insisted on riding the bus and not being driven the four hours to Lincoln escaped Carl, but that was all right by their father, who didn't much care for the big city anyway. He stood apart from them while waiting, as if they were dried cow dung. When the old Greyhound arrived, its exhaust, heavy like freshly laid tar, filled their lungs. Gil practically bounded up the bus steps, exhilarated by the unknown awaiting him. After that, he rarely returned to the farmstead. It was just as well. Gil always said stupid things, as he did following Gwen's death, things like "She's at peace now, Carl." Like she wasn't before.

Perhaps her death was for the better, Carl Steinar thought. Maybe she wouldn't have been happy spending all those years in the country. These days, after all, one could hardly blame a farmer for leaving that life of constant uncertainty: guessing when to plant, watching the sky for storm clouds during dry spells, cursing the gray skies during wet stretches, hoping hungry worms did not devour the seeds, praying insects and disease remained at bay, guessing when to reap. Carl gazed at his dim reflection in the windshield; he appeared drugged, his eyes glazed and body sluggish. Over on Visne Road stood a cottonwood, stuck right in the middle of where the blacktop should be. It would be so easy, he thought, so understandable, to have missed that unnatural curve around it. He could feel his lungs growing with each gust of wind as nearing the turn onto the road but with each quickly advancing mile only found his shoulders dropping. The asphalt passed below him like the tracks of a roaring, out of control train. He fully understood the tale of that old bull who starved despite having two equally good hay bales in front of him – it simply couldn't decide which one to eat.

No, he told himself, the tree would not work. However it is done, there must be a witness to ensure the insurance comes, and Lyle could not be the one. Perhaps then botching in the bathroom was for the better, he decided, and a calmness like the soft silence following a snow covered his disheveled thoughts.

*****

Abbie's face brightened. Her father had agreed to take a walk with her, down to the park with its sweeping field of verdant grass. All summer, her constant pestering of him largely had gone nowhere – even had worked negatively as he grew comfortable with saying "no" each time she asked – but on that one day during her 13th year, he must had heard the slight whimper of anguish that escaped her lips when she cast him the most melancholy of faces. He leaned forward slightly, his hand pressing against the hardwood desktop, and glancing outside at the glorious sun that warmed the soft earth, said he would go. As he rose, the pungent salve that Mary Dawn spread each sunrise across his aching joints wormed across the room. Outside, though, it disappeared into the wide blue sky as their lungs filled with fresh air.

Slowly but certainly they sauntered upon the sidewalk, the light across the concrete brilliant, the summer shrubs bordering their path a lush green. Abbie longed for the days such as those when he showed her the aurora borealis, it glimmering like an iris in the night sky. Perhaps those times had returned, Abbie thought as meadowlarks sang their flute-like songs all about them. She skipped ahead of him then stopped to sniff a goldenrod, the graceful plumes sweet like anise, and inhaled it deeply until he caught up. When with him before the accident, she had always felt assured. She walked alongside with her chin slightly raised, a plucky heroine who had just vanquished a rogue monster, did not notice how he pulled his body in with each step.

Then the park appeared. It spread out before them like a river as it spills into an emerald sea, the wind a trumpet heralding her returned youth. Children twittered and shrieked as chasing one another about the playground. Abbie's face shined as if an infant's, pink and warm. She gripped her father's hand, could almost breathe in the lavender fragrance of days past. The taste of ice cream clung to the roof of her memories, and her lips flared wide.

That was when she first saw it out of the corner of her eye, a puff gliding upon the wind's freed rhythms, jumping and bouncing, just slightly out of reach. Her pupils flew to the white dandelion head as it scurried before them. She swiped at it, but the current of her movements only propelled it farther away. Suddenly she leaped after the puff, like a dog chasing a butterfly; a gust kept it beyond the edges of her fingertips, though. As the dandelion head continued flitting in the wind, her giggles filled the park like the sweet tinkle of chimes, and she ran after it, drawing in the clean prairie air with the sun hot upon her skin. Then the wind slowed. Seeing the opportunity, she flung herself beneath the currents and twirling high into the air with a cupped palm, caught the puff as if it were a softball knocked directly into a mitt. She rolled to the ground, the thick, luxurious grass staining her knees then elbows, laughed triumphantly. Her hand tightened about the dandelion head, and she turned to glimpse her rapidly approaching father.

"Daddy, look what I caught!" she said as extending her closed hand to him. His face glared red.

She let go a slight gasp, and he grasped her arm, the fingers pressing so hard they left bruises.

"What is wrong with you?" he spat between his teeth. "Don't you know how to act your age?" He wrenched Abbie to her feet and pulled her back toward the sidewalk, away from the park.

Her cheeks instantly paled, and she could not shake loose as his legs marched unevenly across the field. Her head swirled back as the puff spilled from the unclasped hand; with two fingers she tried to snatch it back, but his momentum tugged her out of reach. Suddenly her eyes moistened, like leaves dappled with dew.

*****

Though bouncing in the truck, the three Steinars were careful to not graze one another. It was an unspoken rule, that flesh should not touch flesh, and the teenage Peter sometimes wondered from where it came. Enough dust, grease and sweat lined their skin that an accidental brushing against another ensured a gritty smear, but the tenet extended to their clothing as well, even if it were fresh from the dryer.

When the pickup humbled to a stop, Lyle flung the door open, and the dry grass crackled as his boots crushed them. A hot wind blasted across the prairie. Peter pulled the red tool-box from the truck bed, his gloved hands protecting him from the sun-heated metal. His mouth tasted coppery. None of them had drank water for nearly an hour. Carl Steinar then led his adolescent sons toward a pipe linked to the web of irrigation bars and crossbeams spreading across the red field. He held out a hand, and Lyle passed him a hand pliers, as if a nurse responding instinctively to a surgeon. Wind ruffled the hairs upon their necks. Carl twisted the tool about a clamp linking two metal rods, and a slight grunt escaped his mouth as he tugged. Once the pipes came apart, water and a splay of mud trickled onto his hands. "This filter'll need replacing," he said, and then he dropped the pieces onto the dry soil beneath him and headed down the line for the next connection. His acrid scent spewed into the boys' collective space as he passed them. Peter kneeled, and Lyle followed.

With a wrench, Peter plied the filter stuck at one of the openings. The seventeen-year-old would rather that his fingers press into the loamy earth, for he loved how one could burrow into it, grasp it, feel its softness, its life; his hand felt like a stream joining a greater river. He would scoop a handful into his palm, let it sift through until each granule drifted with the wind just as the mist before him passed like a trailing garment. He longed for Laura Jean in this way too, loved the face of that beautiful girl to whom the breeze-blown sand never stuck. Yes, she took the bleakness out of the landscape, he thought. From a corner of the toolbox, he pulled a clean filter, unwrapped its package. He let one hand scoop into the earth until only a thin patch of topsoil separated his fingertips from the clay beneath.

Several yards ahead, Carl glanced at his thirteen-year-old son. "Go ahead and take apart the pipes and check the filter. You saw how I did it back there? Do it the same way."

Lyle crouched before the connection. For a moment, he gazed into the amorphous horizon, his face like a hardened crust of earth, concealing the water and the life deep beneath it. The harsh materiality of their existence angered him, and he saw nothing spiritual in a land once inhabited by prairie rattlers. Wind spooled dust off the flat tract. Still, he preferred the plain's openness to the farmhouse's closed walls. His mouth formed into a frown as he worked the pipes apart.

Carl did not kneel, merely stood above his son, planting his legs into the nigrous soil as if they were stakes. When a child, his father allowed him to explore the homestead, and it built in him a love of the land. His eyes followed the sun-burned field as it gently rolled toward the creek. He remembered walking to it long ago, long before ever meeting Gwen. He would skirt the dusty field, its brown clumps bright in the hazy sunlight, feel the rays' warmth rising upon his neck.

Lyle held the two pipes in his hands as red silt spread over them.

"Just leave it there for Peter to change the filter," Carl said. "I'll show you how to do that on the next one."

The two marched toward a fallow section, it green with weed and grass, and sometimes they'd catch a sweet whiff of prairie bluebonnets. Carl resisted the scent, for it only caused his head to grow slumberous and his feet to drift off the path so his shoes sunk: into the dirt, begriming them. He kept his eyes forward, maintained a straight course. In the distance, a neighbor's tractors hummed and a pickup truck occasionally slashed down the road. With each step, however, those sounds, signs of the real world, diminished. Swirls of soil from the disked field always reminded him of where and who he was.

Eventually Peter caught up with them. The three walked along the irrigation pipe as the sun steadily rose, the wind coating each one with dust, all of them glad to have escaped the womb of the house. Carl avoided heading too close to the creek as they crossed the fields, barren like a bough without leaves, and the wind whispered upon the earth like a long scythe. Then, at a pasture corners, Carl stopped as if to reflect, but he did neither that nor contemplate while the weed stems fluttered across his ankles and the sun, swollen and white, hung over them. He stared at the unfinished horizon then, as if it were laughing at and mocking him, he bowed his head.

Bewildered, Peter gazed his father. Though aware of him, Carl paid his eldest son no attention, only thought of the field's rawness, of how in late August it lay as if the beginning of life, of how it smelled like his sons when they were born. Yet, the Steinars were a family held together – not destroyed – by this thin sheen of land that shriveled beneath the heat. For many years, nothing but that staked him to these prairie furrows, bounded by asphalt and barbed wire; farming wasn't anything but rising expenses and declining prices, certainly no worthy business venture. He knew work was his home, and so long as that remained true, there could be no escape from his suffering.

Then he found himself thinking of the utilitarian yet again, of whether or not to store wheat in the bins, anticipating that prices would jump during the months ahead. The wind skittered across the low grass before him, continuing past him on its unfinished journey, it resistant to linearity, to closure. As the boys moved toward the next irrigation line, Carl Steinar merely stood in place, shrouded in quiet desperation.

Chapter 15

Wind whooshed across the table of red loam with the heat of a shell blast. Peter gazed upon the wheat seed thermometer nailed to the machinery shed, saw that the arrow pointed at ninety-four degrees. After years of working outdoors, he'd learned to tell the time of day by the temperature and where the sun stood in the sky. He glanced up, estimated three o'clock. As the swelter pressed against and expanded the shed's metal sheets, its walls popped slightly, and inside dust rose across crescent shafts of light breaking through where rivets had loosened on the overlap. His father, stinking of motor oil, sauntered past.

"We done for the afternoon, Father?" Lyle called from a pile of gunnysacks.

Carl paused, wiped his cheeks with a dirty handkerchief pulled from his back pocket. He nodded. "Tomorrow will be a long day."

Peter's brow furrowed. Though September had arrived, they still were a week from planting.

"What's tomorrow?"

"You'll find out in the morning," Carl said.

His eldest son sneered. "Why not just tell me now?"

"We're going to replace the auger in the combine header."

Peter's arms flew into the air. "Put on an auger? Whose bonehead idea was that? It'd be easier to just buy a new header."

Carl shot him a dirty look. "I'm getting mighty tired of you arguing with me all of the time."

"How in the hell are we going to put it on? We'll have to tear off the header's sides and reconnect every piece. "

"We've got all year to do it. Cornelius will weld it for nothing."

Lyle stepped between them "We've already got the piece. Picked it up yesterday at the salvage yard."

"Christ," Peter said, shaking his head.

His brother ignored him, headed for their father's pick-up truck. The old man followed, and Peter, figuring he better see what new problem awaited him, did so did as well.

The metal cylinder sat angled upon the truck's dusty bed. Sunlight glistened off the auger's blades curling halfway around the bar.

"If we take one side of the header off, we should be able to slide it right in place," Lyle said as leaning against the pickup's side. "It's just a matter of tightening–"

"Are you crazy?" Peter said. "Do you know how long it will take?"

Carl spoke up. "What's the matter, boy? Afraid of a little hard work?"

Peter crossed his arms. At times, his father behaved so eccentrically, that Peter thought him mad; now his brother had turned that way as well.

"Well, we can't very well take it back," Carl said.

Peter swirled toward his father, hands clenched, found his anger bursting like a monstrous bird that had outgrown its tiny cage. "We can, and you will. Maybe there'll be a loss on it, but if you want to fix the auger, either send it to the implement dealer who has the right tools or buy a whole new header."

As on the porch, Carl Steinar did not move nor did a particle twitch on his leathery skin, it 20 years beyond its age. Peter continued staring into the old man's parched eyes; there was no thanks for even saving his life back in the field, he thought, and his fists tightened. The old man drew back. Peter canted toward him, never let the firebrand of his young pupils off him. Confronting his father buoyed him, as if he were suddenly freed and let loose upon the wind. Yes, he thought, here I am, standing up to the king bull himself. His frame angled away from the old man. That's a metaphor, he told himself, and half-surprised he smiled at using knowledge Abbie had imparted to him.

Then, as if inviting Peter to run up from behind and tackle him for such impudence, Carl simply walked away from the argument and the truck, heading for the farmhouse as his boot heels crunched against the driveway gravel. Legs stiff, the old man's back remained hunched over in defeat. Peter's hands uncoiled; he wanted to say something but could not think of what his words should be. As a child, sometimes he couldn't stand to have his father out of sight for more than a few minutes. The boy panicked when he was late, and sometimes at night even crept into his bedroom and touched his hand, just to make sure he was still breathing. Now he simply wished for his father to disappear but not in this way. The screen door banged shut as his father entered the still, dark house.

Lyle stepped in front of Peter, blocking his view. "What in the hell was that all about?"

For a moment, Peter's mouth fell; his brother had been the quiet one for so long, but now here he was again, speaking his mind. "You heard it all. How could you be so stupid as to go along with such a cockamamie plan?"

"If you don't like it, you ought to leave."

Peter's lips curled. "You're a real bear." He headed toward the house.

"Maybe the problem is you're spending too much time with that reporter."

"Her name's 'Abbie,'" Peter said over his shoulder.

"Maybe you're spending so much time with that 'Abbie' that you're not paying any attention to father."

Peter stopped, but he did not turn around. "You mean 'serving' father?"

"I mean you'd know what he's going through."

Peter spun. He sensed geniuses in Lyle's voice, and this time his brother's grin was neither lopsided condescending. "Just what are you talking about?"

"You'd see that going out with this Abbie bothers him."

"What's it to him?"

Lyle hmmphed. "Oh, why explain it? Of all people, you wouldn't give a damn." Peter grabbed his brother's arm. "Don't you ever say that again, got it?"

Lyle remained silent then nodded. He stared down at the fingers upon his biceps, and Peter let go. Cautiously, the youngest Steinar canted toward the farmhouse. As Peter turned to watch him, he saw his father staring at them from behind the kitchen's Cape Cods.

*****

All Lyle could see was his pursuing father, a wolf licking blood from its lips. The teenage boy pressed a hand to his throbbing temples, tried to quell the image, prayed for the headache to ease. Dusty glanced at him, her eyes compassionate. She peeled the fingers away from his brow, pressed her hand against it. Then two powder blue caplets fell against his open palm, as if dimes shook from a mother's coin purse into a waiting child's hands. Lyle tossed both into his mouth, washed them down with a swig of beer. Pursing her lips, she suppressed a smirk. His head felt increasingly light, like a clearing sky as the moments passed. The bonfire wavered before him, and in its aurora, his girlfriend's face shined bone white. At least I no longer have to lie about being alone, he thought.

The liquor always had blurred Lyle's mind. The next image he remembered with any clarity was of the pickup screaming through the night air, his thin blood hot and churning, he driving crazed and mad as if by bolting across those fields they could be conquered. Should this speed be kept up, he believed, all the world and all of their pasts would whoosh by. Sitting right beneath the rear mirror, Dusty smiled at him, and his lungs tingled in exhilaration. Lyle imagined how he must look to her, to all of them standing about the bonfire and upon the field's edge. He suddenly felt like a mountain as dawn radiates from behind it. Affectionately, they called him Sleepy. Though not fat, he generally lumbered about, and often his friends found him snoozing off a good drunk before the party had ended. To Lyle, however, such sleep was resistance. Dreams did not haunt his nights as they did Peter's. After a half-hour or so of napping, Lyle's friends poked him good-naturedly with sticks, and he'd rise, wet from the damp grass. Dusty would stand at his side, her hair leaden in the bonfire's dim light. Despite the allure, her face remained as pale and withdrawn as Boticelli's Venus.

Dusty hated to wake him, found a sweet innocence in his closed eyes, so still and silent. She admired the handsome jags of his body as he glanced up. "Come on, it's race time," said Lascar Kine, his beckoning gestures like a matador's cape. Knees stiff, Lyle would swipe at the moist blades stuck to his clothes then grab Dusty's hand. Together they'd scramble for the truck. She could smell the clean scent of sweetgrass carried by the winds as he revved the truck's motor and they thrust forward into the night, drowning the crickets' calls for mates. Her lambent green eyes took in his strong limbs as their edges caught the moon glow.

Then a bump would jar them into the next moment as their bodies lurched and her hair flung about. She always came up laughing, like a thrillseeker who'd almost drowned, vainglory with the narrow victory. His headlamps blaring, the field still appeared more dark than light, and then they'd jump the shallow ditch onto the hardpan, tires biting into the dirt shoulder. Vengeance flared in his eyes as their speed rose, faster than the breeze itself, almost to tornadic proportions, and she'd whoop and holler, screaming whenever he swerved to avoid potholes.

Lascar's truck sped evenly with them, and the instant after the drivers glanced at one another, Lyle kicked into fourth gear then shifted back up to fifth and burst ahead, moving so fast that all they could hear was the shouting wind. The asphalt, cracked by Nebraska's steady sun, shone like lightning strikes before the headlights as the wind blew in riptides over them. Then he saw it, the dim red glint of a reflector, the finish line. Passing it, he slowed, spun onto the ungraded road and rounded back to the bonfire.

Like a blue ghost, they drifted through the open fields, the soothing scent of milk thistle calming them. Grass crackled beneath their tires, and the stars seemed to duck away. They slowed even further, came to a full stop.

Lascar ran up to them. "Man, I almost had you!" he said, still ecstatic.

"Yeah," Lyle said, his heartbeat dropping rapidly. He gazed at the oily beyond.

So it was each weekend, the nights soon as indistinguishable as cans stacked on a supermarket shelf, until the day the new kid arrived in town. His name was Brendan. Tall and well formed, he possessed glistening blue eyes. His smile resembled a sparking power line, and his perspiration wafted sweetly, like salt upon an ocean breeze. Throughout the party, the Felton girls kept their gazes fixed upon him except when they glanced at one another, their eyes carbonated and gushed. Lyle once even caught Dusty gawking at him.

At that, the youngest of the Steinars downed a swig of beer and waddled off into the darkness.

All of their fawning bored him. Behind a tree on the tar side of the wooded enclave, he laid himself down, and clasping hands behind his head, closed his eyes. He drifted into sleep, his consciousness like an aster petal fluttering from the stem. Soft light greeted him. As his eyes opened upon this new world, the lead-colored road they drove upon grew increasingly luminescent. He was a boy again, small enough to feel threatened by the vacant stretches of prairie. Ahead loomed an intersection, and his father slowed. The crossroads appeared stained; Lyle could not tell for sure as he barely saw over the dashboard. He felt the truck angling away from it, however, and watched his father gradually turning the steering wheel as if it were the helm of a great ship. Yet, no matter which direction the truck went upon the plain, the intersection remained within sight, always a slight crest just upon the horizon. Lyle tugged at his older brother's sleeve. "Why don't we ever go that way?" he said.

Peter looked down upon him, his mouth a flat line. "That's where our mother died."

Cold prickled the back of Lyle's neck. Death sounded painful, like the moment when one's eyes spring open and the body shudders awake. He felt a sharp pain in his ribs, jumped.

Lascar tossed down his stick. "Brendan says he wants to race you."

Black smudged Lyle's sight as he rubbed his eyes. A dozen teens stared haughtily at him as the sky's heat rippled across a crescent moon. The wind kept striking him, it insinuating like the slap of another's long stare.

"Who?" Lyle said.

"Brendan," they said, virtually in unison.

He scowled. "I don't want to race him. "

For a moment, the clearing fell quiet as an empty room, and then he heard a voice, deep and ruddy. "Why, you chicken?"

Lyle glanced up, saw the new kid's eyes glowing with malice. He rose, stood toe-to-toe with him. "You couldn't beat me anyways."

"So let me make an ass out of myself."

Lyle's brow arched slightly as he stared at the new kid. They eyed one another coolly, like two lions that had come to drink at the same waterhole. The youngest Steinar decided to let silence end the confrontation.

Yet the new boy would not relent. "Unless you really don't think you can beat me."

Lyle leaned toward him. "It starts when both our trucks hit the hardpan. Finish line is Williwaw Road. There's no bumping." The new kid nodded, and the two suddenly were off to their trucks. Lyle liked this new kid, this Brendan. In a way, the new kid reminded him of Lascar, a guy who never backed down. Brendan would have to be put in his place.

Cheers rose like a trumpet blow for Lyle, though some of the girls, he thought, remained oddly quiet. Then one of them he'd never seen before shouted his name, waved a clenched fist of support in the air. He shot a glance toward her, only caught a glimpse of two barrettes keeping bangs out of two eyes before the darkness of the crowd swallowed her. With a wrist, he wiped the sweat from his brow. Lyle passed the new boy's truck, guessed in the dim moonlight that it was fire engine red with stripes, they maybe silver, then as stepping into his own pickup, heard the new kid rev the motor, watched him line the truck head on with his own. A blue haze puffed out of Brendan's exhaust, and Lyle snorted then rubbed his eyes. Ashes from the bonfire flitted through the open window.

Dusty handed Lyle a bottle to help wake him, to ease his own nervousness, which she was certain that he like herself possessed though it did not show. As Lyle brought it to his lips, a scent strong as vinegar filled his mouth, quenching the thirst no better than the blood of a cut finger he'd once sucked into his mouth when a child. The liquor slid fast down his throat and even faster to his head; still, despite the soft trill unfurling in his thoughts, both palms grew clammy. He glanced at his hands then passed the bottle back to Dusty. Her eyes shined coppery green in the headlights' glare. "We'll see who's trailing at midway!" she shouted out the window at Brendan.

Lyle and Dusty pulled onto Visne Road, the asphalt faintly gray, then as he stepped on the accelerator their hair blew back like wheat beneath a gale. A red glow burst from the dashboard gauges as dust and exhaust whirled behind them, and with the booze fueling Lyle's courage, they took the lead. They hit a bump, and their heads grazed the cab roof. Lyle's temples throbbed with heat as the prairie's flat lines warped all around them. He didn't know much about the new boy, just that Brendan had shown up at school on Monday, and that all the girls instantly liked him. The kid was in most of his classes; Felton was small enough for that. Never through the rapaciously hot week had Lyle done or said anything to him. He wondered if that was why the new kid had made the challenge, because he'd been ignored. Big dogs don't pay the small pups any heed, was that what Brendan thought? So, not pissing on his tree is what got me in this trouble?

Suddenly, the nose of Brendan's pickup edged ahead of Lyle. They remained next to one another, each giving a sliver of truck length here and there as both wills strained the motors. Then shards of light from Lyle's headlamps reflected off Brendan's side mirror. Lyle grinned expectantly, and he slipped into fourth. As Brendan's truck bolted ahead, churning like a wild, thronging train ahead of a trackside mule, Dusty gasped. Lyle kicked her into fifth, and pressing his foot hard as he could against the accelerator, shot forward like straw from a twister. The road undulated beneath him as if waves in a storm, and his roaring truck pitched and swayed. Wind slapped his face through the open window as he retook the lead, leaving Brendan to breathe his fumes. Now this was life, Lyle thought, the constant struggle to just stay ahead, a string of moments filled with grittiness.

Ahead, the road curved around a solitary cottonwood, but Lyle did not let off his accelerator, knew from dozens of races that his truck could handle the twist at even faster speeds. As Lyle veered, he lost sight of the new kid, then there he was, no longer on the road but in the field, cutting a straight line to the other side of the curve and nosing ahead of them, Lyle bellowed in laughter; this new kid, he was nervy, jangly. With a sudden bump as pavement turned to dirt, Lyle followed him off the road, the wet grass that wrapped around their axles crinkling like clothes whirling in a dryer. If he could catch up with the new kid, Lyle thought, perhaps corral him off so he had no choice other than brake or slam into the tree, he'd learn his lesson. Lyle's and Dusty's bodies lunged up and forward, bounced down and back as the wheels spanned the furrows beneath them, but the new kid would not yield. Lyle slammed a fist against the dashboard. Then, at the last moment before passing the tree, Brendan braked. A red glow through the cottonwood branches shined against Lyle's windshield like blood across fractured glass. His knuckles locked in place upon the steering wheel, and he felt as if something had caught him by the throat. A chill ran through him. He had three options: hit the new kid's truck, go left and collide with the cottonwood, or turn right, spin out and surrender the race. His thoughts tumbled as if grain shook from a truck bed. He cranked the steering wheel hard right, the stars spinning in the sky before him like numbers on a radio dial.

Brendan crossed Williwaw Road.

Lyle watched Brendan's mud-caked pickup pass as they rounded back to the clearing. Though Lyle did not scream, his voice sounded oddly hoarse. He felt as if he were a stone dropped into an ocean, sinking and sinking until hitting bottom, neither shifting nor floating back up to reach the quiet harbor from which it was flung. Lyle pulled back onto the road, followed Brendan to the teens.

As Lyle and Dusty walked across the scabby ground to the bonfire, each flame shooting upward like the splash of a floodwater, he gazed only at the ground. The wind plucked his bangs with each step. Dusty grabbed his arm, stopped him. "What happened back there?" she said.

The wind quieted, like the moments before a violent storm. He remained silent, was merely a rock in a dry ravine.

She stared into his face then let go, walked several feet

ahead of him. The hairs upon his arm rose as he stepped through the cold grass. They passed amid the crowd like royalty, the teens parting before them in fear, their shadows cast over him.

Among the crowd stood Tina Strom, her hair hanging in two drab waves to beneath both cheeks.

She waited mutely, lips even, and when he glanced her way, she looked at the ground. His eyes lingered when he noticed her reaction, and for an instant he found himself examining every detail about her; the rounded, kittenish nose of a younger girl, the naturalness of her scent, like clear water, the freshness of her lips, as if they were ripe strawberries. Within two of his steps she was gone, lost amid the throng of teenagers as Dusty pulled at his arm and the sharp grass blades of the untrodden field sliced against the dangling fingers of his free hand. He followed.

*****

How many promises to my wife have I broken, Carl Steinar wondered as he inspected Peter's new gate leading to the pasture. He'd never committed any infidelity, had never lied to her, indeed had found their short time as a couple a period of great hope and yearning, all stitched together by vows to never lie nor deceive one another, to forever protect, to forgive always and completely. Their years were built on the immaterial substance of dreams, dreams that with her death were a ruptured balloon.

He lightly shook the new pasture gate. Despite the use of old boards, it held. Carl knew he should have expected as much for his eldest son's handiwork unswervingly was high. Indeed, the boy had proven his self-sufficiency many times over, and if either of his sons' threats to leave the farm were to be taken seriously, it certainly was Peter's. Carl gazed at the thin apple tree stump still standing at the yard's edge.

Peter always had been the more aggressive one, he thought, a Steinar through-and-through. The boy would have no trouble making it on his own, especially with all of the insurance money from his mother's death stashed away. Still, his stomach churned at the notion of breaching his unspoken promise to the boy. Yet, if loyalty equaled dedication, was not the reverse true, Carl asked himself. He sauntered toward the stump, tried to decide what he must do next.

His promises to Gwen had begun the spring he gave the apple tree's first blossom to her. The old trunk was near death, and during dry years half the branches wouldn't even bud. It was a lush May, however, when his fingers plucked a blossoming twig. The smooth stick hung light between his fingers, and like a metalsmith judging his work, he playfully examined the flowers, the color of a tender blush, then arm outstretched he handed them to her. Songbirds whistled a soft trill. He did not try to suppress his grin, and for the first time in his adolescence did not feel embarrassed at such a show of affection. Her face pinkening, she cupped the bough and raised it to her face.

Then Gwen danced a half-pirouette as twirling the flowers in her hand and giggling. The laughter flew at him like a playful breeze, and he caught her as she swung around, pulled her into him. The blossoms grazed his skin, but he could not tell if it were the petals or her cheek that touched him. They gazed into one another's eyes as he caressed her neck, then they kissed, and his body fluttered like wheat tassels upon a light summer wind.

Shortly after she died, he chopped down the tree. The branches crackled like shattered glass as they struck the ground. Carl knew that if he made the decision he was certain would have to be executed, nearly every promise to her also would be broken. No, he told himself, I have to think of the Steinar name for it is all that's left. The name is itself the land that they worked, and to ensure the farm remained, he'd have to pass it on to the son who showed the most loyalty. If it comes to that, he said aloud, I never will break another promise to you will never again let you dissolve like a dream into the night.

*****

Abbie fancied herself a butterfly as she lay in bed remembering the day on the farm with Peter.

They had flitted about, letting the sun warm their backs, listening to the meadowlarks spiritedly chirping upon the unending plain. Holding hands, she found her body suddenly liquid and light. Like the wind, no stillness overcame them, for upon arriving at one place, to sniff a butter-and-eggs wildflower or to pluck then roll a juicy red currant upon the tongue, they realized there were a dozen other delights to experience, and then off they ran. What is it about me that makes him feel like a little boy again, she wondered in the darkness as drawing in the rarified prairie air, blown west from the fields that they had walked. Perhaps Peter had even breathed some of what I am pulling into my lungs right now, she thought, and with it closed both eyes and spread her wings to the realm of dreams.

Chapter 16

Eyes aglow, Abbie believed she'd returned to port after a long, arduous journey. As she sat next to Peter on the dense cover of buffalo grass, the creek, gilded in the afternoon light, flowed gentle and slow. The wind reverberated like a sigh, and she leaned her head against Peter's shoulder, then with every roll of breath drew in his scent; it natural as spring water, and listened to the persistent throb of his heart.

Despite that her hair smelled as if sweet hay drying in the sunlight, Peter's stomach churned, like he were straddling an unsteady rope bridge over a gorge. "You have to let it go," he told himself, but that did little good.

Then her spruce-hued eyes gazed at the sun, golden in the blue sky. "I could spend forever in a place like this," she said.

A lightheadedness almost overcame him as he huddled closer and squeezed her arm. "Well, you'd never be bored – our lives out here are so full of intrigue and daring?" he said, grinning.

She laughed. "What's wrong with wanting to stay in one place for a long time? If that's the life you chose, so be it."

He gazed upon Abbie for a moment, wished it were July so the dormant field above them would be a dusty mauve from all the blooming cornflowers. That he could impress her with. It's one thing I like about her, Peter thought, that she can be enthused. All through childhood there had been no way of impressing his father. The old man had constantly reassured him and his brother that their mother loved them and knew they loved her, but beyond that there lay nothing but stoicism; he'd refuse to show any emotion even if a crop shriveled in front of him.

Abbie glanced up at Peter's sandstone face. He'd grown quiet again, had that look as if he were plotting his own demise. She pressed her head against his dry chest; perhaps it will pass, she hoped.

Peter's thoughts swirled. He knew that this time Lyle was right – he hadn't been around his father lately. Had his eyes always appeared glazed, Peter wondered. Had that voice always been so high-pitched, and I've just never noticed before? No, the old man seemed more irritable than usual, and his face looked excessively worn, as it a barn side stained by years of wind. Peter recalled when his father's brow was not so creased, to when they stood upon the edge of a field and he and Lyle were lectured about how mankind once believed the world was flat but Columbus proved them wrong, that it was round; "Boys, the land isn't flat though it looks it," he said, as if imparting some great truth. The boys merely looked at one another and shrugged.

Abbie pulled her cheek away from Peter's body; though he remained utterly still, she could hear his heart pounding with great ferocity. This time, she would not indulge his self-destructive moods. "Something's wrong," she said, looking up at him. "Would you like to talk?"

He gazed down at her. "A good farmer asks no favors," he said. "That's what my father always told me. 'It's the right order of things,' according to his way of thinking."

"You're angry with him?"

"You've met him. What do you think?"

An eyebrow rose as she mulled how to respond. It was a rhetorical question, she knew, but if they were to continue talking, if he was to open up, she would have to answer. "He has an amazing lack of braggadocio," she said.

"Meaning?"

"He's not arrogant."

Peter laughed. "He's the undisputed leader, the dominant power, on this land."

"Do you blame him for something?"

He stared at the creek ebbing before him. It seemed so petty, but wishing his old man just once would have told him "I know her death hurts a lot" or had mentioned the things she said about him, nullified all the world around him. Yet, Peter knew that a wish had less substance than the wind through his hair, and so he shook his head. "My father is to blame for so much."

His voice rang low and earnest, and Abbie could see how the feeling in his eyes matched his words as he spoke. Perhaps he'd finally come to trust her.

Then she cast a brief look at him, her smile a streamer across the face, and his heart leaped. He imagined himself a little kid, twirling around in the fields, dizzying himself merely to incite a feeling of pleasure. Then the same woozyness as when he wondered what being with his mother was like overcame him. He gazed at the creek as it cantered on, a smoothed voice, and Peter realized he knew so little about Abbie. Did she have brothers or sisters? Who were her college friends? What books had she read? His knowledge of her was incomplete, much like his memories. He drew in the sultry breath of the Nebraska plain – its sweet clusters of phlox, the musty black dirt, those rare but soothing waters –

and wondered for a moment if it was really her and not the farmland's beauty he sensed.

He tried not to let his voice sound chipped. "So, 'A good farmer asks no favors,' 'It's the right order of things' – what do those little downhome sayings mean?"

She shrugged. "They must be lessons that he lives by, maybe that he hopes you'll take to heart." Peter shook his head in disgust. "Do you remember that night of the rainstorm – our first time together – and you said something about wind and stones; it was something your father told you?"

Abbie recited it with exactness. "'Wine will wear down stones as well as can water, but wine makes life richer.' My dad said it to my mother before the accident. Don't ask me why I remember that of all things. I just do."

"What does it mean?"

"Well...it's hard to explain. What do you think it means?"

"I don't know. That's why I'm asking."

Her eyes appeared distant. "Consider the blandness of water's taste. That's like life. Well, if you want to live, if you want to be more than a rock, the best way to do so is not by letting the blandness of life dissolve you but by enjoying its richness, its beauty. I suppose that's what it means. Does that make sense?"

"A little." He stared off at the creek, as if disquietly unaware of all else.

"Oh Peter, what's wrong? Won't you tell me?"

For a second, as if a finger stopping just short of a hot stove, he did not move. "It's my father. He's acting strangely. There are some things my brother has said that make me wonder it there's something to my suspicion, but he lies a lot, or at least he did as a little kid."

"What are you suspicious of?"

"That's just it – I don't know. That there's something going on, something that I don't see.

Maybe I'm wrong – I haven't been spending much time around my father."

"Maybe you just need to talk with him. "

"He listens about as well as a deaf dog. Do you know what it's like to talk to a such a man all your life?"

Abbie sighed. She understood loneliness, of how it was like stepping into the cold darkness on a winter night. Parents and children ought to be able to get along, she thought. Then her mind warmed; maybe she could prove so – perhaps she yet could bring these two errant boats safely to harbor. His father now, she told herself, then his brother. Her big eyes danced over him as she began plotting.

Peter caressed her arm, it creamy like she'd bathed in buttermilk. He didn't want to taint her richness with his problems. Standing, he pulled her up, and without saying anything, she followed though befuddlement filled her eyes. Holding hands, they hurriedly ascended the embankment and headed east onto the field's edge. She squeezed his elbow so he'd stop and she might catch her breath. He glanced back at her, his pupils emotionless. As his head turned forward during their pause, they gazed off at the dust spiraling distantly in a long windrow; the distraction gave reason enough for them to remain silent, for their thoughts to gather. The sun beat mercilessly against their white skin. Even at this moment of impasse, as Abbie crossed her arms tight over her chest, as Peter's eyes hung stonily upon his face, they drew one another's scents into their bodies, let their minds linger upon the exhilaration they offered: for he, her sweet liquidity; for her, his boyish musk. They were man and woman primeval, cast onto a field of thorns and thistles, unable to speak of the paradise they'd lost. The dust cloud rolled closer, and they tasted the bitter earth.

*****

Peter did well enough in high school, got B's, never cared to do better. There was little compulsion to do so for he had no trouble making friends, and their company always was preferable to that of a textbook. Growing up, he'd learned from Aunt Amita a sense of affability and from Uncle Joe a hefty barrage of vulgarities that when used endeared him to his adolescent buddies. He'd also inherited his parents' good looks. Many a time, the older teachers would say in the faculty lounge, "That hoy is a spitting image of his dad," and they were accurate. He possessed peaceful, chestnut eyes that could quiet any inner turmoil, a firm though hushed voice, and the kind of slender yet naturally muscular frame that girls desired to lean into, just as his father owned during his own youth. The boy's unblemished face sparkled like a calm sea, and his gaze, if one could hold it long enough, begged for nurturance.

Despite his relative popularity, an incompleteness drained him until his soul became a dried river, and with each passing year, the grumbling of rebellion grew louder and rose in frequency, like the earth at a fault line. Sometimes he'd lose his appetite for days on end. He refused to visit other children and their parents, never latched upon any classmate's mother. He preferred only the one of his dreams, for her gravity he could to a degree control, and that was a necessity as fluidity haunted him across time's confused ramblings. There were so many shadowed memories, like the one when he told Lyle of where their mother died, as if the two of them were mere tourists upon the prairie road, observing the spot of some event buried in a distant past. Yet, despite Carl Steinar's efforts, time was hardly linear in their lives; it reared itself all too often in the present, and though dissipating it only threatened to return at some unforeseeable moment in the future. Time for Peter seemed more like braids of wind.

Perhaps for that reason alone during high school he clung to Laura Jean, his only girl friend of those days. In the same graduating class as Peter, she always appeared young and dewy, enjoying a face not fully formed. Though tall, she was curvy yet not voluptuous like a full-grown woman. Peter particularly loved the full sway of her hips and her voice, both soothing like a glass of cold lemonade on a hot day, and her charming habit of chewing on the edge of her pinkie. He got to call her Jeannie, a nickname that she would not allow anyone else to use. By all accounts, Laura Jean was perfect for Peter. She never defined him, didn't try to change him. Perhaps that ironically was what bothered him the most about her. Then, one night while half-moonstruck, she said he smelled like patchouli, and with each passing month he found her vocabulary stretching far beyond his own. Still, he liked too many things about her – her long, svelte legs, and her lips, sweet as cotton candy, a rose-colored sugar that melted during a kiss – to say anything. So, he took shelter in her presence. Holding her was like cupping a small bird in his hands, warm and sensuous, but requiring a firmness, a slight squeeze to prevent it from flying off.

So they were an item, and many boys at Felton High were privately jealous of Peter for it, especially when she stunned them at the prom in her formal dress with the small breasts reared in the hip-tight, ruby and taffeta dress, a young woman sweet to the bite but not too rich for their country boy palettes. At the graduation bonfire, as the flames crackled and arced like flashing razors, always shifting in the way it tilled the black space above them, Peter realized he was no more important to her than a letter's rip-ped-open envelope. The kids around them sang and clapped. Then, though doing so felt cold, he removed his arm from her waist, and the bonfire's sparks scattered into the air like sunlit chaff.

As mid-July approached, the hottest days of the year and the most difficult decisions of Peter's life reared. He spent the week before Southwest Community College's reg-istration driving harvested wheat from the fields to the ele-vator; each day the sun seared his back red, and the grip of a shovel and steering wheel blistered his hands. At the end of the twelve-hour day, wheat dust filled his nostrils like black tar, and a Mason jar full of ice water sweetened his gullet like no kiss of Laura Jean's ever could. With each draining of the combine's grain into his truck, the drop deafening like a thousand shaking rain sticks, he left the physical beating of the labors numb his thoughts of her or his future off the farm. For though he held to the notion of escape through the last few lugubrious weeks, his fate was a foregone con-clusion when he had not bothered to apply at a four-year university during his senior year of high school.

He could not trouble his own house, not in fear of in-heritance nor even familial peace, but out of a great anxiety that if he left, only a horrid emptiness would remain behind and ahead of him, an emptiness so monolithic it would over-whelm and swallow him. So, even though all he really knew of Laura Jean was her physical appearance, he decided to convince her to stay.

She had grown too wild for him, though. That last sum-mer together she dyed her strawberry-colored hair a dark black, which he thought better matched her pale com-plexion, but it contrasted too sharply with her light eye-brows and pubic hair. She started listening to alternative music, and though something in the angst-ridden guitars appealed to him, too, he soon found himself bored by the droning vocals. Fortunately, her scent remained the same, like that of a rose sachet hidden in a drawer, but as autumn crawled nearer, she would not allow him to get close enough to press his warm mouth against her neck. Then, as August arrived, she refused to order anything homey or deep fried from menus, saying that she wanted to "branch out," to try new things. In all of Guthrie County, though, there was nothing new to try.

There was no formal break-up, only a mutual sense that they simply needed to end it all, to get the inevitable over with. Perhaps the moment never came because he'd thought of their relationship as brick-solid and perpetual. As the weeks passed, closing upon the day when she'd leave for college, he decided the best thing to do was feel nothing at all. So that last week of August he'd only wished his childhood friends luck as they left one by one for their futures. Peter and Laura Jean said their good-byes by telephone two days before she went. She did most of the talking as his own words stuck in the throat like fingers in a Chinese puzzle. She did not promise to write.

*****

Through Lyle's whole life, he'd never held anyone close to his heart, so the way his stomach sank each time he thought of his father's two attempted suicides disturbed him. The details too strongly reminded him of his senior year when Dusty had OD'd. He'd just finished the chores, including Peter's, who'd dragged their father to some livestock sale, yet even inside the farmhouse, August's hot thermals pressed against him. A stream of sweat split the thick coat of dust upon his cheek as he plopped into the living room chair and let the silent gray calm his body's overworked muscles and pores. Then the telephone rang, its bell careening across the room thrice before he lifted himself from the recliner.

It was Lascar Kine. "My God, Lyle, I've been trying all day to get hold of you. Have you heard?"

Lyle breathed slowly, his eyes halt shut. "Heard what?" "It's Dusty. She's in the hospital."

Lyle's mouth remained straight as a plumb line, his face expressionless. "The hospital? What for?"

The urgency in Lascar's voice rose. "Lyle, she OD'd, mixed those blue pills – a ton of them – with booze. A bender's worth of booze. Oh shit, Lyle, I'm sorry. I must sound damn cold-hearted. Look, can you get to North Platte? That's where she is."

Though eighteen and the owner of a new pickup truck, he didn't have any gas money. He hadn't asked for any either, though. "No," he said.

"I'll be right over."

Then Lascar hung up before Lyle could explain that he didn't want to go to the hospital. For a moment, he cradled the phone against his ear then decided he best wash up.

In the truck, Lascar told as many details as he knew to an even quieter than usual Lyle: how Dusty's parents found her passed out in the bathtub; how Marianne saw the ambulance there; of how she said Dusty's face looked like paste when the paramedics brought her out. Above them, the sun dilated in the afternoon sky. Fearing perhaps that silence might crack Lyle's manly demeanor, Lascar would not stop talking of it the whole hour-long drive to North Platte.

On the hospital's second floor, outside of Dusty's room, her father held his sobbing wife, their backs to the hallway as Lascar and Lyle approached. Hearing the clatter of their feet against the waxed floors, the father turned around, his face red with anger and teeth clenched hard. He pointed at the two boys. "You get out of here, now."

Lascar closed on him. "Is Dusty okay? Is that her room?"

"That's none of your business."

"Dusty is our friend. "

"She's not anymore."

Lascar scowled. "You can't tell Dusty who her friends are, and you can't stop us from seeing her. If you were Dusty, wouldn't you want to see your boyfriend?" He nudged Lyle forward.

"I don't give a damn who you little fucks think you are," the father said, his face shaking with rage. "But I know one thing for damn sure – she's never seeing the likes of you two again. You're the ones who drove her to this, confused her–"

"'Drove her to this'?" Lascar blurted. "What do you mean 'drove her to–" but before he could finish, two nurses stepped between him and Dusty's father.

"That's enough," the older of the two nurses said. "This is a hospital."

"We're here to see Dusty," Lascar started.

"And you're not going to," her father interjected.

The nurse raised her voice above both of them. "That's enough!" She turned to Lascar. "You boys probably should leave."

"But–" said Lascar.

"Dusty is sleeping," the nurse said. "She's all right, but you won't be able to see her for a while anyway."

Lascar's fists clenched. "Oh, Jesus Christ!" He spun on his heel, grabbed Lyle by the arm. "Let's get the hell out of here. "

Outside, the wind crashed over them in great waves. "I'm sorry," Lascar said as they crossed the parking lot. Lyle suppressed a yawn.

"Sorry about what?"

Lascar canted his head, as if to better examine Lyle. "That I couldn't get you in to see Dusty."

"It's okay," Lyle said, and then after a moment, as if to explain himself, "I'm a little tired anyway."

Lascar raised an eyebrow, stared at Lyle. He'd never seen him this way before.

Carl Steinar was sitting at the kitchen table when Lyle returned home shortly after dusk. The young boy's face appeared weathered, like the bowed and grayed boards of an old house. "Everything all right, Son?" Carl said.

Lyle nodded, took a seat across from him.

"Jackie Kine called, told me what happened and where you were."

"I'm sorry, Father. I should have left–"

Carl winced, waved him off. "There's no need to apologize. Just remember, though, in times like this you handle pain, you don't let it handle you."

After a long drought of silence, Carl rose and headed for bed, leaving Lyle alone in the near dark. Crickets chirped incessantly outside. As Lyle sat there, a flame rose inside him, drawing in and consuming all of his wind, yet he was neither angry at Dusty's father nor her for doing this to him but at his own father, for his supposed words of solace. Still, Lyle knew he was right.

Years later, he still believed his father was. Yet, here I sit, he told himself, no longer living by those words. If his old man wanted to kill himself, what business was it of his? If anything, there was much to gain materially from it – the farm, the insurance money – but just as his thoughts never carried a spiritual undertone, so he never valued anything material. His eyes turned dark, cavernous. He suddenly found his shield of apathy cracking. His father's words "You can't trace the wind" finally began to make sense.

*****

Despite the exceptional heat, most shivered at the Allen foreclosure auction. Old Bernie Allen stood off to the crowd's side and crossed his arms as listening, watched evenly while each of his possessions – a cow, a hutch, a pitchfork – were sold, his creased face never wincing for a moment. At times the breeze ruffled the tails of his wind-breaker, and then the nylon puff exhaled as if an old bellows, yet his body did not so much as twitch. Why he wore a jacket on such a warm day perplexed the farmers there; most supposed his torso was a pool of sweat, his skin all melted in the warmth. Still, to those who hung nearby him to quietly demonstrate their solidarity, he did not reek of perspiration. Oddly, he gave off no odor at all, just stood there as if he were a phantom stone. The gullets of those who stared long enough at him ached in admiration.

"People take notice when a main street business boards up," said Edmund Wallace as he stood next to Bernie, "but when a farmer goes down that's just somewhere off in the horizon."

The others nodded, mumbled their agreement. "Just you wait, though," Wallace said. "Everyone else making profit now but the farmer, and that can't go on for long. The pain will spread."

"It's a shame, that's what it is," said Gary Bris.

The men stood quietly for a few moments, waited for Carl Steinar to speak, but he said nothing, merely stared with disinterest at the auctioneer. He found it odd that Bernie Allen had not considered the alternative to such humiliation; certainly an accidental death was better than being served a bill and review right at your kitchen table while sharing coffee with the messenger. Allen had worked hard, raised six kids, coached seventh-grade basketball. He didn't deserve this.

Nor do I deserve what Peter has done to me, he thought; how ironic – old Bernie Allen failed to give what his son wanted, yet he himself had succeeded in giving Peter what his boy did not want.

Edmund Wallace nudged Carl's arm. "Maybe 30 years ago our dads should have organized like that one trouble-maker farmer said, eh?"

Carl merely shrugged, and canting his head into the wind he gazed at the table-flat farmlands beyond the yard. Lyle stood next to him, listening intently to the auctioneer's rattle, and Carl grimaced at the thought of Peter not being with them, he having opted to spend another afternoon with that reporter from the Register.

Buck Sutherland suddenly looked up. "Nah, it's just as well he got out," the old farmer said; his own brother had been smart enough to and now was the newspaper editor. "Look at him – going bald, two of his kids have left the state, and they say down at the Chuck Wagon that he's got ulcers. His town has shrunk, his friends are going broke, and his church is empty."

"Yeah, a farm is a big box," Wallace said. "Can't blame people for not sticking around."

"No, you can't blame him for getting out," Sutherland said. "With global warming and all, pretty soon this'll just be a big desert anyway."

The men remained silent for a long while, listened to the auctioneer. Though barely moving his jowls, the syllables flew from his mouth like bullets out of a machine gun. A gold watch tight upon his wrist flashed sunlight as he pointed to a bidder. The musty odor of sweating cattle in the pen nearly suffocated all present, but the auctioneer continued barking and waving, oblivious to it.

Then he paused for a moment, sipped from a glass of ice water, and continued at his rapid pace.

Carl Steinar remembered back to the day he was certain his own father had made the same decision that he was about to. Sunlight glistened off the sprouts of green breaking through the red furrows as the crop duster dropped white flags at the beginning of each row to mark its course. Gil had been away at college for a year, did not return that summer to help on the farm. Standing along the field's edge, Carl glanced up at his father's parched face, could see how his thoughts ran like a bird turning in its cage, trying to determine a way of escape. They must had stood there for some time watching the buzzing plane as it dipped then rose and circled, for Carl noticed a deep, vermilion patch forming across his father's forehead from too much sun. Those were good days, with the markets opened to Soviet Russia, preserving all of the little towns across the Midwest so every Main Street still possessed its own bakery, café and shops, yet his father remained forlorn, lost. The land hadn't dashed his dreams, nor the wind, drought or even a tornado. Though they said nothing of it, that day Carl learned the unexpected always had a way of rearing itself on the Plains. Working from sunrise to sundown, seven days a week, year after year, strengthened a man physically, emotionally, but one unpondered variable alone could break it all down. There was no time for flights of fancy like those Peter took to the creek as a child or now with this woman reporter. There was just the comfort of a straight furrow to right a man. The plane passed once more, a mere six or seven feet above the ground, then Carl's father turned to him, a needy look of reassurance barely showing in his eyes. "It looks flat, but a man always has to toll up a slight incline, doesn't he, Son?" Carl nodded. He knew his father was right. His father had always been right, about everything.

Chapter 17

The wind slowly curved then leaped across the street as Abbie entered Aunt Amita's shop. As rows of knick-knacks, candles and teddy bears spread before the young reporter, an old fashioned bell rang above the door. The shop smelled vaguely of old newspapers. Amita stood behind the checkout counter, body hunched over an accounting ledger, a calculator to her side. Deep wrinkles were etched across her neck, and the fingers appeared chafed, like she'd been hulling beans all afternoon. This Aunt Amita was the kind of woman who'd ask you to sit on your lap if you were a youngster, Abbie thought, and she also was not one to cower. If not for the curly hair, she easily could be mistaken as asexual, like a washerwoman. In such a presence, Abbie found her own femininity unsettling. She tucked both hands in the pockets of her pea coat and approached the matriarch. Amita looked up, eyed her suspiciously, as if she were an out-of-towner.

Abbie nervously touched her own neck. "Excuse me, but are you Amita Thurston?" she said as sweat beaded upon her shoulders; the young reporter wished she'd not worn such a heavy coat. "My name is Abbie Blaire. I'm dating your nephew, Peter."

Amita's face broke into a smile. "Why, yes, his father

has mentioned you. Peter and I see so little of each other these days that I don't really keep up with all that's happening in his personal life."

"We've been going out for a few weeks now," Abbie said as her shoulders straightened. "We are getting quite serious. I mean serious considering the time we've been together. He means a lot to me. Which is why I have a favor to ask of you, one involving Peter and his father."

Amita drew back and with a hint of skepticism in her eyes examined Abbie.

"Lately they haven't been getting along too well," Abbie said, her words quick, urgent. "It's really affecting Peter, and I think he's too afraid to say anything. Perhaps you could talk to them – get them to talk to one another?"

"Tell me, why you so interested in helping Peter's father, especially when, if you'll excuse my frankness, he doesn't much care for you?" She smelled of camphor, and her almond-colored teeth showed as she spoke.

Abbie's thoughts wobbled, and she glanced away; apparently they'd talked about her. She turned back to Amita. Helping bring Peter and his father together would be her gift to him, she decided.

"I understand what Peter's father has suffered and thinks. He feels I've come between them. Maybe if I can bring them together, he'll accept me."

Amita's eyes glinted with doubt as she fought back a grin. "They're just some things that shouldn't be another person's business."

Abbie carefully mulled her next words; she suspected Amita Thurston was not the kind of woman willing to be led down blind trails. "Peter trusts you. What you did for him as a child helped him deal with his mother's passing, and he appreciates that. Maybe he's never told you–"

"Oh, my dear, flattery is like the wind, now."

Abbie smiled nervously, remained quiet for a moment. Aunt Amita watched her indifferently for some time, as if one of those courthouse statues of oversized ladies representing justice, then she returned to her ledger and calculator. Perhaps I should just go, Abbie thought to herself – if I am to shelter myself in his peace, this simply may not be the door to it. For a second, the only sounds in the shop were Amita's quick strokes of pencil upon paper and the woman's shallow, discordant breathing. Abbie tried to think of something to say, but she knew this Aunt Amita, with her answers brief as the winter days ahead of them, would not help no matter what was said. Her frame slumped. Perhaps, she told herself, inner calm simply was unapproachable, a distant star. A raw heat rose upon her neck.

"Well, thank you for your time," Abbie said. "It was nice meeting you." She headed for the door.

"You're not giving up so quickly, are you?" Amita called, her voice coaxing. Abbie swiveled around.

"He still trusts me, you know," Amita said.

A smile spread across Abbie's face, and she reapproached the counter.

*****

Abbie nervously tucked her legs beneath the restaurant chair and chewed her lip. She wondered what trouble Aunt Amita had gone through to get Peter's father into the café for lunch. Customers filled nearly every table, and as their forks tinked chaotically against plates, they stammered on about crop prices, relatives' poor decisions, and the government's interference.

Peter reached for her wrist. "You're awfully quiet today," he said.

Abbie smiled skittishly. "Oh, I'm sorry. I guess I didn't

realize it."

A few moments of silence passed like the slow, solemn motion of clouds. Peter chuckled. "You keep looking at the window, too."

"It's nothing, really. I–"

But before she could finish, the café door swung open, and Aunt Amita entered, Carl Steinar lagging behind her. Amita glanced about, her frame solid and imposing like a concrete pillar, and spotting Abbie, waved then headed toward her table.

Peter's eyes widened. Still, he rose to greet them. Aunt Amita gave him a meek hug, patted his back. As the two sat, Carl remained standing then hesitantly followed suit. For several seconds, no one spoke.

"Well," Amita quick said, "the wind is rather nippy out there for this time of year, don't you think?"

Peter slouched as his father remained quiet.

Abbie quick chimed in. "And it was so hot just a couple of days ago."

Aunt Amita smiled, and as she did, Peter sat up. "It's just one of many surprises around here lately, isn't it?" he said.

Amita's eyes squeezed disapprovingly at him. "I know what you're thinking. Yes, you're right, this has all been arranged. But I understand a certain father and son haven't been getting along lately. Perhaps the two of you need to talk this out. Well, here's your opportunity."

Abbie surveyed the table. Peter's mouth twitched as he crossed his arms, but Carl's pupils merely glazed over them. Good, she thought, perhaps they're at least open to this, and she turned to Peter's father. "Farmers around town are saying it's almost time to start planting the winter wheat."

Carl Steinar gazed upon her evenly. My eldest son has

thoughts about planting something else, so I don't know if the Steinars will get to the wheat this year."

Amita's mouth dropped, and Peter slammed his fist on the table. The caféteria quieted as he pointed a finger at his father. "You can stop right there, old man!" he shouted, then swirling toward Abbie said, "You were behind this, weren't you? I should have known better than to tell you about my father."

Abbie's stomach tightened She leaned away from him, her face red, uncertain what to say.

Amita harrumphed loudly, sat up straight so she was taller than anyone else at the table. "Well, that's a fine way for both of you men to act. You ought to see yourselves. "

Abbie caressed Peter's arm. "Please, won't you give this a try?" she said, her breath shaky.

Peter suddenly grew quiet as a still pond. He knew with the attack on Abbie that even after all of those years his father's grip held him tight. His hands went slack as he slumped in the chair; he wondered if it was a habit picked up from Aunt Amita, who always seemed to contract in upon herself after reprimanding his cousins. Across the table, a grin reeking of sly righteousness crossed his father's face. Peter's eyes suddenly narrowed. Never once in all of their time together had they said to one another "I miss her."

Talk quickly resumed in the caféteria as the four remained quietly at their table. The waitress hesitantly stepped toward them, tried to hide her anxiety with a cheerful demeanor, asked if they were ready to order. Amita stuck her face into a menu, then Abbie and Peter did so as well.

Carl Steinar stared through the three of them. His fingers, bent tensely at the knuckles, edged toward the table's rim. There was no opportunity here, merely interference, he thought, just manipulation, so much like his older brother's profession. It did not produce but it consumed a staggering profit off of others' efforts. No, he himself lived on the merits of his own hands and determination. His palms pressed against the table as he stood and, face carved with uncertainty, turned toward the door.

Abbie half rose from her chair. "Where's he going?" she said, her voice husky with exasperation.

Aunt Amita looked at the waitress. "It'll just be the three of us for lunch," she said.

*****

Abbie refused to look at Peter as they drove silently back to her apartment, and inside he found her ignominy no different. Neither had eaten much. As she marched to the kitchen sink, he followed. "Hey," he said, but she did not respond as pulling a glass from the cupboard and filled it with tap water. She took a sip as he waited for her to turn around.

When she didn't, he stepped beside her. "Aren't you going to answer me?" he said.

Abbie set the glass on the counter, looked at him. "I've never been so humiliated in my whole life," she said.

Peter's teeth clenched as he tried to hold down his voice. "Well then what did you have to go get her involved for?" he said

Abbie cocked her head to the side, stared at the distant wall with pursed lips. He did not relent in his tirade, and his rambling voice sounded like a series of gunshots. The wind pecked at the kitchen window. She ignored him, fixed her eyes upon the brown grass outside.

"Then you tried to start talking to him about farming," he said. "What was that about? You can't fool him into thinking you know something about farming."

As Abbie crossed her arms, an accusatory stare filled

her eyes. "You have a real heart of stone," she said. Though leaning toward one another, she believed they were farther apart than ever before.

Peter looked at her, straight-faced. "The hell."

"Oh, Peter," she said, "don't you see? All your oppression is internalized. You're crushing yourself from within."

Peter's thoughts rattled like a fence in a storm, but his face turned flat, hard. "I don't think Aunt Amita's interfereence came from 'inside' me."

She shrugged, stood solemnly.

He grit his teeth as curling both hands into fists. She uses silence to fight me, he told himself, why won't she speak? For a long moment, he remained mute, realized he'd not said things the right way. His palms trembled. "Look, it's just not right for her to get involved," he said.

"And why is that?"

He sensed the moment changing, like a stream's shifting currents. "Some things are just between two people and no one else."

Her eyes softened. "But when they affect others, it becomes their business."

Peter's lips parted in surprise. "Are you saying this somehow is hurting you?"

"Don't you see it in the way you act? How you become so sullen? So short-fused at times?" His brow contorted nervously. He gripped the counter, as if to keep himself steady then looked away. If I never meant to hurt you. "

Abbie gazed at him, and he found her eyes, soft as a flower petal, swallowing him. She was always so rational, so in control, and he pondered how she was able to do it. Just let it go, he told himself, and then as he released his grip upon the counter, his hand knocked over the glass of water. Its contents unfurled like a transparent banner across the

Formica.

"I'm sorry," Peter said, turning toward the counter. He uprighted the glass. "Do you have a towel?"

She slid an arm around Peter's waist, threw the other about his shoulder. "Forget the spill," she said.

Cradled against his body, he drew in the freshness of her hair, it sweet like a magnolia bloom, then twirled its ends as she listed deep into him. Her presence burned away his anger, and he nuzzled her creamy neck, brought a hand to her breast. She protested, but as his palm caressed, her voice trailed off. He canted away, unbuttoned her blouse. Reaching behind her untucked shirt, she undid the bra, and he loosened it from her frame, unveiled her breasts, firm and tapered. He kissed each freckle upon her bosom then buried his mouth against her warm chest, as each heard the other's breathing jut upward like a flame. Then they stepped away from one another and undressed, their clothes falling liquidly, gracefully, to the floor. He stared at her naked figure, it thin but shapely, a swimmer's body. She ran the tip of her finger slightly above the skin of his chest, in its wake raising the flesh upon his body, then traced the line of his jaw. Their eyes surrendered to one another, and she took hold of his hand, led him to the bedroom. Upon her peach-colored sheets, she lay like a flower, its petals open, her face a happy pink. His leg brushed against her warm thigh, and as they caressed their entire bodies across one another, passions brimming, he dived into the whirlpool of her body. Like a wind rollicking and quivering, each thrusted toward the other, their skin wet like a sultry midsummer's night, their rhythm like music welling up. Then they let go a mutual gasp, and their beings stilled as they held the other tight.

At length, Peter sensed the dampness of her body dissolving, and he rolled off. They gazed into each other's eyes, and her mouth rounded into a small, maternal smile. Though separated, her presence lingered upon his lips, like a drop of milk clinging to the underside of a spoon, and he placed his hand upon the gentle curve of her waist. Peter knew she defined him, but it was in a way he liked.

"That was nice," she said. Peter murmured in agreement. "Are you still angry with me?"

He shook his head as best he could upon the pillow. "It's hard to stay mad at you."

"Yet you seem to be mad all the time."

"Not all the time."

"Cold then, anyway."

"I don't mean to be."

"That's why I tried to bring you and your father together this afternoon. Because your anger at him is being taken out on me."

"There may be no way to end my frustration with him."

She sighed. "Then you're going to have to let it go."

"Let it go?" He turned onto his back.

"Bear it then."

A sourness screwed across his face as he turned onto his back. "She says to 'bear it.' Who has the heart of stone now?"

She reached for his shoulder, but he flinched and pulled away.

*****

Staring out the kitchen window, Lyle found intolerable the long grasses flowing and bending like ocean waves beneath the morning wind and pondered if his father's suicide threats were authentic. Lyle leaned against the counter, and his balance loped, as if he were spinning upon a whirligig. He disliked the brightness of summer, of how daylight came so early, purging the darkness too soon from the sky. He decided to check on his old man; at least with the upstairs' shades pulled, he wouldn't have to squint. Then, Lyle heard a creaking and paused. A metallic click followed seconds later. He scurried halfway up the stairs, froze.

Standing in the hallway, the old man positioned the cold barrel of a gun at the opening of his mouth. He shifted it about his lips almost playfully, as if testing it out for size, and the gun made a slight whistle as his breath flowed through the metallic gray tube. The burned carbon deep in the barrel and the slick scent of oil from countless cleanings rang pungently as the neighbor dog's barking broke through the house like shards of broken glass striking the floor.

Lyle gasped. "Dad, put the gun down," he finally said. Carl's brow slowly rose as he examined his son.

Lyle's heart bounded, as if he'd suddenly discovered freedom. "Dad, are you listening to me?"

Carl Steinar lowered the gun to his side. "You called me 'Dad.'"

"That's who you are. Now give me the .20-gauge." Lyle stretched his hand toward him.

"Why did you call me 'Dad?'"

"Because that's who you are," Lyle said. He took a step forward.

His father remained lost in the words. The gun hung limp upon his hand, and with another step, Lyle gripped the stock. Slowly, tenderly, he peeled his father's fingers away from the trigger, then held the gun solely in his own arms.

"Dad, you ought to go back to bed, now."

"Bed? Yes ... I am tired."

Carl Steinar slouched off, his body feeble like a quiet wind. The nerves along Lyle's neck thawed, but he winced as holding the gun. Disarming his father had been surprisingly easy, Lyle thought, and he wondered if forgetting the whole affair could be as simple, like shoveling dirt into a hole so the ground would be level again. The springs of his father's bed creaked, and he could hear the old man lie down. Then the youngest of the Steinars headed downstairs, knees trembling.

Lyle knew he'd have to stay. The hairs upon his neck stuck straight up like excited quills at the thought of it. For years, anger had spoken through his idleness; yet now, Lyle knew that he must force himself to possess faith in the world. The wood strained under his step as he headed for the gun cabinet in the living room. There was nothing wrong in remaining on the farm, he told himself; a son's portion is duty. When Jackie Kine called to offer a job, he'd turn it down, say he'd thought about it and reconsidered. The muscles of Lyle's face tensed, while outside the wind built in ferocity. With each step, he grew increasingly certain of his decision, felt as if a window half-frozen shut from a long winter had been cracked open on the first spring day.

He pulled the pair of 12-gauges and the .22 from the gun cabinet, and bundling them in his arms with the 20-gauge, carried them out of the farmhouse. The hot wind blasted and swaggered as he walked against it. He wondered where to hide them, thought of the brick pile in the pole shed then dismissed it for his father would notice the disturbed blocks. The ammunition and bolts jangled in his arms as he broke into a run for the feed shed. The musty smell of its damp lumber swirled at him; he'd never noticed the strange scent before. Kneeling at the back of the shed, he separated each gun's parts. The icy metal stung his hands, and he shook as his pulse rose. He knew the key was to focus, to not panic, and for a second, he paused, caught his breath. After a moment, he continued breaking the guns apart, taking out the bolts then separating the barrels and the stocks. Shoveling old straw over them, he stood, inspected his handiwork. Satisfied, Lyle turned around, headed into the glaring white of the open yard. Before him, the wind braided its way across the prairie.

Chapter 18

Swamped deep in thought over all that had happened with Peter, Abbie found herself staring yet again at the office computer. She pinned back her tangled hair and sighed. Despite a shower, his lavender scent lingered upon her wrist; for a moment she returned to the balm and the comfort it brought. The day with him had begun warm and clear, but by noon, clouds covered the sky as the wind blew with an ever-greater ferocity. Once evening and storm darkened the horizon, he'd left; after only a few minutes alone in the apartment, she'd also moved on.

At last, Abbie's fingers returned to the keyboard. Her typing quickly outpaced the falling rain, but a few seconds later she stopped, dissatisfied with the green lettering that filled the screen. The cursor blinked over and over, stuck in the same neutral gear as her thoughts, repetitive and going nowhere yet demanding that progress be made. Hitting the backspace key, she erased the last sentence. If only the same could be done in my time with Peter, she thought. He'd spoken as if blaming her for his misfortunes, but she couldn't understand why; she wasn't at fault for all the angry years that had passed between him and his father. Those two men were so similar, both acting like sentinels perpetually on guard against...against what, she wondered. Abbie brought a wrist to her face once more, breathed in Peter's scent. Her father had turned that way after his accident, forced a smile as watching to ensure nothing questioned his masculinity, and no matter how she tried impressing him, his shield always prevented the showing of any real admiration or joy until she doubted that he even could feel. For that, she too remained angry.

The rain leveled to a mere drizzle, but as the coolness that came with September showers settled over the room, Abbie crossed her arms. The fecund smell of rain upon the dry humus wormed into the building, persuading her to focus on writing, and she replaced a misspelled word, wrote another line, then paused. It was no use, Abbie told herself, I can't think. She palmed the knotted pulse point of her neck, remembered how Peter's own deft hands so easily relieved the pain. Yet, his behavior also had caused so much of it.

Abbie rubbed her eyes. A story like this should be easy to write, she muttered, and as she stared again at the screen, the rain picked up, whirring like a bicycle wheel spinning down a hill.

I just need to be patient, she told herself, the words will come – it's my own advice, after all, to "bear it." So I also must be patient with Peter. I need to master my passions. I'll take everything slow, and it'll come to me; besides, I really wouldn't want it to arrive in one great rush.

Then Abbie tapped the keys, a slow murmur at first, but gradually a long line of words formed as she progressed. It was not so good as she would have liked, but it was writing nonetheless; eventually it would come to something. Outside, the rain stilled.

*****

When Peter opened the gun cabinet and saw only imprints in the dust of where the stocks once rested, he instantly forgot the overwhelming stench of sulfur that still lingered. Suddenly, his whole universe became the empty cabinet, it void of any silver barrels or white ammunition boxes. He gripped the solid pine doors tight, steadied himself against weakened knees, and blinking with disbelief, looked again. Only light slanted into the cabinet. Then, behind him, he heard Abbie moving closer. Straightening himself, he tried to breathe deeply; there was nothing to be gained by wheeling about in a frantic search for the guns. He had to remain calm or she would start asking questions again, and who knew where that would lead? Quickly, he closed the doors.

"Maybe in front of the house, probably something yellow," Abbie said. "What kind would you like?"

For a long moment, Abbie stared at him then snapped her fingers in front of his face. His eyes opened wide and head thrust up. "Oh, what?"

"Flowers. The place needs flowers," she said, her brow wrinkled. "You looked a thousand miles off."

Peter forced his body into a relaxed posture. "I'm just getting a little tired. Sorry."

Abbie nodded as late afternoon shadows edged up the farmhouse's mint green walls that she and Peter had spent much of the day scrubbing. She walked back into the kitchen, and a ray of light fell upon her face through the window as she smiled and wiped dust off an aspirin bottle half full of blue pills. Take everything slow, she told herself, take everything slow.

Peter thought of the many times he'd pulled a gleaming barrel from the dark cabinet. He tried to imagine the farmhouse without guns – it was like the creek drained of water or the June field void of wheat – and suddenly his own body felt hollow. Where were they, he wondered, and who'd taken them? There was his .22 rifle, a .20-gauge once owned by his grandfather, and two .12-gauges. Had they been sold? All together, they netted no more than a few hundred dollars at a pawn shop, maybe a thousand at best if a buyer were gullible. But what did his father or his brother need money for? He could believe his father selling those that had been gifts to he and his brother – nothing purchased by the old man for Lyle or me truly belongs to us, Peter thought. But his own brother, could he take them? Peter shook his head. There was no good reason to sell the guns; the three men had plenty of cash in the bank and still hunted. Maybe they'd simply been sent away to be cleaned or repaired. He closed both eyes, rubbed his brow. The explanation did not satisfy him, for the guns were not broken and their father always made the boys clean them after each hunt, whether they'd been fired or not. Perhaps the missing guns signified something important, he speculated, something that Lyle was keeping secret from him. Maybe Cornelius Skerry had been wrong after all.

Abbie poured more powdered bleach across the counter, and the acrid green dust bloomed as striking the surface. Despite the lack of cosmetics and toiletries, she found there was no shortage about the house of screws, nails or bolts, usually half-rusted, always grimy. She wiped the counter in tight swirls and as a finishing touch set a shallow basket heaping with apples, oranges and pears upon it. Go slow, and everything will come, she reminded herself.

Not that long ago, Peter always had straightened his room and even did the dishes each night, but as the years passed, he grew tired of picking up after his old man and adult brother. Hell, no one ever visited, he thought, what did it matter? With Abbie coming over regularly, though, that attitude changed. So during their last walk past the blue ribbon of creek, sheltered by leafy branches hanging just above their heads, he asked her to help with a "spring cleaning," to get the farmhouse ready for winter. At first, she resisted; then he explained Lyle and his father wouldn't be there but at the Adams' farm auction. "Trying to make space for all the new stuff they're going to buy?" she said with a sly grin, and when he chuckled, she added, "Well, you are inviting me to rummage through your stuff, so how could I pass on an opportunity like that?"

Starting at the kitchen, they tossed batteries, receipts, old pens that no longer worked, and a corroded flashlight, threw out from the cupboards the dozen different cereal boxes, all of them open. In the bathroom, they cleared the reduced-to-mucous hair clogging the tub's drain, and Abbie scoured the sink until her wrists strained. In the living room, they wiped clean the dust piled upon each picture frame then carried outside to Peter's pickup the stacks of newspapers and old magazines. As the two rested at the dining table, Abbie sorted through a kitchen drawer they'd accidentally skipped. Finding an old farm cookbook of his mother's, she carefully turned its stained pages lest they crumble like dead leaves.

Abbie drew in a long breath. "You know, you never talk about your mother."

"No, I don't."

She raised an eyebrow; perhaps if prodded he'd tell about her. "Why does it bother you? To talk about it?"

"It just was so long ago."

"But you do remember her, right?"

His mouth screwed into a tight ball. "So?"

For a moment, Abbie remained quiet. Slow, she told herself, go slow.

"I'm sorry," Peter said as gazing at her, and turning

away he placed a hand over his mouth, recalled how his mother set gardenia and freesia sachets in the chest of drawers and upon her vanity. "Guess there's just the hallway windows left to do," he said after a moment.

Abbie fought back a loud harummph. "Yes, there are," she said. There was no point in being angry, she told herself, and if I am to maintain the moral high ground, politeness will have to suffice. She sauntered up the stairs after him.

Direct confrontation never had gotten her anywhere. Abbie recalled the Christmas break she'd returned home during her freshman year of college. Mary Dawn had décorated the tiny house in red and silver ribbons, and though she greeted her warmly as an encumbered classmate pulled back onto the street toward his own home, there was no welcome from father. "He's resting," is all Mary Dawn said, and though Abbie wanted to say "Resting? From what?" she held her tongue. At dinner, as the heavy scent of meatloaf covered the room, he acknowledged her but said little more. The next day continued like that, so Abbie spent the time in her room, it blue with cold and virtually empty for most of her belongings sat in a dormitory. So the third day passed, too. At last, she rose from her purgatory and marched into her father's den, did not wait at the doorway for an invitation as she had seven months before. Sitting straight up in chair before his desk, she looked straight at him but did not stare. He only continued to piece together a model airplane.

"Daddy, look at me," she said.

His head slowly canted upward until their eyes locked. She suddenly found her confidence thin as a peel protecting an orange. What has happened to the father that I knew, she wondered, the proud strolling man, his body sleek as if a boat cutting through water, the ends of his bran-colored hair flitting in the wind?

"Daddy, I've missed you," she said.

For a moment, his eyes glistened, though only slightly. "Honey, you've grown up," he said, very quietly. "And I am an old, broken man."

Then his attention shifted back to the model, and as he raised a plastic wing to see how it fit into the plane's main body, she sensed his growing opaqueness. Her thoughts suddenly burned like tinder, and she slammed a fist against his desk. As the model parts bounced, he glanced up. But his lips and pupils did not move, remained monotone. Her heart pounded, then she took a deep breath and twirled around, knew that with him as at that moment with Peter, she must be a slow tide. Spraying cleanser onto the glass pane, Abbie wondered how much she really was like her mother, acting as if there were nothing wrong, both dutifully going about their work. Indeed, they each tidied up the house the same way, preferring a lightness, a breeziness, to their abodes, all except in her father's room, where the blinds always remained drawn and the windows closed. Abbie recalled the story her mother often told of that first date with brash young Lt. A.J. Blaire, of how her heart was taken with him when they went on a hot air balloon ride over local farmland; she'd never seen the world from above: the sea of purple and white alfalfa blossoms, the scent of honey, lemongrass and periwinkle that lingered in the high breeze, the apple orchard that half rolled up the hillside. It so excited her, Abbie supposed, that through him she vicariously cultivated her life of adventure, so much in fact that she was quite content to never leave the housework. Abbie herself had never felt that way toward a man. Her own trials with them had been a steady series of fits and starts, just as it was turning out to be with Peter. Ah, meeting, dating, going steady, breaking up, she asked herself with a grin, who can say when in a relationship each really happens?

"So your brother went to an auction with your father?" she said.

Peter grunted his acknowledgment as he rubbed the window at the hallway's opposite end. "During the interview your brother hardly said a thing." Perhaps talking about Lyle, she surmised, would be a roundabout way to get his mother; Abbie knew she could maneuver faster with words than her feet.

Peter's lip curled, "Don't let his quietness fool you. He has no qualms about doing utterly nasty things, like beating or killing animals. "

Then Peter balled his hands into fists, and after gritting his teeth flexed his fingers. The dirty rag brushed against his leg. The missing guns, he told himself, only proved the need for restraint. Yet, oddly enough even to him, the more he tried to relax, the more it felt as if he were collapsing in upon himself. Peter held his breath for a long moment. Unless you want a fire to rage across the prairie, he told himself, it's best to slow burn only small, controllable swaths at a time. He wiped the last streak of cleanser off the pane and turned around. Abbie also had finished, and without speaking they returned to the kitchen table.

As they sat, Abbie examined how Peter's eyes squinted tight, how he pursed his lips. Her mind turned pensive as she thought what he had said about Lyle. Rising, she opened the unfinished kitchen drawer to see what other treasures loomed inside; the amount of junk the Steinars had collected over the years amazed her. She found a tangle of shoelaces, and bringing the strings back to the table, busied herself at untangling them. Her breathing grew more measured as she focused on the task. Then, unable to undo a knot, her fingers came to a standstill. She dug at the fabric with her nails, but the strings' tightness resisted all effort. She pushed the bundle away, crossed her arms.

"What's wrong?" Peter said.

"These damn shoelaces are all knotted up."

"Well, that's easy enough to fix." Peter rose. I'll find out what happened to the guns, he told himself, if it's the last damn thing I do.

She grabbed the laces, tugged at a string then tried to unbind one end from a tight loop. "Yeah? How?"

Peter ambled to the kitchen cupboards and opening a drawer pulled out a steak knife. In the brightness of the clean room, the metal gleamed like a gilded sash. "Hold it taut," he said. She gazed quizzically at him and half out of curiosity followed his instructions. In a single swipe, he sliced through the string, and its two ends fell limp in her hands. Her eyes widened, and she started to giggle. Peter grinned, then suddenly they laughed together, its pitch rolling out like wind across the plain.

*****

Peter's breath lifted and fell like the sea at the sight of her. As he rounded the corner in downtown Felton the June after Laura Jean had left for college, she stood in front of the sunlight, directly before him. They stopped, stared at one another. How long had it been, Peter wondered, and counting the months since they'd last seen one another, he came up with nine.

Though such little time had passed, he hardly recognized her any more. She'd cut her hair short so that it narrowed in tips along the cheeks and covered the forehead rather than fall in long rivulets past her shoulders as during high school. It remained dyed black and glowed burgundy, not the strawberry blonde he'd known. She said nothing, but he sensed thoughts buzzing behind her pinched lips and slightly squeezed eyes. For a moment he wanted to tell her that she'd put on weight, especially in the breasts and the hips, and how it looked good on her, but knew that wasn't smart. Instead, he gazed stupidly upon her, and shifting slightly forward, tried to determine if her scent had transformed, too. He could not get close enough. At least she still bared her arms in the summer heat, and he relaxed in the comfort that some things never change. Then his mouth grew dry at the notion.

"Hello, Peter," she said.

"Hello, Jean–," but he paused, remembered how in the weeks before they'd broken up she'd demanded that everyone, except him, call her "Laurie." Did that rule now extend to him as well? "Hello, Laurie," he said.

Her eyes remained blank. He cleared his throat, felt like an old husk flittering aimlessly in the wind. "What have you been up to?" she said.

He sensed a mild indifference in her voice. "Still farming. With my father."

"Oh," she said.

Peter shuffled his feet as they stood on the white-hot concrete. "How about yourself?" he said.

"Back for the summer," she said. "Classes ended last week."

He watched Laura Jean form her words rather than listen to them. Her nose had thinned, and the nostrils jutted upward. The nonchalance in her voice revealed a newfound confidence, and she spoke more measuredly, as if he needed time to absorb what was said. Classrooms and textbooks seemed but an indistinct memory to Peter, yet, so it was with every moment of the past, he knew. There never can be any "remember when"; it always must be "from this moment forward" if one is to accept the challenges of existence, especially out on the Plains. The only advantage to memory was if it taught a lesson to get you through the here and now. Peter could think of nothing he'd learned from Laura Jean. She'd merely shared a long portion of the night's darkness with him, that was all. He coughed, clenched his fists.

"I need to get going," she said. "My mother is expecting me to pick up a couple of items for her."

"Say, Laurie," he quick said as she was about to step past, "If you should want to do something or even just talk, give me a call. "

She examined his face, as if it were a curiosity. "It was nice seeing you again, Peter," she said and was off.

That evening, Peter remained sullen at the dinner table. Carl Steinar looked up from his plate of scalloped potatoes, asked him if he was feeling ill.

"No – it's nothing," Peter said, and he forced a forkful of potatoes down his throat.

"He saw Laura Jean in town today," Lyle said. "Laura Jean Strom."

Peter sneered at his brother, but then peripherally he caught his father pausing from the meal and staring ponderously down the table, as if understanding. He turned to the old man; perhaps those eyes held the answer, he thought, for they were still like that of a corpse or a mannequin, were still like his own mind. The young man could not understand how such lifelessness resulted in serenity, but perhaps he was about to find out.

Then his father turned to him. "Son, always remember, you've got to separate the husk from the grain." With that, the old man returned to his nearly barren plate as if nothing had ever happened.

*****

Lyle's nerves ticked as stepping from the pickup truck. He examined the brightly lit gravel his feet kicked up and breathed in the churned dust. The stones crackled as they bounced off one another then the grain elevator's wooden steps. He needed a job, a way to escape the farm. With Joe Audun leaving town, the assistant manager had been promoted, then one of the long-time employees moved to his spot, and so everyone else's duties rippled, leaving a vacancy at the bottom of the mill's totem pole. He glanced up. The elevator's shadow blurred with its gray walls.

A creak swallowed him as he opened door, the reflection of his pickup disappearing in the plate glass window. Puffs of icy air struck, and instantly the hairs of his arm stood on end. A lone girl sat behind the counter at the office's front. She wore a grain elevator shirt, the only crisp one he'd seen on the employees there, and in her sunflower-colored hair were two barrettes that prevented a tangle of bangs from falling over royal blue eyes. He glanced at the elevator's logo sewn across the right breast, didn't see a name. She looked familiar, though, and when she greeted him, her voice quiet like a whisper, he was certain they'd met before.

"Do I know you?" he said, the sight of her taking his mind off the office's grainy odor.

She glanced at the papers on her desk, as if embarrassed.

"Your brother went out with my sister, back in high school."

"Why, you're–" he paused for a moment to think, but only the taste of beer, now distant in memory, rolled through his head. "My, your hair has grown out."

She smiled, even blushed a little as he stared at her. That was not all that had grown, Lyle thought. Her waist was slender like the narrow curve of an hourglass. "Can I help you with something?" she said.

Lyle didn't speak for a moment. "An application form. There's an opening here, right?"

She nodded, twirled toward the file cabinet and pulled out a set of sheets. "Not giving up on farming, are you?"

"Maybe."

Handing him the form, her fingers brushed against his palm, and it hit him like an electric shock.

"That'd be too bad," she said. "You and Peter have a nice spread out there."

"You've been to our farm?"

She smiled. Lyle thought her mouth a bit large, wondered how someone so endowed could speak so gently. "Been by it," she said. "Laura Jean described it enough."

"Just thinking of expanding my horizons is all," he said quickly. "You live in town?"

She nodded again, stared back at him. "Been working here since high school. It's about all one can do in a place like Felton."

He eyed her hand, saw no rings. "A lot of competition for this job, then?"

She smirked. "If you fill out that form, we'll probably be working together."

"Really? You don't do the hiring, do you?"

She laughed. "I wish. Need a pen?"

"Thought I'd fill it out at home."

"Take your time. The job will be open for a while."

"I think I'd like to bring it back tomorrow."

Her face burned crimson as she turned away from him to restock the office shelves with medicines and rat poison. "I think I'd like that, too."

Chapter 19

Carl Steinar tapped a finger against the windmill as he watched his son and the Register reporter from afar, a vantage point from which he often had gazed at his own life. The old farmer could make out the two holding hands and how with aimless steps they playfully bumped into one another. He felt a thick pulsing in his ears as his breathing grew more rapid. In defiance of his own edict, the girl had been to the farm three times during the past week. Then Abbie, who appeared lyrical even at that distance, caressed Peter's bare neck. Long ago, he thought to himself, Gwen and I had acted much the same way. Without speaking, they'd vowed to forever shield one another from life's storms, but there had been no protection for nearly two decades.

Now the time had come to decide their fate.

Carl rubbed his grizzled face. All of their fates, he supposed.

As the two couples ambled across the green before him – one in fact, the other in memory – Carl leaned against the windmill. Its silver metal burned hot, even through his shirt, and on occasion the mill's blades churned, a sound he'd grown to hate. Peter dating that Laura Jean in high school never bothered him for he knew that after graduation she'd leave the county. He wetted his chapped lips then sneered. When she had, his eldest son came back to the farm in both body and spirit, threw his all into maintaining it, the only purpose there was left for him in life. With this Abbie though, he asked himself, what could be done? He wiped his forehead with a wrist, but the acrid sweat merely dampened the once dry patch of arm.

A sudden desire to push overwhelmed Carl. It was the same feeling he got whenever thinking of that other driver, the one who killed Gwen. Each time he remembered her flecks of blood glowing red across the cracked windshield, each time he recalled the tassel of her hair wavering upon the breeze that flit through the crushed car's exposed breaks, he wanted to shake the bastard who ran that stop sign, shake him until all anger spilled out, until he felt giddy and young again. Whenever Carl thought of doing so, though, he simply crossed his arms and caved in upon himself. Then he'd think of the stupid things people said after she died – "Fortunately you and the kids weren't in the car," "It was her time to go," "At least she went quickly" – and his hatred whirled again, like a black stew rising to a boil.

One day the rage so overtook him that without warning he grabbed the sledgehammer from the shed's corner and swaggered like a mad bull toward the windmill. The gravel crunched under his feet as his boots dug in, then with a steady but red eye he honed on a support beam, lifted the hammer over his shoulder as if it were a baseball bat, and swung. The collision of metal cracked across the empty plain like a gunshot. His arms rattled, but he raised the sledgehammer again. It clanged, and iron shavings filled his nostrils as the midday sun simmered, but no matter how many times he struck it, the edifice would not topple. Panting, he dropped the sledgehammer and bent over.

Peter and Abbie disappeared over a knoll. Carl Steinar knew that somehow his eldest son would have to be cut from the farm. How to do it, though, escaped him. He couldn't straight out tell him to leave, for then there would be resentment. Making life on the farm so intolerable that he'd go of his own accord also was unacceptable. Perhaps a middle ground of encouraging him to head to college, of letting fate pull him away was best, but Carl Steinar knew that would take too long, might not even be possible. He backed into the yard, the grass thick from autumn rain. His eyes caught the windmill's supports, golden in the sunlight except for the small dark shadow of where his hammering had dented it.

In the years since that outburst, Carl Steinar had long dismissed any notion that he'd caused Gwen's death by asking her to go so close to lunch that she'd been rushed. His Nebraskan practicality forbade it, though at times the notion still crept into his thoughts, that he was to blame if only by the slimmest degree...yet, he told himself, one must always hold back, must always suppress some thoughts for the better good. So as the years passed, he found the target of his rage growing blank, and a sense of nothingness festered inside him like a malignant cancer he never could rid himself of.

On occasion, there was a girlfriend or acquaintance of Gwen's who came by to pay her respects; the blonde classmate, now living in Lincoln, had appeared once like a dandelion poking from a crevice to check on him, or the church auxiliary lady, who brought a fruit basket on the anniversary of her death. All acted as if they could draw Gwen out of the earth and resurrect her. Yet, for Carl Steinar they did not cast any new nets upon the meaning of her death; he did not need them anyway, for he preferred the anchored dock of his farm. Meeting them on the porch as their cars rolled into the driveway, just when through hard labor and quiet solitude he'd found peace, they'd do nothing but remind him of her.

Carl's breath wove through the air like crackling fire. Who can see and understand our hard labors but one's children, he asked himself, and if they do not, what point is there in enduring those burdens? He thought of Abbie's interference; the young always think they know what's best, he muttered, but look at the shame she's brought to us, the shame Peter has welcomed by allowing her into his life, by putting her ahead of the family. He'd let her in their own home to root through their belongings, to rearrange them, all when he should have been with Lyle and him at the Allen's auction. Certainly, after all I've done for him, he could sacrifice now for me!

During those long days following Gwen's death, Carl had taken on the headiest of tasks, and as taught by his father's example, he set himself fully upon it: the challenge of creating a new family out of the old. He was uncertain how to perform even the simplest of child-rearing chores, though.

Late each afternoon, he'd stare at the cookbook trying to decipher the jumble of numbers and letters; often he forgot how much he put in or which step he was on, and most of the time he didn't have half the ingredients that the recipe required. Then he'd stir when he should blend, grind when he should mince. Or there was cleaning. He found the vacuum cleaner a more difficult implement to run than the combine, and his dishtowel missed crumbs beneath the toaster until they piled high like ashes in a bonfire. At such times, Carl was thankful he had no daughters to deal with all the "female things" – bras, periods, prom dresses, contraception – it was easier to raise boys, to grow what he was familiar with. Still, even they were fatiguing, sometimes so much that he'd find himself eating and drinking slowly or when looking in a mirror would see the color drained from his eyes, but he never allowed it to overcome him, inevitably mustered the energy to make breakfast, to oversee homework, to attend parent-teacher conferences, to remain masked. Exhaustion always trailed him like a shadow.

Perhaps worse, though, the family traditions became alien without his wife. Putting up a Christmas tree, tilling the Easter baskets, wrapping birthday presents – each time he did these it were as if he saw his image in the mirror, a part of the world dislodged from reality. The holidays became vaporous. The loss extended far deeper than a few dreaded dates on the calendar, though. In summer, Gwen would set out a pitcher of ice water with glasses on the dining room hutch; one hot day after the funeral, Carl took a break from his chores and without thinking went to the cabinet for a drink, but nothing was there. Amita had put away the glassware.

He learned to ad-lib. Perhaps that was why he and Gwen had worked so well together: She was a master of improvisation and he an impresario of planning. They balanced one another. Realizing that, he finally understood why he found her love of the wind and of jazz records so delightful. For a moment, he listened to the breeze, to how it rang like the sounds of a great trumpeter playing and composing at the same time, perfecting the art of becoming. It was so similar to Gwen's voice.

Sometimes amid all the loneliness, Gwen would appear, her face white, a stillness to the amorphous body, and help him decide what to do. He found such moments oddly discordant, like songs played out of key. It was as if the blowing wind had opened a blossom then rended the Corolla into shreds. Sometimes the countercurrent would slap a torn petal back into his face as he watched the terrifying spectacle, but occasionally a gust would lift it high into the air, out of sight, then as easing up, let it fall gently upon him. Still, Carl knew that one thing out on the prairie was certain: The wind never remained still.

And then it came to him how he'd get Peter to leave.

*****

The stockyard's lobby appeared like that of any other public building – tiled floors, high imposing walls, all glass and sunshine, busy with the movement of men about their business. Cary Sutherland had sent Abbie there to write a feature on the administrator who was retiring after more than 14 years; the provincial old editor liked what she had done with the Steinar windmill piece and to her delight was increasingly assigning features rather than hard news. As the auctioneer's rapid-pace staccato echoed over the cattle's lowing, she searched for a sign showing where the main offices might be, found one that mimicked a weathered board with words and directional arrow branded onto it. But the rest of the stockyards were unmarked and maze-like, nothing but walls and fences and gates, and after making what seemed like the correct turn, she stepped outside into a blinding light, only to find Lyle Steinar standing on the catwalk before her.

He bore puffy eyes, and his shoulders slouched as if carrying a great burden; Abbie feared it weighed so heavily that the railing he leaned against might collapse. The cow's bellowing and the barks of yardmen rounding them into tight corrals swallowed him while he gazed nonchalantly at the spectacle. Perhaps by talking to rather than ignoring him, she thought to herself, I can ingratiate myself to the Steinar family, and that is important – I am dating his brother. Oddly enough to Abbie, he had kept her away from Lyle and their father; at first, enjoying the attention, she didn't mind. Lately though, she'd found the distancing disturbing. It almost was as if Peter were ashamed of her.

The stockyard's warm muskiness rose about Abbie as she approached Lyle. "Good morning, Mr. Steinar," the girl said.

His pupils brightened in surprise but then almost as quickly dimmed. "Looking for new additions to the herd?" she said.

"Just here."

Abbie glanced downward. She never expected him to fully accept her right away – she wasn't of Felton, after all, and in a small Nebraska town, outsiders had to earn trust. "How are cattle prices?"

"Haven't checked lately."

Abbie resisted grinding her teeth. The Steinars sure are a moody bunch, she thought, but then what had her editor told her? "If you ask any two Steinars, they'll give you two different explanations or none at all; that's what folks around here say about them, anyway." She bit her lip. "Do you know how to get to the administrator's office? I'm supposed to interview him but seem to have taken a wrong turn."

Lyle's head nodded toward the cattle. "It's a pretty bunch down there," he said. "So peaceful and sleepy-eyed. Oblivious to their fate."

Her brow wrinkled. Hadn't he heard what I said, she wondered. "Well, I'm sure I can find my way there. It was nice seeing you aga–"

"I can tell you where it is," he said before she could finish. "I'm just lost in a little reverie, that's all."

"Oh."

"'Reverie' – that's the right word?"

"I suppose it is – I guess I don't know what you were thinking, so–"

Then his gaze fixed upon her, and as Abbie stopped speaking, she saw flecks of warmth in his arctic blue eyes. She glanced down, examined how the denim shirt he wore was discolored like a faded runway and at one spot nearly threadbare, a long seam stretching apart in the asphalt. Regaining her nerve, she looked into his face. He stared back, full of foreboding, as if a man without conviction, a man who'd been separated from the safety of his routine.

"Go back inside, take a left," he said, his voice now luminous. "It's the first left before the entrance."

"Why, thank you," she said, her face blushing a hue. "It's been nice talking with you."

He tipped his chin forward in acknowledgement then turned to the cattle below. In the sunlight, his face appeared round, the hair straw-colored. Perhaps I've been too judgmental, she thought.

*****

For a short time, the Steinar brothers had been close friends. When Peter didn't go to college, he spent his days hanging out with Lyle and the younger teens, and on weekends bought them beer which all of them drank until their breaths reeked like rotten eggs and their heads whirled as if caught up in a twister. It was a simple task, acquiring booze for the parties. In the liquor store, Peter would strike up a conversation, mention that his mother died in 198-, and the middle-aged clerk doing the math in his head would figure he was 21 then say melancholically and with a certain bit of resignation, "Hard to believe it was that long ago," and ring up the purchase. So in this matter, Peter extended his own adolescence indefinitely.

As night fell like a black hood in the grove off Visne Road, Peter would toss back swig after swig, let a rush come to his head until some force deep within his body pulsed and all troubles blurred away. Soon he laughed so hard that his breastbone trembled. Still, letting his whims go where they would was a strangely unnatural release to him, like shoveling off top soil – it served no purpose at all, if anything appeared only detrimental – and sometimes this thought gripped him as he circled the bonfire. Yet, he wondered, how does one intentionally not be deliberate?

Sparks leaped from the cackling flames as he shook his head; that was crazy talk, he told himself, like the words in those songs Laura Jean had started listening to. In any case, the next morning, with tongue dry and eyes red, he always performed the chores just as his old man demanded.

When the buzz hit Lyle's head, he'd imagine that the tree branches parting in the wind were some great bird's beating wings. Lyle fancied himself a cowboy during such moments, untethered to all but his freedom, and would hobble about as if he'd just gotten off a horse, trying to determine what the flying creature was tracking. Then he'd tip the beer back again to his lips. In the bonfire's orange light, the bottle appeared strangely tarnished, even bleared. Still, he'd take another gulp, for by drinking he stayed warm despite autumn's encroaching chill, thus defying the hard winter that would come to his range. These digressions into fantasy filled him with the same sense of glory he felt when exiting the locker room at game time, the verdant green field feathery soft beneath his feet, a rosy glow from the setting sun across all of those faces on the bleachers. Ah, revel tonight, he mumbled incoherently to himself, for tomorrow force and surety will be provided for you. The night dew rose into his nostrils as he stumbled away from the party toward the boughs flashing in the moonlight. Taking another sip, the beer's richness lathered his tongue then flowed smoothly down his throat. He had to admit, his brother had good taste when it came to booze.

Peter did not consider the teens his friends. Yet, ironically through both they and the infernal repetition of his father's words, he gained during the three years following high school a new confidence, and he soon strode easily about the fire, it loud as a crowd's roar. One girl always smiled at him, and when they finally made full eye contact, he nodded and stopped in front of her. Her eyes shined a ceramic blue and in the firelight her face a bright pink, but amid his drunken stupor he saw only thick ragged lines. He could not remember Darcie Allen's name at first, knew only that she was a classmate who also had remained in Felton. As they leaned toward one another, she said something about working at the dry cleaners. He was uncertain how Darcie discovered the parties or who there she might know – it were as if she was a shell that drifted ashore to them – but then he shrugged for all were welcome. He liked the way her vanilla scent swirled about him in the wind as if winter's first snowflakes.

Nearly two years passed before Lyle, with parched mouth and hobbled vision, found himself trying to determine whom all of the kids were at the party. They'd grown numerous, like homesteaders flooding in from the East, breaking up the range. Not one of the girls resembled Dusty, who had been sent away to live with an aunt, and as Lascar talked of joining the Marines after graduation in just seven months, Lyle shook his head. Laura Jean's little sister, only in tenth grade, gazed at him from afar, her cheeks glowing

with a certain calm, eyes gentle, but Lyle found her face soft
and unformed, like a young child's. He turned away, stared
at the black sky, then from deep within his pocket, pulled a
powder blue pill and with a swill of beer tossed it into his
mouth. No sooner had it slid down the throat, gritty as if a
tiny stone dissolving in a creek, when from behind he heard
a girl's voice, a silky thread in the night air. "You shouldn't
take pills for headaches when drinking," she said. He spun
about; though slender and dimpled, her mouse brown hair
had been bleached yellow. In the past if she'd done this,
Dusty would have thrown up her arms, and with a wicked
look in the eyes and a shrill voice stood between the two to
defend what little was hers. Heat swelled through him, and
he stared directly into the new girl's face. "The dog who
turns his nose up at the bone loses it to some other mutt,"
he said. A sour musk of breath followed his words. She harrumphed, twirled away.

Peter took Darcie to a couple of dances at the civic center that first year after graduation, went one afternoon with
her to North Platte on a shopping trip. Though Laura Jean
had returned to Felton for a couple of summers, he hadn't
seen her but the one time downtown. Word got around that
she remanded everyone who did not call her "Laurie." At
least in the diminutive she remembered him, he told
himself, had even kept part of what they were. He stored the
warm thought in the forefront of his mind. As another
autumn arrived, Peter stuck with Darcie, did not notice
when her chest and upper arms thickened. But then paunch
showed in her tummy, chin, and finally the hips, and he
could not help but see. Peter never was one to end something, though, especially if uncertain it had ever started, and
one night, as her shirt stretched about a distended waist and
she swayed from the liquor, Darcie fluttered all eyelashes at

him then undid the top three buttons of her shirt so more space between her corpulent breasts showed. He almost slept with her.

With Peter's embrace of Darcie uncertain, though her hands always cupped his shoulders tight, others saw the opportunity to make a move on her. As stumbling about the bonfire one weekend in late October, the air carrying the breath of anyone who spoke, he could not find her, so he instead stepped off into the trees to piss. Hearing a rustle, he glanced up. There she stood with some guy, bodies coiled about one another, their eyes closed and mouths locked together. Pausing, Peter found he did not feel any anger. Then their arms slid tighter, her chicken-claw hand sweeping across his back, his palm caressing her cocked ass. Peter could tell in the moonlight that she was drunk for her face glowed red, like his neck after shaving. Suddenly a sense of relief overcame him, as if a cool breeze had finally arrived on an oppressively hot day. He walked farther on, out of their sight so they would not see or hear him urinate, decided to erase Darcie from his mind just as he no longer allowed himself to think of Laura Jean or of what she might be doing. "You've got to grab on a hold of the earth, make something of her," he told himself as tottering back toward the bonfire, its flames spreading fluidly into the blackness.

Lyle occasionally wondered what had become of Dusty, if she was thinking of college, it she'd found a new boyfriend. He pondered whether she'd recognize him now that his muscular football body had jellied and voice thickened. Some nights when alone, he merely stared at the few dots of distant farm and village lights on the black prairie. At what would become his last party, he drank nearly a 12-pack by himself to prevent any questions from surfacing, then wandered off behind a bush to sleep. Stepping out of sight of the bonfire, his sense of the world shrank, like the yellow of the sun as smoke slowly covers it. Stable as a two-legged stool, he crossed his arms tight about the body, and the stars struck his eyes sharp in the cold night. Out upon the open plain, his hazy eyes could see little in the dark, yet he still heard much – the tire's crackle, absurd bursts of laughter, the quick crushing of an empty beer can – and the incredible loudness surprised him. Shouldn't all be silent at night? Then his foot caught on a hole in the ground, and he fell across the knee-high grass. Working his ankle free, he curled in a ball, let the pain pass as dew soaked his clothes and bare arms. Huddled and still, buried in the darkness, he closed his eyes. It was so simple, he found, to let the reward of gentle slumber converge upon his senses, like pulling a shade to the sill.

Before his consciousness slipped, though, Peter kneeled over him. His older brother's face had grown hard and angular with adulthood, and Lyle saw a hand stretch toward him. The stars quaked overhead. Peter's eyes gazed mournfully, as if he were ready to return home after a great loss, and Lyle took the hand. He found himself rising. At that moment, the youngest of the Steinars realized how much he both loved and hated his brother.

*****

Boards rattled against one another as Peter haphazardly tossed them into a pile behind him.

Time had pulled and warped their pith until the gray flats scratched against his hands like rough bark. Though sweating profusely, Peter did not stop; the guns had to be somewhere, he knew. Straw and wheat husks floated upward as he lifted each board, and his nostrils pinched tight. Reaching the pole barn's dirt floor, he found nothing but a small beetle scampering away once it became exposed to the light. Peter set both hands upon his hips, caught his breath. He'd looked everywhere: the machine shed, the attic, the ashen cellar, even Lyle's and the old man's pickup trucks. The scent of bird shit from the shed's swallow nests hung headily in the air.

Face splotched brownish-green from perspiration and dust, Peter moved on, passing the currant's arched branches and maple-shaped leaves into the sunlight. It shined starkly upon him. In the distance, Lyle's tractor chugged across the field, dragging a wide disk that broke the earth. Peter suspected his brother was behind the guns' disappearance, that he knew something important.

There would be no confrontation about it, though, not yet anyway, he told himself, not until there was something concrete to level at him. Perhaps Lyle had good reason to take them, but Peter anticipated finding them damaged, maybe poorly hidden, and likely there would arise some other unforeseen flaw in his brother's actions that proved their foolhardiness, that showed Lyle first should have come to him.

Peter sauntered toward the grain bins, their silver metal blinding in the full sun. What have you done Lyle, he whispered under his breath, what have you done? A meadowlark scampered into the air as he reached the end of the bins and paused. There was just one place left to look. His sight dimmed upon entering the hay shed where they stored winter feed for the cattle, but as his vision came back, he spotted near the structure's back disturbed straw, its up-turned stems brassy and uneven. He ran to it. His hands pulled away the loose bedding as if hacking away at jungle branches. Particles of dust and hay swirled into his nose, and digging through the sharp-ended stems, he blinked rap-idly. Then his fingers struck hard metal, and from the hole he yanked a barrel. Specks of rust, like blood on black dirt, clung to the cold, slender tube. He could not believe his father was a coward, yet here appeared to be the proof. Peter wondered why his brother – and he was certain now Lyle was behind this – had not taken greater care to hide the guns. The walls around him swam in the heat. He scraped at the straw again, saw ammunition boxes, the wooden stocks, bolts. Bundling them into his arms, he rose, jaw clenched tight. His eyes narrowed as he re-entered the glaring light and headed for the house.

Chapter 20

Like a snow squall rising out of the Rockies, Peter loomed at the new gate leading to the field.

Lyle eyed him briefly while turning the tractor toward the farmyard for refueling then mindlessly followed the seams carved across the earth. Driving in the enclosed cab reminded him of the times as a child that he spent alone in the closet, the door closed, his eyes tracing the slick edges of clothes draped from the hangers. He remained uncertain why being in such a cramped, dark place appealed to him. All about his tractor, the furrows shimmered amid the heat like sea waves.

The cab, though protective, did not entirely remove the elements from his work. There was the sky gathered above the farm, indifferent to his presence, its infinity enough to incite panic. Ahead of him, dust distorted the sun, limiting his vision, but from the rear, light burned through the glass and upon his neck. He understood now his father's anger when as a young boy he'd run into the fields, seeking a ride. If one could not see a little child, he certainly could not hear him above the din, it clamorous as a blizzard at full fury. Lyle's own being conspired against him as well; his belly sat upon the lap like an overstuffed gunny sack, and despite the cab's cooled air, sweat formed along his waist. Still, the swirls of soil from the harrowed fields always reminded him of where and of who he was. He imagined how the acreage would appear next July, the bronze wheat rolling beneath the wind, each stem yielding golden tassels.

Lyle glanced ahead. His brother remained at the gate, towering even larger, though Lyle knew it was he himself who'd come closer. All morning he'd watched Peter dart about the distant farmyard as if a hawk seeking prey over the open plain. Lyle kept calm by diverting his thoughts to what chores still needed to be done: checking on the cattle to make sure there were no sick, readying the machinery for the fall planting, inspecting the water tank to ensure the pastured beasts did not die of thirst. The two days of disking also had delayed their replacing of the combine header, and the part sat in the back of his pickup truck, collecting rust from the previous night's rain. His father could've started the project on his own, but Lyle had drugged his coffee so he wouldn't off himself while alone; Peter, meanwhile, refused to help. The sun peeked from behind a remnant cloud and burned against Lyle's knuckles. He wondered how long it would be before the mill called him, then he thought of Tina Strom's maize-colored hair and her voice, so airy and teasing.

Lyle suddenly looked up, and there stood Peter directly in the middle of the dirt road before the gate, refusing to move though the tractor was barreling down upon him. Lyle's eyes widened into two white moons, and his foot jammed against the brake.

He shifted the machine into park, clambered down from the running tractor. "What the hell you trying to pull?" Lyle shouted. "I alm–"

Peter brandished a gun barrel speckled in orange. "What's this?" he hollered, eyes overcast with anger. "I want an explanation. Now."

Lyle's face turned wan. He stopped a few feet short of his brother.

"I found the guns buried in the hay shed," Peter said. "What's going on?"

"You wouldn't care. Besides, it's nothing you need to be concerned about."

"Two of those guns are mine."

The gate's thin shadows stretched behind Peter. Lyle glanced at the clouds sliding mutely across the sky above them, found the tractor's roar ironically quieting as his stomach churned. Oh hell, he thought, if I tell him I wash my hands of it. He looked at Peter, took a deep breath. "Father tried to kill himself twice when I was around. Once with a razor and another time with a gun. I think when the truck just about hit him that day you two were working on the fence, he was trying then, too."

Peter shook his head, clutched the gun barrel tightly. "If you're lying to me–"

"I don't lie."

"Why would he do something like that?"

"You know what a crazy old coot he can be sometimes."

"Ah, come on, he always talks pessimistically, but underneath he's all optimism."

"You don't have to believe me."

Sweat dribbled down Peter's temples, and he appeared uneasy, as if standing upon a slippery rock. Smoke the color of black bile wheezed out of the tractor's muffler. "Where's he now?"

"In the house. Sleeping."

"I don't believe you."

Lyle scowled, waved him off.

"If you're telling the truth, then why'd you leave him

alone?" Peter said. "And why didn't you tell me?"

Lyle stormed back to tractor. "I need to refuel," he shouted over his shoulder. "Get the hell out of the way."

Inside the cab, Lyle's hands quivered as they clung to the steering wheel of the moving tractor, it loud as a thousand clashing stones, and he drove straight ahead though Peter remained in the way. The muscles of Lyle's mouth screwed tight as thinking about all those years he'd suffered loss of dignity by living in silence. He'd had enough and stomped on the accelerator. Peter scrambled to sidestep him.

*****

Carl Steinar swam in echoes and dancing shadows. Though the shade remained rolled, the sheets of his bed swirled around him like twilight. He thought there was rustling in another room and the attic above, but the walls about him were no longer uniform and sensible, no longer straight in the lines, and he could not tell if it was his own shifting upon the mattress or the real sounds from another world against which the boundaries of his existence had become ambiguous.

Was it noon? His stomach did not ache with hunger as usual, and though white glared from his window, he found himself unable to make out the cast of sunlight upon the trees or even the sky's color.

For a moment, he sensed surrendering was easier than fighting. A dimness settled over him. The walls faded in and out of view. He tried to remain awake, knew there was just one task left to do, then he could sleep, sleep forever, but his vision grew muted, like steam on a mirror, and he could not tell what time of day it was – perhaps morning, but no it must be afternoon – he no longer could hear Lyle working in the fields, could not even feel the breeze gliding through the screen, for all was motionless.

He found himself holding his breath. That was nec-essary, he told himself, and delighted at his first effort of self-restraint since clambering the stairs and collapsing onto his mattress, fully clothed, boots still on his feet, he did not worry at how the bedroom furniture grew increasingly asymmetrical and rounded as each moment passed.

Staring down the barrel of a gun, its cold tip firm against the root of his mouth...he'd been impressed with his son's courage, talking him out of it, such a good boy, always doing what he's told, then slipping pills into the coffee. Per-haps I've underestimated him, Carl Steinar thought, and his mind fluttered.

The pouches beneath his eyes no longer weighed so heavily, he realized, and in the farmhouse's utter quiet he sank away from the tension, like a pebble dropped into a pool, descending from the hot, sunlit surface, the under-currents dissolving his hard exterior as darkness softly sur-rounded him.

Though it lulled him sweetly – like those many mo-ments of so long ago after he'd held Gwen, when he felt as if his whole being were floating within a sublime luminosity, so warm, so peaceful – even now some force in his head re-sisted, called him back to consciousness, to the steadiness of hard earth, to the ground one could walk upon without tear of swamping, for it held up the unbearable weight of being by providing a firmness, a hardness that one could cling to. His eyes flashed open, and he made out the blue of his bed-room walls.

Within moments, the plaster upon them began to splotch then darken and disintegrate, like paper in fire. His mind retreated from the heat. There was no safe place but the deep pool.

He dove back in; the water's plane sparkled above him, but as he slowly descended, the turquoise shimmer grayed.

Who had started the white blaze, he wondered. He peeked above the waves, and seeing, his blood quickened. There was no choice now, he'd have to get rid of her, somehow, maybe any way possible. First, he whispered, I'll regain my strength.

But as Carl began to slip under, he heard his pickup truck leave – or was it a car arriving? – and for a moment his being made one last grasp for the shore. The sand shifted, and soon the sound disappeared into the porousness of memory, then his heart, anxious for slumber, rhetorically asked, "Does it matter so much what is real and what is not?"

The chemicals that had infiltrated Carl's bloodstream, as it a Fifth Column consuming his will in preparation for an invading army, answered, "No, of course not," and his eyes closed, bringing a darkness like that which comes to a midnight room once the lamp is turned out.

At last, while the world moved about him, he lay very still, as if a branch caught against two rocks in a hard current.

*****

Abbie sat on the Steinar's sofa, delighting in how the aster Peter had picked by the creek glided upon her cheek like his sweet breath when he slept beside her. One of his family's many old photo albums lay across her lap; after coming inside to get out of the chafing wind, she'd spotted them beneath the end table, right where they'd been neatly stacked when the couple had cleaned, and she quietly insisted on looking at them. Peter seemed reluctant, then he sat upon the couch next to her, feigning disinterest. "We haven't looked through those in years," he said, attempting to dissuade her.

"You haven't looked at them in years," she said. "I've never seen them at all."

Dust stuck to her fingers then spiraled into the air as she opened the album, its binding creaking like a rusted hinge. On the first pages were yellowed pictures of pioneers standing before a sod house and afterward gradually less brown photographs of stoic-looking men and women, all decked in the tight, wool fashions of the early 1900s.

"Those are our grandparents, our great-grandparents, and our great-greats," Peter said. "They were from Norway."

"You must have a lot of interesting stories to tell about them," she said.

"Ask my father. He knows all the tales."

"He's never told you any?"

Quietness filled the house, as if they were in a vacuum, while Abbie awaited his answer. Peter's eyes turned inward, but sullenness veiled his face. He kept a hand in his right pocket, she noticed, as it there were something inside it that he wanted to show her. Then the fragmentary chugging of the tractor in the field neared and, once it passed the house, descended into the invisible horizon. "There's the old man now," Peter said, pointing to the open album.

She examined the picture, could make out Carl Steinar's high cheekbones, the shape of his thin lips, yet the rest of him rang untrue to the man she knew. The differences went beyond the lanky, teenage frame. For one, his eyes sparkled, even a bit mischievously, she thought, and his mouth remained partially open as if in mid-laugh. It was not a boisterous exclamation, she sensed, but mirthful. One of his hands ran through the short yet unruly hair as he laid on the grass, torso bare. Likely his lover was nearby, maybe even the one who took the photograph as he tilted his head to the side and gazed up at her. Here rested a boy unafraid of the future, one who'd grow into a polite, unpretentious man. She envied the woman who loved him, imagined the elegant clothes she dressed him in, the firm yet silky hands that would caress her, the clean, uplifting scent she would breathe in as grazing his neck. The teen was a younger Peter, she thought, a Peter of another generation.

"He was so handsome," Abbie said, staring at the photograph. Peter grunted under his breath. She turned the page, its plastic sticky and crinkling, found a teenage couple nuzzling one another. With eyes softly closed, both smiled as if sharing some private joke. Her face was sensuous, like the petal of a lady's slipper, while his was smooth, an unwrinkled, youthful Carl Steinar. They both wore blue, he a button shirt, she a light sweater. "Is this your mother?" she said.

He nodded, a bit despondently, she thought.

Abbie turned through a few more pages, but her mind lingered upon the pictures of Peter's father. She saw his now decrepit body as fresh and masculine, like a field full of blooming lavender. "Why did he never remarry?"

"That old skinflint?" Peter said as chuckling. "Who would have him?"

Her eyes widened as she half-gasped. "Peter!"

He leaned back, hands clasped behind his neck. "The old bastard'll live forever. They all do around here. There's something in the air or water."

"Losing a wife had to be hard on him."

"Who wasn't it hard on?"

"I'm sorry – I shouldn't have asked about remarrying. Not very tactful."

He waved her off, shook his head. "It has nothing to do with you."

"What are you angry about then?"

He paused, as if lost in thought. "My old man...he advances his own interests by appearing to serve mine."

Her brow wrinkled, then she nudged him with an elbow. "He sounds like a regular old politician. Looks as if you need a news reporter around to help you handle him."

Peter glared at her.

"Well, if he's so bad," she said, "where's his braggadocio? He's humble as they come."

He raised an eyebrow as his lips creased. "You just don't understand."

"No, I don't."

Peter sat quietly, stared off into space.

"You're not going to explain it to me, are you?" she said.

Suddenly he stood and grabbed her arm. "Let's get out of here. I can't breathe in this place, not anymore."

Yanked upward, the photo album slipped from her lap. As she scampered to keep up with his pulling arm, the aster flitted into the air.

*****

Peter and Abbie stared at one another from across her kitchen table as the wind outside raked the earth like sharp talons. He remained uncertain what to say, knew that any single misspoken word, even the very tone of his voice, might crack the fissure between them so wide that it could not be bridged. Unable to stand the sounds of Lyle's tractor or her curiosity about the aged photographs, he'd hurriedly left the farm; Abbie followed in her car, only got his voice mail on the cell phone, and when they arrived at her place, she met him in the driveway with a creased forehead. He did not speak as the wind tousled their hair. Inside, she heated a pot of coffee and offered a plate of gingersnaps. They talked of how good the thins tasted despite being store-bought, of how cold the weather was supposed to turn over the next few days. But Peter ate very little, rationalized it by telling himself that he did not want to be sticky-fingered when he pulled the ring from his pocket and presented it to her.

Abbie sensed his anxiety. "I won't press you to tell me what's wrong," she said, cupping both hands around a full mug of coffee so it warmed her palms. He liked the way she broke a narrow piece off the cookie by pressing it against the plate, as if folding a piece of paper, then daintily picking up the morsel with her two fingers and inserting it betwixt her lips. Steam rose from the cup as sunlight glimmered through the window upon her.

A bead of sweat rose above Peter's lip, and for a moment his eyes cast away from her. He thumbed the bantam ring in his jean pocket then pinched it between his fingers, brought it out. "I have something for you," he said.

Extending an arm across the table, his hand unfurled as if parting clouds revealing a star. The ring stood out in his shadowed palm, the multi-faceted, square diamond glimmering. He shifted his hand only slightly so that the stone caught the full sparkle of sunlight. Though tiny in his palm, she knew upon her own diminutive finger it would be enormous. Her face tilted to one side, and she leaned closer to examine it. The metal and marquee smelled of mothballs, yet it shined as if a jeweler had just pulled it from a glass case.

She drew back slightly. "I couldn't–"

Peter nudged it toward her. "Go ahead, try it on."

Abbie said nothing for a moment then smiled albeit briefly. "Well, okay." She fastidiously slid it onto the tip of her third finger, over the knuckle, then snug against the digit's base. The ring fit comfortably, like it had been sized specifically for her. She held her right hand up to the window's light, and for a moment her eyes glistened as if sunlight reflecting off water.

"It's on the wrong hand. Don't you think?"

Her mouth twisted slightly.

"It's an engagement ring. I'm asking you to marry me."

Her face turned white as quartz. She could tell by the nervous crackle in his voice that he meant what he said.

Abbie looked away from him, and her head dipped as both eyes closed. She rubbed her forehead, and for a moment Peter thought he heard her mutter something. Though Abbie's black hair glowed as sunlight streamed warmly across her cheek, he knew the other side of her face was dark. The coffee between them began to sour with cold. At last, she turned back to him. Her face curdled, and yanking the ring off, she pushed it back toward him then shook her head.

Peter fought back a frown as the band sat between them. Unlike the guns, he knew exactly where his grandmother Vann's ring had been kept in the boxes haphazardly piled about the attic, went there after confronting Lyle and as their father slept yet again. Peter could not help but forgive Abbie for trying to bring him and his father together; her intentions were good if not misguided. She cared for him, really loved him, had proved it unlike Laura Jean or Darcie Allen, both of who remained with him only so long as they found it personally satisfying. Abbie had shown her loyalty. As digging through a box in the attic's dark corners, the odor of old dust heavy, all he could think was, "Now I will make my ultimate gesture of love to her." But now...

But now he found his fists, hidden under the table, could not squeeze tight enough. "I'm not good enough for you?" he said.

Abbie's mouth dropped. "Do you know what you're even saying? You ought to listen to yourself sometime."

"I was listening to myself when I decided to give you the ring. Look where that got me."

"Do you think a diamond is all it takes to sweep me off my feet? You've got a lot to learn about people."

"Well, you would know – you've been all around the world."

Abbie stared at a corner of the room and arms folded, shook her head. "Most of the time, you don't even talk. You just close up, like a clam," she said, her voice firm. "No, like a lifted rock dropped back to the ground – except there's something hidden beneath it, something you don't want anyone to see. What is that, Peter? What is it you don't want anyone to see? Your pain?"

"Showing off your learning with a clever metaphor, are you, Abbie? Just back off, okay?"

She threw her hands half into the air, ground her teeth. "Look, I want to get serious with you, but we've only been dating for how long? Seven weeks? And we've already broken up and had how many fights during that time?"

Peter leered at her. What in the hell is it with this girl that I can't get her into the palm of my hand, he asked himself. He swooped the ring from the table, and his chair spun out from under him as he rose then stormed out, slamming the front door shut. For a moment outside, he leaned against his pickup truck, the heat from the sun reflecting off its red surface, and thought of how she'd rejected him. His heart pumped faster, and the back of his throat turned dry. What seemed like such a good idea a few miles back was now a disaster. He stuffed the ring in his pocket, got into the truck.

As Peter started it, his hands trembled.

Chapter 21

The instant Peter's truck passed the screen of yard trees, he spotted his father watching sternly from the porch, body stiff, eyes unwavering. The young man's breathing quickened as the pickup's tires crackled to a stop over the driveway's gravel, and he nervously rubbed his face, bearded with a day's growth of bristles. He wondered if the old man knew about the ring. Peter fingered it in his pocket; despite pressing against his thigh the entire night, the small gold loop remained cold. There was nothing to do now, he told himself, but approach his father and go inside. Stepping from the cab, he swallowed hard then blinked twice to awaken his eyes, splintered with the red of broken capillaries.

"Well, Old Man, you don't have anything to worry about anymore," Peter said as he trudged up the porch's wooden steps. "Abbie and I have broken up, for good this time."

Carl grasped his son's arm above the elbow, held it firmly. "I don't take too kindly to being called 'old man.'"

Peter's lips curled. "And I don't take too kindly to you always telling me what to do."

"What I say is for your own good."

"Is it now?"

"And I don't like how you're talking back to me right

now."

Peter jerked an arm, and as he broke away his father stumbled back. "I'm not a little child anymore," Peter said. "You no longer can speak to me in that tone."

Carl half-gasped. "On my farm," he said, the blush of his cheeks reappearing with each word, "I will speak to anyone I want in any tone I like."

Peter crossed his arms, stared at him. "Is there anything else you want to say?"

"No, there isn't."

"Then I reckon we're done talking to one another." He spat on the porch and swung the screen door open. Its hinges shrieked, then the wood, striking the door frame, clattered as the mesh upon its window rippled.

Though he and Abbie had cleaned the house only a few days before, dirty plates, their multicolored stains like thick smudges of watercolor upon a canvas, already were piled in the sink. Lyle, his arms filthy with red dust, eyed him haughtily from the living room but remained quiet. Heading up the cavernous steps, Peter clung to the loose railing. At the top, a dim glow, diffuse as a phantom's luminescence, flowed upon the walls, and wind buffeted against the hall window while outside gray clouds slowly thickened into a single mass. A cold blue norther was on the way.

The jumbled sheets of an unmade bed greeted Peter as he entered his room and collapsed upon the mattress. He laid there for several long hours, unable to slip into sleep, thinking alternately of his father grasping his arm on the porch and Abbie pushing the ring back toward him as shaking her head. Outside, the sky turned crimson with twilight; neither his father nor Lyle called once for him through the day. Soon, the night sprawled before him like a raven stretching its wings, and he breathed with great difficulty, weak as a small animal with a broken limb. When sleep did occur, it was brief and ended in a sweat-soaked pillow. He spent much of the long, fitful hours staring at his clock, the red lines of its numbers mocking him, making time move only slower.

Through this, he thought of memory, of how his recollections gathered like fallen leaves, then irretrievably scattered as the wind blew over them, only to converge again, newly arranged and mixed with the leaves of other trees in dozens of mounds elsewhere. He knew that likewise his memories somehow also had changed and could even vaguely trace over the years their subtle progressions. At first they appeared gray and amorphous, then more clear but clicking swiftly past – as if an image in a kaleidoscope – and finally growing still though so resplendent that the edges blurred. And what of those memories I've lost, Peter asked himself, of the half-torn leaves carried so far upon the wind that they never are seen again? I must hold on to this one place, to this one time, he told himself, must keep the shadows at bay. But soon he no longer could tell if the images flashing through his mind were dreams or memories. All he knew was a mist, its background a hazy yellow, and he standing, silhouetted upon the embankment, staring at the clear, shifting spring water. He kneeled, dipped his hand into the current to see if it was warm enough for swimming. It was not, so he stepped into it fully clothed. The creek soaked his jeans and within seconds began filling his boots. He waded downstream, beneath a canopy of leaves, his body reeking of fish and algae, of wild water, then leaned forward and broke into a dog paddle, intent upon his destination. Suddenly he no longer could remember what he searched for, and glancing over his shoulder, saw a younger version of himself lagging behind him, and then a yet smaller him trailing that figure.

He swerved to face them, and in his haste a gulp of water filled the mouth. There were dozens of him, all connected as if an accordion, stretching back to the point where he'd stepped into the water. He whirled about, and his eyelids slammed shut at the blinding light of a form gliding through the mist.

Soon the walls began to purple, and he knew sunrise was not far off. He remembered that old cliche his father used to recite, "A quitter never wins, and a winner never quits," supposed he should feel that way now. But what about someone who never tries at all, he speculated. Why bother in the first place – there is so much to lose. Still, he knew what one might gain almost always overshadowed that. He rolled over, stared outside as the growing light of dawn revealed the windmill's shimmering iron bars. No promises ever were made to either Abbie or his father, Peter told himself, only implied. He rose and pulled the shade. Dust flitted from the roller. As he dropped back onto the bed, the windmill blades whirled, its rhythm unpredictable like a jazz improvisation, and he wished it would cease. His jaw tightened as he thought of how Abbie had spurned him. He wouldn't apologize, no not to her. It was insulting not only to me but to the grandmother who once wore the ring and to all those who before me carried my name, he whispered to himself, it dishonored every one of them. And my damn brother, and my god-damned father – they made me angry so I couldn't help but lose my cool; that's why Abbie rejected me – if I'd just been in a good mood, been my usual self, she'd have accepted. Veins bulged along his temple as both eyes darkened. I should have confronted the old bastard about his suicides, he whispered, exposed Lyle for the liar he is. Anger slowly slithered inside him until it filled his great hollowness and hardened.

*****

Lyle thought himself fortunate that he did not have much to pack. All of his personal possessions fit into a milk crate; he had never wanted too much or tried too hard to obtain anything. He rolled a shirt, placed it at the crate's bottom. Once gone, he told himself, there'd be no more dealing with his brother – the gall of Peter to think he'd been lying! – and no more being pulled in two directions by his father.

The wind hummed vaguely, as if a mist covering the moon. Only the hard steps of his work boots punctuated the hazy murmur, and he cast an eye upon them, saw the dry calf shit across the toe. Sure, the mill job didn't pay well, he thought to himself, but I'm a good mechanic, know how to keep things running; later, I can get work doing that. His heart surged at the recollection of that morning when the mill manager had called, and after a few questions, informed him that he could start Monday – if he wanted.

Lyle wondered where he'd live. He supposed in Felton, maybe in Joe Audun's house itself, and if nothing was available, his pickup truck would do fine for a while. The curtains billowed peacefully, like how he remembered a wisp of his mother's hair fluttering across her eyes in the warm, light breeze; he wasn't certain if they really were her strands, but the image welled from so deep inside that he thought they had to be.

He picked up a browned piece of paper filled with a child's handwriting and the crumbling remains of a quashed beetle taped to it. In smooth, perfectly curved and connected red letters were the words "Please see me at recess about this." During fourth grade, his class studied insects, had to write a report on them. He didn't know what to say. So, the night before it was due, he ambled to the pole shed and found a bug crawling up a wooden support beam; crushing its hard shell, he taped it to the paper and wrote "beetel" beside it. The next morning, all bright-eyed when turning the report in, he told the teacher, "I bashed it with my own hand, brought it down like it were a rock, broke its back." All through elementary school, he had rarely looked up when others spoke to him, and when his eyes did glance their way, he'd lean back in his chair as if to maintain a safe distance. Perhaps his fortunes were now changing, he thought to himself. But when she'd handed back the paper with her note, he knew there was no pleasing anyone.

Then, he heard his father's approaching steps, firm against the stairs, not scraping as they had been most of those past few weeks. Lyle steadied himself, would not be dissuaded, vowed there'd be no more shit on his shoes. His father loomed in the doorway.

"Son, what are you doing?"

His eyes tightened. "I'm on to you, Dad. You won't try anything so long as I'm not around. At first, I thought you would, but now I know better. Peter doesn't believe you'd try killing yourself, and if you really wanted to get away with it, all you'd have to do is try when just he was around."

Lyle brushed past him, but Carl grabbed an arm, firmly at first to wrench him into place, then the grip loosened, turned gentle and benevolent like a mother's warm hand upon her infant.

"I'm not certain what you're up to," Lyle said, "but it doesn't matter now. I'm free of it."

His old man let go, leveled desperate eyes upon him. "I'll give you the farm, Son."

Lyle's jaw fell crookedly. "What?"

"You've proven your loyalty to me, to the Steinar name;

you saved me twice, hid the guns. Now someday it'll be your children standing upon the porch, looking out at the wide open plain, and it'll be their farm, too, yours and theirs alone."

Lyle backed into his room, and his stony face twitched like a bull unsure if it should charge. He set the crate down.

*****

Lyle paused for a moment, his lips faltering. Finally he drew in a deep breath. "I've taken a job at the mill. "

Carl's mouth twisted anemic ally; the announcement stung, as if ice splashed into his face by an errant wind. One must keep his promises, he knew, and the contract, even if only verbal, was sacred. Yet, did he also not have an obligation to his wife, to his family name? Blood rushed to his head; I must keep moving, he told himself, must keep Lyle here, to bide time. "Go ahead and work it for now – but you'll need to do your chores around here as well," he said. "There's no shirking one's duties."

Lyle nodded. A moment of uncertain silence passed between them. "Why are you doing this, Dad?"

Carl resisted his hand's urge to tremble. "Is it not enough to simply accept? Why are you angry?"

"This isn't what you wanted."

He shook his head as both eyes sunk mournfully. "Your brother has been unfaithful."

Lyle's brow wrinkled. "You always favored him over me. "

"He always was the one to rebel, who never did what he was told – would run into the fields when he was supposed to be watching you, would go down to the creek when there were chores to do, would tell lies after I told him not to – I had to find a way...a way to make him love–"

"No, Dad."

"–you always did what I asked."

"Dad–"

"He saw her car, saw how her blood spoked across the windshield. You were too young to see, too young to know."

"He at least had her, for a few years. "

"It was better to not have. You can't miss something you've never had, not truly. You can long for it – but your understanding of it is perfect in so many ways: there aren't any flaws between you and her, aren't any regrets of what should have been said, what could have been done."

Lyle's mouth quivered. "This isn't like you, Dad. You're hallucinating – it's those pills–"

"He's always blamed me, Son – that's why he stays away so long." Carl covered his eyes with an arm, fought back a soft sniffle with his sleeve. It was best to let it drip, he decided, better to appear unkempt than weak, and removed his arm. He found the light from Lyle's window blinding. "You, though, you and I, we understand loyalty." Carl's arms opened wide. "We know the value of hard work...of never arguing because families must stick together...of not telling our troubles.

No one knows what I've tried to do – you've kept it secret, even from your own brother. We're men of the land, we understand how what a man does to the earth tells the world who he really is. I'd always hoped your brother would be that way, too, and for a while, I thought he was. Then she came along–" His hands rolled into fists as he shivered.

Lyle did not move. "Dad, you're frightening me."

"She would have been 41 this autumn. Did you know that? She was just 23 when she died. I'm the same age – can you believe it? I don't look it. I don't feel it. My bones, they rattle like they're 61, like they're ancient. I am all dust–"

Carl gazed toward the heavens, saw the bulge of old

paint upon the ceiling's edges where air bubbles had burst and flaked away. Lyle stepped toward him, hesitantly.

"There is not much time left for me," Carl said. "I don't have the strength any more. Not even a marble statue can last; it has to succumb to rain and wind, too. You've seen the statue of Mathias Sutherland in the town square, haven't you, seen how he's discolored, how erosion has smoothed the ends of his coat?"

"Don't talk that way, Dad."

Carl gazed at his son. He examined Lyle's eyes, they gentle beneath the short-cropped hair. The boy stood tall and gaunt.

"My Son," Carl said, "you are so strong. I remember years ago how you handled the suicide of that girl you were with – what was her name? – it doesn't matter."

"She didn't die."

"And neither did you. No, you fought it. You handled the pain, didn't let it handle you! Son, you do love the land, don't you? Aren't you warmed by the bright, languid fields when the wheat is up?"

Lyle nodded.

"And your brother – do you see how he despises it? He always preferred the creek, it so untamed. And you do see how he hates me – and you, too – because we are of the land?"

Carl stretched a hand toward his son. Lyle glanced at the floor, bootprints breaking the dust across it, then his own hand reached outward, slowly but with an ever-increasing certainty, until firmly grasping the old man's.

"There's just one thing," Lyle said. "How will we get Peter to leave?"

*****

As blackness fell outside and the tavern filled with

farmers, mill workers and assorted riffraff, Abbie stared at the plate window bowing from the forceful wind and wondered how the glass withstood the constant pressure. The bartender bantering with two cowhands paid it no heed, acted as if it were an everyday occurrence. Yet that's exactly how disasters happen, she thought, when nobody's paying any attention. All about her, dim light covered the crowd as their feet shuffled across the sticky floor. A nearby couple sat hunched upon stools, their bar rail-kissing elbows propping them up, his mouth coiled into a half-snarl, her eyes seemingly hollowed out. Not so long ago, Abbie had turned to Peter and pointed at the same sullen pair. "They'll probably end up naming their kids after their favorite beers," she had said.

Peter chuckled, slid a hand about his perspiring bottle. He was strangely refreshing, Abbie thought, a man so like how her father used to be. They each sipped from their long necks. She decided to ask him.

"Peter, do you ever feel...betrayed?"

His eyes widened. "Betrayed? What do you mean?"

"Well, like you have been cheated – by someone very important, someone very special to you–" Then she paused, uncertain herself what she meant. Peter's gaze turned toward the television above the bar as his eyes grew mournful. Abbie's brow crinkled, and she fondled his hair. "What's wrong?"

He steepled his fingers, focused even more intently on the television. Then his lips parted. "Cheated – oh yes. All too often."

She smoothed Peter's forehead to ease the tension then hooked a heel into the rung of his barstool and rubbed an ankle against his. He shifted toward her so their arms touched. She smiled; his face no longer was flat, no longer obtuse.

The plate glass window arched again as the bartender stepped in front of Abbie. He eyed her like she didn't belong there. "Waiting for the Steinar boy?" he said as wiping the counter though it was dry.

She nodded.

He moved on. As the waning sun cast an oblique patch of light against the bar's dark wall, Abbie wondered what Peter had seen that night when he looked at the television. She gazed at it. The Nebraska Cornhuskers football team scampered about, red hominids upon a green plain. She looked down, caught sight of a farmhand, his hair drooping and clothes splotched like the coat of a mongrel. You never see any of these guys adjusting their jeans or shirts, never combing their hair so that every strand is perfectly in place, she thought; out here, people just let things be. He was alone – why, all of them at the bar were alone, and then it struck her odd that the bartender would ask why she also was – as if a woman in a bar by herself was wrong.

The farmhand glanced up from his bottle. For a moment, their eyes locked. Her cheeks reddened, and she quick looked away. The glass window trembled once more, but then she wondered if it was merely the tendons of her own face.

The second she'd smiled at Peter that night, he wrapped an arm around her waist, pulled her in tight. She nudged a breast against him, and as their hands interlocked, they squeezed fingers. Despite the crowd's noise, she heard only his breathing, slow and gentle as a stream's flow, as if she were gliding atop a restless rhythm. Her chin nestled against his frame, then she ran a hand through his hair. "I can't believe how soft and thick it is," she said. A stomping version of "Little Liza Jane" cried from the speakers, and she twirled off the barstool. "Spin me once around the dance floor, okay, cowboy?" she said. Peter nodded, tenderly took her palm, and face beaming led her across the wooden floor.

An intense heat burned upon Abbie's neck, breaking the reverie, and she glanced over her shoulder. The farmhand stood mere inches away. "What?" she said, grinning self-consciously.

"You," he said. "You're very beautiful. "

She looked down at her beer, hid a crimson face. Yellowed eyes concentrated on her, and though both of his arms remained at his side, she could see sweat rings emanating from the pits of his white T-shirt.

"I'm waiting for someone," she said.

His mouth dropped. "But you were smi–" he started, then taking a half-step back he snorted.

The heady stink of tobacco smoke spun between them. "This is no place for a woman to be alone," he said and shaking his head walked away.

Abbie shrunk in upon herself, then she peeked over a shoulder to see if he was watching. "Can't be too careful around some of those farmhands – you never know where they've drifted in from," she'd once overheard Cary Sutherland say to a woman who'd told him that items were missing from her house and that the thefts had began shortly after her husband picked up new hired help. Abbie's eyes widened as she crossed her arms; was this the same man? Damn you Peter Steinar, she thought, if you actually were here, none of this would be happening. Just what is wrong with you, getting mad at me when I was trying to help, when I was trying to bring you...happiness? The corners of her eyes tensed, and she glanced around for the farmhand, didn't see him. This fight between Peter and his father was ridiculous, she thought, nothing more than male stubbornness and pride once more at work. Her temples pulsed.

Why, Peter was no better than any of those boys I dated in high school or college, was no better than my own father! They both took something from me that I loved – that I needed – and destroyed it. She rose from the barstool, her teeth grinding, headed for the exit.

Outside, breath swirled from her mouth into the night. A single footstep fell from behind, and she paused. Spinning about, she saw no one, only the tavern's silhouette, black and solid. A wave of heat ran through her body. Abbie picked up her pace, but as the wind punctuated the dark, she couldn't tell if the steps were merely echoes of her own feet. I can't look around again, she thought, or he'll realize that I know he's there and will break into a run for me. Her knees shook. I can buy time – maybe enough time – if I don't let him on to me. A long shadow fell across the dim light of the parking lot's lone lamppost as the wind suddenly roared loud like a waterfall. Her legs weighed heavily, seemed to move no closer to the car than if they were fettered. "This is no place for a woman to be alone," he'd said. She thrust a hand into her purse, franticly dug for keys.

Sweat beaded along Abbie's forehead as she made the last extended steps to her car. The keys tumbled, and missing the opaque lock she slammed a point against the car frame. Her stomach lurched. Then, surprising even to herself, she found the hole and with a twist popped the door open. As her chest labored for breath, she slid into the car, knees scraping the handle, slammed down the lock. Thrusting the key into the ignition, she turned it. Sweat dripped into an eye, and her vision blurred as she gunned the car in reverse. Gravel spun from beneath the tires. She gripped the steering wheel tight, peeled out of the lot, and her lungs rasped heavily as she regained her breath. Glancing in the rear view mirror, only darkness and the rapidly shrinking light of the bar's lamppost appeared. Flames of anger coiled then burst in her. This is no place for a woman to be alone, that drifter had said. How dare he make me feel afraid, Abbie whispered. A bitter taste filled her mouth; she vowed to show them. She would go for the heart, go out with Peter's brother, just a single date, to send him a message he'd not forget. Her jaw clenched, and shaking slowly, she drove into the black abyss.

Chapter 22

A dull primrose stripe fell across the chilled sky as the Steinar children chased one another about the cemetery and Carl stared solemnly at his wife's tombstone. He visited the grave irregularly for her death left a hole inside him that by growing each year threatened to surpass his very form and consume him. That could not happen, he'd decided, so it was best to leave her rest. When Carl did go, however, the boys always came along. Not wanting them to cry, he'd allow the pair to play and run about the boot hill; such insolence on sacred ground was the price to pay for hardening their characters so they one day could survive the Plains. He gazed out at the barbed wire lining three sides of the grassy patch and the unbroken vista of red field stretching beyond. He'd give his farm, even years of his life, to have her back but knew that never could be, for as he often told his sons, "Once a wind has fallen, a new gust must take its place."

Suddenly he felt Peter tugging at the hem of his barn coat. "Father, I'm cold," he said.

"Run along now," Carl said, looking down upon him. "Go play with your brother."

Peter ignored the instructions, leaned into him as if to collect body warmth. The wind blew in crests and troughs across the gray stones and wheat stems, and the little boy gazed ahead. Before him stood an unadorned granite block. He read it: GWENDOLYN STEINAR, BELOVED WIFE OF CARL STEINAR, OCT. 14, 196-, MAY 2,199-.

As if soaked from a cold rain, he shivered. There were no flowers on his mother's grave, yet it seemed to him that bouquets and wreaths lay on virtually all the others. He tried to recall how the flowers she once planted in front of the house looked; he saw pale, saffron blossoms with orange lobes on their lower lips, but the image remained tinted and blurred, as if a browned, out-of-focus photograph. Then he remembered their breakfasts, of how her homemade jellies and jams – plum, chokecherry and wild grape – lathered his buttered toast, remembered her lush desserts of green apple, gooseberry and raisin pies. His face winced, and tears slunk from the eyes, the first trickles of a fractured dam.

Carl shifted unevenly, then he firmed but for a second only to sigh. His hand cupped Peter's head, pressed him against the hip. The boy's hair felt silky as a head of wheat. "Come on, don't cry," he said. "Big boys buck up."

Across the cemetery, a grinning Lyle goose stepped his way over a plot, and coming upon a low tombstone, examined the obstacle. He placed his tiny hands upon its top and with an *oomph* lifted himself The granite's pebbled surface pressed unevenly against his palms and then a kneecap as a leg rose to gain position on the edge. A cold wind, the thick odor of grain left to rot on the prairie floor aloft it, struck his frame, but he paid it no attention. Atop the headstone on his knees, he stood cautiously. Laughing with glee, he turned about to face his father and exclaim his glory.

Lyle's chin suddenly contorted with jealousy. He saw his father holding Peter tight to the waist, heard the solemn wrench of his brother's cry. "What's wrong?" he shouted over the frigid bursts. "Father, what's wrong with Peter?"

Carl's exposed fingers stung as his boy's tears slid upon them, and he found his own frame – huge and thick, slightly hunched – quickly contracting.

"Father?" Lyle shouted again.

The whole world spun about Carl Steinar, and he could not muster the energy to suppress the sensation. His temples etched deep with lines, he looked like shattered glass. He remembered her face, it soft like a rose petal. The image repeated in his head as he lightly clutched the seams of his own trousers. The old man thought himself hanging out over an abyss, in that moment of hovering before the descent. His chest tightened, and as the grief erupted, it crushed him. He pushed his son aside. "Buck up, now. There'll be no crying or we'll go, do you hear?"

Peter choked back a tear, turned tight-lipped as his father's voice bounded over him. Salt clung in the corners of the boy's eyes. He nodded.

Lyle called again, his louder voice now crackling. "Father?!"

Eyes hardened, Carl pointed accusingly at him. "And you shut up! We don't holler in a place like this. Keep it up and we'll never come back here again. Understand?"

Lyle sunk deep into his coat, and his breathing turned thin and faint.

Then Carl looked away and caught the distant scent of cattle being butchered, the salt of their blood thick in the air.

*****

As ribbons of darkness shifted upon the morning sky, Peter found himself growing hungry for the first time in several days. He entered the Chuck Wagon Café after leaving the hardware store, took a seat by the window and stared out. The open blinds formed thin lines across his view. A waitress brought coffee, and he contemplated asking her for pen and paper to write his father a letter but settled on just a menu. He didn't know what to write anyway. As waiting, his stomach ached from the smell of buttered toast in the booth next to him. "I'll find a job, just like Lyle," he thought to himself. "Then I'll move off the farm. I'm done with them. I work and I work, even love what I do, but they'll never treat me as an equal. I'm done with them and all they stand for."

The waitress arrived with his breakfast, and he ate the eggs heartily, then the hash browns, and finishing the pot of coffee asked for another. Outside, lightning zigzagged across the distant horizon like a crack upon a windowpane. He worked on a stack of pancakes as Cornelius Skerry entered the restaurant and who upon spotting him ambled over.

"Well, Peter my boy, how are you?" Cornelius said as sidling into the booth's empty seat. He stunk of stale sweat. "You're the first Steinar I've seen in days – I'm starting to think none of you love me anymore. Normally I wouldn't mind, but business is slow this time of year; it unfortunately gives me a lot of time to think. How's that old man of yours doing?"

The waitress delivered Peter his bill, and Cornelius tapped the coffeepot so she'd bring another.

"Menu, too?" she said, and he nodded.

"You haven't seen my father in days?" Peter said.

"He can't be too busy, either, with you and your brother on the farm. Started planting yet?"

"Two days ago. My father's fine. In days, you said?" He rose, set a ten on the table. "I'm sorry to cut this short, but I've got to take care of something important."

"I understand. That old bastard has always got you two boys running. Just tell 'em I miss him, and if he doesn't stop by soon, I'm getting myself a new girlfriend."

With urgency, Peter headed toward Aunt Amita's shop at street's end. The wind swirled, increasingly dissonant as purpled clouds coalesced atop a glaring white horizon. He still didn't have the answer to why his brother had buried the guns, and thinking of Lyle almost running him over with the tractor, his hands curled into tight fists. He'd find out what was going on, god damn it.

As he entered Amita's store, the bell above the door rang. Tables of glassware, lamps, horse statuettes, pots, old books and hollowware spread before him. Peter thought of all the floors he'd swept and shelves he'd dusted there. His heart relaxed but only momentarily.

"Why, Peter!" Amita exclaimed. She ambled out from behind the cash register, arms half open to him. "This is a surprise!"

"My father," he said, "have you noticed anything strange about him? Has he said anything odd to you?"

Worry filled Amita's eyes as her brow wrinkled. "No," she said slowly. "Why do you ask?"

"How about my brother?"

"I haven't talked to him in weeks. Why? What's wrong?"

"They're acting strange. Both of them."

She smiled teasingly. "Well, I suppose from their point of view, you're the one acting strange."

"What do you mean?"

"Having a new girlfriend and all. I suspect that's mighty odd to them. One of the three musketeers isn't paying that much attention to the other two anymore."

"Abbie and I aren't going out."

Her brow rose. "What do you mean?"

"We broke up. A couple of days ago."

"Over what? If you don't mind me asking."

"I asked her to marry me."

Her mouth fell in a half-gasp. "Why, you two've only known each other for a couple of months."

Peter shrugged. He could not shake the memory of Abbie's face, it framed in wind-blown hair and white collar, propped up by an elbow upon the bar railing, the sepia-hued eyes gazing at him as if there were no one more important in the whole world. She'd titter as listening to him talk, and his words gathered a confidence with each spoken syllable, nearing the boisterous by the end of his story. His father's reprimands and warnings of how Steinar men did not brag tempered him, though, and for a moment as sipping his beer he thanked the old man, for her attention remained locked upon him, the slight smile still bordering on ecstasy even after all he'd said. He wanted to lean into her, inhale the wild rose scent of her neck, let their beings entwine.

Peter glanced about the store. It smelled so familiar, of camphor and oatmeal, and he thought of that day in first grade when he came to the store and could count to eleven, of how he wanted to make change, and she let him while a customer smiled bemusedly as he slowly added up aloud each coin and handed it out. None of her children ever cared that much about the store; they were like their father, always taking everything for granted. Soon it was as if he, a mere nephew, stood as her last hope.

He still trusted her as well.

"When growing up," he said with a hesitant sigh, "you never spoke much of my mother."

Amita glanced at the floor, as if she were stepping over broken glass. "Your father didn't want me to."

"He told you not to?"

"Of course not – and if he had, I'd have put him in his

place. But Carl has a way of speaking without saying a word."

"So why didn't you say something, anything?"

"Because it was for the best. Maybe not for you boys but for him. And ultimately what was best for him was good for Lyle and you."

"I don't understand."

"He needed to get over her. My sister was sweet, God bless her soul, but my brother-in-law – your father – always idolized her, made her out to be something bigger than she really was. That's true love, I suppose."

She looked away, longingly. Outside, the sky shined dully, like the color of tin, as wind pressed against the glass pane. Peter sensed that snow would come early this year, could feel the deep chill settling upon the Plains. He gazed at his aunt. Her wavy black hair of days past had grayed considerably, and wrinkles he'd never noticed before were spread across her face. He thought of how the framed photograph in the living room forever froze his mother's soft and fair complexion.

"Do you remember me telling her 'I love you'?" he said.

"No – how would I remember?" Then, looking at him, her eyes wilted with sympathy. "Oh, Peter, I'm sure you did, many times."

"A storm's brewing. A bad one."

Amita shifted unevenly. "Peter, I'm sorry that I got involved with you and your father when Abbie asked me to. I usually don't do such things, but...well, she was right you know."

Peter canted his head away from her. "I best be going home before the snow starts to fall." He turned for the door.

*****

As dusk's coppery light fell across the sky, leaving only

a wisp of blue dissolving like tobacco smoke, Lyle let his mind file through all of the improvements and changes that the farm needed. First he'd replace each plank gate with a shiny red metal one, ones that actually lasted. The glimmer of Tina Strom's smile, half-covered in the orange glow, distracted him momentarily, but he did not turn to fully look at her as his pickup headed up Highway 83 toward North Platte. After the gates, he'd build a new machine shed, one with cement floors, and maybe install a heater for the winters and ceiling fans for the summers.

She brushed a hand against him. Lyle glanced at his date, admired how her hair sprawled richly about thin shoulders as she sat there, lightly poised. He allowed his eyes to linger then, as if about to fall into sleep's lulling arms, relaxed. She smiled back with round lips. In the face of such beauty, he wondered, how could anyone be cruel? It was not so much the fair complexion but her devotion that de-served a man's loyalty, he thought. He shook his head. His brother didn't deserve what their old man offered. Lyle also knew he would have to rise to new heights of mountainous effort just to maintain the farm. He thought of the past when nothing that his brother worried about had bothered him. Just last week, Peter had whined about how the algae-infested water tank in the pasture needed cleaning. Lyle merely shrugged, answered, "It's doing the job." He understood that attitude would have to change now.

Perhaps Tina could be part of this new order, he told himself. During the first few days of his job at the mill, they always waved at one another with twinkling eyes. Co-workers began mentioning that since Lyle started, Tina was coming back into the granary more frequently, but he said nothing in response to them. Then, at week's end, when Lyle picked up his first paycheck, the scent of spring water wound up from Tina's wrist as she handed the envelope to him. "So, how you going to spend it?" she said. He opened the envelope, saw "$210.18" typed then out below his name spelled out, and his eyes widened into two full moons at how much it was for he'd never possessed so much money. His father always had handled that aspect of the farm. "I don't right know how," he said. A tuft of bangs stuck out from under his grain elevator cap, and dust covered his clothes, which melded more shapely about his frame as a few days of hard labor had sheared some fat from him. Her eyes squinted as she smiled. "Maybe you could help me figure out a way how," he said. "We could go up to North Platte together Saturday night."

The truck motor droned across the long miles, a mere whisper to his thoughts. He liked the straightness of the highway, how it did not needlessly curve as did the wind, idly going where it would. Roads out on the Plains always ran in thin black lines, even-tempered, permanently etched across the crimson fields, he told himself. Now I'll have to resign from the mill. How will she react to that – Will she think me a quitter? Perhaps, once I get rid of Peter, she can join me on the farm. He held a hand to his lips as looking into the brilliant gold horizon.

Tina turned away from him, stared out the window. He did not mind that she'd stopped paying him attention, even enjoyed her quietness and how she was as unassuming as the prairie around them. More people ought to be that way, he thought. He glanced at her as she readjusted the plastic butterfly barrettes holding back her hair. The growing vacuum between them pressed against him as the range ahead rose like a smooth pane of glass. Once I control the farm, he told himself, I'll sell off the animals, will put into crop some of the land near the creek to make up the difference.

Tina lightly tapped her feet.

Lyle chuckled to himself; he'd always imagined leaving the farm, perhaps for a job in Felton or North Platte, maybe even on a football scholarship to Lincoln or Denver. Ever since that day he took the family dog Jesse out to the field during harvest – only eight at the time – he knew the farm life wasn't for him. His father shouted at him over the combine's din, and putting it in park, climbed down out of the machine, massive like a green elephant, marched straight over to him. "You can't be out here!" his father hollered, straw still whirling from the combine's back end, creating a miniature dust devil so that Lyle had to squint lest husks and needle-sized stems strike his eyes. Jesse wagged her tail expectantly, but his father only continued to shout. "Do you hear me?! You can't be out here! It's too dangerous!" Lyle gazed for a moment at his father. Sweat trailed down the old man's stern face, burned a hole in the pure air with its stink. The boy wished he'd brought water, a Mason jar full of it brimming with ice, so he could at least provide a more than forgivable excuse for his transgression.

"Do you hear me now?!" his father shouted again. Now go and git back on up to the house." With that, Lyle and the dog turned away.

He snickered again as the pickup passed the Highway 23 intersection, the last road upon the open plain before North Platte, still 20 miles away.

"What's so funny?" Tina said.

"Uh?"

"You were chuckling. What's so funny?"

He glared at the road, as if a child who'd had his toy taken away from him. "Nothing." Tina's brow rumpled as his head swelled with deep thought. I'm practically running the farm myself anyway, he told himself, have to work the fields alone because Peter is always off carousing with that Abbie Blaire. His eyes narrowed and his breath quickened by the second as the dark of night descended upon the red plain like a purple ghost. There would not be much to do until spring when the cycle of tilling, planting, spraying and harvesting continued again. One could go about the farm life monotonously; it was a simple task, churning loam to nourish and make the soil absorbent, hauling the wagons full of fresh wheat to the elevator. If he left the homestead, Lyle knew he'd miss the power that came with sowing the earth, the satisfaction that followed when one had successfully reshaped it for the next harvest. Such predictability gave his life a contented straight-forwardness, much like a public record: just the facts, never anything personal. Yet, growing up, his skin always felt as it were too tight, like it were squeezing him – and that one season he was always itching, it was the damn animals, he knew, but the dermatologist said there was nothing wrong, and they had to drive all the way to Kearney to see one at that. Lyle's hand clenched like a fist about the steering wheel. He'd find a way to get rid of his brother just like he'd promised his father. His eyes glazed as the truck crossed an uneven section of highway and rattled.

Tina turned toward him. "What would you like to do once we get to town?" His voice cracked like a whip. "It doesn't matter."

She winced. Lyle paid her no heed, and a blackness overwhelmed him as he thought of the house Peter and Abbie had cleaned, like nobody else lived there, reorganizing and throwing away stuff that they had no right touching in the first place. A heat rushed through him, and his nostrils quivered. Coming home, he'd found the photo albums had been neatly piled under the lamp table, and picking one up, rediscovered that it contained pictures of his mother and of her with him as a baby. He tried his hardest but could not remember her. It was as if his eyes had examined pictures of two people he did not even know, but then his father or Peter would appear in one of the other photographs and he realized his emotional escape hatch was blocked. If she'd never died, Lyle thought, perhaps then I could imagine what the next picture would look like. His eyes glowed with an increasing savageness.

Tina gazed at him, saw his pursed lips and how both pupils had constricted again. His profile remained so still not even his breathing could be heard. The truck passed a billboard, then a convenience store, and there at the outskirts of town, her body began to tremble uncontrollably. She gripped the door handle, leaned against it as if readying to jump. "Stop," she said, "stop here and let me out. Now."

His body jolted at her shriek, and with wide eyes he stared at her.

"Stop!" she repeated. "I can't stand being in this truck with you anymore!"

*****

Carl Steinar hoisted the bag of wheat seed onto his shoulder, let out a little oomph as the weight pressed against his bones. Like any task, he thought, it was only a matter of moving a thing from one place to another, whether that be sacks of what would become next year's crop or a man's ideas. Life was little more, after all, than mountains rising and eroding. Slapping the seed bag onto the in the bed of his pickup truck, he flushed a cloud of dust into the air, and though it slowly fell back, some of it still clogged his nostrils and settled between the teeth of his slightly gaping mouth.

Carl stared longingly at the clouds' pregnant shapes,

billowing peacefully as if a young woman asleep beneath white sheets. He had set brother upon brother, would let them sort through it. Like the shifting vapors above, the struggle was not something he could map; he would simply have to let it play out. For several long moments, he pondered why he hadn't sent Abbie away that hour she'd first come to the farm. He leaned against the wall, cupped his face in his hands. His eyes grew sullen at the thought of Gwen's sister getting involved with he and Peter; like he was an old man whose hand had to be taken to get across a street. His shame oscillated with anger, and beneath his breath he cursed Abbie Blaire, an outsider who'd turned his own son against him.

The windmill spun in the sonorous blue sky as an autumn cold settled across the flats. The strongest would survive, he told himself Then Carl remembered his grandfather telling stories of how his own father patiently broke the earth by hand, with horse and plowshare, an acre a day, walking ten miles of long, straight lines that stretched into the horizon. He had much to be proud of; the Steinars weren't the ones who made their fortunes only to move on, weren't the ones who gave up hope and returned to Norway. No, they stayed and surmounted the Plains' great afflictions – drought, blizzards, grasshoppers – proved they were indeed among the fittest.

Their strength encouraged ruin. And just as they had set aside their dreams of quick fortune and everlasting springs merely to survive, so he had consigned himself to the realities of life's harshness and occupied his mind with the day's tasks.

"There's just one thing," Lyle had said as their hands had gripped. "How will we get Peter to leave?"

Carl paused, gazed at his son for a moment. "I will leave

that to you."

A knot ran down Lyle's throat as he swallowed hard. "We can't put this in writing," his son said.

"If we did–"

"It must appear that he left of his own accord."

Lyle examined him cautiously, as if a handwriting expert trying to determine a signature's authenticity. "Then we will farm this land together – as father and son?"

"As father and son."

Lyle nodded, and Carl could see that the boy's eyes appeared sure as marble. He had chosen correctly.

The windmill's blades quivered in the pre-winter wind. Carl ran a hand through his hair, rifling it. People around Felton knew the newborn and the deceased by the land they lived upon, knew which neighbor had worked the soil and which were to one day till it. Whenever someone drove past his farm, showing off the countryside to a visiting relative or a new neighbor, they inevitably said, "That's the Carl Steinar farm – he lost his wife some years back." He knew their words without ever hearing them for countless times he'd said variants of them himself when driving others about: "That's the old Adams' homestead; he passed away five years ago. The son runs it now." Or "There's the Ebenezer ranch; he's been farming it since my own dad was a little boy – it shouldn't be too long now before..." Carl Steinar knew there was no shaking the death of his wife from his being, for her very passing was his identity so long as he stayed upon those 1,842 acres. He remembered a time when a man's name was good enough for credit at the Felton stores; such ideas weren't important to people anymore, the whole world had gone that way. Out here, though, family and honor stood above all else, firmly planted on the land, shining for miles. What had he once said to Gwen, just after they were married? "Our home is fastened to the earth," and she nodded, vigorously. What obligation was there to his sons? Carl shuffled his feet, tapped a finger. Are our ancestors not just as important and isn't our commitment to the land paramount? His hands clenched into fists. If a son be-trays his father, does he not also savage his ancestors and the earth they toiled? A scowl crossed his face, and both eyes turned dark as night. Does the son then not surrender his birthright?

Gravel crackled beneath Carl's heels as he headed for the house, thinking of the hunt, of a time when he did know the answers. He and the boys would cock their heads at the rustle in the knee-high wheat, then freeze, trying to discern a pattern amidst the burnished gold. A chilled breeze snapped at his cleanly shaven face, and for a moment his stomach gurgled in hunger from the long walk. Still, he did not move, only concentrated on remaining steady. The stink of autumn humus wafted toward him.

He opened the porch door, could no longer tell whether he was upon the field at dusk or in the kitchen, devoid of any company, and went to the gun cabinet. The hinges creaked slightly as he opened it. For a long moment, Carl did not move. All of the family guns stood tall and erect, each one reassembled.

Chapter 23

Abbie's eyes tightened in partial thought as she turned the shower handle and the lukewarm water splashed downward. A strange hunger swirled deep inside, and she twitched. Warming, the liquid matted her hair to the shoulders and neck then swayed across each breast. Pulling a bottle of oleander body lotion from the wire shelf, she lathered it about the skin. Water fell upon her frame in streams, splashing unpredictably from the tub floor against both feet, formed a puddle before her that gradually swirled into the open drain and steamed the room. It was something that had to be done, she told herself. Abbie turned off the shower, began toweling herself dry.

As water dripped intermittently from the faucet, she thought of her father, tinted and towering like a bronze statue, knew that her scheme was the only force that could make a stone like Peter Steinar fold, was the only way to assert herself. She dashed on a few sprinkles of perfume, and the warm skin diffused the garden scent as she wrapped a thick terry bathrobe about the body. All her life, Abbie had told herself she'd get what she wanted, and if not, then it wasn't worth having in the first place. She thought this of all but one desire in her life. Her mouth grew dry as she leaned toward the bathroom mirror, plucking a thin line of eyebrow. She recalled the long days after Peter had stormed out, of how her head had filled with confused feelings that leaped to the forefront of her thoughts. Mid-afternoon Wednesday, unable to write, she'd left the office, hoped going for a walk would dampen the fire in her mind. Sand littered the curb's yellow edge as a lone boy on a bicycle rounded the corner, his wheels whirring in the October chill. Peter hadn't called in four days, and she felt tossed away, like the browning core of a half-eaten apple. The wind ticked slowly, as if tired of itself, and she stuffed both hands deep into her coat pockets. Sunshine lit the concrete and asphalt a sickly gray, and a street sign wobbled as the breeze picked up, the scent of withered grass upon it. So this is the quiet life I wanted, she thought.

Granules whirled up from the curb, and squinting she found herself once again in the desert as jets soared overhead. The wind twisted the ends of her hair and scratched at the neck, then once it died, she opened her eyes, only to find Lyle Steinar before her, just as at the stockyards, a mysterious phantom appearing without warning. She looked into the gray of his eyes; they were like burnished nickels.

"Hello, Miss Blaire."

She almost stumbled back. "Hello, Mr. Steinar."

"It's Lyle. You can call me Lyle."

Abbie nodded. She sensed something different about him. Even his shirt appeared new. "What brings you to town?"

"Looking for new stuff – new stuff for the farm."

"Oh." In the chilled gusts, the leaves of a nearby tree fell to the ground almost willingly, as if seeking each other's collective warmth.

"Red metal gates. I'm going to replace all the old wooden ones."

Her breathing paused for a moment then both pupils suddenly brightened. "You've heard about your brother and me?"

The edges of his mouth quivered. "Yes, I have. "

She said nothing for a second, knew the quick realization of how to prove herself to Peter would have to come slowly, as if it were natural. Lyle really wasn't so repulsive, she thought as examining him. The ends of his bangs, peeping from a seed cap, wavered boyishly in the breeze, yet he possessed a bull of a body. A soft heat rose along the back of her neck as she pondered the next step.

He moved first. "I suppose he's told you a lot of things about me. Things that weren't too full of flattery."

"Well, he did speak of you on occasion."

His mouth momentarily flattened.

"You weren't really expecting that he had, were you?" she said.

Lyle shook his head cautiously. "I shouldn't have thought less, I suppose."

"Perhaps we could sit down sometime over a cup of coffee, and I could tell you what he said."

A glimmer came to his eyes, as if knowing he was about to spark a flame after diligently and heretofore unsuccessfully rubbing two sticks together. "Do I get to defend myself?"

She grinned, the first time in four days. "Think that means we'll need a whole pot of coffee then?"

They chuckled. "Say," he said as shifting his feet, "would you like to get out of town for a while? Maybe Saturday?"

Abbie searched his face; both eyes appeared silvery and untainted as he smiled. "Okay, Saturday then. We'll get out of town. I could use that, actually."

As traipsing into the bedroom to dress, Abbie shivered

at the sound of the Saturday morning wind, it harsh like a knife being sharpened on a whetstone. A drip fell from her hair onto the neck, slid coldly across her shoulder before the robe absorbed it. She slipped on a tiny pair of panties and a bra, then surveying herself in the mirror, slowly ran a hand over the padded cups. She thought herself too lank, her breasts too small. Glancing away, Abbie reprimanded herself. She knew this was no time for self-doubt.

*****

Standing before the gray tombstone, Peter listened to the wind rise. All about him, the granite stones remained solid, unflinching; only the leaves of the rose stems propped against his mother's grave wavered. Sometimes the gusts momentarily calmed, and the bulbs' scent would lilt toward him; when it did, he quick breathed in, appreciated it as if warmth pressing against cold hands. He did not move closer to them, though. After some time, the wind grew so steady that he could not capture their fragrance at all.

As the sky darkened, his muscles tightened, and the cold pierced his barn coat. Still, he refused to stir, even as the icy norther numbed the ends of his fingers and chilled his ears red. Finally, he tucked both hands into his coat's pockets, and his chin instinctively ducked inside the collar that flapped amid the breeze.

More than an hour of utter stillness passed before his joints ached from such imposed stiffness and he shifted again. His movements were purposeful. He began with the gravestone to the right of his mother's, collecting the flowers, both real and not, then went to the next marker, and the one after that, and completing the row, turned to the line behind it, stopping at each one like a teacher collecting papers desk by desk. As he progressed, the number of steps between the kneeling at each stone unconsciously became the same and the slinging of the flower stems over his bent arm rote. The wind surged, and his lips slowly purpled. Soon, he came to the end of the cemetery. "What will I do with all of these flowers?" he wondered. "I must get rid of them so no one knows who is to blame." He passed his mother's grave as heading toward the truck, then paused, knew that even if he set them upon her tombstone, the clue did not point to his criminality. It could have been the work of his father or brother, or maybe vandals who randomly dropped them upon the grave of GWENDOLYN STEINAR, BELOVED WIFE OF CARL STEINAR, OCT. 14, 196-, MAY 2, 199-. He scanned the ground behind him for his bootprints. If made, they soon would be frozen into the earth.

A carnation fluttered from his arm. As the wind rushed it eastward, he laughed at the insect-like scampering, at how all of time rolled past a man, no matter how firm he stood. Still, he remained upright, holding the bundles of dead and plastic bouquets and single stems, wishing for the turmoil to die down. "There's no need for haste," he told himself, "no need at all." Kneeling, he found it allowed more wind to strike his wide, exposed back.

She'd always been with him, he knew, a ghostly companion, as gray and unshaped as the future.

It was the curse of the wind, an invisible, oscillating circle, swinging and swelling, always dissonant and unresolved, constantly scorning unity. Unlike water, unlike his memories, her existence could not be guided down a path broken through the earth or inside a steel pipe. A man had to realize that or he'd go mad. Then Peter tried to recall what flower it was that she'd planted outside the porch – orange lobes stood out most distinctly in his mind – and raising his head he began plucking at the array of them about his arm, tossing white and purple chrysanthemums, pink roses, and ivy-colored wreaths into the air, the gust pushing them across the sprawling plain, and his fingers as they grabbed loosened the petals so the wind would rend their corollas and send them whirling into the sky. Then it came to him: butter-and-eggs. She'd called it a butter-and-eggs.

The blue veins upon the back of his hand stood out as he regarded the few flowers still wrapped about his arm. He trembled. A multi-colored array of petals festooned the brown grass like party confetti tossed over a beige carpet. He did not move, only thought of what should be done with the wreaths and flowers collected from the gravestones. And then a snowflake, soft and dappled like a young woman's face, fell upon his shoulder. He brushed it from his coat but another came, melting before he could reach it, and then yet another and as he raised his hand again, still one more descended. Gazing up, it showered all about him like moonlight. He stood, let the flowers slide off his sleeve, all but for one which his palm netted, and he placed it upon the grave of GWENDOLYN STEINAR, BELOVED WIFE OF CARL STEINAR, OCT. 14, 196-, MAY 2,199-.

The pale, saffron blossoms, with orange lobes upon their lower lips, caught the snow as if it were dew.

*****

It wasn't until Abbie pressed her warm face against Lyle's neck that he even thought of them as being on a date. Dusty had only held hands during her deepest felt moments of intimacy, though at times she gave in to his lust. For several miles as his pickup truck ambled down the plumb road, he listened to the rhythm of Abbie's breathing, it never-ending like a musical suite or a wind upon the plains. Then the road curved, following the bend into the river valley, and she shifted. He caught the sunflower scent of her hair and lifted his hand to bring her back in to him, then a quarter way through the motion returned to the steering wheel. His stomach groaned, but a deeper longing than hunger rested there. He tightened. It was a feeling he had not had in years.

"There's a pioneer village over in Minden that we could go to for the day," he said as his truck ascended the opposite banks.

She laughed playfully. "How about going over to Red Cloud to see the Willa Cather memorial?"

"Who? Oh yeah, that one writer we're famous for."

She rolled her eyes. "Yep, that one writer."

He hesitated to speak. She looked at him for a moment then caressed his arm. His breathing smoothed, and he gazed at her, imagined the ends of her midnight-colored hair billowing in the wind. For the first time in many years – perhaps not since the races of his teenage parties, maybe not even since football – he sensed there was a purpose to his life. It had not been thrust upon him but came from within. A new buoyancy filled his thoughts. This Abbie was a gift to him for his perseverance.

"Better keep your eyes on the road, buster," she said. His attention jumped to the windshield and cracked asphalt before them. "The roads are always pretty straight out here," he said after a moment.

She giggled. Ahead of them hung a powder blue heaven, but in his rear view mirror, the sky had darkened to olivine.

"So you want to go to Red Cloud?" he said.

"The pioneer village is fine. Red Cloud is a long drive."

The pickup's motor throbbed, and its tires bumped over the cracks strewn across the sun-broken highway, just as at that moment when Tina had screamed she wanted out of the truck. His brow had risen as both eyes widened into two white saucers, yet when he pulled into the gas station to calm her, she jumped from the pickup and ran inside. He waited a full five minutes, decided there was no point to going in for her. What if she screamed, after all? Crazy bitch, he thought, and then he drove off, headed back to Felton.

His mind tottered at the decision to leave her there. Well, she asked me to, he thought and then harrumphed. What did I expect from a family that spawned the likes of a girl who dated my brother for three years? It was women such as Tina Strom that have held me back my whole life, he told himself, have forced me to think small; she was the same old highway, nothing more than a dead end. I could've been a great football player, could have accomplished so much, if only...I don't need her or the mill job anymore. Why, no more than a week later I've got a far better girl sitting with me in my truck.

Abbie's feet shifted over the floorboard trash – old candy bar wrappers, a crushed bag from his last stop at D-Burgers, empty pop cans – and for a moment he felt a tingle of regret at not having cleaned the truck. A school bus, its dingy windows full of ecstatic kids, passed.

Her eyes trailed it. "School must be getting out early," she said.

He shrugged. All those days of sitting in desks, having to memorize formulas and dates and facts that he'd never use; he did enough to get by, and though never picked on or bullied by classmates who knew he wasn't very bright, a sense of inferiority, of being at the bottom of the trough, always twitched inside him. Oh, but how their eyes would flare once they learned that he alone ran the farm. They'd see he'd proven himself. Lyle knew he would have his father to thank, and at that moment, the youngest Steinar believed he'd been all wrong about him. Certainly the last suicide "attempt" was just a test. He would have to call his father once they reached Minden, let him know where he was; it was a son's duty to.

Then Lyle shivered from the sudden, piercing cold the wind carried. He glanced at Abbie. "Mind if I ask you something?"

She grinned. "Depends on the question."

He didn't say anything, merely squinted as if smoke had come into his eyes. "No, I don't mind," she said.

"Well, what I want to know is why come here? There's a lot happening in the world, and none of it's in Nebraska and especially Felton."

Abbie giggled, and Lyle thought it sounded like crackling ice. "Your brother asked me the same question."

He bristled. "And what answer did you give him?"

"That's private."

He glanced her way again, found her grin lassoing him in, yet he didn't mind being led, even found it inspiring. She was all grace and poetry, he thought as examining her smile, it warm and lucid. He wondered if they ever could move together as one instrument. Well, she's with me now, isn't she, he told himself, and sat up straighter.

*****

The phone's ringing burst through the house, exploding the silence, then faded to stillness only to blast again like fireworks ballooning in the sky. On the third peal, Carl rose from his chair. Serenity covered his face as the sweat from the day's work lay cool upon the skin and an utter certitude that the world was ordered and measured hung in his eyes. Peter had broken up with that Abbie – perhaps once the boy lost the farm, his inheritance, he'd realize the foolishness of impudence – while Lyle had found a new girl, the Strom gal who'd stayed behind on the Plains. His youngest son had even left the mill, had been back on the farm all week. Fortune worked in his favor; all he ever had to do was persevere.

Carl picked up the phone. From the wind that blew through the earpiece, he knew whoever called was using a pay phone. "Hello?" he said.

"Dad? Is everything all right?" It was Lyle.

"But of course, Son. Why wouldn't it be?"

"I'm in Minden right now."

"Minden? What for?"

"Abbie and I went to see the pioneer village."

A cold shiver shot down Carl's spine. He paused for a moment. "Lyle? Is that you?"

"Yes, Dad. It's me – Lyle."

The old man's knees began to waver. The phone in his hand suddenly gained a great heaviness.

"Dad? Is Peter there?"

"Peter? No, I...don't know where he is. You're in Minden?"

"Yes, Minden."

Carl gazed at his overalls, examined the grass stains circling his knees. Washing had darkened the green into murky splotches. "Who are you with?"

There was no response for a moment. "It's hard to hear, Dad, with the wind."

Carl regained his composure. Yes, the wind – because of it he must not have heard right. His son was with Tina Strom. He was such a good boy, calling to let him know where he was. "A blizzard is coming in. There've been storm warnings on TV."

"It's too early in the year for snow, Dad."

Carl glanced out the kitchen window. Cold gusts swirled up debris and loosened the cottonwoods' leaves. He remembered the early October storm when snow struck the farm like water from an unleashed dam and furiously covered the whole prairie. He and his father spent a good part of the night bringing the cattle back into the barn so they'd not freeze or starve. Lyle was in Minden; perhaps that far east the sky had not turned so gray and chilled. "Who are you with?" he said.

"With Abbie. The reporter–"

The phone slipped from Carl's hand. It bounced against the wall, denting the plaster, then struck the floor where it spun. Carl found himself sinking.

"Dad? Dad?" Lyle's voice shouted from the receiver. "Dad, are you all right?"

On the tile, Carl picked up the phone, raised it to his ear. "Son, are you still there?"

"Yes, Dad. Are you all right?"

"I thought you were with the Strom girl."

"That was last weekend. I...I haven't talked to her since I quit the mill."

The old man's eyes paled.

"Dad?"

"Yes?"

"I'm going now. I just wanted to let you know where I was and to see if you were all right."

Neither spoke for a moment.

"Okay?" Lyle said.

Carl's voice almost choked. "Okay," he said, meekly.

"Okay then. Goodbye."

The phone at the other end clicked, and the sound of the wind disappeared. Then the loud, computerized drone of a dead telephone line filled the earpiece. Carl Steinar curled into an unmoving ball.

Chapter 24

As Carl Steinar gazed out the window, snow sprang and swirled from all directions, masking the windmill and sheds, and he could not help but think of the farmhouse as a bubble. With Peter likely stuck in town and Lyle on a date, he finally could do it. Rising, he went to the gun cabinet as wind struck the farmhouse with scorn. His pupils glowed red like two burning embers, and he opened the cabinet's doors.

Light slanted against its wooden frame and then, as if a spark traveling along a wick, up the long rods. He plucked one from the velvet rest; the rifle lay naturally in his hands, he thought, like the long handle of a hoe or a rake, an extension of his arm, of his very being, as a truth that could be held. Then the old man gazed down the barrel's length and set the gun upon the living room chair.

He unbuttoned his shirt. Gently placing it upon the chair's back, Carl Steinar kneeled, and as he undid his boots, he reflected upon how the one thing that made him a man was forever out-of-reach, like fruit on a branch that the wind had blown upward. He unbuckled his belt, measuredly pulled it through the pant loops, then they came off. He stood only in his underwear, and without a pause he slipped out of them as well. At last, he took off his wedding band, the peeling skin below it pale like the white about an egg yolk.

He chambered a round in the gun. His body straightened as he raised the barrel tip to the mouth.

The cold metal slid past his lips and reached the soft palate like a needle to a suture, and his tongue wrapped around the smooth bore as if to hold it in place.

"One man can't keep a house," he told himself.

His thumb pressed the trigger. The shot resounded through the rooms like a boulder breaking, and he flew back.

*****

Abbie saw the note lying on the plate as soon as she entered the kitchen. She picked it up, read its instructions for dinner. Beside her dish sat a dirty one, the remaining grease and juice congealed upon the surface and stinking. It belonged to her father. She collected it, an encrusted fork, and a glass, empty but for an inner ring of dried milk, placed them in the sink. Then she returned her own place setting to the cupboards and sat at the table. The clock above her said 10 p.m. She would wait.

After an hour, the college senior began to wonder if her effort would be futile. Still, she knew to not speak could be just as dangerous. The only real question was what words to use. She had time to think about them. In a sweat-stained blouse at 2:18 a.m., Mary Dawn would tiredly unclick the front door lock and traipse across the vast darkness of the kitchen, where by moonlight she'd fill a glass of tap water to drink before heading off to bed. It was a pattern to which Abbie, by her fifth day home that spring break, had grown to despise. Sometimes she wondered how her mother could exist in such a state, working two low-paying jobs as taking care of a husband who unnecessarily behaved like an invalid.

Four hours later, just as Abbie predicted, the lock snapped and the door slowly creaked open and closed. Shoes shuffled across the floor, gaining in volume until reaching the kitchen entry. Mary Dawn paused, and a trickle of perspiration slipped down Abbie's spine. Their eyes fell upon one another as for several moments only the tick of the clock filled the empty space between them. Abbie knew she did not have to speak first. Her mother would find this break in the order of things odd, would inquire. So Abbie sat and waited, arms folded across her chest, as Mary Dawn, like a moth with torn wings, remained standing and inert, the house's darkness her backdrop. She limped past Abbie to the sink, the steps mere whispers.

For a few seconds, tap water surged. Then she turned around, leaned against the cupboard and with static and dull pupils examined Abbie as if trying to gain strength for a confrontation she knew was inevitable and ultimately fruitless. "Why, Abbie," she said, "what's keeping you up so late?" She paused for a second and rolling her eyes let out a hoarse giggle. "Now what is bothering you?"

"Mom," Abbie said, voice wavering, uncertain again if she would listen, and like a muffling gray fog, a quietness settled between them. Mary Dawn finished her water, set the glass in the sink with a loud *clink!* "Mom, sit down."

"I'm tired."

"Please, sit," Abbie said. "What I have to say won't take more than a few minutes."

"Really, Abbie, I'm tired."

The girl leaned forward, her eyes intense like an archer as drawing back his bow. "Mom," she said, "what's the real reason you won't talk? What I have to say is important."

"All right, I'll sit," she said, taking a chair opposite her. "But please be quick."

Abbie sat up straight. "Mom," she said softly, "working two jobs a day, it's killing you. What few hours you have off is spent cleaning the house and cooking meals. You don't spend time with your friends or even on yourself." She paused for a moment, careful to choose her next words. "It doesn't have to be that way, Mom."

Mary Dawn remained quiet for a moment, her face pale and weary. "Doesn't have to be what way?"

"Have you talked with him, Mom? About how the accident doesn't mean his life is over?"

Abbie contemplated stopping but knew if she did not continue, she might never speak again. "There are many things a disabled person can do, many satisfying jobs, many that make good money. Many that..."

"Your father isn't disabled."

"Of course not, and that's exactly what I mean. It's not as if he's incapacitated or–"

"He wants to fly."

"There are a lot of things he could do with planes – maintenance, designing, buying and selling them–"

"He wants to be an officer."

"With a little schooling he easily could go into management–"

"'Management' is not the same as being an officer. Far from it."

"You just can't go on–"

"Yes, I can."

"Mom–"

"Abbie, let me ask you something. Do you know about loyalty? What the word means?"

She half rolled her eyes.

"No, really now, do you? Have you heard of 'til death do us part'? Do you understand about vows and oaths?"

"Mom, this vow is killing you."

Mary Dawn rose to her feet. "No, you don't understand, after all. You don't know about how a promise can give meaning and purpose to one's life, so much in fact that they can suffer through almost anything. Well, for many years – when your father could walk and fly – he never let me down. And now, in his time of need, I won't forget that. He suffered a great indignity, but I won't hurt him even more with disloyalty."

"How is it disloyal to ask someone to share in the responsibilities?"

Mary Dawn only shook her head slowly. "I can't believe my own daughter is talking like this. I thought I raised you right. "

"Mom!"

Her mother headed for the living room. "I'm going to sleep now. When I wake up in the morning, I will assume this conversation was just a bad dream."

Abbie stood, wanted to scramble toward her, fall against the tall legs and into her embrace. But Mary Dawn Blaire only disappeared into the darkness of the house, a shadow dissolving as the light gave way.

*****

Abbie's tone was insistent. "You can't drive anywhere in this," she said. "You can barely see a few yards."

Still, Lyle remained at the door. Their date had gone well – her eyes glittered whenever she smiled, even during the long ride home through the snowstorm – yet he found himself uncertain, as if stuck on a school exam question, unable to decide which letter to circle. Why was she so persistent, he wondered. Did she hope for something more? Perhaps she really cared that much for his safety, for his well-being. "I suppose," he said. "We could see if it clears off."

"We could," she said as brushing off the chunks of snow that clung to her hair. Then she motioned to the sofa and after handing his coat to her, he sat there, staring out the picture window at the blizzard around them.

The storm reminded him of that story his father once told about the blizzard of '76, when only a child, of rescuing a cow half-buried by snow. He shivered whenever thinking of that tale, not so much from the story itself which was frightening enough, but from the way his father, always so strong and silent, told it with passion and precision, as if it were the one event that forever shaped his life. The week had been mild enough, so the cattle were left to graze in the pasture, but unexpectedly one October night, like a stampede of white devil horses, the storm swept out of the Rockies across the prairie, instantly deluging the land in harsh winds and several feet of snow. Through the darkness and blasting winds, his grandfather and the two sons herded them back into the farmyard. But as daylight broke, a lone bellow resounded across the field, growing weaker with each cry. They waded through three-foot drifts toward the cow, until reaching the struggling brown mass. Caked with ice, its breath felt cold, smelled dry like parched dung, but the grandfather was persistent; no cow would die from his lack of trying to save it. So they dug out the animal and then a path across the pasture, harassed at every shovelful by straying snow, and pushed the cow until it reached the barn. A companion, grateful to see its friend returned, licked the ice clean off. The cow survived, and Lyle knew that probably somewhere in their herd, nearly half a century later, its descendant, dumb to the past plight of its line, grazed and bore young that provided for him.

With the snow gone, Abbie's hair hung flat and wet. Her

face paled in the cold, and she folded her arms, tightening her small frame. She disappeared into the kitchen then the vacuum of the refrigerator door popped as a rectangle of yellow light flashed upon the wall. "Would you like some wine?" she said, but before he could answer, a cupboard had clapped open then shut, and a beverage plashed in first one then a second glass. He watched her shadow flow to reality as she re-entered the living room, her hips swaying like wheat in a field, curving in and out. She handed him a glass full of wine. The zinfandel's sweetness filled his nostrils as he sipped it.

She sat on the hassock before him. "So," she said. The lamp's dim yet warm glow framed her, and Lyle could feel the heat in her apartment rise.

"So," he said.

She giggled, took another sip from her glass. "Good wine."

He examined his glass, supposed she wanted to talk. It did not bother him. "It is good. I'm not much of a wine drinker, though."

"Beer mainly?"

Lyle nodded. "It is good, though."

She smiled playfully at him. "Beer or the wine?"

"Both really." They laughed. He glanced outside, the wind and snow furious as an angry voice speeding with rage. "Say, you never said why you came out here."

Her brow wrinkled. "'Out here'?"

"You know. To Felton." Then he paused, as if thinking better of what he was saying. "I mean, you're smart; you seem like the kind who should be living in a big city or someplace where something is happening, like Florida."

Her eyes brightened as she tittered. "Florida? And what would I do there, collect seashells?"

The edges of his mouth curled. "You'd write. For a paper."

Abbie said nothing, gazed out window, fathoming what he implied.

"So, what gives? Why'd you come out to a nowhere town like Felton?"

She smiled mischievously. "Because I hate seashells."

Lyle leaned back on the sofa, took another sip of the wine.

"So tell me," she said, "about what growing up on the Plains was like."

His thoughts faltered. "Well–" Lyle started, but before he could think of what else to say, Abbie canted forward, cheek resting in the base of her palm, gazing long and hard at him Her complete attentiveness startled him; he found his pulse rising as his face flushed with heat. Glancing back at her, those lips so wet full, the vanilla scent of her milky complexion swirling, he could not concentrate on his words. He chuckled nervously. She only grinned back as the wind and snow outside wrapped itself about the apartment.

He quick regained his composure. "And that's about it," he said. "Quite a story, eh?"

She laughed, and rising unevenly, her knees wobbled. It was all going faster than anticipated, but she couldn't risk slowing down. "Oh my," she said, "I think I'm a little tipsy."

Giggling, she stumbled into him, he laughing, too, as her warm cheek fell against his face and her nimble fingers rested upon his shoulder. Instinctively, his arm slid around her small shoulders, and he nuzzled the crown of her head, the hair sweet like a warm April day. She closed her eyes, pressed closer to him, and as his free hand caressed her ribs just an inch below a breast, her chin glided upward, across his rough neck, and their lips met, burning with passion and the taste of fermented fruit.

*****

Peter stared through a small opening in his window just above the dashboard. Ice lay crusted across all the glass but for a small oval that his defroster barely kept clear. Amid the whitewash, he squinted, pondered the cold years with his father, so unwilling to provide any warmth to him. He had spent the whole night driving about the Plains through the snow, wondering. The old man always had been that way, he thought, even before his mother's death. It had not much bothered Peter then; his mother provided enough affection on her own, and in any case, a hardened father provided the appropriate balance against her mellifluousness. Still, certainly in her presence, he thought, the old man must have understood the need for affection, must have even learned how to express it. There could be only one reason his father did not: If consumed by hatred for him. Peter rarely had experienced that passion himself, and should someone reveal it, he'd never fail to turn away. Even as wind buffeted the truck and he tried not sliding into the rising snow drifts, he did not curse the storm or the land he lived on for its merciless weather. He had felt anger frequently, of course, always had admitted as much to himself, but he believed such flares hardly were tantamount to hatred's violent blaze. Indeed, he regarded them as quite different, for one was surface and momentary while the other ran deep and perpetual. Peter shook his head, tried to concentrate on driving. This is what happens when a man spends too much time thinking to himself, he whispered. The snow snapped about him like a whipman's unceasing lashes.

As the windshield's clean spot shrank, Peter could see the bank of cottonwoods, their white tops wavering in the wind that marked the Steinar homestead. He was on his own land now, surrounded by fields his cattle had pastured, soil that his own hands had broken and watered. He figured himself safe. Of course, he had heard stories of grown men who'd become lost in such blizzards, even in their own yards, and of how they walked in circles unable to see even the front doors of their own homes until they collapsed from exhaustion and froze to death. The tales went back to the pioneer days, and though he knew they were grounded in fact for such deaths had indeed occurred, he found their details wildly exaggerated. Certainly, if I can guide my own pickup home, he thought, I can walk there just as well. As the malevolent snow fell in straight-line winds at his truck, he'd forgotten how a man standing alone amid it, without the aid of any of his tools or machines, was a very lonely figure indeed. The wind by itself could skin a man alive. He flipped off the heater, whose fan only blew cold air and snow crystals into the cab, then closed the vents. At last, he reached the driveway, and able to tell where it was only from memory for snowdrifts concealed it, he cranked the steering wheel hard and gunned the truck. It slid slightly, the motor whirring, but soon was righted though the tires spun as they hit low spots in the snow and touched ice.

He parked askance to the porch, but in the storm's mad rush thought it quite perpendicular. As he descended from the dry cab, snow pellets buffeted his face, and squinting he brought a hand to his face to ward against the onslaught; though it reduced the stinging, it could not silence the wind's roar. His feet sunk into the drifts, and before he could lift his legs for the next step, snow already had covered his boot's toes. Still, he refused to grunt any disapproval. Raising the knees high and bowing his head, he forced himself toward the house, then reaching the porch, also covered in dunes of white, stretched his hand for the doorknob.

Frozen to its frame, the door stuck. Peter yanked again, and when it would not give, he rattled the handle, hoping his very might would unleash it. The ice crackled along the door's top, and the undone corner flapped in the wind as if a snapping banner. Fearing it could break, he tugged gently, but growing impatient soon wrenched hard. The frozen edge split from the frame, and the door flopped about in the wind as he wedged inside.

Silence met him.

Peter shivered, hesitated taking off his coat. The kitchen was bitterly cold, as if the heat had not been turned on, and he made his way to the thermostat. He wondered where everyone had gone. Entering the living room, a brilliant light from the open curtains blinded him for a moment as his soaked boots squeaked against the wooden floor.

Then he stopped, shuddered.

Encircled in a pool of red, his nude father lay like a toppled stone at the room's center, a rifle on the floor next to him.

A chill ran down Peter's back, and he felt colder than when outside in the storm. Half of the old man's head was missing. "Father?" he said, then stepped toward him and at his side kneeled. "Father?" From the start, he did not suspect murder, could tell from the way the gun lay on the floor that it had fallen from the old man's hands, knew from what he'd denied all this time about his father that the only explanation could be suicide. The toe of his boot reddened. He raised his father at the chest and pressed the old man's face against his own beating heart. Blood and clots of brain oozed onto Peter's hands. "Father," he said, "I don't hate or blame you for what you've done, but like so many of your decisions, it was just plain wrong – just plain wrong."

Chapter 25

As Lyle gazed into the bright horizon, a brutal wind swept across the white plain. He squinted, and his pickup truck turned onto Visne Road. Amid the glare of sun and his long night with Abbie, he could barely make out the sign warning of the road's quick bend. Mounds of snow rippled then shifted beneath the gusts as traces of blue highway presented itself under the swirl. He wished to be in bed with Abbie, her hair burnished in the lamp's glow, voice hushed and overgentle; after sex, she'd have held his head and gently stroked his hair until he fell asleep. That morning, though, only Lyle's sour breath hung in the cold air.

His Merle Haggard cassette and its broken box slid across the dashboard as the road wended into the river valley. An invisible glaze of ice covered the asphalt. It did not faze him, for as his truck gained speed down the hillside, he imagined himself a jet fighter pilot screaming into battle. He caught a glimpse of himself in the rear-view mirror, but his rumpled hair didn't bother him, either; he held no fear of his father saying to comb it as was so often the case during childhood. He stepped on the accelerator.

Suddenly the pickup skid, zigzagging across the road, and Lyle's heart suspended a beat. He did not react at first but instead wondered at his own failure to do so, wondered if he'd been slowed by daydreams of Abbie. As the pickup gathered speed even while he let off the gas, the highway whorled into a wild trail, and the windswept snow fell like a reign of arrows. A crushed bag from his last stop at D-Burgers flew up, and the truck spun as if caught in a twister – he saw first white snow, followed by blue sky, white snow once more, blue sky again – until finally the pickup straightened, and he realized it was sliding backwards.

Then Lyle bounced, like he'd hit a lineman in front of him, and his head struck the steering wheel. Though the truck had stopped, the world continued twirling around him, and the quick sting of a hundred broken capillaries crossed his forehead. As the shock wore off, he understood what had happened. The truck rested askance in the road, its back end half buried in a snow bank. A horrid throb filled his head. He stepped on the accelerator, but lacking traction, the tires only spun. Placing the shift stick in park, he got out. As the snow shimmered blindingly, the wind lashed at him. Wincing, he kicked away white clumps from the tires, his boots knifing through the snow as if it were merely wet sand. The leather over his feet moistened, and in the cold hardened instantly. His hands gripped the truck's bumper. With a grunt, he raised the pickup, could feel his spine stretching as anger gave his muscles increased strength, then he pushed it forward so it sat out of the drift. He walked back to the cab like a cop marching off the measured beat of his footsteps, and getting in decided he would go out again with Abbie, if only to make Peter leave the farm, for upon finding out, his brother would run, just like he always did – going to the creek as a child, staying away from Aunt Amita's basement and their cousins, walking away from Darcie Allen when she was making out with that guy. Why, Peter's spending time with Abbie in the first place was just running, too. He restarted the truck, backed up in a Y, and took off again down the road, but driving more cautiously as if expecting to run over a booby trap or a land mine. He found a certain purity, a magic, in his concentrated effort. Last night, he had wanted to leave Abbie's immediately after she'd abandoned the living room, but the apartment's heat, the vanilla scent of her soft neck, the wine, it had all made him so sleepy, had so eased his mind. He thought of the first day he'd seen her, how she stepped from the car, the tight T-shirt beneath the blazer flattening the breasts, her breathing like a lake's lap against the shore, the white clouds reflecting in her calming green eyes as she held a pen in her hand. It was unfair that Peter always got the women, always got the attention. Now he would show them all that he was capable. "You've got to grab on a hold of the earth, make something of her," he whispered to himself, "because that's how a man's worth is measured." For the first time in his life, he truly understood his father.

Arriving at home, he followed the vague trail his brother had cut through the snow. The gusts grew more pointed as he stepped, but inside, a quietness like the sky as it turned a bruised green and utterly still before a tornado, met him. Then, he heard a whimper from the living room. Lyle stepped into its entry, froze. His sobbing brother held the lifeless torso of their father, a patch of hair hanging from the old man's skull as if attached by a hinge.

*****

Redness filled the Steinar farmhouse as never before. It covered the floor and walls; droplets clung to the chairs and the table legs; the color streamed down the walls and across the rugs. Window light illuminated the corpse, dried the spilled blood encrusted into a maroon reef about it. The Steinar brothers, all pink drained from their faces, sat next to the naked body, their pants dampened by the pool of vital fluid. They trembled as staring into their father's barren pupils, listened closely for even the dimmest of breath. His body only paled, and as it did, the red slowly ceased to flow from it.

Finally Lyle spoke, his words a stutter. "Has anyone called an ambulance?" Peter shook his head. He had been the only one who could.

Lyle headed for the phone, his boot heel leaving crimson imprints upon the floor. As if in slow motion, he dialed 9-1-1. He asked for paramedics, gave the address, explained their father had shot himself, that he was dead.

Peter remained at the body's side, mouth locked open. "Where are we going to put it?" he said.

"Put it?" Lyle said, returning. "Put what?"

"The body. Father."

"We're not going to put it anywhere."

"We can't leave it like..." He grimaced. "...like this, all crumpled."

Lyle stared at the body, considering. He kneeled over it, and they straightened the corpse so their father would be more comfortable, if only in their own minds. His glassy eyes gazed upward. For a long time, Peter and Lyle simply took in the body. They noticed the calluses on the old man's hands, the soiled collar that smelled of stale linen, the gray stubble. Peter refused to look at the redness for fear it would blind him. He fidgeted, had always thought of red as the color of the world ablaze, not of suffocation. We must at least move it out of the light, he thought, though he did not know why that mattered as his father certainly didn't feel the brilliant whiteness shining through the window, certainly couldn't appreciate being shaded from it. The lace curtains hung moth-like across the glass pane. At last, Lyle went upstairs and returned with a blanket to lay over the body.

Peter wondered what would become of their father's memories. Upon his mother's death, it was as if his recollections of her were mere petals in the wind. Then he thought back to a time when a child, when like red dust floating upon the wind he did not know where he would fall to rest. The fence line unfurled beyond the eye's limits, and if not for the many times he'd walked it, checking the boundaries of his existence, he would not know where he stood upon the expansive earth. The scent of dry grass and puce dirt rose indifferently from the timeworn ground. After several more steps, the field descended toward the creek. Peter admired its green lushness for a moment. Plowing through the land, cutting its way across rock, the stream possessed purpose, remained persistent even when exhausted in August's low waters, always returned to the task after winter's long slumber.

Lyle stretched the wool blanket over his father's body, allowed some of the fabric to drape across his brother's arms. His eyes muddied, became a nebulous void that he could not see with, and his nostrils pinched tight for all around him the air smelled acrid, like a burned wire. Kneeling next to the body, he tried to remain steady on his feet, but his ribs ached as if a linebacker had smacked him once he'd hit the line of scrimmage, leaving him winded. His hand reached for the bloodied rifle, picked it up. He swore silently at his damn brother; he'd hidden the guns for his old man's own good. On the barrel, the blood had dried like spilled syrup. He shook his head. His father, as his dreams, was now reduced to a clump of moist clay.

Then the red lights of the ambulance as it pulled up flashed through the lace curtain. Lyle rose to answer the door.

*****

Abbie was not one to witness her revenge. She thought of her comeuppance as spinning a top then turning away; eventually it would come to rest, to a point of equilibrium – one did not need to see it to know so. Such behavior presented itself as if she was a mischievous child told not to touch a toy but when left alone to her own whims could not resist picking it up, and should it be movable, would push it for a few seconds to satisfy an urge to defy so her own individuality might be asserted. That no one knew of her rebellion or success was of little consequence as it was for her satisfaction alone any way that such resistance had been expressed.

Outside, the wind swirled like a white wheel. She wondered why Lyle felt compelled to leave once dawn had broken, before she'd even awaken, especially in this weather. They'd made out, and he'd touched her breasts, but when she rose and went to the bedroom, he did not follow. After undressing, she peeked around the hallway wall, saw him curled upon the sofa, fast asleep. His body appeared sad and shrunken. She had not wanted to go farther anyway. Quietly opening the hall closet door, she took down an old blanket from the top shelf, and tiptoeing toward him, set it on the hassock and switched off the light. She returned to her own bed, it vast and cold, satisfied that he'd boast to his brother of the night.

For men, she thought, bragging was natural, some evolutionary mechanism that allowed the weaker ones to raise their value in the eyes of others. During college, she'd dated such boys, always had to endure the smirks and ribbing elbows of his friends who'd been told of their experiences, of her passion. In her sophomore year, she'd met a man of twenty whom smelled of lavender as he canted toward her, grinning boyishly. Recognizably handsome at first sight, his lake blue eyes shined so deep and clear, always looking out at the sky, and as he often guessed as going along, beheld a certain sense of adventure in the spontaneity of it. He doesn't make me play the fool, she told herself, this must be the one. She believed during her hours apart from him that he thought of her as much as she did of him. As they lay in bed together at night, the dorm room bed cramped and muffled sounds of heavy metal music playing through cinder block walls, they'd tell each other of the day's most trivial details, listening not so much to the words but to the sweet sound of the other's voice. She'd lean close to let him smell her, press against his warm, oily skin. He'd lightly trace the curve of her hip, just as she had dreamed much of the day that he would, and she shivered beneath his fingertips, found her eyes half-closed in a swoon as her heart beat faster. They pleasured in the soft richness of the other's youthful body, of physical beings in their prime. She'd shift across his gleaming ribs, smooth as flowing air, plant her knees against his waist and sitting up smile brazenly as tossing her head back, the hair flailing like the lines of a whirlwind. What Abbie did not know was that though she had occupied his thoughts much of the day, the images in his mind were of they naked and entangled, of her breasts rising like twin islands out of an undulating sea. Unlike the other girls he'd slept with, she did not merely lie there but fed frenzy with her own excitement, as if a wind that builds into a storm out of its own increasingly rapid spiraling. She would not have believed that his thoughts of her consisted mainly of this, and so as she abandoned herself to the fantasy of true love and the pure, raw emotion it begat, he decided that during her days she also imagined only the nights. Then, when she told him that only he could ever make her feel that way, he came to believe that his prowess alone was responsible for her outpouring of passion. Before they'd met, such narcissism never would have entered his thoughts, and that trait in particular was what she had found attractive about him. But as she tipped her chin down, offering the neck to him while he gripped her buttocks, his certainty that such newfound pride was justified only grew.

Soon his vanity allowed for an overeagerness to enter his hands whenever they met. She playfully fought him off, made him wait. He took it as a sign of manipulation, her way of regaining power in a relationship where she could not help but surrender to his physical deftness. He grew rougher with her, and she, thinking it merely a variation, perhaps even an experiment in their deep intimacy, initially allowed in. He viewed such surrender as further proof of her gamesmanship and of her inability to resist him. Gradually, as the tenderness turned to tight grips that left bruises on her arms and a soreness rather than fulfillment between her legs, she took less interest in their lovemaking. She did not broach the subject to him, simply convinced herself that this was merely a phase in his desires. After a few days, though, during her hours in classroom desks and writing for the student newspaper, she did not think so much of as merely feared him. Eventually, she found ways to avoid him at night – a made-up excuse about being ill, the desperate need to study for a test, expecting an important phone call from her parents. Such forced separation only increased the violence of his hands and of his thrusts when they did meet; one night, she wept afterward.

The next morning, as she sat at her dorm room desk skipping classes and contemplating how to break it off, she began to write a letter despite not knowing what to say. She feared both him and the loss of him; while the prior rang more brutally real in her existence, the latter ran deeper, like the roots of a weed that tore at one's hands as it was pulled out and once vanquished only left behind a gash of upturned soil.

Though inertia had driven them to this point, she decided her own force must quickly bring it to an end. Abbie called his best friend, asked if they could talk. They met in a bar near campus. She expressed her love for the boy she feared, inquired if something was bothering him, exaggerated how he'd physically hurt her. His friend listened to her voice, liquid and lovely, with growing intensity watched her glistening eyes as they drank glass after glass of beer, though she discreetly paced her sips. As twilight descended outside, she found his attention alluring, and in the cold of a January night, they huddled against one another while their drunken frames stumbled back to her dorm. Outside her hall, they paused, an urgent gaze in each other's eyes, then their warm mouths touched, softly at first, but lingering as he gently and momentarily tasted her lower lip. When they parted, Abbie saw the boy she feared, his mouth tight and narrow, the eyes flaming. Suddenly, she no longer was afraid of him. He had a new enemy now, and that former friend, who'd angrily blame her for perverting his sense of reason and morality, never would bother her either. She turned for the quiet of her room as the deafening voices of two angry men swirled at one another in the opaqueness of night.

*****

As the car door clicked shut, Abbie stared at the funeral home's lawn where snow had pebbled from ceaseless blasts of wind that pushed about miniscule mounds with each passing second. She sighed, tucked both hands deep into her pea coat. The straight, half-frozen steps of those who'd came before her – the tiny imprints of a fragile woman's heel, the heavy press of a young man's tennis shoe, the nondescript bottom of a man's rubber boot – stretched along the walkway's slush. A honeyed shimmer emanated from the mute white house, its columns holding a roof high over a grand porch, as if a marker erected by the Plains' men to stand against the wind's onslaught. Cold stung the insides of her nostrils as she walked, face slightly downcast, toward the monolith. I've never done this before, she thought, have never turned back toward those I've gotten revenge on. Her throat suddenly tightened and mouth grew dry, but she pushed on.

That day at dawn, the sun's orange glow lit the prairie's snow-white landscape so it glittered like a field of gold. Perhaps, she told herself, this great sheath under the twilight blue was the mirage that had given rise to Coronado's Seven Cities. It remained serenely quiet but for an occasional ground-laden gust that swirled icy flakes off the drifts. As Abbie sipped her black coffee, it warm upon the lips, she found it little comfort against the windowpane's cold. Between whiffs of the drink's awakening stearn, she still could imagine Lyle's faint scent, it musky upon her skin. A barren tree trembled distant on the horizon.

She arrived at the office early. Outside, the light slowly grew, its progress marked in sheets of yellow as it rose up the paneled walls. The coldness did not correspondingly fall, however, but unveiled by the day's brightness struck with an even greater fury. Then, as she typed a cutline for a photo accompanying her story, Abbie heard the name "Carl W. Steinar." Her head jerked up from the screen as she focused on Mrs. Lierley, who recited back the obituary just taken from Regier Mortuary. When finished, Abbie inched over to Mrs. Lierley's desk, spoke slowly. "Did you just write an obit for Carl Steinar?"

"Why, yes, did you know him?"

Abbie nodded timidly.

"Oh, of course. The windmill piece you did was about his farm. Yes, he died last night."

"Did they say what from?"

Mrs. Lierley's brow pinched. "No, they didn't. They often don't, you know."

There had been no mention of Carl Steinar in the village traffic reports, no fax from the sheriff's department saying he'd been killed in an accident. As she sat in the office that afternoon trying to organize meeting notes into a story of worth, she found herself wondering why he had hated her. From what Peter had said, he seemed to possess a sort of rustic horse sense, and that was a quality she could admire. Soon, the girl wondered how she herself could have felt so vile toward Peter – he'd only wanted to spend his life with her, only made the humblest of gestures that a man of genuineness could offer: of marriage, of saying "I need you to make me complete." But Peter had never directly said he'd needed her, had only made the symbolic offer. She wanted to hear those words to be certain, to feel them as if they were a warm wind brushing her cheek.

Abbie cautiously entered the funeral home. She knew about the loss of a father, could not leave if she wanted. Inside, a half-dozen farmers and their wives stood silently, backs slumped, faces more dour than usual. She glanced around for Peter and Lyle. Perhaps they would come to meet her, save her the agony of stepping before the watchful eyes of all those people. For some time, she stood at the back of the room, waiting to see if that might happen.

When Lyle left the funeral director's office, he found himself staring at the floor. The swell of his paunch blocked his view as he walked, his brother's shoulder almost beside him, Aunt Amita and Uncle Joe close behind. At least I'm unruffled by all of this while Peter hasn't even shaven in two days, Lyle thought himself. Then the younger Steinar glanced down at the sleeve of his starched white shirt that Aunt Amita had virtually demanded he wear for the wake, scratched at the itchy fabric across his forearm. He saw his hands trembling like loose plates on a running machine; in his mind he ordered them to stop. Within seconds both hands steadied. Grinning victoriously, he marveled at his own self-control even after he'd lost so much. He quickly pressed his mouth into a flat line once they entered the chapel. The four stood there silently, and cold air blew from a wall vent, prickling the back of his neck. He shivered. Gazing at the dozen or so people in attendance, he saw Edmund Wallace and his wife, cousin Brady, the banker Mr. Bart-mas, and then he did a double take. At the far entry, just behind Mrs. Wallace, stood Abbie. His mouth parted to speak, but he hesitated, knew he couldn't or Peter would see them together.

"I...I have to go back to the director's office," Lyle said. "I left something there."

He slipped past Aunt Amita, the smell of cooking lard rising from her, and went into the hallway. He paced it, keeping an eyes on the other entry to the chapel for her. Fluorescent lights shined dully in the windowless hallway. Then there she was, her soft blackberry hair falling over the black pea coat's collar as she stepped toward him.

"Why Abbie, it's good to see you – thank you for coming," he said. His hand stilled for a moment.

"My God, I'm so sorry about your father," she said. "Are you all right? How is Peter taking this?"

"He's not doing so good, as you probably saw, isn't

handling it quite as well as me."

So, Peter was right, Abbie thought, his brother does lie. "Your father – what...how did he–"

Lyle raised a hand to quiet her. "Suicide."

Abbie's hand flung to her mouth as she gasped. "Oh my – I..."

A darkness encircled Lyle's eyes. "At least I still have you in my life," he said. He raised a hand to caress her, but she stood just out of his reach.

Her lips quivered. "Maybe – maybe it wouldn't be a good time now for that. Your brother, he–" Then she paused, as if thinking better of what to say. "You two need each other right now. I don't want to come between you."

"You wouldn't–" But before he could finish, she began walking away. He took a step in pursuit, started to call her name but stopped. I can't afford to let Peter hear me, he told himself, not now. His hands clenched into fists, and he thought himself an empty can discarded along a trail.

Chapter 26

Peter's heart pounded unremittingly as the gunnysack filled with the family guns jabbed into his back and the wind bellowed across the snow-encrusted plain. Above him, the sky shined like a well-polished onyx. He chuckled at the irony of his trudging, though as doing so the icy air nipped the inside of his mouth; only a few weeks before amid the oppressive heat of Indian summer, he'd searched every shed and room for the guns, and now here he was trying to be rid of them. All night he'd thought of how that might be done, and then an hour before dawn he rose from his bed and decided it did not matter so long as it was done. He dressed quietly to not awake his brother, and from the pole shed brought a bag into which he loaded each gun kept at the living room cabinet. The dried streaks of his father's blood smeared onto his gloves as he picked up the rifle. Despite being worth several hundred dollars, he refused to think of selling them, could not stand the thought that they even existed. By burying them in the very earth from which their metal and wooden parts sprang, he surmised they might be exorcised from his memory.

As Peter slogged across the white field, he set his sights upon a distant blinking radio tower, it like a needle, the tip red-hot. For a moment, his lips quivered. Despite the blowing wind, the antenna's light never distorted, and he found odd how the array of air currents did not affect his vision. Still, only when he stood still and fixed his eyes upon a thing could he ever see something more in it, like the whorls of a thumbprint or the irises of a woman's eyes. Maybe it's just the growing tiredness upsetting my vision, he thought as continuing toward the far horizon. Peter gazed at the spread of snow-covered land, it glistening like a field of jagged diamonds as a frail crescent moon hovered above him. "I've given myself away to you and to this farm," he muttered, half-believing his father would hear. None of it made any sense, everything happening at once – his father's death, the breakup with Abbie, fighting with Lyle.

Why hadn't I taken the signs more seriously, Peter wondered as his feet pressed into the drifts.

He found the mystery of his own decisions impenetrable; like water washing against solid rock, it would take much wearing down to get at its core, perhaps more than even he had patience for. For several weeks, the old man seemed to stumble about zombie-like, as if in that stage between consciousness and sleep, yet who didn't when working out on the Plains under the brilliant sun and hot ripples of wind? But then there was the way his face hung heavy, as if a storm about to break, and how he'd sometimes wash his arms up to the elbows, over and over, several times a day. And what about the day they were fixing the fence together? Peter's teeth clenched as his pace quickened. Damn that Cornelius Skerry and his advice, he muttered to himself, what did he know about anything? Then the chilled wind tempered his broiling blood. His father was not an easy man to know, never confessing or denying, often leaving one hanging in ambiguity. His make-do attitude always led to the sparest of a life, yet he supposed there must have been much more buried underneath that sheath of stone. The guns clattered against one another as his knees stepped high through the snow. It's another good mess you've left us, he whispered as pondering what would happen to the farm. His brother lacked the self-discipline to run it with him; he'd have to take on a greater share of the work.

Panting, Peter reached a small depression, a circle like that of an old, filled-in well beneath the field's white cover. Kneeling in it, his legs sank through the snow until they touched the buried wheat's pointed stems. He dropped the gunnysack to his side, and for a moment the muscles of his arm sighed in relief. As his lungs rasped, he gazed at a distant prairie bush, covered in hoarfrost, wavering in the blackness, then behind him at the snow pulled up like rubble about the craters of his footsteps, stretching in a long line back to the yard. Peter hoped the gusts would erase his footprints so his brother could not follow. He still had no idea what to do with the guns, tried to think of a place they could be tossed. He decided to march on. Slinging the gunnysack over his shoulder, Peter stood. The wind wore against his cheeks already flushed with exertion, and continuing, he tried to conjure good memories just as when washing his father's blood from the living room floor.

He imagined standing before his father, telling him that there was nothing to be ashamed of in needing help, that he still was the strongest person in the family, that taking medications to deal with the loss was okay. "Now that is disapproved of," his old man would have said. Peter understood what he meant then placed a hand upon the old man's back and said, "Don't do it for yourself or for me – do it for the land our forefathers broke." His father would hesitate for a moment then hold out his hands, palms up. If only they had something in common, beyond loss, to bind them, Peter thought. Then he added, "The land is who we are, Father. It is our destiny." The old man would chuckle nervously. "Guess I'm just a stubborn old Norwegian," he'd say as if to explain away his resistance. The two men would laugh heartily.

With the back of a glove, Peter wiped the frost along his stubble. He shook his head, knew his father never could have been persuaded like that; why, talking to him was pointless, no better than driving in circles. As he sighed, the first pink of dawn ringed the horizon. If only I could quilt together this hodgepodge of emotions into a coherent whole, he thought, then glancing at the tower's red light fading in the early morning glow, abruptly turned west for the creek.

There was but one way to get rid of the guns, he realized, and with that his body warmed and his pace quickened. Ahead of him, the bare tops of cottonwoods and willows appeared like cracks across the bottom of a windshield. The wool of his stocking cap scratched against the hair and forehead, soaked with the sweat of his efforts. At the bank, he sidestepped down the ravine, no longer paid any attention to the coldness encasing his toes. The frozen creek's milky surface meandered through a still woods. Reaching the shore, he dumped the guns from the sack and picking up the heaviest one, the shotgun, raised both arms over his head and hurled it at the water. Its stock smashed through the thin ice, splashing up chilled water then sinking. Peter grabbed the rifle, repeated the throw. The butt broke away a chunk of ice then drowned as well. The current below the frozen surface clutched the guns, forced them along downstream. In turn, he threw each of the remaining firearms into the water.

Peter left the gunnysack there and ascended the hill. Snow clung to the calves of his denim as the dampness of breath gave way to the dry air. Upon the plain, the sun glimmered like a copper penny at the lowest point on the cold horizon. Released from the cargo, his shoulders relaxed, but the muscles in his thighs ached from high stepping through the deep drifts. Still, he pushed on. It was the one great lesson his father taught him: The path to happiness was constant planning and unceasing labor in accomplishing one's aim. The problem all my life, he thought to himself, is that I never shared the same goals as my father. Ironically, with the old man's death, he also could not help but feel as if a great boulder had been lifted from him. He resolved to get Abbie back. As dawn fully arrived, shadows pooled in the field.

*****

Lyle awoke when an orange ray of sun poked through a pinhole in his browned roller shade. He rubbed his eyes, planted both feet on the cold floor. Outside, gusts sent the windmill alternately clacking and whirring. The wind must just be starting up, he thought, for the night had been relatively calm, oddly peaceful. Sluggishly, he headed down the stairs, hoped his brother was still asleep. Without their father, he needed time to think of what to do next. Probably nothing would happen that day; Peter and their aunt and uncle would see to that. After calling the ambulance, the trio had taken over: Aunt Amita handled the cleanup of their father's blood, Uncle Joe made arrangements with the mortuary, Peter hovered over him to ensure he'd no time to be alone. The funeral would not be for another day, and he found little was expected of men who'd lost their father except to spend the hours waiting.

In the kitchen, Lyle tapped the grounds from the coffeepot into the trashcan. The death of his father and the loss of Abbie would be too much for almost any man to take, he thought as spooning fresh grounds into the filter. Its aroma swirled upward, snapped him fully awake. He heard her words again: "You two need each other right now. I don't want to come between you." Already he missed the way she swayed blissfully, like a sunflower. He filled the coffee vat with water, let its *swoosh!* overtake his ability to hear his own thoughts. I don't need to remind myself that I feel more remorse for the loss of her than of my own father, he told himself. He clicked on the coffeepot, listened to it percolate as the base heated and brew dripped into the vat. Still, despite living all of those years with him, Lyle admitted he barely knew the man who was his father.

The old man was frugal, that much Lyle understood; how many years had he balked at spending money on painting the kitchen until both boys themselves grew used to its tattered appearance and did not want to see it changed? He also was a stern judge. Upon hearing what he believed was a bad idea, he'd sniff the air and say, "There's something in the wind," and should you persist, he in no uncertain terms would tell you what he thought and the way it was going to be. Still, Lyle sensed there was something more to him than just that, as if some pain were compressed so tightly inside his frame that it could hardly be contained.

At times, Lyle tried to bond with his father, tried to show that he being caged also hurt. He remembered being ten and standing by the creek with his father as two banks of gray clouds reduced the sky's blue to a mere strip overhead. His father wiped the band of sweat from his forehead, leaned against a spade fresh with the muddy scent of red clay. The cottonwood leaves rustled as Lyle stared at the rectangle of upturned dirt between them. Then his father headed for the path leading to the pickup.

Lyle half-gasped in amazement. "Father…" he stuttered

in a strained voice, then he repeated himself, louder, more firm.

Carl paused, glanced over his shoulder at him. "Come along now. We've got work to do."

"But the insides of his mouth grew bitter in taste as the choked-back sniffles dripped into his throat. "But we haven't given Jesse a headstone."

"A what?"

"A headstone, to show who is buried here."

His father swore under the breath, retraced his steps to the grave. "It's a dog. Dogs don't get headstones. "

Lyle gazed up at him. "Why?"

"Because they're dogs."

"But...I loved Jesse."

His father stared a long moment at him. The old man's eyes softened, Lyle thought – years later was certain of it – but then his mouth hardened. "We all did. But we didn't let Jesse eat at the table, either, did we? Dogs don't get headstones, that's all there is to it."

Lyle cast his eyes down at the soil, it brilliant in the day's remaining sunlight. He wondered if Peter, off on some afternoon with the local 4-H, would have insisted on a headstone. Likely his elder brother would have sneered and sided with their father. If Jesse was to be properly remembered, it would up to him alone.

"Just a cross then?" Lyle said. "We could make a cross out of sticks." He quick picked up one, showed it to his father.

Carl rolled his eyes. "All right, we'll plant a god damn cross for the dog." The old man kicked lightly at sticks on the ground then grasped one. "Run up to the truck and get some twine," he said, and as Lyle did, he overheard his father mutter, "The god damned dog is buried in a nicer placer place then his mother."

Lyle spun around. His mother – he wanted to speak just then but words escaped him. Perhaps, he thought, it was because I had nothing to say.

Lyle poured coffee into a mug, watched it steam upward in the early morning chill. As staring out the window, he brought the drink to his lips. Its bitterness hung in his mouth even after swallowing. The wind blew eroded crystals of snow across the drifts as the windmill clattered away. All my life I've tried to reach my father, and just when I think I have, he kills himself, Lyle whispered. And then, as the sun's glow stretched across the yard, he saw the broken line through the smooth drifts. He leaned close to the window, felt the chill upon his nose even as the half-raised coffee warmed his chin. They were footsteps, leading from the house to the pole shed then back again, and finally out into the field, west toward the Bris property, made just that morning. Lyle set the mug upon the counter and headed for the entryway. He pulled on his overalls, then his coat and boots.

*****

The morning Carl Steinar killed himself, he believed that dawn's orange glow bathed the farmhouse in peace and warmth. But winter merely had chilled the world into dormancy. The yard's bare-branched trees remained still, the tightly packed snow lay undisturbed, and the icicles upon the rain gutters hung indifferently. Having flown to Mexico for the long, dim months, no birds sang, and even the cats kept to the hay shed, unwilling to leave the heat of their collective slumbers. Smoke languidly curled from the chimney.

Inside, Carl's alarm rang, and he rose ploddingly but certainly, pausing only at the edge of his bed before taking the first step onto the cold floor and into the day. A gray hue filled his room, but he could sense sunshine about the curtain's sides. He rubbed his eyes, the rough balls of his hands scratching him awake, and yawned. Standing, his wool socks barely deflected the wind's bite, and he ambled to the door, the wood boards creaking below him. Time to wake the boys, he thought to himself, as he had every morning for almost 20 years. It used to be Gwen's job, but that like all else in his sons' two worlds had become his duty. It was the task he dreaded the most, though like any sentinel sworn to uphold his post, he bore it well, without emotion. To wake into the abyss of another day was a horrible enough trial for any man, but to force others into that great chasm seemed heinous, beastly.

He entered the hallway. "Boys!" he said. "Time to wake up!" But then he paused as the loose board beneath his foot moaned. No sound came from either bedroom. He stepped into the doorway of Peter's room, saw only a made bed, its brown spread tattered at the edges. Turning around, he glanced into Lyle's room, found the same scattering of sheets he'd noticed when passing the room the night before. His eyes sunk. Sluggishly, he headed for the stairs, gripped the railing tight as taking each dizzying step downward.

At the living room, he sat in his chair, gazed out the window. Snow twisted and snarled upon writhing currents, and the old man saw he'd been wrong about the sunlight. The freak autumn storm had continued through the night and showed only the slimmest sign of letting up. He straightened himself, patted the armrest. "Better put on some coffee, Gwen," he said, "it's going to be a cold one." But as Carl Steinar rose, he realized there was no spouse to share coffee with. There were no sons to wake. There was only him.

He climbed slowly up the stairs as the gusts hissed outside. In his room, he drew a shirt from the closet. He thought of the cruelty of memory, how it constantly reminded him of loss. Opening a drawer, he found a pair of jeans and slid each leg into them. Her death stood as a dividing line, he knew, the edge between the lightness of sky and the blackness of a great abyss. Pulling a belt through his jean's loops, he pondered how long he could fall before clattering like a great stone against the pit's bottom. Lastly, he sat upon the bed and put on his work boots, foot by foot, lacing each one in stride.

The blast of the telephone ringing broke the silence, and he spoke briefly with his youngest son.

At last, he returned to his chair, watched the spiraling snow outside his window, wondered if the cattle needed feed, if any were stranded in the pasture. Then his face warped and twisted like the lumber of an aged cottonwood. The same fate ultimately befalls both man and beast, he thought. Each rises from the same dust, both breathe the same air, each return to the same ground. Outside, a shrieking white covered the window. Who really knows if a man's spirit goes upward or if a beast's soul returns to the earth, he asked himself His stomach churned slowly, painfully, until he grew immune to it the way numbness overtakes a man being whipped to death.

For a long time to Carl Steinar, the hours stood still, as if he were a great boulder carried all that way by Ice Age glaciers and was merely waiting to return. He thought once more of Gwen, of how she always sang ahead of or behind the notes, but her voice, sweet as melted butter, made it all forgivable. She no longer was there, he knew, could no longer lift him up. Each night since her departure, he'd lay cold and alone. A man by himself might prevail against adversity, but two together surely would withstand them, he told himself Once I had been strong, very strong, and he set upon warming his heart with thoughts of who he once was, of when he still could hold his beloved wife and of when his sons did not despise him. And so, as the memories of his past curled and withered like sun-baked paper, he found himself staring forward in time, at his own body, at his flesh and ideas reduced to wind-blown ash, forgotten and unimportant, until the emptiness of his endeavors filled and solidified him, until all he had left was his great, meaningless bulk, uncaring and unconcerned about the present. At best, he thought to himself, I am sand, a layer for all the future to build upon, the weight of its infinity burying and crushing me.

Though the house remained cold, no chill ran through him. "Gwen, I just can't feel the pain anymore," he said aloud, "even when you're sitting right there before me." Carl stretched his hand outward like a drowning man deperately hoping someone would grasp it and pull him to safety, but there was only emptiness. He gazed out the window. Snow sprang and swirled from all directions, masking the farm buildings and windmill from his view.

*****

With the lights off, Abbie dug through Mrs. Lierley's middle drawer for the extra key to Cary Sutherland's office. Usually he left it wide open, but on weekends it was locked, if only because it had become part of the editor's Friday night closing ritual. The Guthrie County Register never had been broken into during all of its years of business, and Mr. Sutherland often joked that it was bound to happen as the odds were now against him. Why he believed a burglary would happen only on the weekend escaped her, and she chalked it up to some small town fiction. At last, she found the key, half-buried beneath a sheath of loose papers. It was a charming notion, Abbie thought, that people were too busy doing an honest day's work to commit a crime on a weekday, and yet, here she was, entering his office without permission on a Saturday morning.

As the lock unclicked, Abbie slowly pushed the creaking door open just enough to slip inside.

Careful to not disturb anything, she set her purse upon a clear space on the carpet and eased into his chair. She snapped the computer on, and as the whir of its drive rose, the screen cast a blue glow across her face. Though she had a computer at home, it wasn't hooked to the Internet – nor on her salary would it ever be – but that was the only way to find a job in journalism anymore. She did not mind, fully knew that the quiet life did not require connection to the broader, urban world that the Web provided. The Register, being a small paper, could not afford the Internet for each of its terminals, but Cary Sutherland was not one to ignore its potential. He had installed a modem on his computer – and his alone – in the office.

A tick sounded from the front entry, and Abbie's eyes shot up. She sat utterly still for a moment, heard the rattle again. It was only the wind, she realized, pressing against the glass of the front door. Her attention returned to the screen, and the modem whirred and beeped as she logged on. Sweat trickled along the back of her neck, but she resisted taking off her coat in case a fast break was needed. All she needed to do was go to a couple of sites, make some quick printouts. She could read the list of job openings at home, in comfort.

Home. Abbie sighed at the feeling that she considered her tiny Felton apartment a "home." As the search engine scrolled slowly onto the screen, she thought back to that morning when she awoke. Leaning against the bedpost, she locked an arm around the smooth cedar. Its scent mingled with her night sweat, and she smiled. For a moment, her delicate frame sat perched, ready to rise, then she yawned deeply, her mouth a great maw, and as the lips closed, she ran a hand through her brunette hair and stretched like a cat. Her eyes gazed murkily out at the dim room. "I need coffee," she said.

In Cary Sutherland's office, she typed the name of a job bank. As it downloaded, she stared at her reflection on the screen, tried to see the brown hues of her pupils just as she had when in the bathroom washing up. The sink's water warmed her skin, like her body felt when she and Peter laid curled tight to one another. The coffeepot percolated, and she caught the first whiff of its aroma as the automatic timer clicked the machine into brew mode. Droplets of water eked down her chin. She hadn't wanted it to end as it did.

Abbie knew nothing at all ever could resolve her differences with the Steinar brothers.

Apologies and giving in would go only so far, and at that she'd have to be the one to make the first overture. Well, she thought to herself, it's not as if I wanted reconciliation anyway – just retribution. Still, it seemed to her misplaced. She thought of her father just then, of his fine hewn body silhouetted in the sun, of his trembling as learning to walk again during physical therapy, of his flabby limbs hanging from a husk of a man. For some time she had not talked with him. Nor did she any longer want to see the look of despair upon Peter's face after his lying brother told him that he'd slept with her. Yet, is that not what revenge is about, she reasoned, the pleasure of seeing the victim suffer? She laughed aloud. And who was the victim here, really?

She hit the print command on the computer, listened to it drone in the newsroom. If anyone came in now they'd certainly hear it, and without any of the computers on, easily could deduce that she'd been in Cary Sutherland's office. She hoped for the best.

The only other option was to waste away, like she had after washing up. Head drooping, she'd poured herself a cup of coffee and limped back to the bedroom. There, she set the cup on the lamp table and fell again into the sheets. For a half hour or more, she lay backward in bed, an arm half dangling off the mattress, her silky knees bent against the pillow, eyes staring askew at the ceiling. She'd never rested in that position before and wondered if there was some reason the headboard always was positioned against the wall rather than in the middle of the room. The kitchen clock ticked as the gauze curtains shimmered in the sunlight. She brought a wrist to her face, but even with eyelids closed there was no scent of him, only the milky perfume of her own soap. Swallowing hard, she found moving difficult. Letting time sip one up seemed easier, preferable.

She printed another job list. On it she caught the names of cities and newspapers – Boise, Carlsbad, the News Journal – with reporter openings. Most were dailies, all were out-of-state. Leaving Peter behind would be difficult, she admitted. Despite her anger at him, not all men boasted – her father never had, nor had Peter Steinar. She knew Lyle would, could sense it in the way he spoke of how he was going to improve the farm – the red metal gates, the new shed with its concrete floor – certainly, she understood, he wasn't going to do that, not so long as Peter and their father remained there. Real men did not speak of their visions, she knew; they acted upon them.

And then at that thought she sat straight up as her face finned. She would move on, search for the quiet life elsewhere. Felton merely had been a wrong turn, but one that had made her stronger, more certain than ever before. There was much to do.

A list from a third job bank printed, and she supposed there were enough leads. I've tempted fate too long, she told herself, then shutting off the computer, grabbed her purse by its handles and tiptoed out of the room. She discreetly closed the door, turned the lock. After what Lyle would tell Peter of her, she knew there was no going back to him. She returned the key to Mrs. Lierley's drawer and gathering the printouts, folded the paper in half and stuck them in her purse.

Chapter 27

The day before Carl Steinar's funeral, somberness lingered in his household like a deep bruise.

Aunt Amita, Uncle Joe and Brady sat with dull eyes upon the living room sofa, as if patiently waiting at the station for a bus to arrive while Peter stared into the empty expanses between them. At length, he rose from the couch, and head drooping limped past Lyle to the phone. There, his hand hung suspended for several long seconds above the receiver. The time is all wrong, he told himself, yet she kept moving through his mind like water, fluidly and gathering force with each thought. If I just apologize...Withdrawing his hand, he leaned against the kitchen counter, examined the pear rotting beside him.

The tarrying pressed against him like a murderer's pillow slowly suffocating its victim. Steinar men pushed back, did not cower even if their last breaths were leaving them, he told himself. If there was one thing worthwhile he'd learned from his father, it was that. Lyle watched him from the kitchen chair as if a cat waiting to see which way the cornered mouse would turn. Peter picked up the phone, dialed.

It rang once, then twice. On the fourth ring, an answering machine clicked. "Hello, you've reached 574–" He slammed down the receiver.

"Who you trying to call?" Lyle said.

Peter crossed his arms. "Abbie."

"Now why would you be trying to call her?"

"Because I want to talk with her, what do you think for?"

Lyle studied his brother's furrowed brow. "I don't think she'd want to talk. I hear she's already got somebody else."

Peter's eyes ballooned then his lips twisted into a sneer. "Who?"

Lyle waited for a long, measured moment then smiled crookedly. "Me. She's gone out once so far with me."

Peter's eyes widened again, then as if a river rising higher and higher, his jaw pointed up and shoulders bulked. He grabbed Lyle by the V of his shirt.

Lyle's face transformed into a sheet of white. "Turn loose," he said, his arms open.

Peter jut his face directly into Lyle's. Even when working side by side, the two brothers had not been so physically close to one another in years, and the weight of Peter's presence loomed. Lyle had touched many cattle as herding them but rarely Peter under any circumstance. He thought his brother smelled familiar, like earth, like himself.

"'Turn loose' nothing," Peter said. He raised his fist.

Lyle did not crouch, knew Peter wouldn't punch him. Then, he saw the arrows in his brother's eyes, and as he probed them with his own, like a poker player trying to gauge a bluff, Peter's fist hit him squarely on the mouth. Lyle stumbled back, and lifting an arm to strike with his wrist inadvertently blocked a second blow. Suddenly Lyle felt Aunt Amita's hot breath upon his neck, and she pulled him away as Uncle Joe and Brady grasped his brother.

"Here now, what's wrong with you two?" Aunt Amita

said as standing between then, her camphor scent strong. "That's a fine way to act, after what has happened to your father. What would he say if he caught you like that, if he were here?"

Glaring, the two brothers backed off from one another; Peter ignored the spittle on his chin, Lyle the smart running across his mouth.

Aunt Amita's voice snapped like a willow switch. "What was that all about anyway?" she said. "I've never seen you two fight, even when you were children."

Lyle ignored her, ran the back of his wrist against a cut lip. The blood glistened like the cast of red sun across rippling water. "You still haven't said why you went outside this morning."

"I told you, I was taking a walk."

Lyle's mouth twisted haughtily. "Right."

Peter's lip curled as his uncle and cousin released him. "I don't believe it about you and Abbie."

"You oughta. We went pretty far." He watched the anger bubble on Peter's face until it reached the point of almost boiling over. "In fact, I fucked her."

Peter's fist swung again, like the head of a blunt club, and striking Lyle's eye his brother plummeted to the floor, the shoulder bouncing on the tile.

For a moment, Lyle's vision blackened. His palms pressed into the gritty tile as he tried to raise himself, but his head swooned. He glanced up at Peter. The light struck only half of his brother's face, but that was enough to show the anger in it. Wind blew at the door.

And then, as Lyle's head dropped to regain his equilibrium, he felt the swift displacement of air from Peter's leg as it swung toward him. The foot slammed into his ribs, rolling him onto the side. He pushed against the floor to stand, only to sense the same gust of leg shifting again and the sudden thud of foot catching his abdomen. He let out an *oomph!*, found himself rolling onto his waist.

Aunt Arnita shrieked as Uncle Joe and Brady grabbed Peter then pulled his body and flailing legs away. "Stop it! It's like a civil war in here!" she hollered.

A chair bounced as Lyle heard his brother's frame thrown into it. For a minute, the younger Steinar lay un-moving, allowed his mouth to regain its moisture. But, even down on the floor, he refused to wince.

*****

Despite rubbing his eyes, Peter could not bring himself to sit down. He paced the length of the room again, stepping upon the very floor where only days before his father's body had lain, found himself questioning. Aunt Amita had cleaned the mess with some help from him, but it had only stoked the already roiling inner turmoil.

After Uncle Joe had thrown him back into the kitchen chair, Aunt Amita nudged Lyle upstairs.

Peter found himself ready to spring after his brother, but Uncle Joe loomed like a bull before him, and with Brady standing only a few feet away, the eldest Steinar decided it best to stay put and so merely crossed his arms. Perhaps it's the little boy in me that fears this hulking man with the foul mouth, he thought, but then his mind wandered; maybe I really did go over the line.

Uncle Joe's chin shifted. "You're going to stay there now, damn it – right?"

Peter nodded.

"Cause I don't want no god damn trouble anymore, you hear?"

The two men eyed each other evenly, then Peter sheep-ishly glanced away.

"Good then," Uncle Joe said. "You're getting too old to be stood over, and I'm getting too old to keep standing." He stared at Peter for a moment then returned to the dining room, Brady closely following him. They sat at the table, hands folded before them as if waiting.

As Peter lingered in the wooden chair, he heard water running intermittently from the bathroom.

His brother was washing up, he suspected. He harrumphed; there was no amount of water that could cleanse Lyle of his lies. Uncle Joe and Brady looked up at Peter, and he flattened his grin. As the minutes passed on the clock, he listened closely for the faucet, for Aunt Amita's voice. No words came though, only the tick of the clock, the wind outside blowing in great huffs as if it were running a marathon, and the water oscillating between being on and off. The cast of sunlight slowly drifted down the farmhouse's walls. Amid the breaks of silence, doubts flashed through him like a thousand candles chaotically lit and extinguished. He wondered about the memory of his own mother: Was it an illusion I believed in, a ghost no more substantial than my breath? An image as empty as the air she floated upon? His nose crinkled angrily, and he rose.

Uncle Joe and Brady shot up in the dining room, Midstep, Peter paused, raised his hands in surrender. "I just want to stand, okay?" he said. "I won't leave your sight."

Uncle Joe examined his eyes then nodded and slowly sat. His son followed in turn.

Standing amid the gray room, Peter kept hearing a thin cry in the air, knew it was merely the wind, yet thought for a moment that it might be the phantom of his dead father lingering upon the earth, unable to accept his demise. He stared out the window as if to search for the image, saw only a whirling swarm of snow blown off the drifts. What is memory but a spray of images and ideas, he asked himself. Yet, perhaps it is as real as the chair I sit in, for father must had decided he no longer could stand being without such perfection. His heart slowed as the heat of anger cooled. Peter knew that throughout his life, when his understanding of the world expanded, he reinvented his vision of her to survive. In a sense, he thought, his memory was like the wind: realigning, shifting and adjusting to places and pro-portions, just as it was doing now to the billows of snow out upon the prairie, just as his own mind always had done to the memory of his mother since she'd died. He folded his arms to ward off the house's chill. Well, what is life then, he asked himself, but a constant going back and forth between memories and the reality of the earth beneath us? If only we could still our recollections, could find equilibrium, a state of peaceful rest. Perhaps that was what father had always wished for.

The hot water pipes shuddered as the water ran again upstairs. He shook his head. Here I am, he told himself, crawling again before my old man, but this time through my brother, still believing all their lies. He cast his eyes to the corner of the kitchen where a dust ball, gray and fuzzy, rested. His lower lip curled with uncertainty: Had Lyle deliberately set them against one another for all those years? The heat of a long stare flushed across the back of his neck, and he whirled about. Aunt Amita stood in the doorway, her arms crossed.

"Are you two going to act that way tomorrow, at the funeral?" she said.

"It depends what he–"

"Don't take that tone with me," she said. "'It' depends on nothing."

Peter bit his lip. "What do you expect of me?"

"What I expect of both of you, of course."

"Which is?"

"That you act like a family – like two brothers – should. I'm certain that's what your father would have expected. And your mother, too."

Peter's face paled slightly. He remembered his mother singing but heard a distorted melody.

Aunt Amita was the only flesh and blood link to her. He nodded.

*****

As pain flared across Lyle's bruised ribs, he found tempering his emotions difficult. Yet, such control was necessary he told himself, for without it his body only would suffer more, only would make foolish decisions like taking the ravine side too swiftly as he was doing at that moment. The embankment was not particularly steep, but at his quick pace in the downreaching snow – despite Peter's half-concealed tracks – the chance of tumbling rose exponentially. Still, even in reason's face, his thoughts and heart would not slow and he believed himself a wind smashing into a building when it should logically guide itself around the structure. His leg muscles burned as both feet bound through the drifts covering the uneven surface of dead grass and glacial rock.

At last he reached the ravine's bottom and paused. A gunnysack lay caught in a chokeberry bush's stripped branches, a plastic edge flapping in the light but chilled breeze. Panting heavily, he examined the white ground about it, compressed by dozens of boot steps. His own feet bristled from the mix of cold and sweat, and kneeling he scanned the bag. It could not have been outside for long, he surmised; barely any of it was covered by snow, and none of it had been browned by the elements.

He rose. Before him lay the creek, it motionless and white like a midnight moon, and then he saw how a section of the ice was thin, a freshly-formed layer beneath which blue spring water gurgled. In a few days there'd be no sign at all of the break, he knew. Lyle remained motionless: an exhausted man and the wild creek, creatures of two unique planes, one rushing about indifferent to the larger universe about it, the other silent and contemplative, attempting to discover some sense to it. He stared at the gunnysack, sensed that somehow it was connected to the new ice. His hand grasped the bag's flopping edge, tore it from the snow and bush; with a screech, a side of the sack ripped. Opening it, his hand felt for anything that could be grabbed. Then, as gazing inside, searching to see if his hand had missed something, he caught the strong waft of cleaning oil and gunpowder.

His heart stilled.

Lyle's eyes scanned downstream, hoping to still spot them. They'd come up next spring, he knew, and if seen early enough could be fished out. But, even now, after only a few hours in the chilled water, they were severely damaged. His gloved hands rolled into fists, and a new energy surged through him. Despite the ache along his hips, he scurried up the snow-encrusted embankment, refused to take Peter's half-made trail. I may be bulky, clumsy, even a quitter, he thought, but I am not fragile, am not beaten.

At the top, the Plains' blinding whiteness scoured his eyes. Perhaps not all the guns were gone, he thought, just the one father had used. Father, he thought, not dad? Before him, windswept snow high off the drifts so it floated like clouds against the brilliant blue sky. Twice I'd been able to stop him, and just when I'd come to trust the old man, he does himself in. Perhaps giving the farm to me was just a ruse. As he stepped through the drifts, swirls of snow streaked about his feet then upward. Yes, it was all a ruse, he told himself, my existence had never meant anything to him or Dusty or Peter or Abbie. The cold ate at his nostrils then the insides of his very lungs as he breathed harder with each step. Why, the only person it probably would have mattered to was gone, he told himself, gone long ago, gone before he even had a chance to remember her.

Pain shot across his torso, and grasping his side, he found his vision blackening. A warm dizziness flushed through his head, but he resisted stumbling, continued onward. The snow crunched beneath his feet; for a moment he found it deafening. He remained proud of himself for not showing fragility when knocked down by his brother, and the memory of such success boosted his resolve. He grit his teeth. Tramping over the snow was easy, he told himself, was no more difficult than in summer when he'd work his way through the knee-high wheat, their tassels bobbing like a flame's pointed tips. I don't need them, he whispered, and then he said it again but much louder, and finally he screamed it, "I don't need them! I don't need them!" until it resounded over the empty prairie like rifle blasts.

Suddenly Lyle stumbled, saw the horizon go askance. His gloved hands caught the fall, but snow sloshed against the exposed break of his wrist and slipped inside the sleeve then across the palms. He panted hard. Must get up, he told himself, must get up. Snow matted along his pant legs, and he found himself shivering. With rest, his senses returned. Must get up and do what, he asked. Go back to my brother? Farm the land with someone who despises it and me? Be surrounded by walls of lies and hatred? For a moment, the wind died, leaving a clear though cold sky about him. I need to get away from here, he told himself, not so much to sort things out as to simply get away from them; North Platte probably would not even be far enough. As the compacted snow beneath his body began to refreeze, he found his frame shifting like a boulder carried aloft a great glacier. Crouching, he regained his breath, in his mind blocked the pain the best that he could. Yes, go back, he told himself, go back and propose to Peter that once the estate is settled they sell the farm. He stood, cautiously stepped forward. Yes, that is what I'll do, he thought as taking a second then a third step. Frozen sunlight spread across him and the lustrous field while he marched.

*****

Sitting in the stolid pew watching the pastor make the sign of the cross from the mount, the Steinar brothers found themselves uncertain. Neither moved, nor did either glance at the other. Above them, the pastor recited numbers, and as the rustle of turned pages filled the church, he spoke: "Moses lifted his hand, and with his rod he smote the rock twice: and water came out abundantly. "

The Steinar brothers had not been in a church for many years; after Carl had broken up with Mina, he simply stopped going, gave no explanation for it, just as he never did for any of his decisions. To the boys, it did not matter for church always had been a place of uncomfortable, formal clothes and reprimands to sit still in hard, oak seats as a man droned about concepts and notions they did not understand. So the boys did not question why. Instead, they spent their Sunday mornings as they did each day of the week when at home: first breakfast, then chores in the cool morning followed by lunch, a continuing of work through the hot afternoon, dinner, and finally a short reprieve before the night's sleep. The old man supposed they did not ask because of the self-discipline that he'd taught them. To a degree he was right, but they mainly did not inquire for fear that he'd rethink his decision and make them go back to church. At that tender age, they still believed his primary interest was ensuring their happiness.

A somber ray of light spread through a stained glass window as the audience rose for the commendation. Peter and Lyle stood a second behind Aunt Amita, her body obese and graying, and the churchgoers read aloud the words on the sheets printed for them. Their voices began as a mumble, the frayed end of a thread, then grew louder and more coherent as the syllables weaved into a smooth string. Both Steinar brothers found the standing a relief upon their sore backs. Then, they heard the pastor, his tone a stark, cold timbre: "...you created me, saying 'You are dust, and to dust you shall return.' All of us go down to the dust; yet even at the grave we make our song..." The musty odor of old wood filled the church. Their throats dry, Lyle and Peter swallowed hard. The organ's gothic pitch rose as if some supernatural exorcising of their father from this world.

Carl figured that through the farm he could teach the boys all they would have learned anyway in church. There wasn't much difference between country life and the Hebrew bible, he told himself: both were either milk and honey or red desert land. As for the New Testament, he didn't half believe it himself, found the cry for compassion an unacceptable apology for weakness, had thought the assault upon the temple's moneychangers a brash, radical action. The Christ he most admired was the one perched upon the donkey, riding into Jerusalem, ever hopeful though the reader knew certain death awaited him. The ministers and pastors never made enough of that tale, he thought. They always preferred to talk of charity, mercy and glory.

And then Peter found himself standing when everyone

else had taken a seat; Aunt Amita tugged at the hem of his suit coat, which scratched like a thornbush against his skin, and looking about he realized his error. Peter sat slowly, as if he'd intended to remain on his feet for that long. All there would forgive him for his transgression, all the men with weary faces of reddened flesh, all the women with hair somberly pulled back and dark maroon lipstick painted upon their mouths. It was a sign of how much he grieved, they'd say, of how his pain ran so deep that he'd been separated from the real world.

No sooner had he sat than the pastor dismissed them with his last words: "...Make you perfect in every good work to do his will, working in you that which is well-pleasing in his sight; through Jesus Christ, to whom be glory for ever and ever. Amen."

"Amen," the audience responded and then rose.

But Peter remained in his pew for a second, his body still and cool as if once half-buried and covered with dust, now freed from the earth and polished. As he stood, Lyle shuffled ahead of him. They worked their way past pained eyes, dropped shoulders and red blotches on women's faces from crying. Neither of the brothers could entirely make out who was there, only caught glimpses of Amita's daughter Gretel, of Mr. and Mrs. Edmund Wallace, of Cornelius Skerry. Then, as they stepped into the white sky of outdoors, cold struck them like a rock slammed across unsuspecting fingers. Lyle shivered. Their eyes readjusted to the light, and each examined the trail of footprints angled across the flat lawn of snow, misguided attempts at obtaining a short cut. The wind blew harder at them, as if they suddenly stood in a vacuum, then glancing over their shoulders saw the crowd parting as the pallbearers made their way down the church's center aisle. The brothers stepped aside. As the coffin passed, they thought of the man inside it, of his powdered face, the stitched lips, the closed eyelids. They did not believe the corpse real.

Around them, people milled about as if birds scattered across a beach. Uncle Gil stepped up to Peter, patted his back. "He's at peace now, boys, he's at peace," their uncle said, and then gazing at the frozen ground, the snow upon it thin as white hair on an old man's head, he nodded and walked off.

The hands of the Steinar boys trembled. Each knew everything had suddenly changed.

Chapter 28

Despite not knowing where she would go, Abbie had boxed most of her belongings. Such uncertainty little mattered to her; she'd decided to leave even if a new job wasn't certain. Still, she packed her belongings with the utmost care, delicately wrapping each dish in newspaper, perfectly fitting each item into boxes, cautiously thinking of herself as a woman learning to walk again. A driving anger toward Peter and Lyle raged inside, forced her to press onward; how can I ever face either brother again, she thought. In the few months of living in Felton, she'd learned the rhythms of small town life all too well; rumor stuck to one's identity as if it were mud to a shoe. Soon all of the townsfolk would talk of her bedding both Steinar farm boys, whether it be true or not.

Abbie put her mind to the task at hand: first she had to pack. As arranging a suitcase, she mulled over possible destinations. There were jobs in Lincoln and Omaha, the suburban papers of Denver. She shook her head at each idea. She wanted to race across open fields, the grass green and soft beneath her bare soles. I need to go somewhere I've never been before, she told herself

A knock on the door startled Abbie's slow march. She pulled aside a living room curtain; the heat perforated the snow and reduced the icicles to long, dripping lines as the sun's warmth burned against her face. At the door stood Peter, the grass iridescent between them. Then his eyes locked on to hers, and he turned to the window. She quick shut the curtain, stepped back from it. It did not deter him; he shouted her name through the window, asked that she let him in.

Silence hovered for a moment, but she still could sense his presence there, could feel the slush upon the grass dampening his boots. "Come on Abbie, please," he shouted once more. "Let me in. We've got to talk." Her mouth wrinkled as she searched for a direction. She knew he wasn't the violent type, wouldn't hit her. Slowly, she un-chained the door and turned the dead bolt.

As the door creaked open, Peter entered hesitantly, hands stuffed in coat pockets. He gazed at the gapes and holes in her decor, the piles of boxes, the paneling nails jut-ting from the plaster walls. "What's all this?" he said, his voice unsteady as meekly waving at the array.

"I'm moving. To another town."

His eyes widened.

She closed both eyes, massaged her temples. "So, what did you want to talk about?"

His pupils firmed. "I understand you went out with my brother." He paused for a moment. "What was that about?"

"What do you think?"

"I don't know. You tell me."

"I'm not sure if I can explain. And even if I could, I don't know that you'd understand."

"What does that mean?"

"It means–" Her brow crinkled in thought, and she turned away. "Look, maybe it was a stupid thing to do. I hon-estly didn't think you respected me, and I wanted to show you, somehow, someway, that it hurt me. I know that prob-ably doesn't make any sense to you but–"

He stared at her for a long moment. She frowned, and in the mirror upon the wall, her face appeared as did his upon the windowpane with the onset of winter pasts.

"Not respect you?" he said. "What about when we made love? It was like...like we were singing. Didn't that mean something?"

Her eyes seemed to tremble. "That was special," she said slowly, her voice choking. "But there's so much more. You just won't open up to me."

Peter sneered. "I've got nothing to hide."

"Maybe not to hide but to find."

Peter's hands flew to his hips. "So did you or didn't you?"

"Did I or didn't I what?"

"Oh Christ, do I have to say it? My brother. Sleep with him. Did you sleep with him?"

Her face paled. "What do you think?"

"I can't believe you would."

"Yet, you're asking."

He held up his hands. "No. It's just so incredible that you would that I...well, everything that has happened these past few weeks is too impossible for me to accept. It would shock me it you had, but–"

"You don't have faith in me then."

"I have faith that you wouldn't deliberately hurt me."

"So why did you run away from me?"

"I wouldn't call it 'running away.'"

"Then why won't you get close to me, beyond sex? If you know I won't hurt you–"

Peter's eyes glazed, as if he wasn't listening.

"Is it because what I say or what I do still does hurt?

Why? How?"

His head cast downward, and his chin trembled. For several long seconds, Abbie watched him, and soon she found her own heart quavering. Her eyes glistened tenderly; they suffered from the same ailment, she knew. She wanted to caress him, to soothe away his despair and fears, felt that desire as if it were a warm commotion of wind enveloping her. Going out with his brother had hurt him, and her eyes gazed down, too. Then, she reached for him, her arm like the beam of a lighthouse offering to guide a ship upon the dark sea. "Please tell me. I want to help, Peter."

"I don't need help. I need to remain strong."

She shook her head. "We all need help sometime in our lives – that doesn't make you weak."

Peter stood his ground for a moment. "Weakness? Is that what you think I fear?"

"Isn't it? If not, what then?"

Peter stared off at the ceiling. "Why, it's..." He paused, thought of his mother. Her voice, a delicate, wind-chime soprano, sang to him.

She stood still for a long moment. "Why won't you tell me, Peter?"

He backed away. "Because, Abbie, I feel with such passion..."

She nodded, stepped toward him. "I know you do, Peter. I know. I sense it when we make love."

"I – I can't let it...overwhelm me."

"Why, Peter?"

"Because–"

"Because of what you fear?"

He gazed directly at her, and for a moment Abbie thought she saw disappointment in his eyes.

"Abbie, I'm sorry for all I've put you through."

"It's all right, if–"

"I should be going now."

"Peter–"

"It's for the best."

He turned the doorknob. She did not move. Then, as the door closed, she ran to the living room window, and from its corner watched him go. The ice upon the driveway's mud crackled beneath his feet. Yes, she told herself, it's painful, but I must bleach them from my life.

*****

If not for the windmill's silver blades glistening gold as the sun set across the prairie, no one would have understood what Peter watched through the window. Sitting in the kitchen chair, he stared at its girders clenching the earth, examined how it subtly captured the current and collared it into a freewheeling line, if only for a moment, acting much in the same way the mind formed a memory. Then the wind was let go, allowed to return to its twisting and turning, as if on a never-ending odyssey. Peter found himself caught in the vice of his own fear, and it crushed against him. On his way back from Abbie's, he'd stopped at a convenience store, bought a 12-pack of beer – just a little something to steady the nerves when at home, he told himself – but a mile out of Felton, he popped open a can. Peter hadn't drank in so long that it tasted like hot vinegar, but as he took a second gulp and then a third, its fire came back. Soon the swigs of heat soured his breath so it smelled like stale sweat, yet with each drink he imagined that his heart grew larger. Halfway through the pack, he heard Lyle's footsteps, slow and sonorous, move to the table behind him.

Lyle waited a long moment for his brother to acknowledge him, and when no words or even a glance came, he spoke. "Uncle Joe is the executor of the will."

Peter's eyes did not waver from the windmill. "I know."

"It shouldn't take long to settle the estate."

"Father's will is pretty clear."

"And to the letter of the law. I know Jerry Brudd wrote it for him." Lyle hesitated for a moment. "Guess that means we'll be owning the farm together."

"Guess so."

Lyle gazed at the window, tried to determine what his brother was studying. The younger Steinar saw only a collection of metal beams, an obstacle that stood in the way of quickly mowing the lawn, an impractical implement for modern farming that always clattered when he tried to sleep and never offered shade of any worth from the red sun when he was awake. He glanced back at Peter. "Does that bother you?"

Peter wrung his hands. "What are you proposing?"

"That we sell it. Split the profit, fifty-fifty."

Peter brought a can of beer to his lips, and as the bitterness slid down his throat, the edges of his life softened again. For a moment, he savored the peace. "Is that what you want?"

"It's what's going to happen."

"You're going to force me to sell?"

"You can buy my half if you want."

"And if I don't want to?"

Lyle snarled. "Peter, I'm leaving the farm."

Peter's eyes steadied upon the windmill. He found his heart surging; though the wind moved unpredictably and without reason, the windmill always stood firm, like an ageless principle offering continuation, security.

The bastard is ignoring me, Lyle told himself, just as he had after secretly tossing the guns in the creek. "Did you hear?"

Peter rose, turned about to face his brother. They glared at one another. "I heard you."

"I'm surprised you're not happy that I'm going."

"I don't care what you do."

Waves of blood throbbed in Lyle's temples. "You've never liked me, Peter."

"No, I never have, not since mother died. It was your misbehaving that caused our father to be so hard, to be so intolerant. You always were running out into the field after him, never following instructions, always starting fights. He wouldn't have been so strict if you'd just shown some self-restraint."

Lyle bared his teeth for a moment then compressed his anger. I've done nothing but show self-restraint my whole life to please our father, he said to himself, then in a moment of inspiration he rubbed his bruised eye. "It doesn't hurt as much as I expected it would."

Peter grunted. "Good. That means next time you still won't be smart enough to hit me first." Lyle's eyes blazed. His arm swung upward like a mallet, smashed his brother squarely in the eye. Peter's breath escaped him for a minute, and regaining his balance, he drew away like he was suddenly blinded by light. Then his lips rose as he revealed clenched teeth. His right arm slung outward, but he was still off balance and the errant punch only hit Lyle's forehead, a strike no more harmful than when their old man had taken the sledgehammer to the windmill. The younger of the Steinars raised his fists, ready to strike again.

Peter slowly backed off as his eyes twisted with shock, a retreating soldier cautiously watching his flank. I've become my father, he thought as peering down at his hands. He decided to leave Nebraska – I won't be left alone here to run the farm by myself, he told himself – but before he could utter the words, Lyle spun toward the door, each step thunderous, and fled the house. Peter found himself standing alone, his shirt damp with sweat.

*****

Lyle's truck sped full bore down the gravel road, spitting icy stones high upon the air as storm clouds gathered to the north. Towering toward the heavens, they steadily coalesced as their gray bottoms formed a blanket across the sky. The kick Peter had laid him in the ribs hurt too much to notice the approaching turbulence, though, and the angry throbbing of his temples as his jaw clenched tight prevented him from hearing the wind's ever rising pitch. His bare hands gripped the steering wheel tighter, as if that would get him to Abbie sooner. Twenty minutes before, he had thrown his beer-laden brother off him and in a rage made for her apartment. The bile in his mouth firmed into a ball. He would show Abbie what her little pet Peter had done to him, show her what she had done to him through rejection. The roadside reflectors blurred by him like the needle of a radio dial spun across the spectrum.

Lightning cracked about the sky, forking like a lit artery, its thunder roaring at him as if blood rushing to the ears. For a moment, all the world – farm buildings, the plains, cars upon the road – lit up. Hair stood the length of his arms, and his mouth went dry. The air reeked like a burned wire.

Then, there she was, he was certain of it, a cranberry-colored car heading in opposite lane toward him, it like a blot of blood against the sky's gray. Suddenly he yanked his steering wheel hard to the left, and veering his pickup in front of her, stopping the truck crosswise on the road. Her brakes squealed as she stopped but yards short of him. Lyle leaped out of his truck, and as he stormed toward Abbie's car, her pupils widened and she gasped.

Then her face firmed, and she rolled down her window. "Are you crazy?" Abbie shouted. "We could've been killed!"

He stood at her car door. She looked perfect, like the bride statuette atop a wedding cake, even though he hated her so.

Abbie shrunk back. "What happened to you?" she said, staring directly at the bold purple bruise under his eye.

Lyle's eyes gleamed. "Oh, don't worry – I gave Peter one that's just as bad looking."

Her eyes squinted as she looked away. "It's barbaric."

"You don't understand – Peter always got the beautiful women, it wasn't fair. But finally, he's proven for all the world to see what kind of man he really is–"

Abbie's mouth gaped, then a harrumph shot from her lips. "So is that all I am to you – a beautiful woman, a prize your brother can't have? Both of you disgust me. Now get your god damn truck out of the middle of the road before you kill someone."

She pressed on her accelerator, and gravel spun up from her tires. Lyle jumped back a step, and his face paled, as if it were void of blood. Momentarily too surprised to feel the cold air stinging his bare hands, he watched the car cut across the shoulder then disappear into the distance.

Anger whirled in Lyle like winter winds; years of self-control suddenly flew aside as he ran to his truck. The pickup took off in a squeal, and he soared after Abbie's car. He grit his teeth as the snow banks blurred and the prairie lost its cardboard flatness. "Just one more race to win," he whispered as lightning wishboned across the sky. He knew the truth about Peter, even if she refused to accept it, knew that he deliberately had brought the guns back into the house – why, his grieving, it was all just a show – then, for a moment his heart surged as her red brake lights loomed larger in his windshield. When she slowed to curve around the cottonwood, they grew even brighter.

He pressed on the gas, watched the tree so he knew when to corner. The cottonwood slanted eastward so its branches and leaves hung to one side, which covered by white ice appeared then in the opening blue sky to hover like a cloud. Out on the open plain, it had taken the brunt of wind for many years, all its life really, yet it endured, albeit in this twisted, malformed shape. A gust buffeted at his truck as he neared the tree. Never had a moment of silence fallen across this flat stretch, he realized. The cab's temperature fell slightly, and he turned the fan on higher, but it only blasted all that much more lukewarm air as clattering fanatically. Frozen dust particles slapped his face from the vent, and his humid nose sucked them in. The air about him grew desert dry, and as he passed the bent tree, it wavered in the merciless wind, too taken up by its own struggle to pay him any heed.

Suddenly, he slammed on his brakes, and the pickup spun. After nearly a full turn, it stopped.

This was ridiculous, he told himself, what would be proved if I caught up with her? It's my damn father again, chasing after me from inside my head; the old man's power extends from even the grave. He breathed hard as a voice told him to be steady, to persevere, to fight by enduring; it was like the boxer that just kept taking punch after punch until his opponent grew weary of hitting – but did he ever weaken so much as to collapse?

He turned off the motor, glanced in his rear view mirror, watched Abbie's car vanish like a star into the morning light.

*****

Abbie was right, Peter told himself as he threw a duffel bag of clothes into his pickup truck, maybe I have nothing to hide, but I certainly have something to find. For years my efforts have staked down the whole farm, or at least a corner of it, but in all of that time, one stake has been missing. He had thought perhaps Abbie might be that paling, but now the possibility of it had cracked beyond repair. Getting into the truck, he revved the motor, gunned out of the yard. As the windmill whirred behind him, he rolled down the window, letting cool air into the sun-drenched cab. For a second he thought of Lyle leaving, of how he bolted from the house to his pickup truck and took off, but then Peter told himself he didn't give a damn what happened to the farm; Aunt Amita could run it for all he cared. Though fenced, the farm was not walled, he whispered as the afternoon sun beat against his face.

High lines and transformers stretched across the prairie out ahead. Though Abbie hadn't directly answered him, he did not believe his brother's claim of sleeping with her, even though it had been the night of the blizzard when he'd not returned home. The clouds lumped together in the distant horizon, and his shirt clung in the rising humidity. Even if she had committed this great betrayal, he could not bring himself to blame her.

He rubbed his aching eye, tried to concentrate on the road. Five miles ahead of him rose the first sign of Felton's grain elevators, just their white, conical tops at first, but with each passing moment they grew taller and more distinct, soon three towering projections, then the thin, capital letters proclaiming the village's name, and finally even the miniscule railings atop each silo. Behind them loomed a black sky, and lightning streaked across it as thunder echoed over the prairie. With the window rolled down, he could smell the moisture as it swelled in the air, chilling the wind's swirls. Rounding a bend into the outskirts of town, he caught a whiff of the café's greasy lunch.

Nausea swirled through his guts, as if a knife were cutting him from the inside out. He began counting the fence poles bordering the highway, just as he had done when a boy walking the fence line, measuredly stepping between the narrow poles, careful to not brush against the taut metal threads and their intermittent thorns. On occasion, he'd pretend to be a grown man who had been named farmer of the year, and his mother, still appearing as she did in her young 20s, was there to congratulate him. Sometimes he'd carry the cutout news picture of her, the slippery ink sliding across his bare belly as he tucked it beneath the shirt so no one knew he possessed it.

Leaving town, the sky, marbled purple and dark blue, appeared bruised as if repeatedly beaten.

A cold wind gusted beneath the mass, and Peter could make out the distant rumble not of thunder but of clouds coalescing, their intense weight groaning like continents as they rubbed against one another. He gaped in awe at the approaching onslaught as the dry breeze evaporated the spit from his mouth. It was an upside down world they lived in, Peter thought, first an October blizzard then a November thunderstorm. But there were reasons to things, he decided, for if not then all of the principles behind his practicality were naught.

He resolved to determine them. After Lyle had left, Peter went through every drawer in their old man's bedroom. He hadn't been in the room for years, yet remembered its constituent parts – the quilt upon the bed, the oak dresser, the brass lamp upon the nightstand – each now faded, nicked or dusty as if items abandoned in a junk store.

With each opened drawer, though, nothing appeared but the sound of rubbing wood and the sight of old clothes. Peter frowned. His father had left no diaries for him to read and explore; perhaps by understanding him, Peter surmised, he might cool the pain weltering inside. But with every drawer pulled and each box unstuffed, there was only Gwen's death certificate, buried beneath a pile of tattered long johns. His body wilted; what good would a diary have been any way, he asked himself, the old man probably would have just kept a record of daily temperatures and precipitation. And so, he spread out the only clue remaining.

The certificate was yellowed and deeply creased, as if it had been opened and folded several times. Peter mulled over it for a long while, rereading his mother's full name, the date of the accident, the cause of death, the coroner's signature in barely legible handwriting. He imagined showing the paper to Lyle, who would give it a cursory glance then hand it back, so Peter brought the certificate to his room and placed it between the covers of a nursery rhyme book he'd received as a child when she'd still been alive. In it were the flattened remnants of the newspaper picture describing his mother's 4-H success, a high school love letter from Laura Jean, and a ticket stub from the most recent county fair. It would be easy to pack, he knew.

From there Peter crept into the attic, the triangular slant of light from the open door barely enough to unveil the new chamber, and he muddled his way to its center until walking into a chain of cold metal beads hanging from the ceiling. He pulled the cord. A diffuse yellow glow covered the boxes haphazardly piled on the floor of thin wooden slats. He scanned each container, knew the top one to the left only held white and blue plates, and he vaguely recalled eating from them before his mother purchased a new set; it was so like a farmwife to keep the old ones, to not squander any resource. The box to his right stored her china. As a small child, he often sneaked into the attic to look at them when his brother and father were out of sight, and would admire the intricate details of leaves and flowers along the delicate pieces. He sighed, sat upon a third box, buried his face into his hands. The scent of old things, like autumn grass that had gone brown and began to decay, wafted about him.

He thought of that day not so long ago when after breakfast the three Steinar men shuffled and limped through a wavering mist rising out of the ground to examine the irrigation systems that hung over the furrows like the jointed legs of monstrous spiders. Moist dust reddened their work boots, but they paid it no attention.

At the edge of one field, Lyle stooped then gazed into the amorphous horizon, his face like a hardened crust of earth. Wind spooled dust off the tract before him, and his mouth formed into a frown. Peter took a knee as well, appeared gaunt next to his stout brother, and his fingers pressed into the loam. He loved how one could burrow into it, grasp it, feel its softness, its life; whenever doing so, his hand was like a stream joining a greater river. He scooped the red soil into his palm, let it sift through his hands. Each granule drifted with the wind as the mist before them passed like a trailing garment. He longed for Abbie in this way too, loved all he could recall of that beautiful woman to whom the breeze-blown sand never stuck. She took the bleakness out of the landscape. His palm scooped deeper into the earth until only a thin patch of topsoil separated his fingertips from the clay beneath. Their father did not kneel, merely stood above the two lads, planting his legs into the ground as if they were stakes. His eyes followed the sun-burned field that gently rolled toward the creek.

Then the three walked on as the sun steadily rose, the wind coating each one with dust, each glad to have escaped the womb of the house. Their father seemed to steer them, Peter thought, away from the creek as they crossed the fields, barren as a leafless branch. The wind whispered upon the earth like a long scythe. At a pasture corner, the old man stopped while the weed stems fluttered at his ankles and the sun, swollen and white, hung over them. He stared at the unfinished horizon, as if...as if what, Peter wondered. Bewildered, he gazed at his father. The old man paid him no attention, though, as the wind skittered across the low wheat before him, continuing past them on its unfinished journey, resistant to linearity, opposed to closure. As the boys moved toward the next irrigation line, he merely stood in place.

It made no sense, Peter muttered to himself, as he opened another box of his parents' belongings in the attic. A stack of 30 to 40 records, some of their edges frayed, filled the box, and he pulled one out. A smoky blue image of a black man blowing the trumpet festooned the cover as the plastic of the still left-on wrapping crinkled beneath his fingers. He tipped the record case to its side, and a warped round disk slid from the slipcase, caught a gleam of sunlight through the attic window. Peter set it on another box then grabbed a stack of records, shuffled through them as if they were playing cards. He'd not heard of any of the musicians, didn't understand how his mother had come to know about them. And, as he drew each album from its sleeve, the disc's edge sharp against his skin, he found each one warped. Heat and cold had worked their power on them like they did the road. It was not much; the records told him little about her, at least directly. Still, the collection was better than his father, who left no note, no will, no clues, just a body, the blood from its torn skull spoked across the far wall and the desert of their living room. Now, the cavernous role of Carl Steinar's life loomed before him. There were so many things he did not know about his father despite all of the years with him.

The horizon hung like a precipice before the road Peter drove; if only there were rolls, not bumps, to break up the great flatness, he thought. Ahead of him, the puddles reddened as reflecting the brake lights of turning car. North Platte was only 20 miles ahead, and he'd have to decide there which way to go: west toward Denver or east to Lincoln. "We all need help sometime in our lives – that doesn't make you weak," Abbie had said to him. No, she doesn't understand me, he decided, but the realization that she wanted to nagged at him. She'd reached to him in ways his father refused to, in ways he'd wished his father always had, and regret over the mistakes he'd made with her pricked at him as if a thorn. He momentarily withdrew his bare hands from the steering wheel, rubbed them together to overcome the cold; it would turn to snow again, he knew.

Chapter 29

Off a gravel back road west of Felton there is a small plot full of wind and stones. Many would say that during late October silence reigns there: Birds have flown to the warmth of Mexico, widows find the air too chilled for their weekly cries, the machinery of a neighboring field locked in a farmer's shed awaits spring. Yes, all is silent, unless one counts the wind and the stones. But men of the Plains often become deaf to the ceaseless wind, and few take stock in stones making any sound. Listen closely, though, to the gusts howling across the open prairie and against the thin barbed wire that like a frame about a canvas marks the cemetery's limits. The wind plays off the granite and marble heads as if breath blown through a flute. It is upon such stones that men attempt to permanently etch history so they will not exist in a vacuum; it is the final statement after a lifetime of scratching out divisions upon the ground, over ephemeral time itself, merely to give their short journeys meaning, to tell others "I was here – do not forget me, do not let my brief blast dissolve into nothingness." Then, as new gusts blow over and between those stones, each spiriting of air finds itself tempered and reshaped as offering its own soft-colorings, harmonized open-fifths, simple duets and plodding bass marches, all forming a great collage and patchwork of song as they make their inexorable movement onward, quickly casting eyes to witness what is beside them, of what came before. And so, if not for the stone in that plot where Carl Steinar is buried, there would be no sound at all upon the earth but a howl.

*****

Without makeup on, Abbie found the wrinkles of her skin readily apparent, like crop rows as seen from an airplane, no depth to them but lines nevertheless. She drew in a heavy sigh as glancing once more in the rear-view mirror; the creases at the edges of her eyes where they met the nose and the skin about her dimples were not so flat. She needed sleep but unable to wait any longer, she continued driving as a crescendo of gray dropped rain upon the empty red plain.

Abbie knew that if she stayed in Felton her hopefulness would burn off like a moon mist as sunlight broke. Her car's tires whooshed over the road's slush, a faint reminder of the recent blizzard that noontide's heat and midnight's chill alternately melted and froze. She'd put her belongings in a storage shed, left in the apartment the furniture she couldn't move – it was all second-hand, anyway – then amid a nearly empty living room placed the keys into an envelope and slipped them under the landlord's door. In the car, she steered north toward the Dakotas, if only because its very emptiness seemed pregnant with solitude.

Then, outside of North Platte on Highway 83, as the rain muddied the brown fields and sloshed across her windshield faster than the thwacking wipers could keep up with, her car began to sputter, like it were out of gas. She pulled on to the shoulder, the gravel crackling beneath the tires until the vehicle died. She rolled the ignition, but other than a red glow and sonorous dong from the dashboard, there was nothing. Her teeth ground tight. "Damn car – never working when it's wet!" she spit out, and then swinging the door open she stepped onto the road. Before her stretched a sea of wheat stems, each no more than an inch or two high, barely able to conceal the red loam beneath. Wind whirled across the open plain, and with no grass heads to rustle, it sounded horridly angry, as if a two-year-old denied his wishes. The rush stung against her face like a slap, dry and flat, and she longed for a glass of water. Above her, the gray sky darkened with the onset of autumn's early evening.

The car hood creaked as she lifted it, the weight pressuring her wrist. Streams of cold rain twirled downward, and hitting the motor, a hot steam rose. Her chin furrowed as both hands rolled into fists. She stuck her head into the vehicle's maw, and though it kept her head dry, the stink of oil soon covered her face and coat. From what she could tell, the wires, belts and blocks of metal appeared all right. Her stomach curled; there was nothing to do now but sit and wait for help. Dropping the hood, it slammed into place, splattering raindrops onto her as she slid back to the driver's seat. Inside, she pushed both hands deep into her pockets to fend off the chill. A copperiness filled her mouth as she closed her eyes. All I want to do is get away, she thought.

Then, no more than a minute later, headlights from a pickup truck washed the interior of her car in a yellow glow, and blinker lights flashed red against the dashboard. She stared in the side mirror, watched a swaddled figure distorted by rain approach. Slowly it came into focus, a man she could tell by the way it walked, the legs straight and no bounce to the hips, and suddenly her mouth widened, as if a part of her face had been scooped out. It was Peter. Her neck brimmed with heat. Had he followed her, decided to come to her rescue, to be her knight in shining armor? She scoffed at the notion, knew that she wasn't the one who needed to be saved.

Peter crouched over the driver's door. "Abbie, are you all right?" he shouted, his voice muffled by the wind and glass, but she could tell that he already knew. She rolled down the window, and an icy rain spat at her. His right eye puffed. "Come on, I'll take you into town," he said.

"I'll be all right," she said. Breath streamed from her mouth as she spoke.

"Is your car broke down?"

She said nothing.

"Abbie, you can't just sit here in the middle of the prairie, car broken down and a snowstorm brewing."

Her thoughts hovered for a moment; Abbie knew this might be the last time she'd get help out here where not even her cell phone had reception. Her fingers began to stiffen in the cold. "Just take me to the nearest farmhouse."

He nodded, and backing from the door, she got out. Rain sprayed across her like water shot from a hose, and she ran for his truck, jumped inside it. As she stared at the moisture smearing her view through the windshield and the regular gushes of high wind that blinded her with white, droplets streamed along her temples. The metal cab dulled the rainfall's drumming, its snap against the wheat and asphalt so clamorous outside. It also blocked the downpour's scent, strangely fresh like mountain snow, and she thought for a moment of cracking a window. Then the glass darkened with the steam of her own breath, and the stuffy vapors of her sweat which she inhaled clung to the roof of her mouth.

Peter maneuvered the truck through a Y-turn, headed back south away from North Platte. Rain obscured the plain's eastern horizon as if thousands of gauze strips hung suspended from the sky, but gradually as her eye shifted westward, the whiteness faded into the steel gray of snow clouds. The wind remained absent from the neutral zone that the truck rode through, and other than the motor's churning, the cab was utterly quiet. Abbie sat pressed to the door, her face straight ahead, hands folded in the lap. She said nothing though he stared at her for several seconds, his black eye a purplish-green crescent under his bottom eyelash. Droplets of ice began to strike on the windshield.

"Would you like a comb?" he said.

"A what?" Then she glanced at him, ran a hand through her hair. The strands swirled about her fingers, mostly flattened by the wetness though the ends haphazardly curled as they dried in the pickup truck's warmth. "It's not that bad," she said, turning away.

"You could get sick with all that dampness."

She found her throat growing dry again. "Okay, pass it over here." She held out her hand. Peter lifted his rump slightly from the seat, pulled a thin black comb from a back pocket. "Do you mind if you tell you something?" he said.

She remained aloofly quiet as running his comb through her hair.

"Well, I'll tell you anyway. While driving this truck when the snowstorm struck last week, I decided that if I ever had the opportunity, I'd give you another 'chance.'"

Her raking of the comb slowed, but still she said nothing.

"Well, I've since realized that's a downright stupid notion. I've done you wrong, so you're the one who has to give me another chance."

They closed upon a drive leading to a farmhouse, but Abbie's lips remained together as she watched the buildings pass from the corner of her eye. Wind rocked his truck as the rain turned to sleet like a whisper rising in volume. She glanced at him, could see his face was scrawled with desperation; perhaps it was the same look her own father possessed for an instant when his plane crashed and he felt the first bones of his leg fracturing into more pieces than an eggshell splattered against tarmac.

"Abbie, if you'll still let me, there's a lot I have to tell. If I don't, I'll end up just like my old man."

She said nothing, thought herself groping down a dark hallway. Now that the moment she'd always wanted had finally come, Abbie didn't know if she was ready for it.

"I'd rather tell you because – well, you're the one person...the only person...I really trust."

Abbie glanced meekly at him. "Do you really mean that, Peter? I hope you do."

Peter nodded, slowly. "The problem is, I really haven't thought it all through enough to know exactly what I have to say. It may not make a lot of sense if any at all. "

Her eyes brightened as she smiled, then cupping her chin in a hand she stared into the horizon.

"What did a war vet once tell me during an interview?" she said. "You begin with the vowels, and the consonants will follow."

*****

In the pickup cab, Peter's words unspooled over the long miles as if water rushing down a dry run. "All my life, nightmares of the accident have haunted me," he said. "In one, my body as well as my mother's were entangled in the wreck, except we were not on a road but sinking in half-frozen mud; during another I was a fisherman, casting a net into this unending sea, but as I did, the water boiled red, and my mother rose from it. I never talked to anyone about those dreams. My father wouldn't have allowed it any way. For him, only constant, hard work mattered. I figured the old man would just keep laboring on until he fell. But I really didn't know what to be more afraid of – my father abandoning me or dominating me. Later on, the old man never fought back, never got angry, just sat there so solemnly, so smugly. Eventually I gave up arguing with him; what was the point when his temperament remained hard as stone?"

Abbie's chin puckered then trembled in understanding. "That's what hurts the most, that he can no longer be counted upon."

"What you said some time ago about my father and me, well, you were right – I do blame him, but it's not about her death so much as the way we lived afterward."

"I know what you mean – after my father's accident, he ceased to be...nourishing, he–" but then she stopped in fear of scaring him into silence.

Peter nodded, as if he didn't mind where she was steering the conversation. 'To think, all of these years I've been deaf to the wind." His skin itched. "I...I have a long way to go...I think, well...I think I need your help."

Abbie smiled lightly; between the water of her persistence and the Colorado storm, his rock-exterior had worn some. Fragments of red brick from the elementary school at Felton's outskirts were barely visible amid the whitewash. Abbie knew she could not stay angry at him; he'd had a vision of them together and had acted upon it. "I'm glad to be back with you," she said, and though he did not speak:, she believed his quiet was an indication that he, too, considered them a couple once more. And as several seconds passed and she still had not heard him talk, she glanced at him, and his face against the backdrop of blindingly bright, wind-swept snow, crinkled, then the eyes winced and she thought he even wept for a moment.

He suddenly found himself growing lighter. Why hadn't I told her this before, Peter wondered, and yet he found himself more confused than ever, the lines of his beliefs suddenly gray. The past weighed heavy as stones. Near the railroad tracks ahead, at the massive Victorian house built long ago by the son of Mathias Sutherland, the squall appeared to ease. Perhaps hatred and anger are only different hues of the same consuming fire, he thought, but still he did not say it aloud, feared it would only break the trust he'd regained with Abbie. Yet, he also knew the wind never blew in quite the same direction twice, and so also it was with other people, that one never knew what to expect next.

As he stalwart Victorian grew in size, it remained horridly vulnerable amid the unending sky whose gray had only begun to part, Abbie thought. Her hair bristled at the thought that it had stood for all those years without the banshee roar of a twister toppling it; perhaps its time was near. The pickup paused at the tracks. Cold, purple shadows fell across the side of the house askance from the sunlight while the other bathed warmly in the late afternoon glow. She could smell her sweat from beneath the heavy coat but dared not pull it off in the overheated cab for fear that it signaled a comfortability and hence acceptance of Peter. The truck bumped over the tracks, passed the old Vic, its glass windows steely with shadow and light.

"We're almost to Felton," Peter said, his words hesitant, unsteady. "Where do you want me to let you off?"

She fidgeted, hadn't thought of that. "I – I don't know. I don't have keys anymore to my apartment. "

"Well, there's no motels in Felton; I'd have to take you back to North Platte." Fragmented blasts of snow-filled wind crossed the windshield. "You can stay at my place for the night, if you want."

Abbie rubbed her wet palms together. "What about your brother?"

"He's gone."

Her stomach knotted. "Gone?"

"He's left the farm. He doesn't want anything to do with it, even offered to let me buy him out of his share."

"How can you be so certain he hasn't come back?"

"I know my brother."

"Oh."

The snow showered about them. "So is my place fine? Just so we can get out of this storm? In the morning, you can figure out where to go."

Her mouth arched mischievously. "I suppose it beats staying for the night in the storage shed I rented."

He began to laugh, and as she did also, their eyes grew wet, as if rising a wave's crest. Finally, they quieted. "So it's okay then," Peter said, "staying at my place?"

She nodded.

They remained silent during the last few miles to the Steinar farm. At each passing fence post, the snow swirled with increasing ferocity, and Peter found himself slowing so that the time of their travel stretched endlessly into the blazing white chaos. Finally, he spotted the windmill, its blades whirring frantically above the yard's snow-capped trees. Stopping the truck in the drift-filled driveway, he turned about and slightly pulled up his seat; reaching an arm behind it, he yanked out a blanket, its olive green dark in the cold brightness. He motioned for her to come toward him, and when she sidled over the gearshift, they slung it across their shoulders. Then with the blanket wrapped around them, they scurried from the truck toward the house. Peter watched their step, careful not to run too fast lest they slip on ice. Though the chilled wind struck him along the neck, he found her cheek nestled against his shoulder and her hand curled about the ribs warm. Then he paused. She raised the wool over her nostrils. "What is it?" she said, her teeth starting to clatter. His eyes followed the windmill's elongated shadow over the snow, then as they reached the metal structure itself, his head canted upward. He was home.

*****

Rays of sunlight slivered across amorphous snow clumps strewn across the Steinar yard and fields. As Peter leaned against the cold window pane, he imagined the white clumps lining the windmill's horizontal beams, the slant of his pickup's hood, the long furrows where wheat seed lay safe underground, as wind solidified, as the air's ever-twisting flow captured as if in a freeze-frame photograph. A drip fell past the glass, plopping onto the ground outside, reminding him that nothing was permanent. He straightened his back, stretched his arms over the head until the muscles of his naked body grew taut. The brightness warmed his exposed ribs. The taste of Abbie's perspiration from a night of lovemaking hung in his mouth.

He watched the windmill blades slow in the downturning current, thought the breeze straightening like a knot unbounded. Then her light footsteps approached him from behind him, and as he turned his head to look, her naked frame slipped against his chest. He wrapped his arms around her warm tummy as she leaned her back into his torso and purred. Through the window, sunlight falling upon them, and he nuzzled her head, took in the scent of her hair, it like blossoming sunflowers. For a moment, his head swooned, and he thought his existence formless and darting. When they'd returned the night before, their faces pale from the cold, the stench of ammonia left during the cleaning of his father's blood greeted them. They let the blanket flutter to the floor, but she remained in his arms as they stood motionless in the still kitchen. She tended to his black eye, told him it was barbaric, but as accepting her scolding, he explained how after striking his brother he was astonished at his own violence. Her eyes softened, and as they stared into one another's eyes, he noticed the redness of her cheeks as warmth returned to them. He rose, undressed himself. She merely watched, said nothing, and her quickening breathing as his angular frame and erect member unveiled itself. He scooped her up, carried her to his father's room, where she also undressed as he silently watched. Finally, her lithe, unclothed body curled against his as they slid under the bed's covers. For a moment, he listened to her breathing, it low and soft like the creek's gentle summer flow. His hand traced the curve of her hip, and her eyes half closed. Then, without thinking, he pulled her atop him, kneaded her shoulder blades as their chests pressed against one another. She wriggled slightly, and suddenly they gasped in unison. He found his mind swirling. Their lips met, and her mouth tasted of wine. His back arched as her long hair swung across his neck in a wild rhapsody. Then she too froze, and for some time their oiled frames rested against one another as both hearts slowed. She shifted off him, nestled her head upon his chest. She smelled of baby's breath, he thought, and they fell asleep in one another's arms.

In the darkness, he found himself at the creek, standing in the waist-high water. A gust rustled the cottonwood leaves overhead, and then before him appeared a white, translucent visage. The scent of algae, thick as if in late August, rose about him. This time, he told himself, he would not reach for her. Then a chilled wind swept over him, brushing his hair back, and the form grew increasingly opaque. "It is time to move on," he said over the swirling water, and as the ghost nodded, its skull-masked face looked directly at him. He gasped. Then, stretching his arm out, he found Abbie's wrist, it lambskin soft, and as her hand unconsciously curled into his, he nuzzled closer until his pounding heart calmed.

The next morning, he found himself shifting tight once more against her bare frame. She nestled her head against his arm, looked back at him, and they gazed at one another in the sunlight. For the first time in all of those weeks that he'd been with Abbie, even when they were intimate, he noticed the range of hues in her eyes, how though mainly brown a light green burst ringed the black of her pupil, and how even amid those two colors appeared slender lines in varying lengths of blue. "What?" she said, girlishly as a hot flash of red spread across her cheeks. "Why are you staring at me like that?"

"Your irises," he said, "they're...they're beautiful. They're not flat and solid, but...but something more."

Slowly they leaned closer to one another. His neck smelled of freesia, and his thoughts whirled. She let him stare a moment longer then giggled and rolled away from him, headed for the kitchen. "Do you mind if make coffee?" she said, looking over her shoulder, the smooth, unblemished mounds of her breasts swaying as she turned. He shook his head, thought their beings amorphous now that they were with one another. Life was not a series of furrows, plowed in straight lines across the earth, as his father tried to make it; no, life was wavering, at times frenetically, at times peacefully, but always it was swirling, rising and dipping, reaching new heights and despicable nadirs. It was a fool's errand to remove, weigh or dissect any of it, as if some mineral pulled from the earth.

The burst of a telephone ring interrupted the morning quiet. Peter picked it up. "Hello?"

Aunt Amita spoke rapidly. "Peter? Is everything all right? I tried calling you all afternoon yesterday but then the lines when down – must have been the storm – Lyle had phoned me, said he was in Julesberg, on his way to Denver – do you know anything about it?"

"Everything is all right, here."

Amita paused, then her words came, hesitantly. "And Lyle? Why – why's he going to Denver?"

"I couldn't say."

"Peter?"

"He'll have to be the one to tell us – when he's ready."

Amita said nothing, then before she could, Peter gently placed the phone back into its cradle. Abbie, hair falling over her bare neck, handed him a cup of coffee. "Is something wrong?" she said.

He nodded. "It was Aunt Amita. She says Lyle has gone to Denver."

Her eyes dropped to the wall beside them. "You're alone now on the farm. What will you do now?"

Peter nodded. Yes, it seems I'm always alone, he told himself. He gave out a long sigh, thought about the future for the first time in many years. "I think I'll build a new house, one that overlooks the windmill." He said nothing for a moment. "I've lived in this one for too long."

Abbie smiled at the notion as she looked back at him and took a sip from her mug.

Peter gazed upon her, thought of her as a magnolia among the dust, and at that instant he would have liked to stroke her hair. "Say, you don't have an apartment anymore do you?"

She shook her head no, grinned. "Probably no job either."

"I suppose there's a room here for you."

She put hands on her waist, mocked a contemplative look. "I suppose it wouldn't be too bad staying here."

"It will be risky. For both of us."

"And if it works, also richer."

He set the coffee upon the counter, returned to the bright window, thought of the uncharted world before them. Then he heard her the soft clatter of her coffee mug as it was placed next to his, and she joined him, leaned her back against his chest. Their hands interlocked, and they snuggled. Outside, the windmill blades whirred as if a fluttering dove.

"I'll need to check on the cattle tonight," he said.

She nodded. "But that's tonight."

They smiled, watched the mist roil off the melting snow and clear. The wind's subtlety and beauty intertwined as he spread their arms out to the light.

Epilogue

The field lay blue in silhouette as the orange sun descended beneath the horizon, leaving but a curve of purpled clouds above it. Peter shivered as a cold breeze swept against him, carrying the scent of dried wildflowers, yet he paid it no heed, merely stood solid upon the frozen ground, as if a great boulder half buried in the earth. Somehow in the enveloping darkness the rustle of iced grass beneath his feet sounded more ominous, and he pondered if the other creatures of the prairie felt this way, too. After a moment, he wiped his cold lips with the side of a hand. The salt of his flesh startled him.

About the Author

Rob Bignell is the owner and sole editor at Inventing Reality Editing Service, which meets the editing and proofreading needs of writers both new and published. During the past four years, he's helped more than 50 novelists, poets and nonfiction authors obtain their publishing dreams. Several of his short stories in the literary and science fiction genres have been published, and he is the author of the popular and highly acclaimed nonfiction "Hikes with Tykes" guidebooks. For more than two decades, he worked as an award-winning journalist, with half of those years spent as an editor. In addition, for seven years he served as an English teacher or a community college journalism instructor. He holds a Master's degree in English and a Bachelor's degree in journalism and English. "Windmill" is his first published novel. He resides in Hudson, Wis.

WANT TO BECOME A BETTER WRITER?

Follow the author's blog, where you'll find:

Tips for making your writing stronger

Lists of great ideas for getting published

Questions about writing
and marketing answered

Product reviews

News about the book series
and author

And more!

Visit online at:
http://inventingrealityeditingservice.
blogspot.com/

www.ingramcontent.com/pod-product-compliance
Lightning Source LLC
Chambersburg PA
CBHW060142260626
47160CB00001B/93